Veronica Henry has worked as a scriptwriter for *The Archers*, *Heartbeat* and *Holby City* amongst many others, before turning to fiction. She won the 2014 RNA Novel of the Year award for *A Night on the Orient Express*. Veronica lives with her family in a village in north Devon.

Find out more at www.veronicahenry.co.uk, sign up to her Facebook page f/veronicahenryauthor or follow her on Twitter @veronica_henry and Instagram @veronicahenryauthor

Also by Veronica Henry

Wild Oats
An Eligible Bachelor
Love on the Rocks
Marriage and Other Games
The Beach Hut
The Birthday Party
The Long Weekend
A Night on the Orient Express
The Beach Hut Next Door
High Tide
How to Find Love in a Book Shop
The Forever House

THE HONEYCOTE NOVELS
A Country Christmas (*previously published as* Honeycote)
A Country Life (*previously published as* Making Hay)
A Country Wedding (*previously published as* Just a Family Affair)

A COUNTRY WEDDING

Veronica Henry

First published in Great Britain in 2008
by Orion
This paperback edition published in 2017
by Orion Books,
an imprint of The Orion Publishing Group Ltd,
Carmelite House, 50 Victoria Embankment
London EC4Y 0DZ

An Hachette UK Company

1 3 5 7 9 10 8 6 4 2

A CIP catalogue record for this book is
available from the British Library.

ISBN 978 1 4091 6094 6

Typeset by Input Data Services Ltd, Somerset

Printed and bound in Great Britain
by Clays Ltd, St Ives plc

www.orionbooks.co.uk

A COUNTRY WEDDING

Prologue

*T*he little church at Honeycote was bursting at the seams. *Toned buttocks vied with broader beams for space on the slippery wood of the pews. Shafts of golden sunlight pierced the stained-glass windows, shining on the congregation. The organist, confident now she was in her stride, shifted her repertoire up a gear. Usually, the service was over before she'd even had a chance to warm up, so she was taking advantage of this rare opportunity to demonstrate her musical prowess.*

Every alternate Sunday, the stone walls were host to nothing more exciting than dull tweeds and gabardine. Today, the church was crammed with a veritable rainbow of colours in every imaginable stuff – silk, chiffon, velvet, linen and lace. Hats, it seemed, were back with a vengeance, from straw cartwheels trimmed with fruit to ostrich-feather headdresses to dainty pillboxes. And the scent! Most of the seven deadly sins were represented, and several more weaknesses besides – Envy and Obsession and Passion mingled with the woodier base notes of the men's cologne.

Everyone was seated now. The initial cocktail party atmosphere had settled, the ritual two-cheek kisses and squeals of recognition over for the time being, although guests were still peering over their shoulders to see who had come in behind, wiggling their fingers surreptitiously in greeting. And raising eyebrows. Shrugging shoulders, as if to say 'I don't know what's going on. Do you?'

In the front row, the mother of the bride took a deep breath, thanking God she had dropped two diazepam with her lunch. She'd chosen to wear a cream brocade coat dress woven through with metallic threads, picking out the bronze for her accessories – St Laurent courts and a matching clutch. Which she was now clutching, knuckles white with anxiety. This eventuality hadn't been in her list of possible disasters. She had contingency plans for every technical hitch and natural disaster, but this hadn't occurred to her in her wildest nightmare.

Achingly handsome ushers were stalking the aisles, exchanging worried glances whilst trying not to cause alarm. The organist ploughed valiantly on, drowning out the rustle of hymn sheets and the occasional cough. The vicar conferred with the best man. Not that he was in any hurry. Honeycote was a quiet parish; this was the first wedding he had presided over this year and he was determined to enjoy it. He was particularly looking forward to the reception – he'd been asked back to Honeycote House afterwards, and the Liddiard hospitality was famous. And he was partial to a pint or two of Honeycote Ale, which was bound to be on tap even if there were rumours abounding that the Liddiards were as good as bankrupt – again! – and the brewery was about to be sold off.

Ten minutes later, even the vicar was starting to have doubts. Twenty minutes was the longest he'd ever been kept waiting. The church clock struck the half-hour solemnly. As if anyone needed reminding of the time; the invitation had stated two o'clock quite clearly.

Outside the church, the bride's fingers tightened around her bouquet. Her father gave her arm a kindly pat, and she tried to feel reassured. She wasn't the hysterical type, but it was hard not to feel a little disconcerted.

After all, it was the bride's prerogative to be late for the wedding, not the groom's.

I

Six months earlier

Kay Oakley stretched out on her sun-lounger, wiggled her toes and decided that the deep plum polish the beautician had talked her into really was too dark. The nails looked bruised, as if someone had stepped on her foot. The infuriating thing was she'd known all along she wouldn't like it, but had given in. Now she'd have to go back tomorrow and have them re-varnished her usual pillar-box red.

Then she sighed. Was this what her life had come to? When the colour of her nail polish constituted a crisis? It wasn't as if another trip to the salon was even an inconvenience. She genuinely didn't have anything better to do. And when had she lost the ability to paint her own toenails? When had the prospect of lifting a finger to do anything herself become inconceivable?

From an outsider's point of view, she had little to complain about. The twenty-metre pool rippled in front of her, blue and inviting. The gardens were lush and well kept, the stone of the terrace glowed warm in the afternoon sun. The nearby poolhouse provided a wet room, a huge fridge stocked with beers, wines, and soft drinks, and a stack of fluffy towels that was replenished daily by the maids. A walkway sheltered by a vine-covered trellis meandered back up to the house, with its whitewashed walls and cool tiled floors. Her daughter Flora and her little friend splashed in the children's pool under the watchful eye of the nanny.

She looked down at her body. Kay had never had a problem with weight, even after giving birth, but she had to admit she was in tip-top condition for a mother just on the wrong side of forty. Her stomach was flat, without a stretchmark in sight, and thanks to her healthy Mediterranean diet of meat, fish, vegetables and fruit, she had no cellulite. Her white Gucci bikini showed off her even tan – not too dark, for Kay was vigilant about not overdoing the sun. She knew from their social circle that there was nothing more ageing, except perhaps a forty-a-day habit. She didn't want to look like a tortoise. Furthermore, there wasn't a superfluous hair or skin cell on her. Every day she looked for some imperfection that could be ironed out, just to give her a challenge. She longed for a hairy mole or an unsightly bulge that she could get her teeth into, but thanks to her daily gym and salon visits there were none.

She reached out a languid hand for the tumbler of mineral water filled with ice and wedges of fresh lemon she'd picked off the tree earlier. Here she was, leading the perfect magazine existence, in a luxury villa on a luxury complex in Portugal, and she was bored out of her mind. She'd thought about getting a job, but there were none. At least nothing that would make it worth her while. She could get a job as a manicurist. Or as a guide, showing potential purchasers around the new developments that her husband Lawrence and his cronies were throwing up overnight. But neither of these opportunities was what she had in mind. She wanted something that would shake her out of her complacency. Something that would make her feel excited. Afraid, even. Something that would enable her to justify her place on this planet. It wasn't as if they needed the money. At the moment, they couldn't get rid of it fast enough. What she needed was some mental stimulation.

A few months ago, in desperation, she'd tried setting up a book club. Kay was no boffin, but she longed for some banter, some witty repartee. For the inaugural read she'd chosen *Chocolat*, because she didn't want to put the other women off with anything too erudite. But out of six, only three managed to finish it, and the ensuing discussion revolved around the calorific content of the subject matter and the casting of Johnny Depp in the movie. Hardly an intellectual debate. Kay, who'd devoured it, adored it, and been enchanted by the concept of magical reality (which she'd read about in the reader's notes on the website), realized she was onto a losing wicket. There were no like-minded women in her social circle. Kay had never been one for close friends, but she found that for the first time in her life she was lonely.

Added to which, she missed England dreadfully. She'd never considered herself particularly at one with nature, but she missed the changing seasons. The relentless Portuguese sunshine was driving her mad. She'd give anything for a sparkling frost, or a brisk autumnal breeze, or even a torrential downpour.

In her mind's eye she longingly imagined Honeycote, the tiny village in the Cotswolds she and Lawrence had lived in before they moved here. It would be hunkering down for winter now, shedding its leaves, putting on its mantle of mist, the air crisp and sharp. And she was fairly certain its inhabitants could have managed more than five minutes of discussion on Joanne Harris before moving on to the inevitable salacious gossip about who was bonking whom in the local hunt.

Kay jumped to her feet and marched over to the children. The nanny eyed her warily, wondering if she had inadvertently put a foot wrong – were the children being too loud? Were they splashing too much? But no – Mrs Oakley was smiling at her.

'You might as well have the rest of the day off. I'll look after them.'

The girl blinked in astonishment, then panicked that she was going to be given her notice. The English never came out with what they were really thinking. Was this Mrs Oakley's way of saying her services were no longer needed? Would she have a curt phone call that evening telling her not to bother coming back?

'I'll see you tomorrow.' Kay was getting impatient. The nanny was dithering – didn't she know a good thing when she saw it? Eventually she went, and Kay took the two little girls into the kitchen to make them milkshakes. Kay wasn't a natural hands-on mother, but anything to stop the tedium.

She wasn't sure how much longer she could endure this way of life. Swimming pool. Shopping. Beauty parlour. Shopping. Cocktail parties and barbecues. Shopping. There was nothing to strive for. Nothing to think about, except what to wear and whether to go one shade lighter or darker with the highlights. And what to throw on the barbecue each evening for the so-called friends they entertained night after night. Even though they could hardly be described as anything more than acquaintances. They were all indistinguishable from each other, the people that she and Lawrence mixed with. They all had the same values. Or lack of.

She took a carton of ice-cream out of the freezer and a box of huge ripe strawberries. If they were in England, she could be leading Flora round the paddock on a fat little pony. There were stables here, of course, but it wasn't the same. She longed for trees and hedges and hills and valleys and ponds and streams. And air that was fresh, not air that hit the back of your throat.

Kay hulled the strawberries, throwing them carelessly into the blender. She wanted a change. She'd had enough. Nearly four years, they'd been here. Surely that was long enough? Surely they could go back to England now? Any gossip would have died down by now. They could start again afresh. Not that she cared about rumour-mongering, but she knew Lawrence was sensitive. He was the one who'd wanted to move away to escape the wagging tongues. Brazen Kay would have happily faced the speculation and scandal, but she gave in to his wishes. After all, he had made a pretty big sacrifice, taking her back when she'd given birth to another man's child. So she had capitulated, initially seduced by the picture he painted of life in the sun. What wasn't to like?

A lot, it now turned out. She flicked the switch on the blender and watched the fruit bounce wildly in the glass jar, spurting out red juice, staining the white of the ice-cream, until eventually the two mingled into a satisfying deep pink. She poured the unctuous liquid into two tall glasses and topped it with sprinkles. Sitting on a chrome bar stool, resting her chin in her hand with her elbow on the granite work surface, she watched Flora and her friend giggling and spooning the concoction into their mouths. They were happy enough. But Kay was worried how Flora would turn out, brought up in this sterile environment. She missed the English class system, the little giveaway clues that allowed you to pigeonhole people. Here, you were simply judged on how much money you had, and people speculated on the state of your bank balance interminably. In England, you could be top dog without cash; even the wealthiest person could slide to the bottom of the pecking order if they weren't seen to be spending their money on the right things. Kay loved the nuances; the way you could never be quite sure of your position. The way it was always the people who didn't care who came out on top; the ones who did care often languished at the bottom, desperate to make their way up the greasy pole to recognition and respectability.

Kay took no comfort from the fact that here, she and Lawrence were at the top of their social ladder, simply by dint of their perceived financial success. She really didn't care that she was the queen bee, for she didn't value the opinion of any of their associates. She wouldn't care if she never saw anything of them again. She picked up a perfectly ripe strawberry and bit into it savagely.

She'd talk to Lawrence when he got home this evening. She was starting to suspect that he too had had enough of paradise. He had been restless of late. A bit heavy on the vodka and tonics too, which she didn't like. It was often the way, when you had the Midas touch. Money didn't always make life easier. Maybe they should cut their losses, get out while the going was good, and settle for a quieter existence. She pictured a small house back in

Honeycote – well, not small small, but certainly not as big as the palatial manor house they had once lived in. Flora could go to a decent school – she pictured her in the red and grey uniform of the prep school in Eldenbury, the nearby market town. And she could have a proper conversation, with a man who wasn't a sexist git drenched in Hugo Boss, trying to paw you under the dinner table at every opportunity. Not that men in the Cotswolds didn't have wandering hands, but they were more subtle about it. Kay allowed herself a little smile, both at the memory and the prospect, and felt a flicker of adrenalin. Perhaps they could be back in time for Christmas? Images of roaring log fires, flickering candles and intoxicating mulled wine rushed through her head. Surely Flora deserved a proper English Yuletide? Perhaps that was the tack she should take with Lawrence? Flora was his Achilles heel, after all.

Something had to happen to get them out of this anodyne existence.

At half past four the doorbell rang, the chimes echoing through the marble of the hall. Kay automatically checked her appearance in the mirror and swiped a lipstick across her mouth, because you could never be seen to look anything other than your best – that was when the rumours started. She put the lid back on the lipstick and sighed. She'd been brain-washed. Why should she care what people thought?

She walked through the hall, discerning two shadowy shapes through the thickly frosted glass of the front door. Bulky figures. Definitely men. Disconcerted, for a moment she thought about not answering, but something drew her forward.

As she opened the door and saw the solemn expressions, then recognized the uniform of the police, a warning sprang into her mind. What was that irritating strap line that people seemed so fond of these days?

Be careful what you wish for . . .

2

Lucy Liddiard woke with butterflies and a smile on her face. A trickle of golden sunlight was filtering through the curtains, the sound of birdsong hinting that spring was on its way and the long winter was at last coming to an end. She estimated that it must be about half past six – the house was quiet, which meant the heating, still necessary to take the edge off the morning chill, hadn't come on yet. The pipes usually rumbled and groaned for the first half-hour of their wakening.

Next to her, her husband Mickey was still out for the count. In the half-light, the few silver threads in his dark curls couldn't be seen, nor the laughter lines that were just starting to deepen at the corner of his eyes and around his mouth, now he was approaching fifty. One year closer today. She considered waking him and wishing him a happy birthday, but decided against it. It was still far too early – she'd take advantage of the peace and quiet. She had a lot to do.

For the fifth time she added up how many she had coming for lunch. For months, it had been just the two of them for Sunday lunch at Honeycote House, which had been horribly strange. In the end, Lucy had stopped bothering doing a roast, because it was hardly worth it. But today, everyone was coming round for Mickey's birthday, and she couldn't wait.

Her stepson, Patrick, and his girlfriend Mandy would probably arrive first. They usually rushed off somewhere glamorous on a Sunday. To the races, or shopping in Bath, or for lunch with friends at a rowdy restaurant in Cheltenham. But then they were young and in love and with no real responsibility, although Lucy knew that Patrick had taken a lot on board at Honeycote Ales. He'd stepped into Mickey's shoes straight after the ghastly accident that Lucy didn't like to think about any more, now it was becoming a distant memory. Even now Mickey was back on form Patrick seemed to manage more than his share of the workload. God knows where the boy had inherited his sense of duty from. Certainly not his father – Mickey was notoriously irresponsible, only marginally less so now he was undeniably middle-aged. And not his mother either. She had been by all accounts a hippydippy flake, which was why Mickey had managed to get custody in the end. Lucy had brought Patrick up as her own, and she thought the world of him.

He was so like Mickey in some ways. They both had the devil-may-care insouciance that only the truly handsome can carry off, combined with boyish charm, immaculate manners and a fondness for the good things in life. But Lucy knew Patrick had hidden depths. He was not as transparent as his father; he took things to heart, though he was always desperate not to show it. Mickey, on the other hand, was a bona fide ostrich. If he could pretend something bad wasn't happening, then he would. Patrick did the worrying for both of them.

Which made Lucy wonder if Mandy was quite the

right girl for him. She was very sweet, but perhaps a little
. . . well, superficial seemed an unkind description. But
Lucy couldn't help feeling that Patrick needed someone
who could unlock whatever it was that lay underneath
his beguiling exterior, someone who understood his com-
plexity. On the other hand, perhaps someone like Mandy
was good for him. She was a simple soul, straightforward
and relatively undemanding, not like a lot of girls these
days, who seemed to expect everything their own way
with gold-plated, diamond-encrusted knobs on.

Next to appear would be Mandy's father, Keith.
Lovely, cuddly Keith, with his ready smile and the broad
Brummie accent he would never lose. He'd come for one
of their infamous Sunday lunches a few years ago, just
after his ghastly wife had left him. Disillusioned with the
empty life he was leading in soulless, suburban Solihull,
he'd fallen under the Liddiard spell immediately, plunging
all his money into the ailing brewery, which had been on
the verge of bankruptcy at the time. He was virtually one
of the family now. He would be bringing Ginny, his . . .
what would you call her? Girlfriend? Lover? Mistress?
Other half? Lucy wasn't sure of the official term. She'd
introduced the two of them to each other three years ago,
when they had both been abandoned souls licking their
respective wounds, and they had been living together ever
since.

Lucy's younger daughter, Georgina, was also coming
back from university in Gloucester for the day, bombing
over in her clapped-out Fiesta. Madcap Georgie – the
phrase 'jolly hockeysticks' could have been coined just for
her. She was halfway through her degree; Lucy had never
quite got to the bottom of what it was all about, but it

seemed to involve hospitality and sport and tourism – perfect for the sporty, bossy Georgie. Lucy was eternally grateful that she'd chosen a university close enough for her to pop back for the day if she felt like it. Her older daughter, Sophie, was on yet another jaunt to Australia with her boyfriend Ned, and it was Lucy's greatest fear that they would never come home.

Last of all, and late, because they were always late these days, would be Mickey's brother James, his wife Caroline, and their three children, who were all under five. Lucy prayed that James and Caroline would be on speaking terms. Their relationship was pretty strained at the moment. James, it was safe to say, was not a new man, and Caroline was volatile at the best of times. At least everyone would muck in today and look after the kids so she could have a bit of a break.

All in all, that made a total of twelve for lunch. Lucy wasn't fazed. She preferred catering for large numbers. It was what she was used to. She'd been hopeless at cooking for just her and Mickey; half of what she prepared had ended up in the bin or the dog's bowl each night. Today she was cooking two enormous fillets of beef – one medium, one rare – and her mouth watered at the prospect of the beetroot-red velvety slices. Batter for dozens and dozens of Yorkshire puddings was already resting in a jug in the pantry.

She padded down to the kitchen. Every time she walked in, it still gave her a shock. The kitchen at Honeycote House had long been legendary. Hundreds of meals, impromptu parties and spontaneous celebrations had taken place around the enormous table in its midst. No one cared that the doors of the antiquated kitchen units were hanging off their hinges, or that the plaster was falling off, or that the walls hadn't been redecorated for years. But two months ago Lucy had finally decided that enough was enough. If you looked at it in the cold light of day, and not through a fug of wine and smoke and laughter and cooking smells, it was a disgrace. She had looked around one morning and seen nothing but grease stains and cobwebs. Time for a makeover, she'd decided.

Lucy was no princess. She gutted the kitchen herself, manhandling the old units out into the tack room where they could be used to store animal food and cleaning equipment. Then she'd been through all her old gadgets and utensils, chucking out anything broken or out-of-date. The process had been exhausting. She'd found mementos and treasures from years ago. Postcards from long-lost friends. An old Rimmel lipstick, the smell of which brought the past rushing back to her so vividly it turned her stomach. Cocktail sticks and paper cases that reminded her of all the sausages on sticks and fairy cakes she'd done for children's parties over the years. A gingham bun-holder trimmed in ric-rac that Sophie had made for her, which Lucy had proudly displayed at dinner parties for years, even though her guests had looked askance at it. Tupperware boxes that still smelled of the picnic food they'd once held. Lucy felt flayed alive emotionally as she forced herself to rid the kitchen of anything remotely rancid, which was pretty much everything.

She'd sat for hours looking at the row of empty champagne bottles that used to sit on the top shelf of the dresser, the occasion they had marked inscribed on each label in thick black pen. Why was she so desperate to hang on to them? Would life change one iota if she took them to the recycling centre in Eldenbury? All they did was gather dust, and, if she was honest, remind her of times that could never be repeated. She forced herself to drop each bottle into the bin in the supermarket car park, wiping away tears with her remaining hand, hoping desperately no one would spot her. As the glass shattered, it occurred to her that over the past couple of years nothing had happened worth celebrating. It had been a period of farewells, as first Patrick had moved out to live with Mandy, then Sophie and Georgina had flown the nest, leaving Lucy and Mickey to rattle around in Honeycote House, which had always been large but now seemed positively cavernous.

One wall in the kitchen had been smothered in photographs. It was a veritable rogues' gallery – Mickey dressed as a woman, the girls on a toboggan being pulled by Patrick; Lucy in a flapper dress for the Great Gatsby party they had for her fortieth; a toothless Georgie on the family pony. They were cracked and faded. Lucy took them all down carefully, annotated them as well as her memory allowed, and took them to a girl who specialized in photographic collages. The snapshots had come back beautifully mounted and framed in a chronological unfolding of life at Honeycote House. It was a work of art, but Lucy still preferred the slapdash version that had been stuck to the wall with browning sticky tape.

Then she commissioned some simple cupboards in oak tongue and groove, held together with huge black hinges she'd found in a reclamation yard. The walls, once a cheery egg-yolk yellow, were now painted a calm and restful duck-egg blue. The ancient Laura Ashley curtains were replaced with a smart Vanessa Arbuthnott roller blind – the fabric had been screamingly expensive, but Lucy had got a remnant and made the blind herself, which had involved a fair amount of swearing. Then she'd treated herself to some new appliances. A new fridge, for a start, with a freezer that defrosted itself. All she'd had before was an ice box that got so full the peas invariably slid out every time you opened it.

By the end of the project she was even more unsettled. There was no doubt the kitchen was stunning. Decluttering it had seemed to double the size and the light, but to Lucy it didn't feel quite right. She felt faintly embarrassed every time she cooked in it, rather as if she had a new dress on that she wasn't quite sure about. Everyone who had seen it had exclaimed how fantastic it looked, but she could tell deep down they preferred the previous incarnation, as did she. She sighed. She would get used to it. It just needed distressing; perhaps today's celebrations would take the gloss off it and make it feel more lived in.

Lucy felt as if she'd been treading water for ages, waiting for the next phase of her life. Surely it didn't just fade into complete nothingness? She'd heard of empty-nest syndrome, but didn't that belong to women of a different age – menopausal, grey-haired creatures with thick waists and no dress sense? Technically, Lucy could still have another baby if she wanted. She'd been barely in her twenties when she'd had Sophie and Georgina. This solution to her ennui had occurred to her in a wild moment when she'd folded all the girls' baby clothes away one afternoon and put them in the attic, but she'd dismissed it fairly rapidly. If not a baby, then the traditional route for a dissatisfied, middle-aged woman was either an affair or an Open University degree. Neither of which particularly appealed.

She checked the warming oven of the Aga to see if

her pavlovas had dried out – three dense, chewy discs of meringue as big as dinner plates which would be piled on top of each other with dollops of whipped cream flecked with raspberries – madly out of season but now she had the facilities, she could take advantage of frozen fruit. That would keep the sweet-toothed brigade happy, while the rest could delve into Stilton or Brie. There was a whole one of each resting on a marble slab.

At the prospect of the banquet to come, Lucy felt like her old self again. She sang as she put on the kettle, dancing round the kitchen in her striped pyjamas and bed socks, lighter of heart than she had been for months.

Mickey Liddiard stood in the doorway of his transformed kitchen, smiling. His wife still did it for him. Lucy had never used anything more exotic than Ponds Cold Cream, but it had done the trick – her skin was smooth and glowing, her treacle-brown eyes unlined. Her tousled chestnut hair fell to her shoulders, without a hint of grey. She was still as slim as a reed; riding kept her waist trim, her buttocks taut, her arms toned.

He knew she'd been struggling over the past few months. She hated the house when it was empty. Lucy thrived on company, the more the merrier. When the children were young, there had been a constant stream of friends in and out, coming for tea, sleeping over, sometimes staying for days on end. Patrick's girlfriend Mandy had been one such guest – she'd come to stay for the weekend with Sophie and to all intents and purposes had never actually left. But with Patrick and Mandy now in their own little cottage, Sophie in Australia and Georgina at uni, the stream had dried up. Mickey had watched Lucy almost wither away.

Once or twice he'd offered to find her a job at the brewery, but she'd batted away the idea with what was bordering on scorn. She'd be no use at the brewery. She had no idea how it was run. And as she'd never done a day's work in her life, she'd be a liability. Lucy had no confidence in her own abilities.

And now, thought Mickey, he was glad she hadn't taken him up on his offer. Business was pretty grim, and he preferred to protect her from the harsh reality of belt-tightening and redundancies. Had she been working for Honeycote Ales, he'd have found it hard to hide the truth.

'Morning, Mrs Liddiard.' He affected a cod bumpkin accent.

She turned round with a start. He grinned at her, lounging against the wall in his chambray pyjama bottoms, his shoulders still as broad and his stomach still as flat as the day she had met him, then gave her a lascivious tradesman's wink as he held up the bottle of milk he'd retrieved from the doorstep.

'I brought you your usual. Will that be all today, or was there something else you were after?'

'Oh, thank you.' She played along immediately, her eyes sparkling. 'Actually, I wouldn't mind one of your specials today.'

'Ooh, right, Mrs Liddiard. I'll see what I can do.'

She giggled as he unbuttoned her pyjama top, then scooped her up and carried her upstairs, dropping her on the bed in a heap.

'They don't call me the fastest milkman in the west for nothing,' he murmured as he ravished her amongst the rumpled bedclothes.

An hour later, Lucy woke with a start. They'd fallen asleep, tangled in each other's arms.

'Come on, Mickey. Get up. They'll all be here soon and I've got mounds of potatoes to peel and the table to lay.'

She flew back down the stairs to the kitchen, put the kettle back on the hotplate and drew breath. It wasn't quite nine by the clock on the wall. She leant back against the Aga for a moment to wait for the water to boil, breathing out a little sigh of contentment. Spring in the air, a quick roll in the hay, followed by a houseful for lunch. It didn't get better than that.

By midday, everything was under control. Lucy stood back to admire her handiwork. It was unusual for her to be so particular; at Honeycote House, meals and celebrations seemed to evolve by some sort of osmosis that took no planning, underpinned with a slight air of chaos. Today, because there was no one in the house to distract her, no dilemmas to deal with, she could concentrate on the task in hand, which was making her nervous. In the old days, the phone would have been ringing continuously, dogs would be barking as people came and went, an argument over clothing would break out between the girls, Mickey would slope off at the last minute, just when she needed him to carve or bring in some logs . . . but today peace and order reigned.

The table looked stunning. When she'd finished the kitchen, Lucy had reflected that she and Mickey had been using his parents' old crockery all these years, old-fashioned and chipped and mismatched. They had Wedgwood and the Waterford for special occasions, of course, but in the kitchen they had always made do. It had never seemed to matter before, but now the plates didn't fit at all. So Lucy had rushed out and bought a dozen cream dinner plates – rustic Provençal china with scrolled edges. And a dozen chunky wine glasses with square bottoms that she'd fallen in love with – for years they had drunk out of the boring goblets they got from the supplier who did the pubs, because glasses at Honeycote House always got broken and there was no point in having any nicer ones.

Now, all her purchases were laid out on the table. There were also soft linen napkins trimmed with lace that Lucy had found in the airing cupboard, and laundered and ironed, another legacy from Mickey's mother – they didn't usually bother with such niceties. A huge wrought-iron candelabra sat in the middle, stuffed with proper beeswax candles. Lucy reminded herself to remove it at some stage during the meal or it was bound to get knocked over. Two enamel jugs were stuffed to the gills with white tulips.

Sunlight shone in through the open kitchen window, lighting up the whole room, and Lucy could hear the peal of bells as the Sunday service at the little church in the village finished. Lucy sometimes went, because she knew the church might be in danger of closure if it wasn't supported, but today she hadn't had time. She slid a tray of cheese straws into the baking oven of the Aga and rushed upstairs to get changed.

In recognition of spring, she put on a pale yellow linen skirt, a white cashmere cardigan, and white ballet flats. She had a moment to look in the mirror just as the front doorbell jangled madly, shook her hair out with her fingers, and ran down the stairs to greet the first of her guests.

*

It was Caroline and James who arrived first, which was unusual. Their oldest, Henry, hurtled in through the door with a bloodcurdling Red Indian war cry and a plastic tomahawk. James followed, looking awkward with Percy in his portable baby chair. He had never been at home with baby paraphernalia but as someone pointed out, Chippendale didn't do car seats. Caroline brought up the rear with two-year-old Constance, who stumped over the gravel and up the steps clinging on to her mother's finger, solemn beneath her ginger pudding-bowl haircut.

'Happy birthday. And for Christ's sake, open it quickly,' James muttered to his brother, thrusting a bottle of vintage Veuve at Mickey as he deposited the car seat on the kitchen table. Lucy promptly picked it up and put it on the floor. Percy had once rocked his chair so hard it had fallen off the kitchen work top, a fact James never seemed to remember. She popped open the buckle and scooped Percy out. He promptly puked over her.

'Welcome to my world,' said Caroline, puffing with exertion, even though there were only three steps up to the front door of Honeycote House. She was terribly unfit.

'Don't worry,' Lucy reassured her, dabbing at her cardigan with a tea towel. 'It's only a little posset.'

James looked as if he might be sick himself. Mickey sniffed, wrinkling his nose.

'I think Connie might have done a poo.'

'Your turn,' said Caroline to her husband.

'How can it be my turn?' asked James acidly. 'I changed her just before we came out.'

'Well, I changed her fifty-nine times last week. So you've got a lot of catching up to do.'

'I'll do it,' said Lucy, popping Percy back into his seat and holding out her hand. 'Come on, Connie.'

'You're a saint.' Caroline flopped into the big chair at the head of the table. She had on a black wrap dress that had fitted perfectly once but was now two sizes too small. As soon as she sat down the fabric strained, revealing hold-up black stockings and an impressive cleavage. Mickey's eyes nearly popped out of his head.

'It's OK. I've been there.' Lucy grinned in response. 'It must run in the family. Mickey didn't change a single nappy when my lot were little.'

'Quite right. Women's work.' Mickey worked the cork out of the bottle of champagne. It flew obligingly across the room. Caroline promptly picked it up and threw it back at Mickey, who ducked.

'I know you're only trying to wind me up,' she shouted. 'But there's no need.' And she promptly burst into tears.

Oh dear, thought Lucy.

'Nappies? Baby wipes?' she asked hopefully.

'Shit!' Caroline wailed. 'I forgot the changing bag. James, you'll have to go home and get it.'

James already had his paw around a chilled glass of Veuve Clicquot.

'No way.'

'Don't panic,' said Lucy. 'I'll phone Patrick and Mandy. They can stop off at the supermarket in Eldenbury on their way through. Connie can go without for half an hour.'

'She'll piddle on your tiles,' warned James.

'She won't be the first,' said Lucy cheerfully, 'and I'm sure she won't be the last.'

Once Connie had been divested of her soiled nappy

and everyone had a drink, Georgina bounded in. Georgina, it was safe to say, did not have her finger on the pulse of fashion. She really didn't care about clothes, just threw on whatever was closest to hand. Today that was an outsize rugby shirt (Lucy didn't like to ask whose), a denim miniskirt, opaque tights and pink clogs. Her hair was tied up in two stubby bunches.

'Glad to see you've dressed for the occasion.' Mickey kissed his daughter absently on the head and handed her a glass.

'You should have seen what I had on earlier,' retorted Georgie. 'Anyway, it's just Sunday lunch, isn't it? No big deal.' She relented, grinning, and thrust a parcel at her father. 'Happy birthday, Dad. Sorry about the crap wrapping paper.'

Mickey duly unwrapped it. It was a book.

'*Fifty Places to See Before You Die?*' Mickey raised an eyebrow. 'I'm not quite sure how I'm supposed to take that.'

'I thought it was about time you and Mum did something,' declared Georgina. 'When's the last time you stepped foot outside Honeycote?'

'In case you'd forgotten, I'm forking out for your university fees at the moment,' Mickey shot back. 'Which means we'd be lucky to afford a day trip to Weston.'

'But thank you, sweetheart.' Lucy shot her husband a warning look, not wanting dissension amongst the troops. She'd almost forgotten what it was like when they all got together. And they weren't even all here yet.

'Wow!' said Mandy. 'I had no idea. Barbie or the Little Mermaid. Which do you think?'

Patrick rolled his eyes. They were in the middle of the supermarket in Eldenbury, following an SOS call from Lucy. It was astonishing, he thought, how Mandy could turn the most mundane of shopping trips into a retail experience. She was dithering over the choice of nappies as if she was choosing a bracelet in Tiffany's.

'Can't you just get plain ones?'

'That's boring!' Mandy reached out a decisive hand, and Patrick sighed with relief. 'The Little Mermaid, I think. Or maybe I should get both.'

'No!'

Mandy gave him a reproachful look.

'They won't go to waste. She'll use them.'

Patrick smiled, despite himself. Mandy could justify any purchase on God's earth.

'Come on, then.'

He went to walk off, then realized that she was staring at the rack of baby clothes with a strange look in her eyes.

'Mandy?'

'Aren't they sweet?'

'Those are too small for Constance. Or even Percy.' He sensed he would have to be firm.

'I know . . .' She trailed off wistfully.

Patrick frowned.

'You're not . . . ?'

'No. But it makes you think, doesn't it? I mean, look.' She picked up a tiny red and white striped babygro. 'It's just adorable.'

'Very nice. Now come on. Connie's running round without a nappy on, remember.'

Mandy hung the little outfit back up reluctantly.

Patrick found himself staring at it.

27

A baby.

Why the hell hadn't he thought of it sooner?

Patrick had no concrete evidence, but he had a funny feeling that Mandy's father wanted out of the brewery. After Keith Sherwyn had come on board, nearly five years ago now, things had gone swimmingly for a while. He had brought a much-needed lump sum and a significant amount of business acumen to the table.

Now, they had run out of cash. Keith's investment had allowed them to completely renovate and refurbish the Honeycote Arms, make a few long overdue improvements to the brewery itself and do some very basic running repairs to their other tied houses. They had just about managed to break even for the past two years, but now it was clear that if they wanted to move into substantial profit they would have to do for their other pubs what they had done for their flagship. Traditional pubs were all very well, but people expected tradition with a twist these days, not faded banquettes and the offer of a cheese and onion bap at lunchtime. Mod cons and luxury had become the norm; style and design were the buzzwords right down to the last knife and fork. And this couldn't be brought about on a shoestring. A decent refurb was, on average, a hundred grand. To transform all their pubs into successful gastropubs like the Honeycote Arms meant a budget of more than a million quid.

Realistically, they had three options.

The easiest was to limp on as they were. Honeycote Ales itself sold a reasonable amount of beer, as the brew had a good reputation and a loyal following, albeit locally. The pubs had their established clientele, who weren't big spenders but were regular enough to ensure a steady income stream. But they would only be prolonging the agony, postponing the day when the pubs finally fell into total disrepair and the ancient equipment gave up the ghost.

The next option was to sell off a couple of pubs, giving them an instant injection of ready cash which they could then spread around the rest. But the Liddiards had always firmly resisted this path, as it diminished their property portfolio, and once you gave into that temptation where did you stop? The tied houses were their collateral, what made them millionaires on paper.

Or they could sell up completely. They had offers all the time, from bigger breweries that would have the means to do everything needed to turn Honeycote Ales into a cash cow almost overnight. It would be tempting to take the money and run. But to Mickey and Patrick, that was anathema. Honeycote Ales had been in the Liddiard family since the middle of the nineteenth century. And even Keith, who had no such ties, had been drawn to the brewery in the first place because of what it represented – family values and age-old traditions. If he urged them to sell he would be hypocritical.

But Patrick had sensed in him a certain malaise of late. Keith had been withdrawn and distracted. Never rude or uninterested, but he definitely had something on his mind. And the last time Mickey, in a moment of despondency when they had a quote in to underpin the subsiding Peacock Inn, had mooted flogging the whole lot, Keith hadn't demurred. Which was tantamount to capitulation, in Patrick's book. Keith was a fighter, bullish to the end. If even he was losing hope, well . . . then there wasn't any. Patrick felt a tight ball of worry in his stomach when he thought about it. Keith could easily get rid of his share and walk away. He bloody well hoped he wouldn't, but one of the first lessons Keith had taught him was not to be sentimental about business.

Patrick knew he couldn't manage without Keith on side. Keith was always calm. Practical. He didn't mind facing problems head on. If Keith jumped ship, Patrick knew he wouldn't be able to manage. He didn't have the experience, the vision, the power of his own convictions that came with years of being hands on.

And Mickey was useless. He just put his head in the sand. He didn't have a fucking clue about business; he wouldn't know a strategic alliance or an early adopter if he fell over it. Patrick might not be Alan Sugar, but he read the trade papers and surfed the internet religiously to see what their competitors were doing. Mickey didn't even have an email address, and only just about knew how to go online. Some might think it was an affectation, a pretentious attempt to appear a Luddite, but Patrick knew it was pure laziness. If Mickey didn't have an email address, then he didn't have to deal with anything.

Patrick sighed. Sometimes he thought he was a lucky sod. After all, not everyone was handed the chance to go into the family business. And a brewery was slightly glamorous and romantic. Everyone liked a drink, after all, and there was a history to Honeycote Ales that filled him with a sense of pride. He adored the old buildings, whose very bricks and floor-boards were suffused with the sweat of his forebears. It was one of the reasons why he was so desperately keen to hang on to the brewery and not see it slip out of the Liddiard family. It would be a crime against their heritage. People like them had a responsibility to the nation. If they didn't fight tooth and nail to hold on to their history, the whole country would become homogenized, dominated by a handful of brand names, all the character wiped out and replaced with wipe-clean, EEC compliant machinery.

At other times, however, Patrick wished fervently he'd never been handed this legacy, or had chosen to walk away from it when he'd left school, when he'd been free to make a choice. But a lack of academic qualifications had left him with few realistic alternatives, and now he was too firmly entrenched. He was emotionally attached, as well as financially beholden. And he had a genuine interest. He loved the pubs, their place in local society, the fact that everyone from the merest farmhand to the grandest landowner for miles around rubbed shoulders at the bar and drank thirstily from their pumps. He'd learnt a lot in the past four years, once he'd started taking his position seriously and hadn't just spent his time drinking and womanizing.

Now Patrick had a very clear vision of where Honeycote Ales should be headed. But he couldn't do it without Keith. If Keith was disillusioned, if he had fallen out of love with Honeycote Ales – which he had every right to do, for he wasn't a Liddiard and owed them no loyalty – then Patrick had to take steps to convince him to stay.

If he married Mandy, then Keith would stay loyal to the brewery to protect his daughter's interests. And if there was a baby too . . .

Patrick emerged from the supermarket, blinking in the unexpectedly bright sunshine, swinging the carrier bag containing not just the nappies but a huge box of Belgian chocolates, a tub of Maltesers for the kids, a bottle of Bollinger – it was his dad's birthday, after all, so they needed a toast – and a copy of the Eagles' Greatest Hits. One of Mickey's party tricks when drunk was a heartfelt rendition of 'Hotel California'. This would sound great on the state-of-the-art sound system Lucy'd had put into the kitchen.

The new kitchen was a further cause of anxiety for Patrick. Lucy's extravagance was evidence that Mickey hadn't even hinted to her that times were hard. Lucy wasn't a spendthrift, but she'd thrown herself wholeheartedly into the project and hadn't held back at all. Patrick knew that some of the invoices for materials and work still hadn't been paid, and were sitting in the in-tray at the brewery office. Lucy would be horrified if she knew.

Never mind, he thought. He wasn't going to worry about unpaid bills today. He had a far more interesting item on his agenda.

It was the first day to remotely resemble spring, so they put the top down on his Austin Healey. As they drove out of Eldenbury and along the road that led to Honeycote, Patrick turned his idea over in his mind. Today would be the ideal occasion to announce an engagement, he thought. He felt a flicker of excitement in his belly, and the corners of his mouth turned up.

They reached the crest of Poachers Hill, with its dizzying view of Honeycote below. Patrick could see the church, the tower of the brewery and, if you followed the road carefully, the golden walls of Honeycote House peeping through the bare branches of the trees. In a month or so, when the trees were green, you wouldn't be able to see it at all.

He pulled over into the lay-by that served as a view-point for tourists. He switched off the engine and turned to Mandy, clearing his throat.

'I've had an idea,' he said casually. She looked at him quizzically, and he gazed at her for a moment, remembering the first time he had kissed her. He'd only done it to wind her up, wanting to punish her for transforming his sister Sophie into a total trollop for the ball they'd gone to that evening. Patrick had wanted to make it quite clear to Mandy that no one messed with his family without his say-so, that giving Sophie a cleavage and a fake tan and a ridiculous hairdo had been totally inappropriate. But as soon as their lips had met he had been lost. Tearing himself away from her, leaving her breathless and gasping and desperate for more, had been an act of iron will. In the process of teaching her a lesson, he'd fallen in love himself.

She was smiling back at him now, the little dimple flickering in and out of the creamy flesh at the corner of her mouth.

'What?' She was intrigued. Patrick wasn't one for ideas. He was never conspiratorial. But he was grinning at her, his ice-blue eyes, which could be so cold when he was displeased, sparkling in the sunshine.

'I think we should get married.'

Mandy blinked. Once. Twice.

'It's about time, don't you think? We've lived together long enough. We love each other . . . don't we?'

Patrick looked at her, suddenly anxious. She burst out laughing. Patrick was rarely anxious or unsure of himself.

'What's so funny?' he asked indignantly.

'You. You're nervous! I've never seen you nervous.'

33

'I'm not bloody nervous. I just . . .'

Patrick trailed off, feeling foolish and exposed. He hadn't expected Mandy to laugh at his proposal. Was it so ridiculous?

'I'm sorry,' he said stiffly. 'I thought it was a logical step. Obviously I was wrong.'

Mandy bit her lip, realizing he had mistaken her laughter for derision, not delirium.

'I'm laughing because I'm happy, you idiot!' She flung her arms around his neck. 'I think it's a fantastic idea. Of course I want to marry you.'

Patrick felt the tension in his shoulders melt away at her touch. His worst fear was always ridicule; any suggestion that he was being laughed at or undermined meant the barriers went straight up. But now he knew he'd misunderstood, relief flooded through him and he managed a smile.

'Good.'

She frowned. 'You do mean . . . soon, don't you? You're not just going to ask me and then make me wait for ages and ages?'

'Of course not,' said Patrick.

'And we don't want a fuss, do we?' she asked anxiously. 'A nice service in the church, of course. And then everyone back to the house for lunch.'

That was what he loved about her. She might love her labels and her shopping, and she might spend an inordinate amount of time on her appearance, but Mandy was surprisingly down to earth. Anyone looking at her would think she'd want the full works: Sudeley Castle, an army of bridesmaids, vintage cars, a Robbie Williams lookalike to serenade her. But it seemed not.

'Everyone makes too much fuss about weddings these days,' she went on. 'I think it would be much more fun to keep it low key. Though obviously . . .' she leaned forward with a mischievous smile. 'I want a fuck-off dress.'

Patrick pulled her to him, suddenly turned on by the fact that here they were, engaged.

'I can't wait,' he murmured, his voice hoarse with desire. 'Let's do it as soon as we can.'

'I've always wanted to get married in May.'

'Bloody hell,' said Patrick. 'That quickly?'

'Why not?' Her eyes were shining with excitement. 'The longer you have to wait, the more of a nightmare it becomes. If we've only got a few weeks to plan it, it can't get too complicated. And if anyone can't make it, they can't make it. But Sophie and Ned will be back from Australia by then—'

Patrick suddenly looked at her, aghast.

'I forgot about the ring,' he said. 'I should have done that whole flip open the box thing . . .'

Mandy brushed his worries away with her hand. 'Listen, I've got more rings than you can shake a stick at. Let's save the money and put it towards the reception.'

Yet again she surprised him. Most women would be gagging for a rock. And how sweet that she instinctively seemed to know that money was tight. Patrick smoothed her hair in a gesture of affection, appreciating her unspoken consideration for the depths of everyone's pockets. Or should he say shallowness.

'Are you OK with us telling the others at lunch?'

'Definitely,' grinned Mandy. Patrick turned the keys in the ignition, slammed the car into first, and they whizzed off down the hill, their hair streaming behind them in the spring breeze, she in her Prada shades, he in his Raybans, the absolute picture of happiness.

It was going to be fine, Patrick told himself. He was going to marry the woman he loved, thereby bringing about the union of two families for the benefit of the business. It was terribly old-fashioned, but in some ways – despite his musical tastes and his dress sense, which were both bang up to date – Patrick was.

Minutes later, the car turned in through a pair of Cotswold stone pillars that seemed to be missing their gates and roared up the rutted drive, following the line of grass that grew through the middle before screeching to a halt before the front door. The house was glowing a mellow gold in the spring sunshine – it was large and rambling, with mullioned windows that begged to be peered through, a mossy roof, and stone as crumbly as home-made fudge. Of course, on close inspection a surveyor would have a field day, but to Patrick, who'd been brought here when he was barely as tall as the two urns that stood either side of the front door and held a cluster of primroses, it was perfect.

And one day it would be his. His fondest memories were of the kitchen at Honeycote House, of all of them together round the table. Him and Sophie and Georgina. He had always presumed that he would keep the Liddiard bloodline going. For a moment, he allowed himself a vision of his own offspring sitting round that kitchen table, bashing the tops off their boiled eggs. Then he jumped out of the driver's seat and went round to open the door for Mandy. As he took her hand, his heart burst with pride, and he couldn't resist taking her in his arms once again.

'I love you,' he murmured as he kissed her, running his fingers through her sleek, dark mane. Moments later the front door opened.

'Ugh! Cousin Patch! Stop snogging!' Henry stood in the doorway, his snub nose wrinkled with distaste, and Patrick and Mandy pulled themselves apart, laughing.

Ginny and Keith arrived bang on half past twelve, delightfully prompt as ever. Ginny was carrying a wicker basket stuffed with offerings – she had the knack of remembering things that no one had thought of. Not that Lucy ever forgot anything when it came to entertaining, but Ginny was super-thoughtful, without being saintly. Anyway, she'd been to the Liddiards' enough times to know that things could get a bit, well, heavy on the drink front, and the children might be glad of a diversion.

'I made some Rice Krispie cakes for the little ones. White chocolate, so they don't get covered. And some homemade lemonade.' There had been an incident once when a thirsty Henry had drained the dregs from everyone's Pimm's glass, with ensuing panic.

'You're an angel.' Lucy took the basket off Ginny and gave Keith a kiss. He was wearing a pale green lambswool sweater and beige cords, a totally different man to the besuited, swaggering powerhouse that had arrived on their doorstep to collect his daughter five years ago. He was softer, more relaxed, and looked younger for it, though Lucy knew that beneath the gentle exterior were nerves of steel. Keith was the archetypal iron fist in a velvet glove. Lucy had given thanks over and over when he had taken the helm, for the brewery had been adrift on very dangerous seas. Keith had put them firmly back on course.

'The twins might pop in later, if that's OK?' Ginny looked apologetic, as she always did when she was about to inflict her nubile and ebullient daughters on any social gathering.

'Of course it's OK. It would be lovely to see them.'

Kitty and Sasha were by Ginny's marriage to David, a philandering dentist who had run off with his hygienist. Cruelly ousted from their family home as a result of the ensuing divorce, Ginny had come to Honeycote with the twins to make a fresh start, renting a tiny barn conversion in the village. Lucy had found her in the village post office looking woebegone, and had promptly adopted her as her latest cause. Lucy was always looking after neglected horses or abandoned dogs, but she specialized in people too, healing them and putting them back on their feet.

Now, Ginny was a changed person. She was no longer a victim. It had taken her a long time to recover from David's selfishness and cruelty, but she'd had the last laugh in the end. David often appeared on her doorstep at the weekends, his daughter Chelsea in tow, desperate for assistance because Faith the hygienist was off shopping somewhere. Ginny hardened her heart. She let him come in and drink coffee and nodded politely while he bemoaned his situation, but she never gave him what he really wanted, which was to offer to look after Chelsea while he buggered off and did his own thing. In her previous incarnation as a doormat, Ginny would probably have had the little girl for the whole weekend, but she'd learnt the value of standing up for herself. Much to David's annoyance.

As a result of this transformation, Ginny was also now running Mrs Tiggywinkle's, an extremely successful business with an impressive turnover. When she first came to Honeycote, she had supplemented her meagre income by taking in ironing. Its immediate success soon led her to spot a gap in the market for good old-fashioned housekeeping. The area was stuffed with wealthy people who were so busy working that they were prepared to pay over the odds for someone to take on the running of their homes completely. Now, Ginny had a team of girls working for her who swooped in pairs through the front doors of the barristers and consultants and film producers and property magnates who disappeared off to London or Birmingham every day. Beds were stripped and replaced with freshly laundered sheets, every surface was swept, polished or dusted, taps, tiles and mirrors gleamed, wood was buffed with beeswax until it shone. Lightbulbs were replaced, loo paper and soap replenished, dirty towels and bathmats were removed and fresh ones put in their place, bins were washed out and bleached, every inch of grime was scrubbed from the insides of the ovens, fridges and microwaves . . . even the rinse aid and salt was topped up in the dishwasher. Finally, fresh flowers were distributed and each room lightly spritzed with a delicious citrus room spray. As the team left, they took with them any suits and dresses that had been left out to be dry-cleaned, the bed linen to be laundered, shoes to be polished and re-heeled, all of which would be returned immaculate within forty-eight hours. For this clients were willing to pay two hundred pounds a session, safe in the knowledge that they would come home to a pristine, sweet-smelling, well-stocked house.

Ginny called each client every week to make sure they were happy, to see if anything had been overlooked or to find out if there was any other detail she could add to her service. Suggestions came thick and fast from her wealthy and overworked customers. As a result, Ginny had already arranged delivery of consignments of fresh organic meat, fruit and vegetables, which would be unpacked by her team and put into the fridge or cupboards. Now she was expanding into weekend entertaining, sending girls round to lay up the dining tables, serve and then clear up afterwards. People were prepared to pay quite ridiculous prices for stress-free entertaining. Ginny paid her girls well, creamed off the top for herself and still had enough left over to keep reinvesting.

To keep up with demand, she had rented a unit on the industrial estate just outside Eldenbury, where her team of girls did the laundry and the ironing. She was considering bringing out her own range of room sprays, linen water and soaps, so even if you couldn't afford her, your home could smell as if you could. She already had a list of people waiting for her life-changing services. Clients phoned her regularly to say what a difference she had made to their lives, how uplifting it was to walk in after a hard day's work and find the place spotless and a brace of organic sirloin steaks in the fridge.

Ginny's daughter Sasha helped her in the business. Sasha was brilliant at training, as she knew every trick in the book herself, and was also on hand to step in should any of the staff call in sick. Which they rarely did, as they were well looked after, and Ginny was at pains to fit work-loads around childcare commitments. Once a week she did a working breakfast for them all, with Danish pastries and freshly squeezed orange juice and the chance to swap notes, grievances, worries and suggestions – something

Keith had introduced at Honeycote Ales and found very successful.

Thus it seemed Ginny had absorbed some of Keith's grit and determination, while Keith had taken on board her happy-go-lucky attitude and sweet nature. They were a contented, easy-going couple who seemed to have the perfect work/life balance. Lucy adored the fact that they sometimes held hands, without being in the least nauseating.

Today, though, she thought Keith looked tired and worried, and Ginny rather subdued. Lucy bit her lip, hoping that it wasn't the brewery that was the underlying cause. She'd had her suspicions of late, suspicions that were worsening because of Mickey's cheerful reassurance that everything in the garden was rosy. Whenever he did that, she knew there was trouble on the horizon, and she suddenly felt rather guilty about her extravagance in the kitchen.

Determined that she wasn't going to let this niggling worry spoil today's lunch, Lucy pulled the joints of beef out of the Aga and left them to relax on the top for half an hour, then shook the roast potatoes in their tray. As she dropped handfuls of Gruyere into the sauce for the cauliflower cheese, she looked around. Everyone was chattering madly, swigging champagne and munching on the cheese straws she'd wisely put out to line their stomachs. Pokey the red setter circumnavigated the room gobbling up the plentiful crumbs, with Connie tottering behind trying to grab her tail.

Lucy picked up her own glass and took a sip, breathing a sigh of relief. All her hard work hadn't been in vain. All the kitchen had needed was people.

Two fillets of beef and several pounds of potatoes later, everyone looked rather glazed. The magnificent feast and plentiful booze were taking their toll; eyelids were getting heavy and blood was pumping slowly as Lucy came in bearing the pavlova, which she had crowned with long, slim golden tapers. A raucous, drunken round of 'Happy Birthday to You' ensued, with Mickey pulling Henry onto his knee to help blow out the candles.

'Make a wish!' shouted someone, and Mickey obeyed, looking at Lucy and giving her a meaningful smile. She blushed.

'What did you wish? What did you wish, Uncle Mickey?' demanded Henry, jiggling up and down on his knee.

'I'm not allowed to say, otherwise it won't come true,' Mickey told him. Besides, he wasn't going to admit to hoping for cold, hard cash. It was so mercenary and unromantic.

Lucy sliced up the pavlova into thick wedges, the cream oozing from between the layers before she could get each slice onto the appropriate plate. Despite protestations of fullness, everyone managed a piece. As spoons scraped against porcelain, there were sighs of satisfaction.

'What time do you think Kitty will get here?' Mandy asked Ginny. 'Because there's something I want to ask her. Something important I want her to do for me.'

Patrick shot her a glance. She was positively bursting with the news. She looked back at him, as if begging him to divulge the information before she exploded. He supposed now was as good a time as any. He hadn't wanted to overshadow Mickey's birthday celebrations, but it would probably be some time before he could get this many of his family under one roof. And besides, he was excited too. He tapped his pudding spoon on the side of his glass.

'Um, by the way, everyone. While I've got you all captive . . .'

Everyone turned to look at Patrick, puzzled. He wasn't one for self-important announcements. He looked rather sheepish. He ran his hand through the lock of black hair that fell habitually over his eyes, a gesture that everyone who knew him recognized as a sign of nervousness. What did Patrick have to be nervous about?

He put out an arm for Mandy, and she slipped under it, looking rather coy herself. As he hugged her to him, she smiled up, glowing with adoration.

'What's that saying . . . in spring a young man's mind turns to fancy?' Patrick affected vagueness. 'Well, there was so much spring in the air as we drove over this morning that it must have got to me. I stopped the car and did something rather rash. Rather . . . impulsive.'

He couldn't resist a dramatic pause as he looked round the table.

'I asked Mandy to marry me.'

There was a moment's astonished silence, and then all hell broke loose.

'Did she say yes?' roared Mickey above the hubbub.

'Of course I did!' cried Mandy, as Patrick picked her up and swung her round. Georgina pounded the table in glee.

Keith got up from the table and came round to shake Patrick by the hand.

'Congratulations. I'm delighted. I know you'll look after her.' His voice was slightly gruff, as if he was finding it hard to speak, and as he stepped away Patrick thought he saw the glitter of a tear in his eye.

'Thank you . . . sir.' He wasn't one for deference, but the occasion merited respect. He felt sure that Keith's congratulations were genuine.

Only Caroline was lukewarm in her enthusiasm, but luckily the soon-to-be-bride and groom weren't aware of her mutterings.

'I hope he doesn't turn out like his dad or his uncle,' she slurred into her glass. 'These Liddiards look like a good catch, then they turn out to be utter bastards.'

'If you can't say anything nice,' said Lucy icily, 'then don't say anything at all.'

Caroline looked at her with the aggrieved innocence of the totally sloshed. 'You should know better than anyone,' she riposted hotly. 'Anyway, there's no need to get all indignant. It's obvious it's only a marriage of convenience.'

There was an audible gasp from Ginny. Luckily only she and Georgina had heard Caroline's spiteful remarks. Lucy was about to give her a piece of her mind, when Caroline defused the situation by bursting into noisy sobs.

'I'm sorry,' she wailed. 'They just look so happy. I can remember feeling like that once . . .'

'Mummy,' said Georgina firmly. 'I think I should take Caroline upstairs to my room for a lie down. She needs a rest.'

Ten minutes later, Georgina collared Lucy in the pantry.

'Mum, what's the matter with Caroline? She looks really awful and she's behaving like a spoilt child. And James is being a pig.'

'She does give him a hard time.'

44

'But he doesn't do anything to help.'

'James is old-fashioned.'

'What sort of an excuse is that?' Georgina looked outraged. 'You don't believe that lets him off the hook, surely?'

Actually, Caroline did look dreadful. Overweight, pale, spotty. Bloated. Her hair was lank and dull. Lucy remembered the voluptuous, flame-haired, feisty creature James had fallen in love with: karaoke queen, fearless horsewoman, career girl.

'She's got her hands full with the children.' Lucy tried to reassure Georgie, who hated dissension of any kind. 'It'll get easier.'

It was just a phase. And it would pass soon enough. Lucy remembered desperately trying to dry baby clothes on the Aga, getting up to feed Georgina in the cold of the night, then hoping to snatch some sleep before Sophie woke up at the crack of dawn. She remembered always feeling as if she had left her brain in another room, a permanent state of empty headedness. But before you knew it they were sleeping through, walking and talking, going to school, leaving home . . .

She knew that would be no comfort to Caroline. And Georgie wouldn't understand either. Dear Georgie. So matter-of-fact and positive. Everything to her was black and white. She had no real clue about what lay ahead of her, the grey areas, the dilemmas, the compromises.

Lucy decided she'd have to talk to James, if it was so obvious even to Georgie that things were badly wrong. Lucy carefully unwrapped the Brie from its waxed paper and prodded it experimentally. Perfect. Runny, but not actually running away. Just how everyone liked it.

She managed to corner James half an hour later, just as he was coming out of the loo that led into the back hallway. She blocked his way, arms crossed.

'James. I'm sorry, I've got to say it, but your behaviour towards Caroline is unforgivable. Can't you see she's struggling? Give the poor girl a break.'

James stared back at her, his eyes cold.

'I never wanted three children. Two was enough for me. She's made her own bloody bed.'

Lucy took in a sharp breath of disbelief. 'You don't mean that.'

'I do. We don't have the room. I don't earn enough money. It's bloody selfish.'

'You're not telling me you don't love Percy.'

James looked irritated. 'Of course I love Percy,' he snapped. 'But I don't like being cornered. I didn't get the choice. Percy was a fait accompli. I don't feel good about resenting him, I can assure you. But the bottom line, Lucy, is we can't afford three kids. Caroline isn't going to be back at work for at least another four years at this rate.'

'Hang on,' said Lucy. 'You're the one who keeps an Aston Martin in the garage.'

'Why the fuck should I give that up?' James exploded. 'I love that car.'

'James . . .' Lucy wasn't quite sure how to get through to him. 'Being married and having kids is all about compromise. And making sacrifices.'

'Do you really think you're fit to preach to me?' James sneered. 'If my memory serves me correctly, your marriage doesn't exactly stand up to scrutiny.'

Lucy's voice was low as she answered. 'If my marriage wasn't perfect, it's because you Liddiards have no idea about anyone but yourselves.'

She glared at him as he raised a supercilious eyebrow. How could she ever have thought herself in love with him, even for a moment? She shivered in self-disgust as she remembered their frenzied coupling on the Aubusson rug in his oh-so-tasteful living room, that desperate revenge fuck, the payback for Mickey's infidelity and feckless behaviour. She'd shut the memory out, as she and Mickey had gone on to mend their marriage, which to her mind had only been slightly damaged, not totally destroyed. She had forgiven him, and he had never known the full truth about her and James.

But now James was taunting her, reminding her that she had been weak. And perhaps he was right. Perhaps she wasn't fit to preach. But Caroline definitely didn't deserve the treatment she was getting. When had James become such an out and out sadistic bastard? He'd always been measured and self-contained, but he'd had a more gentle and sensitive side than Mickey, which was why Lucy had once been drawn to him. But that softer side seemed to have vanished into thin air. James was unrecognizably harsh. She tried desperately to see life from his perspective, for Lucy was always fair. OK, so they'd had three children in quick succession, and as James had spent the best part of his life as a rather sybaritic bachelor, pleasing himself in his immaculate house, no doubt the ensuing chaos was rather a shock to his system. But that didn't mean he had to be cruel . . .

'Just grow up,' she hissed. 'Don't be like your brother, shirking his responsibilities at every opportunity. Why don't you break with the Liddiard family tradition and be a man?'

James surveyed her coolly.

'Perhaps it wouldn't be so hard,' he drawled, 'if the women we attracted didn't see us as a meal ticket.'

Lucy had never slapped anyone in her life. But she was so incensed by James's arrogance, his cruelty and, of course, the guilt he'd stirred up inside her, that before she knew it she'd dealt him a stinging blow. He grabbed her wrist and pulled it away.

'Get off me!' she snarled. His fingers circled her slender wrist and he held her arm tightly as she struggled to get away. 'I'm warning you, James—'

'What's going on?'

The two of them turned to see Caroline staring at them accusingly, swaying at the end of the corridor, her eyes wild and her hair even wilder. James let Lucy's arm drop.

'Lucy was just giving me some advice.'

Caroline's eyes were swollen from lack of sleep, too much drink and the occasional bout of sobbing. They darted beadily from James to Lucy and back again.

'About what?'

'I was asking her if she knew anyone in the village who could give us some help in the house. I can't afford Ginny's rates, unfortunately. But I think it's about time you had some help.'

'Oh.' Caroline seemed instantly mollified.

'I know it's been hard for you since poor Mrs Titcombe's knees finally gave out,' James went on robustly, referring to his old housekeeper. Mrs Titcombe had actually given notice because she couldn't cope with the chaos Caroline left in her wake, but had been tactful enough to blame her dodgy knees.

'I'll ask around,' Lucy added, playing along with this blatant lie, but thankful that a scene had been averted. 'I'm sure there'll be someone glad of some extra cash.'

She smiled at Caroline, and was rewarded with a look of pure malevolence. She turned and hurried back to the kitchen, feeling rather sick. Too much food, one too many glasses of champagne, and the guilt of her secret swirled round in the pit of her stomach. She swallowed down the bile, blinked back the tears that were threatening to spill, and steeled herself to go back into the chaos of the kitchen as if nothing had happened. But she couldn't help wondering how much of their exchange Caroline had witnessed. She didn't want her as an enemy. Lucy didn't scare easily but Caroline was a frightening adversary.

Back in the kitchen, Patrick was doing magic for Henry. Utterly appalling magic that anyone over five would have seen through, but as Henry was only four and a half he got away with it. Georgie was walking round the kitchen with Connie balanced on her feet, and Ginny was bouncing Percy up and down on her knee. Kitty and Sasha had arrived, and were bubbling over with excitement at Patrick and Mandy's announcement.

'Can we be bridesmaids?' demanded Sasha. 'Because we're almost related. I mean, Mum is practically married to Mandy's dad. Which makes us almost sisters. And twin bridesmaids – hey, how cool would that be?'

'For heaven's sake, Sasha,' protested Ginny. 'I don't suppose Patrick and Mandy have given any thought to bridesmaids yet. And even if they have, I don't suppose you and Kitty are top of their list. There's Sophie and Georgina for a start.'

'No way!' protested Georgina, who had been a brides-maid when James and Caroline got married. 'Sorry, Caroline, no offence. But first and last time. I can't cope with the responsibility. '

Caroline had come back into the room and claimed one of the comfy chairs by the Aga.

'Quite,' drawled Caroline. 'Anyway, it would probably be terribly bad luck. Having a bridesmaid who'd already attended at a wedding that was doomed to failure.'

'I think I'll put the kettle on,' said Lucy quickly. 'I'm sure everyone's gasping for a cup of tea.'

Mandy turned to Kitty.

'Actually, Kitty,' said Mandy, 'I did want to ask you a favour. Will you do the dress?'

Kitty's mouth dropped open. Mandy was always in the latest gear. Kitty was at the local college doing fashion design, and although she specialized in catwalk knock-offs for all her friends, she didn't think Mandy would take her attempts at not-so-haute-couture seriously.

'Do you mean it?'

'Yes. I want a one-off. A total original. And you've got such great ideas.'

Kitty was overwhelmed. 'Mandy – I'd love to. But if you change your mind, I understand. I thought you'd go for a real designer.'

Mandy shook her head.

'Why line their pockets? I want all my friends and family to be as closely involved as possible. And everything else will be local.'

'Just tell me you're not going to get that awful Fleur

Gibson to do the flowers.' Sasha, who always said what everyone else was thinking, had got herself a Saturday job at Twig, the florist in Eldenbury, and had lasted precisely half a day before locking horns with the notoriously difficult owner and flouncing out.

Mandy made a face. 'She is good.'

This was true. Fleur, or to be more precise the nineteen-year-old genius she kept locked in the back room, had a wonderful knack with arrangements.

'She's a bloody menace.' Everyone looked surprised. Lucy never said anything nasty about anyone. 'She's not happy unless she thinks every man in the room fancies her. Which, of course, they do.'

'Actually, I don't,' Mickey interjected. 'She's my worst nightmare. Clingy, manipulative, dangerous.'

'She's always reminded me of Kay Oakley.' James swirled his wine round in his glass casually as he spoke.

There was an awkward silence.

'Kay wasn't that bad,' said Lucy stoutly. 'I always quite liked her.'

Which, given it was Kay that Mickey had had an affair with, was pretty loyal. But Lucy knew that James was just stirring, because he hadn't liked being reprimanded, and she wasn't having any of it. Bringing up the past when they were all intent on looking to the future was totally out of order.

'Anyway,' she said, trying to steer away from the subjects, 'I think it's up to Mandy to choose. Where are you having the reception?'

Patrick and Mandy looked at each other.

'I don't know,' Patrick admitted. 'We only thought of it this morning.'

'I know it's traditional to have it at the bride's home, but our garden at Kiplington isn't really big enough. Is it, Dad?' Mandy turned to her father anxiously.

'Not really,' said Keith. 'You'd be very limited on numbers. And parking would be tricky.'

'I definitely don't fancy having it in a hotel. It's not very personal, is it?' Mandy wrinkled her nose.

'I can't think of anything worse,' said Patrick. 'Lukewarm Bucks Fizz and swirly carpets.' He shuddered.

'Why not have it here, then?' said Lucy. 'There's bags of room.'

'You honestly wouldn't mind?' Mandy's eyes were shining. 'All those people traipsing through the house and ruining the grass? Although,' she added hastily, 'we are hoping to keep it small. Ish.'

'Mind?' said Lucy. 'I'd be thrilled. I'll help you organize it. I haven't got anything else to do.'

Patrick was secretly delighted. Being a bloke, he hadn't often fantasized about his own wedding, but now he'd given it some thought he couldn't imagine holding it in some impersonal venue still warm from the previous incumbents, the confetti and cake crumbs hastily swept away in order to make way for the next arrivals. It seemed right to have it here at home. And now he knew the entire proceedings were being left to Lucy and Mandy, he could concentrate on the matter in hand. Getting the brewery back on its feet. He needed to speak to Keith as soon as possible. He was still very subdued, though Patrick was sure he was delighted by their announcement. And now they were officially engaged, Patrick could have a man-to-man chat about how each of them saw the future.

Realizing he'd drifted off, he drew his attention back to

the rest of the room. James, Mickey and Keith were half-heartedly passing a bottle of port amongst themselves. Caroline was dozing in the big chair, Percy snuggled up against her having just guzzled his afternoon bottle. Ginny, bless her, was tackling the nasty pans that wouldn't go in the dishwasher, despite Lucy's protestations. Lucy was busy making the tea she had promised earlier.

The conversation had moved back to dresses, as it so often did. Patrick was relieved that he had little choice on the sartorial front. He had a morning suit. All he'd need to worry about was a new pair of shoes.

'Gypsy punk,' Kitty was saying, leaning back against the Aga, her hands gesticulating as she waxed lyrical on her favourite subject. She had wild curly hair, and was wearing a baby-doll dress over a Led Zeppelin T-shirt, dizzyingly high wedges and striped over-the-knee socks. For a moment, Patrick debated the wisdom of Mandy's wedding dress being in Kitty's hands. 'Or Fifties starlet-harlot. Or flamenco? No. Those are all too . . . urban. We need something pastoral. Hardy meets Larkin. As in H. E. Bates, not Philip. With a bit of Midsummer Night's Dream thrown in.'

'Stop!' Mandy was laughing at the enthusiasm her invitation had unleashed. 'I've got no idea what I want yet. Patrick only proposed to me this morning. The only thing I've set my mind on is the colour.'

'Oyster pink?' Kitty sounded hopeful. 'No – pale grey.'

'Scarlet!' said Sasha lasciviously. 'You could easily do scarlet with your colouring.'

'Too tarty.'

'It doesn't have to be.'

The twins were soon arguing the toss. They were so

different. Sasha was the antithesis of bohemian Kitty, all gloss and glimmer in designer jeans and a sparkly halter-neck top that showed off her fake tan, her hair poker straight and gleaming.

'Sorry,' said Mandy firmly. 'I'm going to be dead boring, I'm afraid. I want to get married in white.'

She smiled round as everyone stared at her. Caroline snorted. James raised an eyebrow. But Mandy stood her ground.

'I've always wanted a white wedding.'

'Then you shall have it,' said Lucy soothingly. 'There's nothing boring about being traditional. I think it's a lovely idea.'

'To a white wedding,' said Mickey, raising his glass. He loved any excuse for a toast.

'A white wedding,' everyone chorused, raising their glasses in response.

When everyone had gone, Lucy paced out the lawn from the bottom of the stone steps that led down from the terrace at the back of Honeycote House. She'd already ignored the fact that the steps were crumbling. They couldn't afford to repair everything that needed doing. Not that anyone would notice, for Lucy was an expert at making everything look just so.

She felt light of heart as she walked down the garden. She absolutely wasn't going to be the interfering mother-in-law, but having the wedding here was going to give her something to get her teeth into. It would take her mind off her ennui and stop her going completely bark-ing mad. Even though Mandy and Patrick were insisting that they wanted things kept simple, Lucy knew that this meant as much hard work as something more elaborate. If people weren't going to be distracted by gimmicks, then everything had to be perfect. In an understated, rough-round-the-edges way. She wasn't daunted, for so many things that seemed to be wedding prerequisites these days were superfluous and, usually, rather tasteless. As long as the food was delicious and there was plenty of booze, everything else would fall into place.

Lucy looked back up at the house from the bottom of the lawn and smiled in satisfaction. Mother Nature would provide most of the decoration. The bank that was studded with snowdrops and crocuses would be a brilliant green by May. The soggy ground would be dry, the lawn soft and lush, not yet parched. The countryside would be glowing in shades of emerald and lime interspersed with pinky-white blossom, the air thick with its heavenly scent. Why look any further for a source of inspiration? Mandy was right, decided Lucy. A white wedding. There was no point in trying to be clever about it. It was absolutely perfect.

Not far away, at Keeper's Cottage in Kiplington, Keith slipped into the bathroom to freshen himself up. He looked at his reflection critically. He didn't look as bad as he felt. He kept his hair clipped short these days now it had all turned steel grey, and there was no doubt it took a few years off. His face was slightly pink from rather too much to drink at lunch, but other than that he looked the picture of health.

Tomorrow might contradict his reflection. Tomorrow would bring the truth . . .

He brushed his teeth vigorously, spitting the foaming

paste back into the sink, wondering if all the rich food would stop him falling asleep later. He hoped not. When he didn't sleep, the nights were long and full of terror. Worst of all were the nights when he did drop off, then woke with a start at about three, drenched in sweat. There was no rhyme or reason to it.

He put his toothbrush back carefully, splashed water on his face and towelled it dry. He'd go back downstairs and watch the Sunday-night drama with Ginny. He often tried to slip into bed early these days, so he could feign unconsciousness when she got in beside him and thus avoid any embarrassment. But it wasn't fair. He was pushing her away, just when he needed her most.

Given the choice, Kay would never have plumped for a metallic purple Nissan Micra. But her father had insisted on buying her a car. She knew he couldn't really afford to part with five grand, but he'd wanted to do it. And now she had Flora, she understood how, as a parent, you would make any sacrifice for your children. Besides, her father knew a bloke who was selling his wife's runaround, and he knew it had been looked after from brand new. So here she was, bowling along the road out of Eldenbury with Flora in a child seat that her mother had bought from the local paper and steam-cleaned until it looked like new, in a car that had 'one careful lady owner' written all over it, when what she was used to was a motor that screamed 'reckless speed freak'.

But, as she reminded herself, that was what had got her where she was today.

Lawrence had only had his car for two weeks when it had left the coast road on a notorious bend. Forensics said he had been doing over a hundred and had lost control. She found it hard to believe. Lawrence was a good driver, and he knew that road like the back of his hand. Her unease grew when her lawyer outlined the bare facts to her rather gravely after the funeral. Lawrence had left her without a bean. Every last penny, including the money he'd raised by remortgaging their villa, unbeknownst to her, had been invested in his latest development project. This had gone mysteriously bankrupt at the time of his death. Even more mysteriously, his partners had emerged unscathed, somehow managing to get their money out before the project crashed.

Kay knew Lawrence had been unhappy with the way business had been going just before he died. The latest project was not to his taste: cheap apartments that were being thrown up using low-grade materials and badly finished. And the sales tactics being used went against the grain. Extremely high pressure techniques being used mercilessly on people who didn't know better; people who had been lured out on free flights and promptly cornered by ruthless salespeople who filled their heads with the promise of a better life. Lawrence knew that nobody was actually held at gunpoint, but he didn't agree with the mind games being used. His partners scoffed at his protestation that their customers were being exploited. Strangely enough it was the female salespeople who were the most aggressive, using a combination of their tanned sexuality and innate cunning to secure the most names on the dotted line. Lawrence loathed them, and refused to have anything to do with rewarding their success.

Kay wondered if he'd threatened to pull his money out. He'd had a meeting the week before he died, and come home in a very dark mood. Unusually, he hadn't wanted to share his misgivings with Kay, whom he often used as a sounding board. Instead, he'd taken her and Flora for a meal at their favourite harbour-side restaurant, and his mood had soon lightened when Flora ordered for them in perfect Portuguese. The little girl always managed to make him smile. So Kay hadn't grilled him any further, which she now bitterly regretted. Had she known what was troubling him, she might now be able to prove her suspicions – that his partners had sacrificed Lawrence to their own ends. Money was king in their world; loyalty meant nothing. Had they forced him off the road or done something to his brakes? Or was she being completely paranoid?

It was a better theory than the other possibility. That Lawrence had found the pressure too much and taken the only way out. She didn't believe he would have done that; he loved Flora too much. So in the end, she came to terms with the fact that it was an accident. Any other theory was too difficult to cope with.

And life was hard enough. She learned with a shock just how fickle the circles they moved in were. At the merest whiff of scandal all their so-called friends had withdrawn hastily. None of them had attended Lawrence's funeral. Not a single woman who had lounged by Kay's pool, drunk her champagne or eaten at her table phoned to commiserate. No one asked how she was, or offered to have Flora. She was a social outcast.

She got through it. Kay was tough, and the doctor was kind enough to give her something to soften the harsh reality. Nothing too strong – she wanted her wits about her, if only for Flora. Her heart ached for the bewildered little girl, who didn't really understand that her daddy had gone for ever.

Each day got worse and worse, until the day her solicitor told her gravely that, after the house had been sold and the debts paid off, she was left with the princely sum of just over five thousand pounds. Kay couldn't help thinking it would have been better to be left with nothing. Somehow that would have been easier to take than the paltry sum she had to start a new life with. Penniless somehow rang truer than merely poor.

She'd got away as quickly as she could. There was nothing keeping her in Portugal, after all. And it was pretty humiliating, being ignored in the supermarket, walked past in the street. Kay resisted the urge to march up to her old acquaintances and accost them with a cheery greeting. As soon as all the paperwork was tied up, she'd taken the first plane out and landed on her parents' doorstep in Slough. Just as she had a few years before, when she'd found out she was pregnant with Flora, and Lawrence had kicked her out. Unsurprisingly. For what he'd failed to tell her throughout their marriage was that he was infertile. She could hardly pass the baby off as his, when he'd been firing blanks all along.

It had been all right, in the end. Lawrence had come to find her, just after she had Flora. He wanted her back. He admitted he'd been wrong to withhold the information from her. That didn't excuse her infidelity, of course. But in a funny way two wrongs had made a right. The incident had brought them closer than they'd ever been. And he had become a wonderful father to Flora.

As she turned off the main road and drove into the village of Honeycote, a lump rose in Kay's throat. Perhaps they should never have left. They had never openly discussed it, but they had both felt that bringing up Flora in such close proximity to her biological father was not a good idea, and so they'd left for Portugal. As far as she knew, no one in Honeycote was even aware of their reconciliation, or the truth about Flora's parentage.

Kay's sharp eyes raked the landscape around her for signs of change. It was getting dark, but she noted a development of rather splendid new houses behind a set of gates. Honeycote Grange, read the slate sign. The best part of a million each at the very least, she estimated. She'd once been an estate agent, and her instincts had never died.

As she passed the driveway to her old house, her throat constricted. Barton Court Spa, it announced. For a moment she was tempted to check in. Whereas once she had tired of her weekly massage and exfoliation, now she longed for soothing hands to ease her aching bones. She had never felt so exhausted. It was the emotion, of course. And the uncertainty. The horrible, horrible fear. She'd lost over a stone since Lawrence died, and the one thing Kay didn't need was to lose weight. But there had been a knot of worry in her stomach – the knot that had materialized the second she'd seen the shadowy figures of the policemen through the door, and hadn't gone away since. And it seemed there wasn't room for a knot and food.

If it had been just her, it wouldn't have mattered. Kay was a survivor. She'd always kept her wits about her. But with a five-year-old child to look after, she was incredibly restricted. She needed somewhere for them to live.

It was a catch twenty-two. A vicious circle.

Of course, what it boiled down to at the end of the day

was money. Which was why she was back in Honeycote. Kay hadn't asked herself too many questions about what she was about to do next, because she didn't have any choice. It was the easiest way she could think of to get her hands on a decent lump sum, and she wasn't proud.

She pulled into the car-park of the Honeycote Arms. The crunching of the tyres on the gravel woke Flora up.

'Where are we?'

Kay was almost tempted to say 'home'. For Honeycote felt like home. She'd never been one for sentimental attachments in the past. But somehow here she felt safe. The Honeycote Arms had undergone a total transformation since she'd left. Then, it had been a typical English village pub, complete with horse-brasses and hunting prints, inoffensive but uninspiring, smelling of stale fags and the faintest whiff of wee. Now it was completely stripped out, with polished flagstones, creamy walls, and low sofas. A huge glass vase crammed with brightly coloured birds of paradise stood on the bar, behind which was a chalked-up menu and wines by the glass. It still felt traditional and English, but with a contemporary edge.

This boded well, thought Kay. Honeycote Ales had clearly got their arse into gear.

'Did you want an extra bed for the little one?' The land-lord was polite. And rather gorgeous. Early thirties, she guessed. Quite posh. Things had definitely changed. She smiled at him, wondering if he might be a useful source of information. Not now, because she was exhausted. But perhaps tomorrow.

'No. She can share with me.'

It was a habit she had got into, and one she knew would be hard to break. But it gave her comfort, to have

Flora's warm little body next to her at night. And the urge to protect her was enormous. Flora had almost stopped weeping for Lawrence, but she still talked about him, her little face screwed up with anxiety as to where exactly he was and what he was doing. And Kay knew that one day she was going to have to tell her the truth.

'Fine. Well, I'm Barney. Barney Blake. My wife Suzanna runs the kitchen. So if there's anything we can do for you during your stay . . .'

His welcoming smile reached his eyes, and Kay felt heartened. She knew she probably couldn't afford to stay here for long, but while she could, she was going to enjoy the luxury. She decided to have supper sent up to her room. She didn't quite have the nerve to go down to the bar to eat, even though they had assured her she was welcome, as she couldn't be sure who might pop in for a Sunday evening pint. She refrained from telling Barney that she used to live in the village, explaining that she was in the area on business. Which wasn't so very far from the truth.

Half an hour later, Flora tucked into boiled eggs with soldiers and Kay devoured sausage and mash. It was the first time she had felt hungry for months. She almost felt relaxed, snug and protected from the real world. Flora had laid her teddy carefully out on the bed they were to share. When they'd finished, she chucked Flora into the bath then into her pyjamas. The little girl was soon asleep, and Kay snuggled down next to her with the Sunday papers and the telly on quietly. It might be unprepossessing March, with a bitter wind outside, but Kay felt as if she had come home.

If only Lawrence had come clean to her. She felt sure

he had been hiding his problems. He would be furious with himself if he knew how things had turned out. Flora was his princess. But he was dead, Kay reminded herself, and nothing was going to bring him back. It was up to her. And the moment of reckoning was getting closer and closer. She couldn't put it off much longer. She could only afford to stay here a week, for a start. Strictly speaking, she should have checked into a bed and breakfast at thirty pounds a night, but she'd had enough of candlewick bedspreads and Glade air freshener at her parents'.

She looked at the phone, trying to screw up the courage, but her resolve trickled away. She was drained from the drive, not to mention the emotional turmoil of coming back to Honeycote and all the memories that had unleashed. She decided she would leave it until tomorrow. Monday morning was a good time to get things done. Not Sunday night.

After all, you could hardly ring someone during the *Antiques Roadshow* and tell them they had a long-lost daughter. And that you were expecting them to cough up.

3

Angela Perkins' mother lived at the end of a semi-circle of council houses on the Eldenbury side of Honeycote. There were dark red quarry tiles on the kitchen floor, and a larder cupboard, the shelves covered with stickyback plastic, and iron window frames. Had Elsie still been a council tenant it would have had central heating and double glazing fitted by now. But some years ago Angela had persuaded her husband to cough up for a mortgage so they could buy the house for Elsie, which was worth far more than the council was asking. Angela was shrewd; adept at feathering her own nest and making it look as if she was doing her mother a favour. She'd got the solicitor out pretty quickly as soon as the purchase had gone through, to ensure she was the sole beneficiary of Elsie's will, and had watched beadily from the other side of the room as Elsie had signed it in her old-fashioned, sloping cursive.

This particular Monday morning, however, she was trying to get her mother out of her house and into a home. Elsie was riddled, virtually crippled, with arthritis, and could scarcely do anything for herself. Angela couldn't take the strain any longer. She lived right the other side of Evesham, in a sprawling, ranch-style bungalow with a pair of rampant eagles on the pillars outside, and checking up on her mother in Honeycote was highly inconvenient, especially when she had virtually full occupancy at the kennels twenty-four/seven/fifty-two. The Barkley was the ultimate in luxury canine accommodation, and it was hard work meeting the exacting standards required by pedigree-dog owners these days – air-conditioning, organic food, dust-free bedding and homeopathic beauty treatments. The last thing she needed was daily visits to her mother, lugging bags of shopping and taking away dirty washing, thankless and tedious tasks and really quite unnecessary when the answer was staring them in the face. If only Elsie would accept her offer of a place at Coppice House, which she'd had to pull serious strings to get, life would be so much easier. Angela couldn't understand for the life of her why the old lady wouldn't cooperate.

'Mother . . .' she cooed. 'You'll get hot dinners, all your laundry done, other people to talk to. They have fabulous social evenings. And a mobile hairdresser.'

'Not to mention interfering nursing staff,' retorted Elsie. 'Interfering in more ways than one, if you believe the papers.'

'It's not a nursing home. It's a residential home. There's a difference.' Angela took one of her mother's gnarled hands and stroked it. It was all Elsie could do not to snatch her hand away. 'Can't you understand I'm worried sick about you? You can't cope here on your own.'

'Yes, I can.'

'Look, Mum.' Angela's voice was low and soothing, the voice she used when she was trying to reassure one of her snappier over-bred guests. 'Joyce has told me there's a lovely room coming up next month. Looking over the gardens. Light and airy. She'll move you to the top of the list if you want it. People wait years to get in.'

It was typical of Angela, who lived on favours and bribes and backhanders, to have someone willing to shove Elsie to the front of the queue. Elsie knew Joyce Hardiment, the owner of the home. Angela looked after her disgusting pug dogs while she went off to the Bahamas three times a year. Which said it all, really. Elsie was not going to subsidize Joyce's Caribbean jaunts by taking a room in her horrible establishment, which stank of wee and cabbage no matter what the brochure said. She tilted her chin defiantly.

'The only way you're going to get me out of here is in a pine box.'

Angela dropped Elsie's hand, all pretence of affection over, and lit a menthol cigarette. She sauntered over to the mirror that hung over the mantelpiece and inspected herself. White jeans, tight pink blouse, diamanté belt, freshly extended blonde hair that now fell past her shoulders, and a new set of square-tipped nails. Looking good, she thought to herself. She inspected her arse. Taut as any teenager's. Roy had been right about that exercise bike. She hadn't been impressed when he'd bought it off eBay, but she'd done as he said – hopped on it in front of *EastEnders* three times a week – and you could see the results.

She turned back to her mother, shrugging her shoulders in exasperation.

'Well, if you're not going to listen, then you're on your own. I can't come running over here at the drop of a hat. Roy and I never have time for ourselves as it is, what with

the kennels, and Mason and Ryan. They've got tourna-
ments every weekend now. We've got to support them.'

Elsie stifled a snort. Angela never did anything she
didn't want to. If she was happy to drive Mason and Ryan
round the country, it was because of the attention she got
from the other fathers on the motocross circuit. Roy, bless
him, did all the donkey work while Angela paraded round
the other motor-homes, swapping notes on performance.
And as for the kennels, Elsie knew perfectly well Angela
had a raft of dog-loving teenage girls who came up at
the weekends and were happy to clean out the runs in
return for peanuts. She wasn't exactly wading through dog
muck herself. She just made sure she was there to greet
the owners when they dropped their precious pooches off,
to reassure them they were having the five-star treatment
they deserved, given her outrageous prices.

Five minutes later Elsie heard the door slam, and
watched her daughter flounce up the garden path in her
skin-tight trousers and get into her car.

Elsie sighed. She didn't know when it was that Angela
had turned from a sweet and loving little girl into . . .
well, a spoilt madam. Perhaps that had been their mistake,
she and her husband Bill. Spoiling her. Not with things,
perhaps, but with time, indulging her every little whim,
because they had waited so long to have her and when she
had arrived she had been so breathtakingly beautiful they
couldn't ever bring themselves to say no to her.

It was ironic that Elsie had been nearly forty before she
had had Angela, and then Angela had gone and rather
carelessly got herself pregnant at the age of seventeen.
Carelessly – or deliberately? The alleged father was a
titled tearaway from Warwickshire she met when serving

behind the bar at the local point-to-point. Angela had sworn that she was in love with Gerard, and he with her, that they were going to make a go of it, and that she was going to have the baby, who would apparently inherit its own title: she was going to give birth to a baronet! Elsie waited with a sinking heart for it all to go wrong. She didn't see Angela for five months, as she was apparently ensconced in domestic bliss in a cottage on Gerard's estate in Warwickshire, being waited on hand, foot and finger by his ageing retainers.

Angela turned up distraught a month before the baby was due. When she went into labour two days later, Elsie was surprised that the baby looked, if anything, rather overdue. In a flood of postnatal hysteria, the truth came out. The baby wasn't Gerard's at all. Angela, finding herself pregnant by a boy from school, had seduced Gerard behind the beer tent at the point-to-point, and thought she had found her ticket out. His family, however, weren't so easily fobbed off. His astute and protective mother had eventually bullied her into a confession and, rather coldheartedly, booted her out, swollen belly and all.

After the birth, Angela fell completely to pieces, unable to pick the baby up, unable to bond with it. She just lay in bed for days, staring at the ceiling, complaining that she felt ill. The doctor assured Elsie that her motherly instincts would take over before long, but Elsie was shocked to find Angela couldn't even summon up the enthusiasm to give the baby a name. So Elsie named her Mary, a name that was so plain and ordinary that Angela was bound to want to change it, if only out of sheer bloody-mindedness.

Eventually, Angela dragged herself out of bed because she was bored. She complained of total exhaustion, but

Elsie chided her for not eating. Angela was desperate to get back to her pre-baby figure and ended up even thinner than before, to her triumph. And to her glee, as not long afterwards she was offered a modelling contract, which meant moving to London. Elsie had already resigned herself to bringing up the baby. Angela had reassured her that going to London was the best thing for all of them.

'I'm going to make enough in a year to make sure we don't have to worry again,' she promised her mother.

She didn't, of course. Angela was pretty, but not that pretty, and after an initial flurry of success she found there were lots more girls out there who were thinner, taller and with bigger breasts. When she had to come back to Honeycote with her tail between her legs, she had lost the ability to bond with her daughter completely. Little Mary squealed every time her mother picked her up, an ungodly ear-splitting shriek. It only occurred to Elsie, in a suspicious moment some years later, that perhaps Angela had pinched her whenever she was put into her arms.

True to form, though, Angela soon used the baby as a tool. Being a homeless single mother, she managed to get her own council flat in Cheltenham, as it definitely cramped her style to be stuck in Honeycote, which after the bright lights of London felt like the arse end of nowhere. At this point, Elsie's husband Bill put his foot down. The two of them weren't to look after Mary any longer. For the odd afternoon, of course, for they loved seeing her. But not for nights on end, to suit Angela. They were getting on, after all, and it wasn't right for a child to be brought up by her ageing grandparents. Plus it was unsettling for a small child never to be quite sure where she was going to wake up in the morning. Mary's rightful place was with her mother. Elsie bowed to his decision, albeit reluctantly, for she knew that if they had care of Mary then at least she would have decent food and her clothes ironed. Angela seemed to feed her nothing but Dairylea triangles and Frosties. Elsie spooned rose-hip syrup and Haliborange down the little girl surreptitiously whenever she did come round, and piled her plate high with proper meat and vegetables.

When Bill keeled over in the back garden while picking runner beans one sunny afternoon and died, the distraught and lonely Elsie was only too glad to have someone to lavish her affection on, so it wasn't long before she allowed Mary back into her life and her home. It made the pain so much easier to bear, not waking up in a house that rang with emptiness. Angela was delighted to have a reprieve. At last she could have a social life again. Soon she was dropping Mary at Elsie's on a Friday night and, still yawning from her weekend's revelry, collecting her on a Sunday afternoon. Half terms and holidays, Mary was there all the time, and was much happier riding her bike up and down the lanes of Honeycote and eating her granny's home-cooked food than cooped up in a flat with an endless supply of chicken nuggets.

When Mary was eleven, Angela persuaded Elsie to let her use her address in Honeycote so she could apply for a place at the secondary school in Eldenbury. The school Mary was due to go to on the outskirts of Cheltenham was rough, with shocking exam results. Angela was no academic, but she knew she could use Mary's education as a lever on her mother. Before Elsie knew it, Mary had been enrolled at Eldenbury High, and spent most of the week at her gran's – the travelling got to her, explained Angela, and by the time she got home she was too tired to do her homework. Elsie knew she was being used, but she didn't mind. And neither, which was more to the point, did Mary.

By the time she was fourteen Mary lived at her grandmother's virtually full time, for she and her mother disagreed on everything. They were polar opposites. Mary was compassionate, always rooting for the underdog. Angela was ruthless and self-interested. As Mary became more opinionated and sure of herself, putting the two of them in a room was like slinging two pit bulls together. Angela bewailed her daughter's behaviour, claiming she was out of control, rude, antagonistic. But Elsie found Mary perfectly obliging and sweet-natured. It was just that Angela brought out the worst in her, perhaps because she sensed her mother's neglect of her when she was young. Perhaps she had felt her mother physically recoil when she held her? Perhaps she remembered Angela thrusting her tiny body at Elsie, shouting 'Take her away from me. I can't stand her!'

Perhaps babies weren't quite as forgiving as one might think.

In some ways, it broke Elsie's heart that the two of them didn't get on. But in other ways it gave her a new lease of life. She loved having Mary around. She was lively, sparky, bright. A rebel with hundreds of causes. It didn't worry Elsie that Mary dyed her hair any number of colours and wore outlandish clothes. She knew she had a reputation as a bit of a wild child. She had become a party animal, no doubt about that. Many times she'd waved the girl off on the back of some motorbike, dressed in leather and fishnet, her black hair back-combed and her eyes dark with kohl. But Mary had always phoned Elsie just before she went to bed at ten, to tell her she was all right, that she'd got a lift home arranged and if she wasn't back not to worry. And she was always back home the next day, to help around the house, never seeming to suffer from a hangover or sleep deprivation. And when Elsie had rather timidly tried to talk to her about birth control, Mary had hugged her and said, 'Don't worry. I'm not going to make the same mistake as Mum.'

One day, Angela and Mary had the most terrible argument, during which Angela had slung the cruel fact that she'd hated her so much as a baby that she'd been given a temporary name.

'I didn't even want to give you a name. I didn't choose Mary. Your grandmother called you Mary, because she didn't want to call you "it" any longer. And I never bothered to change it because I didn't care.'

Mary had spent the weekend in her room, trying to come to terms with the shock, and had emerged with a new identity. It was the spring bank holiday, and she took that as her inspiration.

'This is the first day of the new me. I'm going to have nothing more to do with that woman. If she couldn't even be bothered to name me, I'll name myself. From now on, I'm going to be known as Mayday. I like the rhythm. I like the way it rhymes. And May's my favourite month. It smells of blossom and sunshine.'

Elsie thought it was a strange choice, and wondered about the wisdom of naming yourself after a distress signal. Nevertheless, the new pseudonym suited her grandaughter. Mayday was a strong individual with a dress sense designed to shock, no fear of authority and a well-developed sense of what was right and wrong, which often got her into trouble. She was no sheep. No one was ever going to tell her which way to go.

Not long after her mother's brutal revelation, Mayday left school without bothering to do her exams. She'd been predicted good grades, especially in English, which she loved – she always had her nose buried in a book, whether it was Jackie Collins or Virginia Woolf. But, she told Elsie, she wanted to stand on her own two feet. She didn't want to live with her mother, yet she didn't want to be a burden to her grandmother, either. Mayday was proud, independent . . . and stubborn. Despite Elsie's protests that she could stay with her as long as she liked, all the way through university if she wanted, because she was clever enough, Mayday had begun work as a barmaid at the Horse and Groom in Eldenbury. She became so popular that she was soon working nearly every shift and was given her own room at the top of the pub, becoming as much a part of the fixtures and fittings as the long, low oak bar and the inglenook fireplace.

Angela, in the meantime, without the encumbrance of her daughter, had calmed down, and met and married Roy, a market gardener from Evesham. Not long after, her two sons, Mason and then Ryan, were born. Perversely, Angela became a natural mother overnight, doting on the two boys and tending to their every need. Elsie, rather bewildered by this volte-face, came to the conclusion that Angela simply didn't like other females, viewing them as competition for the male attention she craved.

Now, looking back, Elsie felt in need of a large slug of

Bill's rhubarb wine. There were still half a dozen bottles lined up in the larder, the labels inscribed in his felt tip capitals. She didn't have the heart to throw them away, and she knew the thick, syrupy sharp-sweetness would take the edge off her feelings, the regret, the guilt, the wondering if she should have done things another way.

Suddenly, she missed Bill more than ever. He'd been a man of few words and a creature of habit, but he had always had a way of reassuring her. Without Bill there to tell her she was being silly, Elsie didn't feel quite so sure of her own mind. She couldn't peel a potato, open a letter, put on a pair of tights. Simple everyday tasks. Maybe she should go into a home . . . ?

She felt tears spring to her eyes. She missed Bill so much. It had been over ten years, but the grief could still catch her breath and take it away completely. She missed him, with his silly flowerpotman hat, his thick brown jumper with the holes in the elbows, the armfuls of fresh vegetables . . . she rarely had fresh vegetables now. It was all she could do to get a bag of free-flowing frozen peas and carrots out of the freezer and pour them into the saucepan. She was useless.

One thing was certain. Rhubarb wine wasn't the answer. Besides, she probably wouldn't be able to get the cork out. She moved over to the range and shifted the kettle onto the hotplate by hooking her whole hand through the handle and lifting it with her wrist. Everyone was happy enough now, she told herself. Mayday and Angela kept out of each other's way for the most part, only meeting occasionally and managing to be civil. Mayday was still ensconced at the Horse and Groom; Angela doted on her boys. Elsie was the only real problem, and she would manage.

The next minute she sat down heavily at the kitchen table and put her head in her arms, sobbing. A new box of teabags sat on the side unopened. She had tried and tried to pick at the blue tape that would unravel the cellophane. But she couldn't get at it, not with her useless crippled fingers. She'd meant to ask Angela to open it, but had been so upset by her suggestion that she had forgotten.

After five minutes' sobbing, Elsie fell into an exhausted slumber. She'd slept badly the night before, because of the pain in her legs. As she slept, the kettle bubbled merrily away, not seeming to mind that no one had noticed that the water had come to the boil ages ago.

The doctors' surgery in Eldenbury was always full to bursting on a Monday morning, harbouring all the gripes and complaints that had gone untended over the weekend, both real and imaginary, and providing a haven for all those who couldn't face going into work. Elderly gentlemen and prune-faced spinsters sat alongside belligerent toddlers and weary pregnant mothers, everyone in their own bubble of self-absorption, totally uninterested in anyone else's plight.

To look at him, Keith had no visible signs of complaint. He looked like a perfectly healthy man in his early fifties, with no running nose or hacking cough or weeping sores. Only the white of his knuckles gave a hint that anything was wrong, as he gripped the side of his orange padded seat and waited for his name to flash up on the screen overhead. This was a recent innovation, replacing the bored tones of the receptionist whose job it had been to announce the next patient. Somehow, seeing one's name emblazoned in red letters seemed even less discreet than having it bellowed around the waiting room. It was there for everyone to see and mull over until the consulting-room door was reached, when one's name was replaced with an anodyne 'Good morning – welcome to the Eldenbury Practice.'

Keith had seen six names flash up already. He was fifteen minutes early for his appointment, which he knew was totally pointless as the surgery always overran by at least five minutes, even if you were first in the queue. But somehow being in the waiting room represented positive action. He was trying to make up for the fact that initially he had been so negative. He was compensating. Or should that be over-compensating? He didn't know. All he knew was that the situation was out of his control.

He tried to take his mind off things by gazing at the fish tank. There were four fish in there, gliding round in ever-increasing circles. Last week, he was sure there had been five. He clenched his hands. The last thing he needed reminding of was mortality, whether his own or that of a fish. He was just thinking that the practice manager might have been tactful enough to replace it, when he noticed that the fifth fish was there after all. It had been nestling amongst the pebbles at the bottom, just behind a rather garish plaster sunken ship. His heart gave a little skip. Maybe this was an omen; a reminder not to lose hope.

To be honest, all he really wanted was a straight answer. If he knew what he was dealing with, then he could take action. That was how he had always done business, after all. But somehow he suspected that it wasn't going to be as straightforward as that. It wasn't how health worked. In business, you could look at the figures, see them in black and white, and work out exactly how much trouble you were in. But he was already discovering that bodies were not bank balances. It took a frustrating amount of time to elicit information, and in the meantime you had no idea whether you had a clean bill of health or were looking at choosing your funeral hymns.

He sighed heavily, earning himself glances from several other patients ranging from agitated to startled. It didn't do to show emotion in the waiting room, as if anxiety was somehow contagious and might set off mass hysteria. But Keith had kept his emotions in check for long enough. His stomach was tied in knots. All night long, he had vacillated between calm and panic, playing over every possible scenario in his head. He imagined Dr Keller's pleasant, round face as she imparted the diagnosis, wondering if she had a different expression for each degree of severity, or if she remained the same regardless. How did doctors do it? Was it part of their training, not to let their features give anything away? They couldn't let it get to them. After all, it was common enough.

Cancer. Everyone knew about it. Loathed it. Feared it. But the mere sound of the word changed as soon as it became personal. Or even just a possibility. Keith wondered how exactly it was that you were singled out. There were all sorts of contributing factors, of course. Genetic predisposition. Diet. Lifestyle. Unwitting exposure to some deadly carcinogen. Or flagrant dicing with substances known to cause it. But why did some sixty-a-day smokers die peacefully at ninety, while seemingly clean-living innocents could be struck dead within days of their initial diagnosis? There must be some element of fate, some all-powerful finger flicking a little switch that set the cancerous cells multiplying regardless of how you lived your life. Had that switch been flicked in him, or was he suffering the intense paranoia that comes from any unexplained lump, bump, swelling, ailment or feeling of malaise when you reach a certain age?

It had taken him weeks to pluck up the courage to visit Dr Keller. And before that, it had been some time before it had occurred to him that something might actually be seriously wrong. An increased need to pee in the middle of the night wasn't instant cause for alarm, after all. He was getting on, and it was one of those things people joked about, middle-aged men bobbing up and down for a slash. But then there was the other symptom.

Erectile dysfunction. The butt of many a comedian's joke, but actually, it couldn't be less funny. Keith's penis had been pretty obedient for most of his life. It popped up and down as and when he needed it, rising up obligingly when the moment was appropriate, and not rearing its head when it wasn't wanted. But for the past few months there had been nada.

Not that he and Ginny were at it like newlyweds, exactly. But there was a soothing rhythm to their relaxed rather than frantic bedroom activity, when they demonstrated their affection for each other, both emerging satisfied. There was nothing experimental; they had both wordlessly accepted that they knew what worked for each other and they didn't need to enter into forbidden territory, even though if you read the Sunday papers most couples donned rubber masks or wielded multi-headed dildos on a nightly basis.

Suddenly, however, Keith had found himself incapable. No matter how he tried, with internal fantasies or external manipulation, his knob was not interested. Keith was mortified, and agonized that Ginny would somehow think she was responsible for his inert member. But he couldn't find the words to express how he was feeling. And so he withdrew, so to speak. After several weeks of surreptitiously trying to nudge himself into life under the sheets, he gave up. Perhaps if he stopped trying it would get bored with playing dead, and would leap up again triumphantly, as if to say 'Ha ha. Fooled you!'

Ginny, being Ginny, didn't say anything about the lack of bedroom activity. They had just sort of drifted into mere companionship. Keith studiously avoided synchronizing bedtime, either scuttling up after the news and making sure he was fast asleep by the time Ginny slipped under the duvet, or waiting till she was slumbering before he climbed in. Then, of course, he lay there for hours, wondering if she was feeling rejected, but not quite able to say what was on his mind.

What he couldn't decide was if he was in any pain or discomfort, because once you were trying to establish that the merest twinge became a searing pain. A full bladder became agonizing and disposing of it felt like white-hot needles, but Keith was sure it was all in his mind. Having a pee felt no different than it had done all of his life, he kept telling himself firmly.

In the end, he had to pluck up the courage to sit in front of his pretty little GP and mutter his ailments, as if speaking them quietly meant they didn't exist. Her response, to Keith's horror, was to slip on a pair of latex gloves and ask him, politely but firmly, to bend over.

Her verdict was neither reassuring nor an immediate cause for alarm. Yes, he had a slightly enlarged prostate gland, but that could mean a number of things. There followed a list of possible explanations, some of which Keith remembered from his tentative trawl around the internet. He'd gone online at the office, even though he knew that was the quickest way to self-diagnose a terminal disease and find several more you hadn't thought of.

To pin it down, Dr Keller had explained at his first visit, he would need a PSA test. 'PSA is a protein produced by the prostate, which gets released into the bloodstream. When there's a problem with the prostate – for example, but not necessarily, prostate cancer – more and more of this protein is released. With a simple blood test, your PSA levels can be easily detected. And we can decide where to take it from there.'

'Let's do it, then,' Keith had said, with false jollity. He didn't mention that he couldn't stand needles, because he suspected that this was probably the beginning of a number of painful procedures, and a blood test was probably the least invasive. He'd stuck his arm out bravely, and Dr Keller proved to be extremely gentle.

He was here today to get the results. Keith heard the buzzer indicating it was time for the next patient, and looked up to see his name. His stomach lurched, and for a moment he wanted to turn and walk out of the surgery. Perhaps it was too late? He'd heard stories about people who were riddled with cancer, walking around completely oblivious until they'd gone in with an inconsequential symptom and discovered the awful truth.

He stood up, telling himself not to be neurotic. It might be nothing. Or it might just be the early signs, in which case something could be done. It was irresponsible to bolt. He threw back his shoulders and went to meet his fate.

Dr Keller was typing something into her computer as he walked into her room. She gave him a perfunctory welcoming smile as he sat down, then finished off whatever she was typing. He wondered what was going through her mind, if she had looked at his notes yet, if she was debating how to break the news or if she hadn't yet had a chance to see what card fate had dealt him. Probably not, if you believed what you read in the papers about how overstretched the NHS was. She was probably used to picking up a patient's results and giving it to them straight.

'Hello, Mr Sherwyn.' She smiled again, and Keith marvelled at how young she looked, with her blunt-cut bob and her pale freckled skin, her generous breasts under a turquoise cheesecloth blouse which she probably didn't realize showed the outline of her bra. There was an agonizing few moments as she scanned the letter. Was the frown that appeared on her forehead a result of concentration, or concern at the result, or her inability to comprehend what was written there?

'Bad news?' Keith managed to croak, desperate to prompt some sort of response. Anything was better than not knowing.

'We spoke about PSA levels when we took your blood, if you remember. PSA levels under four are usually considered normal; anything over ten is high. Your level is nine.' Keith swallowed nervously as she paused. 'As I explained, a high level can indicate the presence of prostate cancer. Or it could have another cause, such as prostatisis. Nine isn't alarming, but I wouldn't be happy letting you walk out of here without some sort of further investigation.'

He felt his heart plummet. Not a death sentence, but not a reprieve either.

'I think what we need to organize is a biopsy. It's a question of removing some cells from the prostate and sending them off to the lab. It's an outpatient's appointment – you'll just need a local anaesthetic. It shouldn't hurt any more than my initial examination.'

The only thing that had been hurt then was his pride.

'How soon can I have it done?'

'I'll write a letter straight away. You'll hear from the hospital.'

Clickety click went the keys on her keyboard.

'And then what?'

'The biopsy will tell if there is any cancer present, and if so what grade it is. Whether it's confined to the prostate, or if it's spread.'

Keith put his face in his hands for a moment. 'You mean you won't know . . . I won't know . . . exactly what's what . . . for a while yet?'

'I'm afraid it takes time. I'm sorry. I know it's frustrating.'

'And if . . . ?'

Keith couldn't bring himself to say the actual words. Any of the words relating to his fear. Cancer. Or tumour. Or malignant.

Dr Keller swung round in her chair, moving away from the computer screen to face him, her eyes flickering momentarily towards the clock, clearly inwardly assessing how much time she could afford to give him. Keith suspected she had decided to forfeit her eleven o'clock coffee break in order to allow him a few more precious minutes. Either that, or gallop through a couple of her other appointments, perhaps not give the conjunctivitis or tennis elbow quite as much consideration as she otherwise would have.

She spoke gently. 'Have you spoken to your wife about this at all? I know it's sensitive, but it is much better to have someone to talk things over with, especially in this period of uncertainty.'

Reconcile your differences, Keith felt sure she was saying. Make the most of your time together while you can.

'My wife and I are divorced.'

Dr Keller's face clouded over with confusion. Keith remembered he had revealed his more intimate secrets to her when he had initially come in. She must have assumed he was married. But he didn't want to mention Ginny.

He didn't want to bring Ginny into this scenario at all.

'I see. Well, there are a number of excellent support groups who can put you in touch with other people who've been through the same experience.'

'We don't know I've got anything yet, though, do we?' Keith spoke as heartily as he could manage.

'Don't be afraid to discuss it. That's all I'm saying.'

She turned back to her screen. Dr Keller had clearly decided to claw back the extra time she had allocated. There might be someone else out there who needed it more than Keith.

He got to his feet. 'I'll wait to hear from the hospital, then.'

'Yes.'

'There's no way of speeding things up?'

'I'm afraid these things take as long as they take.'

Her smile was polite, but dismissive. Keith took the hint. He didn't need her time today. There was no point in wasting it when they didn't have a definite diagnosis.

He walked out into the car park, the bright spring light hitting him. He climbed into his Jaguar, breathing in the smell of leather, a smell that had once reminded him of his success, but which now taunted him. All you were ever interested in was money, it seemed to say, but now you realize how unimportant that is.

He felt disinclined to go back to the brewery just yet. They were meeting at three, he and Patrick and Mickey. It wasn't quite a crisis meeting, but they had some serious issues to discuss, and decisions to make. He decided to go home and take stock for an hour or two.

Keeper's Cottage looked idyllic as he swung into the drive. Keith tended the grounds himself at the weekend. He didn't find it a chore, but a means of relaxation, taking pleasure in the results – the fresh paintwork, the hedges neatly clipped, the gravel evenly raked. The house wouldn't be hard to sell if he died, he found himself thinking. He suddenly saw it through the eyes of its next inhabitant. How long before it was on the market? What if he had a galloping tumour that had spread through his lymphatic system? He could be dead by the end of the year.

Don't be stupid, he told himself. Your result was bor-derline. Dr Keller is just being cautious. He went into the house, and went through the motions of making himself a cup of coffee, wondering if perhaps he should be avoiding caffeine. A lot of the websites he'd visited had stressed the benefits of a healthy diet in the battle against cancer – fresh fruit, whole-grains, super foods, whatever they were. And tomatoes – they were particularly good for you, apparently. They contained lycopene . . . or was that good for testicular cancer, and not prostate? Oh God, he should never have gone on the internet. It was all too confusing. His brain felt like mush. He hesitated before spooning the coarsely ground Colombian grains into the cafetiere, then went ahead. One more cup wasn't going to make any difference, just while he got his head around things.

His overwhelming feeling was one of disappointment. He had expected to go into the surgery this morning and be given a definite diagnosis. Instead he was setting himself up for another agonizing wait. How long was this biopsy going to take? He knew the system was slow. You always heard horror stories about referrals being lost in the post, records being mixed up, people waiting weeks for an appointment until they realized they'd been lost in the system. And in the meantime, if it was cancer, it would be given a chance to spread, to creep from local-ized to terminal all because of someone's inefficiency. Not that he thought Dr Keller inefficient – she was charming, but she couldn't be expected to track his medical journey every step of the way. It was up to him to take charge, Keith realized. Time was of the essence. After all, he had more important things to focus on.

Mandy, for a start. He wanted all this done and dusted as quickly as possible, so it didn't overshadow his daugh-ter's big day. Not that he had any intention of telling anyone what was going on, because no one could do anything about his plight until he had the full picture, and so there was no point. Ginny had enough on her plate, what with running the business and keeping on top of the twins, who were delightful but high-maintenance emotionally, and took up a lot of time. He'd become very fond of Kitty and Sasha, and did his best to treat them if not exactly the same as Mandy then certainly not to make them feel second best. When Mandy had moved out, he'd had no hesitation in letting Sasha move into her room. Ginny had been touched by the gesture, but Keith didn't see the point in letting the room sit empty when Kitty and Sasha were squashed in together, and they could always re-think if Mandy decided to come home for any reason. He secretly loved the energy they brought to the household, even if it did remind him how dull and restrained Mandy's upbringing had been, largely because he had always been working and his wife Sandra had been – well, Keith didn't like to dwell on it too much, because it left a sour taste in his mouth. But luckily Mandy didn't seem to have been scarred by the lack of attention she'd had during her childhood. Besides, he had made up for it since they'd moved to the Cotswolds; he and Mandy were closer than ever. Which was why Keith was determined that nothing should overshadow her wedding day. He was going to deal with this on his own.

The coffee brewed, Keith poured himself a cup carefully and sat down at the kitchen table. It was strange being in the house when it was quiet. He was rarely on his own, and it was unusual not to hear music blaring, or hairdryers going, or the telly on. But he found the silence disconcerting. He couldn't think straight, couldn't focus at all, and he had so much to think about. He had to put his life in order and make some decisions. But how could he, when he didn't have a definite prognosis? He was still no clearer as to whether he was absolutely fine or destined for months of gruelling operations and chemotherapy.

It was no good. He wasn't going to be able to bear this waiting and uncertainty. He put down his coffee, went out to his car and headed back to the surgery. He managed to persuade the receptionist to let him back in to see Dr Keller just as morning surgery came to an end.

'Dr Keller?'

She looked up as he walked in, her smile polite but puzzled.

'I know it's not right, just because I've got the cash,' Keith said firmly, 'but I want to go private. There's a clinic up near Birmingham. I've seen it on the internet. I want the best man, and I want him tomorrow.'

Dr Keller nodded wearily. 'I'll do you a referral,' she said, without protest. Private clinics existed for people to whom time meant money, and who had money to buy time. She could see his Jag in the car park. She wasn't going to get an attack of the guilts or show him any disapproval. Besides, if Keith Sherwyn went private it freed up space for someone else.

Mayday looked over at the last couple in the dining room, and estimated that as they were on their second pot of coffee, it wouldn't be rude to present them with the bill before they asked for it. Once they'd settled up, she would be able to go. She never liked to leave the hotel until she was happy that all her lunchtime customers were satisfied. They had been unexpectedly busy for a Monday, which was great, except that she wanted to get away early to go and see her grandmother.

She always liked to take Monday afternoons off, after the chaos of the weekend. The Horse and Groom now did a roaring trade for Sunday lunch, since Mayday had introduced a magnificent carvery boasting ten different vegetables, all you can eat and children free. It was always packed to the gills, and by the time the lunchtime crowd had faded away, people began to trickle into the bar for the Sunday evening pub quiz. Mayday compiled, compered and judged the quiz each week, brooked no arguments as her decision was final, and presented the winning team with a much-coveted trophy. Competition was cut-throat and alcohol-fuelled, the competitors sustained by plates of free sandwiches and bowls of crisps. As a result, Mayday was always exhausted by Monday and longing for an afternoon away from the hotel.

The bill paid, Mayday went into the kitchen and plated up three portions of leftovers that Elsie could pop in the microwave. Then she ransacked the fridge for the remains of the puddings from Sunday lunch, which the chef always kept for her.

'There's nothing wrong with any of it,' he said, 'but I can't serve it up again, so you might as well make use of it.'

She appropriated half a bowl of sherry trifle, sticking it in the cool box she had bought specially to transport her Red Cross parcels. It was the best way she knew to help Elsie, for Mayday couldn't cook to save her life. And she knew her grandmother loved traditional food – roast dinners and proper puddings. There was no point in stocking up on ready meals from the supermarket. Elsie was suspicious of anything pre-prepared. Mayday looked upon it as one of the perks of being the manager. It wasn't pilfering, because it would all go in the bin if she didn't have it.

She lugged the box out to her old 2CV. Bright green with a striped roof, it scraped through its MOT year after year, but she adored it. Today was cold but bright, and she needed no encouragement to fling the roof back and let the sky in. She drove off, singing along to the B-52s at the top of her voice, earning herself bemused glances as she bowled along Eldenbury high street out of the town and onto the road to Honeycote.

She loved going to her grandmother's house. When she wanted comfort, or reassurance or advice – which wasn't very often, for if Mayday knew anything it was her own mind, but she was only human – then she slipped into the kitchen by the side door and hugged the little figure who would usually be sitting by the old range. The kettle would be lifted off its hotplate, and the stout brown teapot filled. Mayday's special cup – pink flowers with a gold rim – would be plucked down from its shelf on the dresser, and two custard creams placed ceremoniously on the saucer.

Her grandmother's face was incredibly lined now, her bones frail, her hair thin and white. Mayday knew this deterioration had come about because of the pain. Elsie had aged ten years in two, and seemed to become smaller and more wizened each time she came to visit. But in defiance of her suffering shone a pair of sparkling eyes that held within them such love and wisdom that Mayday felt sure her gran would be there for ever.

She parked on the road outside and walked up the path, noticing with pleasure the joyous ranks of daffodils. She'd have to see about a gardener soon. Elsie had kept on Bill's legacy as best she could, but there was no way she would be able to maintain a full-to-bursting cottage garden in her condition. Mayday was sure there would be someone at the brewery who would be glad of some extra cash, either one of the young lads or one of the old codgers who'd been at Honeycote Ales since the dawn of time. She'd get Patrick to ask around, maybe stick a notice up in the staff room.

In the kitchen, her grandmother was sitting at the table, looking rather dazed, and there was a strong smell of burning. Mayday rushed over to the Aga, where the kettle had boiled itself dry. She stuck her hand in an oven glove and pulled it off.

'Gran! What happened?'

'I must have fallen asleep.' Elsie blinked. Her eyes were unnaturally pink. Mayday peered at her.

'Have you been crying?'

'No, no. It's . . .' Elsie cast round for an excuse, but was still too groggy to think of one. Mayday pressed her lips together.

'Mum's been here, hasn't she?' Her mother was the only person on the planet who could upset Elsie. And who chose to upset her. 'What did she say?'

For a moment, Elsie considered saying nothing. She didn't like stirring up trouble between her daughter and granddaughter. But she wanted reassurance that Angela's suggestion was outrageous, because the more she thought about it the more sense it seemed to make. After all, how could she carry on the way she was? At Coppice House, she would be fed and waited on, there would be somebody on hand to help if she couldn't reach something, or open something. Even now, she had to resort to shapeless tops and elasticated skirts to avoid fiddly zips and buttons. Elsie was no fashion plate, but she liked a nice crisp cotton blouse. And shoelaces – who would have thought that shoe laces would become a luxury? She suddenly loathed the cushioned slip-on shoes she'd bought from Marks and Spencer.

She decided she would retain as neutral a tone as possible when mooting Angela's idea to Mayday.

'Your mother thinks I should move into Coppice House.'

Mayday's response was immediate, as she dumped the cool box on the table and put her hands on her hips, tossing back her black hair in a gesture of indignation.

'What? Is she mad?'

Elsie immediately felt mollified. The idea was preposterous.

'That dump?' Mayday went on. 'You'd be better off in one of Mum's dog kennels, which is really saying something. Joyce Hardiment is only interested in one thing and that's profit. Not the welfare of her patients. If it was up to her they would lie on a plastic mattress wallowing in their own wee all day, being fed on a drip so she didn't have to pay any staff. They've had E-coli there three times, it's so filthy.' Mayday pulled off the lid of the cool box and took out a plate of chicken casserole, going over to the range and sliding it into the top oven to reheat. 'No, Gran. If you want to go into a home, we'll find you somewhere nice. Not somewhere run by a money-grabbing old cow.'

Elsie looked down at her hands folded in her lap. So it was Coppice House that Mayday objected to, not the idea of a home. She blinked hard to stop the tears of self-pity betraying her. For the first time since he died she thought perhaps Bill had had a lucky, if premature, escape. At least he hadn't undergone the indignity of being a crippled nuisance, packed off to an institution for the elderly and infirm. That's what she was: elderly and infirm.

'I expect Joyce is short of takers or something.' Mayday was busying herself round the kitchen, refilling the kettle. 'I hope you told Mum where to shove it.'

She picked up the teabag box, and Elsie watched in envy as she peeled away the cellophane in one easy movement, then lifted down the brown teapot from its place on the shelf.

'Tell you what.' Mayday lifted the kettle, which had by now reboiled, and poured the hot water in a steady stream. 'Why don't I do your hair? You deserve a bit of pampering. Have your tea, then we'll give you a shampoo and set. You won't know yourself.'

'Lovely,' said Elsie, and obediently ate her chicken.

She couldn't quite pluck up the courage to ask Mayday to help her with her bed. Mayday had only changed the sheets on Friday. But last night Elsie had woken in the early hours desperate for a wee. The pain in her knees had been so excruciating, she couldn't face getting up. She'd tried to ignore the persistence in her bladder, and had eventually succeeded, falling back to sleep. But when she woke that morning she realized that she hadn't conquered her need at all. She'd wet the bed. If she admitted that, even to Mayday, then the search for a home would definitely be on. She'd have a go at changing the bed herself, she decided, later on tonight. Even if she just got the bottom sheet off, and slept on the bare mattress . . . she'd just have to pray there wasn't a repeat performance. Or perhaps she should try not drinking so much during the day.

So when Mayday passed her a cup of tea, Elsie waited until her back was turned and poured it quietly down the sink.

4

That afternoon's meeting at Honeycote Ales wasn't exactly official. But all the board members were going, and Elspeth, the brewery receptionist, had laid out proper cups and saucers for tea and a plate of shortbread, which lent an air of formality to the proceedings.

Patrick arrived first. The afternoon sun was slanting in through the windows, making the wood of the mahogany table gleam. The whiteboard had been wiped clean from the last sales meeting. Patrick put his notes down on the table in front of the space he had chosen for himself, and wondered whether to write his bullet points up on the board. No, he decided. He'd wait and see where everyone else lay before he showed his cards.

He looked through the notes Elspeth had printed out for each board member: the balance sheets, the quotes and the projected sales figures, a gloomy collation of pie charts and graphs that showed their profits were plummeting. His stomach churned slightly. The writing might not actually be on the wall yet, but they weren't far off it. It seemed as if they continually took one step forward and three back. No sooner had the Honeycote Arms won Gastropub of the Year in one of the Sunday papers, than they were hit with an industrial tribunal from one of their staff for unfair dismissal. The case had clearly been a set-up, but times being what they were, and employers evidently being evil and exploitational, they lost the case and had to pay a hideous amount of compensation.

Then they had won a contract with a new chain of pizzerias to supply their bottled beer, only to discover that the Peacock Inn was subsiding and threatening to slide down its own beer garden and into the river – they'd had to close it immediately, and lost its comparatively substantial income. Added to that, there was absolutely no doubt that a lot of the machinery in the brewery was tired and worn; they had reached the point where it was counterproductive to keep repairing it. They needed a complete refit, and goodness knows what would be uncovered in the process – the brewery was held together by years of dust and cobwebs, and to disturb it was asking for trouble. And, of course, they were still trying to recover from the ghastly incident with Roger Sandbach, landlord at the Horse and Groom.

He should have listened to Mayday, thought Patrick. She had phoned him any number of times with dark warnings about Roger's drinking and gambling habits. But every time Patrick had called in to see him, Roger had been perfectly steady on his pins, and the books had been in order.

'You think I'm crying wolf.' Mayday's dark eyes had been accusing. 'But why would I? People talk, Patrick, and you'd do well to listen. He cashes up, takes the money down to the bookies on the way to the bank, sticks a load of bets on, collects his winnings, puts back what he borrowed, takes our money to the bank and keeps the rest. OK, so he's got some great tips, and nine times out of ten he cleans up. But it's going to go wrong, Patrick. There's no way he can keep it up. And you know gamblers. They get greedy. One day he's going to make a bet he can't afford to lose.'

It wasn't that he didn't believe Mayday, who he knew had her ear to the ground and was privy to the secrets of most of the great and the good of Eldenbury, as well as the not so great and the downright bad. It was just that he didn't want the landlord of his biggest establishment to be putting the hotel takings on the three-thirty at Cheltenham. So he had ignored her warnings, until the day Roger had received a tip for a dead cert and put two weeks' takings on a horse that fell at the first fence. Roger promptly blew his brains out in the back office, not simply because he'd lost the money, but because everyone would know that he'd been on the fiddle as he hadn't kept back enough to cover his losses.

Mayday was astonishing. She'd found the body, poor girl, but hadn't batted an eyelid. As she said afterwards, she'd been waiting for disaster to strike for so long, it was almost a relief when it happened. She'd dealt with the situation with incredible calm. She had contacts with the local police, who arrived as discreetly as they could so that the hotel guests were oblivious to the tragedy. The ambulance had slipped quietly around the back without all sirens blazing and removed the body. Then she'd called the staff into the dining room and quietly informed them that Roger had shot himself. By the time Mickey and Patrick arrived, it was as if nothing had happened. The hotel was preparing for evening service with an air of serenity that was almost unnatural. Mayday, it seemed, had put it to them straight, pointing out that everyone's livelihoods would be in jeopardy unless as little fuss as possible was made.

It was Patrick who suggested that Mayday take Roger's place. The staff clearly respected her, and if anyone knew how the hotel worked it was Mayday who, it emerged, had been troubleshooting for Roger almost since the day he arrived. Keith and Mickey had both been wary and unsure. The Horse and Groom was one of their biggest earners – when its staff weren't gambling with the profits, at any rate – and they were reluctant to put it into the hands of a young girl with a less than conventional sense of dress. But, as Patrick pointed out, most of the customers came in to see what Mayday was – or sometimes wasn't – wearing, and she was pretty astute. He finally persuaded them to appoint an assistant manager who had qualifications and a quiet taste in clothing, and hand over the reins to Mayday. They'd given her a three-month trial period.

That had been eighteen months ago, and the takings had nearly doubled since Roger's demise, which went some way towards recouping the substantial loss he'd made on their behalf. Ironically, the Horse and Groom became the place to stay for Cheltenham racegoers – Mayday had organized a courtesy bus to and from the racecourse for the key meetings. The amount her guests drank in the hotel before and after more than covered the cost. At other times the hotel was packed with city dwellers arriving for her Cotswold Experience weekends, which included a hot air balloon ride over the breath-taking countryside. And she didn't forget the locals: she had devised a special loyalty card for commuters who got off the Paddington train. Between six and seven the lounge bar was stuffed to the gills with suited executives enjoying a glass of her 'Wine of the Week' together with a selection of nibbles, before going home to their lovingly prepared suppers. Lunch on market days was booked for weeks ahead, and she'd introduced a special high tea for children at five o'clock, as she had noticed many harassed mothers en route from Brownies or ballet or swimming who were only too glad not to have to cook for their overtired offspring and brought them in for organic sesame-coated chicken goujons, sweet potato wedges and stir-fried broccoli spears.

Patrick was relieved that his gamble had paid off. He would have been more concerned about his loyalty to Mayday than his loyalty to the brewery if things had gone awry. For she was his rock, his sounding board. It was Mayday Patrick turned to if he had a dilemma, or a brainwave, or if he needed a second opinion, for she gave him a totally objective point of view, and she had a great gut for what was right and wrong. Sometimes he felt guilty, and thought it should be Mandy he turned to for advice, but he rather thought Mandy told him what she thought he wanted to hear when it came to business. Besides, with Keith being her father he sometimes had to be careful what he said. He didn't have to pull his punches with Mayday. They were always honest and upfront with each other. They always had been, since the day they'd first met.

He'd been fifteen, home from boarding school one hot June weekend. The fair was in town, sprawling all over the market place in Eldenbury, which usually harboured nothing more exotic than Volvos and pick-ups. The air was hot and heavy, filled with promise and the smell of frying onions. Patrick was bored. He'd come here with his best mate Ned, who'd promptly run off with some rabbity-faced girl he'd met at a Pony Club Disco.

He was idly taking pot shots at the rifle range when he felt sure someone was staring at him: the hairs on the back of his neck rippled. He turned, and saw an extraordinary creature with a mane of teased black hair, eyes ringed with kohl, and the fullest, plumpest lips he had ever seen, painted deep purple. She wore a black velvet bodice, ripped jeans and staggeringly high stiletto boots.

'I've always wanted a giant giraffe.' The voice trickled from between her lips like honey falling from a spoon. Patrick swallowed hard, and attempted a laconic smile.

'Whatever the lady wants . . .'

He turned to take aim. The star prize, the giraffe in question, stood lopsidedly against the stand, mocking him. His hand shook. He could feel her beside him, imagined he felt the warmth of her breath on his neck. Her perfume was as sweet and alluring as the candy floss from the next stall. It made Patrick feel quite giddy as he squeezed the trigger. The pellet whistled past the tin and missed.

'I thought that's all you posh boys were good for. Shooting things. And killing foxes.'

Oh God, thought Patrick. Not a bloody animal rights fanatic. She probably knew his dad was a stalwart member of the Eldenbury hunt. He really couldn't be bothered to get into an argument about it.

'Who says I'm posh?' he asked, trying desperately not to sound it.

As an answer she smiled, reached out a finger, and brushed the tell-tale long fringe out of his eyes. He jerked his head away and brushed his hair back with an impatient gesture, not liking this invasion of his personal space, but suddenly wanting more.

'And so what if I am?' he demanded.

'Quite,' she answered, not taking her eyes off him. 'So what if you are?'

He could feel himself going red under her scrutiny, until eventually she dragged her gaze from him and cast a longing glance at the giraffe.

'Shame,' she commented wistfully. 'I could just do with him to cuddle up with at night.'

Before he knew it, she had gone, gliding like a ghost amongst the crowds. Vainly he tried to catch a glimpse of her as she moved through the fair, but she had vanished without a trace. He wondered for a mad moment if he had imagined her.

He turned back to the shooting range. He had one chance. If he could get the giraffe . . . But he was a lousy shot. He always had been. He beckoned the stallholder.

'Listen, mate.' The stallholder curled his lip at Patrick's attempt to come down to his level. 'How much for the giraffe?'

The bloke looked him up and down, chewing thoughtfully on his gum. 'Cost me fifteen,' he said finally. 'So call it twenty.'

Twenty quid! Patrick knew it was bullshit, that he'd probably got his entire menagerie of acrylic stuffed animals for half that, but it was a small price to pay. He dug in his wallet. Thirteen. That was all he could manage. He thrust it at the man.

'Take this as a deposit. I'm going to find my friend. Please – don't let anyone win it.'

Patrick pushed his way through the crowds, desperately searching for Ned. He always had wads of cash, because his dad paid him to do the milking on their farm and Ned never parted with a penny for months, then blew it all in one night by getting totally bladdered. He had to get to him before he spent it.

He found him on the dodgems with his Pony Club partner, who was looking rather green.

'Lend me seven quid,' begged Patrick. 'It's a matter of life and death. Actually, no, make it a tenner.' He'd need a bit over if he found her. Enough to buy her a drink.

Ned didn't quibble. He knew his mate wouldn't ask if it wasn't urgent. He thrust a hand into his jeans and pulled out a wad of crumpled notes. Patrick extricated two fivers, then went for a third. He didn't want to look a cheapskate.

'Make it fifteen. I'll pay you back tomorrow.'

Stuffing the money into his own pocket, he ran back to the rifle range.

The giraffe was gone. As was the stallholder. Bastard. Patrick steeled himself for a row. He bet he wouldn't get his money back. Gypsies, tramps and bloody thieves, the lot of them.

Suddenly the stallholder popped up from behind the barrier, brandishing the giraffe. 'Didn't want anyone else taking a fancy and winning him.' He grinned. 'There's some good shots round here.'

Patrick settled up as quickly as he could, then grabbed the giraffe. It was nearly as big as he was. He pushed through the throngs, looking right and left, every song that blasted out seeming to mock him: 'She's Gone', 'Who's That Girl?', 'Beware the Devil Woman' . . .

She was there, sitting on the bonnet of a truck, swigging scrumpy out of a bottle, surrounded by a crowd of youths Patrick suspected were dropouts from Eldenbury High, an unsavoury bunch who wouldn't take kindly to a posh git stepping forward with a giant cuddly giraffe and stealing one of their own.

She saw him. He raised one corner of his mouth in a rueful grin and leaned his head against his newfound companion's. She nodded her head in recognition, a slight smile playing on her lips, then jumped down off the bonnet. Patrick prayed he wouldn't be spotted by the others, but she said something to them, some muttered excuse that they seemed to accept, then made her way over to him.

'Is that for me?' she asked.

'Well,' said Patrick, 'to be absolutely honest with you, I've already got an elephant and a rhino. There just wouldn't be room for us all in one bed.'

Her lips twitched, and he looked longingly at her mouth. He thought to kiss her would be like eating the first blackberries of autumn.

The evening passed in a blaze of colour and sound and incredible sensations. Whirling merry-go-rounds, pounding bass, the stench of diesel and the roar of the generators. The feeling of her fingers on his lips as she pulled off tufts of candy floss from a pink cloud and fed him, the sugar melting almost immediately on his tongue. Patrick felt elated as she pulled him from one experience to the next. They didn't pay for a thing all night, as Mayday seemed to know all the swarthy, earringed youths that ran the rides. Patrick was soon to learn that Mayday rarely paid for anything, that she could get things done, that she had a network of contacts starting from the local chief of police downwards, who were willing to bend over backwards for her. And it wasn't hard to see why. She had a natural but enigmatic charm, and she treated everybody the same. She was disarmingly honest and frank, but never unkind.

Patrick found himself utterly bewitched. He'd had dalliances before, girls with thick blond hair and names like Suzi, Tash and Harriet – usually daughters of friends of his parents. Next to Mayday, they seemed interchangeable and incredibly dull. Mayday promised danger, excitement – and the one thing Patrick hadn't quite plucked up the courage to do before now.

As the fair came to a close, he found himself with her in the back of a pick-up being driven out of town, the ridiculous giraffe between them. A small part of him niggled that he should have told Ned where he was going, but then Ned hadn't bothered worrying about him earlier. He didn't know where the pick-up was going, but he didn't care. He was with Mayday.

Eventually they pulled up at a tumbledown farm, where an impromptu party threatened to carry on well into the early hours. Mayday was obviously familiar with her surroundings. She took him by the hand and led him to a barn filled with sweet-scented bales of the summer's first cut. Talk about a roll in the hay, thought Patrick, as she pulled him towards her.

When he finally kissed her, she tasted of apples and vanilla, as the cider she'd been drinking mingled with the perfume she wore. He wasn't going to tell her he was a virgin, no way. Besides, he felt all-powerful, more sure of this shot than the one he had attempted earlier. Her clothes seemed to melt away as if by magic; she lay naked beneath him, her skin pale and glowing like opalescent moonlight, her black hair cascading over her shoulders. She pulled him out of his jeans and into her, locking her legs around him, pulling him deeper and deeper inside. And when, moments later, he found himself crying, she kissed away his tears and made him taste them on her blackberry lips.

'I won't have crying,' she whispered to him. 'Save your tears for when there's something to cry about.'

Later, they lay entwined in each other's arms. As Patrick drifted off, Mayday began to sing, in a soft husky croak that was only just in tune but all the sweeter for it:

> *My young love said to me, my mother won't mind*
> *And my father won't slight you for your lack of kind,*
> *And she stepped away from me and this she did say,*
> *It will not be long love 'til our wedding day.*

The tune was haunting; the lyrics made him shiver. Patrick could see the stars through a hole in the roof. He'd only known her a few hours, but he felt as if he had found his soulmate. In just the short space of time they had spent together, he knew he wanted it to last for ever. He turned to her.

'Shall we?'

'What?'

'Get married?'

She gave him a gentle shove.

'Don't be daft. We'd never work. You're from the big house, and I'm a worthless bint born the wrong side of the blanket—'

'So was I,' said Patrick eagerly. 'Born the wrong side of the blanket. Well, almost. My dad only married my mother because she threw up her pill after a dodgy curry and got pregnant.'

This confession caused him a moment of guilt. His father had warned him often enough about getting carried away. 'Look where it got me,' Mickey had said, then added hastily, 'Not that I would be without you, of course.' His marriage to Patrick's mother hadn't seen out a year.

Mayday was shaking her head. 'We're poles apart, you and me. Your family practically own the village I grew up in.'

Patrick frowned.

'You grew up in Honeycote?'

'My nan lives in the council houses. She brought me up. Or as good as.'

Patrick looked surprised. Mayday gave a twisted little smile.

'You see? You never even noticed me. Why would the likes of you notice the riff-raff from the bottom of the village?'

'You're not riff-raff—'

'I watched you drive past in your big car. Ride past on your horses. But you never saw me.'

'So you knew who I was all along?' Patrick suddenly felt set up. As if he'd fallen into some trap. Had she deliberately seduced him, just to prove she could? He felt sick. 'You did this on purpose,' he said angrily.

Mayday bit her lip. The dark purple had long been kissed away.

'OK,' she said. 'I admit it. I dared myself. I wanted you

to want me, to get you back for all those times you drove past without noticing me.'

For the second time that evening Patrick wanted to cry. So his seduction had been a trick, a little diversion for Mayday's amusement. He'd just been a pawn in her game, her pathetic attempt to redress the class barrier, because everyone was the same lying down. And to think he'd felt this was the most important thing that had ever happened to him. He clenched his jaw, not sure whether to walk off into the night. This was a first for Patrick, being made to feel awkward, foolish, unsure. He usually had the upper hand in his relationships, and he knew he could be thoughtless and possibly a little bit selfish. But not premeditatedly cruel.

'Well, I hope it's made you feel good,' he said in a strangled voice.

She cupped his face in her hands, stroking his cheekbones with her thumbs.

'I was wrong,' she said softly. 'You're not what I thought you were going to be at all. And I'm sorry. Will you forgive me?'

She drew her face towards his and kissed him again. And how could he resist? He had tasted pleasure and he wanted more, even if it brought with it the pain of humiliation and rejection.

Some time later she looked up at him, eyes glazed with satisfaction.

'I guess that means we're friends again?'

Patrick propped himself up on one elbow, smiling.

'More than friends, surely?'

Her face clouded. She shook her head.

'No. That would spoil it.'

'Spoil it?' He sat up in alarm. 'We can't do what we've just done and walk away from each other. It was . . . amazing. How can you not want this to go on for ever?'

Mayday signed. 'Sweetheart,' she said. 'That's sex for you. It's not me that's made you feel like that, I promise you. You'll feel like that with the next person. And the next.'

Patrick felt himself blush. She'd known it was his first time.

'Trust me,' she went on. 'It would end in tears. And I don't want to hate you, Patrick. I want you as my friend. For ever.'

Ten years on, and they were still firm friends. Patrick was no longer in awe of Mayday and her sultry allure. And he was no longer the embarrassed schoolboy she had seduced; far from it. He'd gone on to learn that she was right, that sex was pretty bloody amazing whoever it was with, unless you were very unlucky. And their relationship had endured the test of time; their loyalty to each other knew no bounds. They could trust each other with secrets, share their misgivings and give their honest opinions. And occasionally, very occasionally, if they found themselves alone together and the mood took them, then they went back to rediscover that magical night, because there had been a chemistry that was hard to forget . . .

Patrick snapped out of his reverie as the others filed in. First his uncle, James, in a beautifully cut tweed suit and a lilac shirt, his features so much more chiselled than his brother Mickey's so he always looked rather arrogant and haughty. Which he was a lot of the time, though Patrick was very fond of James, who was his godfather. He'd given him sound advice on several occasions.

Then Mickey, in a Honeycote Ales polo shirt and a pair of jeans. His dark hair was dishevelled and he was badly in need of a shave. He always spent Mondays with the men, checking over the brewery and seeing what maintenance needed doing. Mickey loved being hands on, and as the master brewer, the keeper of the secret recipes which gave Honeycote Ale its reputation, he liked to keep things clockwork. For someone who couldn't organize a piss-up in his own brewery, he was surprisingly meticulous about the machinery, and spent hours ensconced with Eric the handyman, who was familiar with its workings down to every last nut and bolt.

Then Keith, in the v-neck and cords that had become his uniform. His face was usually cheery and smiling, but Patrick noticed immediately that Keith didn't look himself. There was a set to his jaw and a dullness in his eyes, and his face looked drawn. Was he unhappy about the engagement? His congratulations had seemed sincere the day before, but perhaps now he'd slept on it he didn't think Patrick was good enough for his daughter? Keith doted on Mandy, after all. And Patrick was banking on his approval of the marriage to ensure his continued support of the brewery. If he was against the wedding . . .

The next moment, Patrick felt mollified. Keith patted him on the shoulder on his way past, in a gesture that was both fond and reassuring. If he looked tense, it was probably because he knew this meeting was going to be awkward; that they were all going to have to face facts.

Mickey called the meeting to attention.

'Basically, we're up shit-strasse. Again,' Mickey said, surprisingly cheerfully. But perhaps he was used to it by now – staring disaster in the face and being dragged back from the brink. 'Due to a number of factors that we are all aware of.'

Everyone nodded, looking rather gloomily at the balance sheets that Elspeth had printed out for them.

'The question is – what is our priority? A temporary overdraft, to prop up the Peacock and get that going again? Every week it's shut we're losing money. Or do we cut our losses and sell it? Even in the state it's in, it's a prime piece of riverside real estate. There's a lot we could do with the cash.'

'Once we start selling off pubs—' Patrick began to object, but Mickey held up his hand to stop him.

'Just hear me out. Let's run through our options. That's option one. Option two is a whopping great loan, which means we'll have to find the money to cover the interest every month and we're struggling as it is. Option three, find another white knight . . .'

His eyes flickered over to Keith, who had come to their rescue before. Keith was running a hand over his face wearily.

'And we all know what option four is,' Mickey finished heavily. 'I took the liberty of getting a valuation. We'd all do quite nicely.'

He passed a copy of the valuation to each person. Everyone stared at the figures, doing the mental arithmetic.

James whistled softly. 'Tempting.'

'That is assuming we find a buyer. But I'm pretty confident we would. There have been enough breweries knocking on the door over the years.'

Patrick chucked the paper on the table in disgust.

'It might sound like a lot of money,' he said. 'But when it's gone, it's gone. There's nothing to fall back on. No bricks and mortar, no income stream.'

Keith spoke up. 'Patrick's right. He's the next generation, after all. It's OK for us, with our mortgages paid off—'

'Speak for yourself,' snorted James.

'OK,' demurred Keith. 'But we have got to think about the younger ones. Patrick and Mandy are about to get married. They need to know they are secure.'

'I wouldn't have minded starting married life with a million quid in the bank,' James observed drily.

'A million quid doesn't go far these days.'

'Try me.'

Keith frowned. James was being irritatingly flippant.

'Patrick and Mandy have got to be our priority. We have to safeguard their future as well as our own.'

Patrick cheered inwardly, delighted that his strategy had worked. Keith was definitely on his side.

James sat back in his chair, tapping his fountain pen on the table. 'Just remind me – when is the wedding? I thought we were tightening our belts.'

Mickey shot his brother a warning glance. Why the hell was James being so mealy mouthed?

'Second Saturday in May, didn't we decide, Patrick?' he said heartily. 'We should get some decent weather by then.'

'Listen, the wedding doesn't have to be a big deal,' said Patrick. 'In fact, I'm beginning to wish I'd never said anything. We should just have nipped off and tied the knot somewhere quietly.'

'Bollocks to that,' said Mickey. 'We need a reason for a party. And I can't think of a better one.'

Patrick smothered a smile. Good old Dad, running true to form. Focus on something entirely irrelevant; find an excuse to spend money rather than saving it. Though actually, the last thing Patrick wanted was a fuss, and he was sure Mandy felt the same.

'I think we should just do a picnic in the garden and get everyone to bring a bottle of champagne instead of a present. I mean, Mandy and I don't need anything for the house.'

'No way. I'm going to put my foot down. You're having the full works whether you like it or not. Don't you think, Keith?'

'I think they should have whatever they want.' In his mild-mannered way, Keith was gently reminding Mickey that this was not his gig.

'Aren't we straying off the subject?' asked James impatiently. 'Much as I would love to discuss the order of service and whether to have matching hymn sheets, Caroline will have my balls for bath plugs if I'm not home to help with the children's tea.'

'I thought you'd rather like the excuse not to go home.' Mickey's tone was loaded.

Keith looked around the table, worried. The Liddiards always seemed to collapse under pressure. They should be pulling together, not sniping at each other. He sighed. He was going to have to take control. He rapped on the table.

'Enough of this back-biting. I know we're all under pressure and we all have our own issues.' Fucking prostate cancer, in my case, he thought, a trifle bitterly. 'But if we're going to come up with a strategy we need to pull together. Let's get all the cards on the table, air all our grievances. James, you seem particularly rattled.'

James had the grace to look a little shamefaced. 'OK. I'll be honest. I was rather hoping one of you lot would buy me out.'

There was a stunned silence. James had always been a valued member of the board. Not interfering, but a steady head who often had a valuable opinion, when he wasn't bitching. Not being directly involved with the brewery, his objectivity could be incredibly useful.

'I'm rather up shit-strasse myself.' He smiled wryly. 'I'm the first to admit I've overstretched myself with this new house.' The house adjoining James's antiques shop in Eldenbury wasn't big enough for a family of five, so he'd rented it out and bought a rather nice coach house on the road to Honeycote. At huge expense. 'And business is . . . well, frankly, I don't understand why anyone wants to go to Ikea. But it seems they all do.'

'Because most people can't afford eighteen grand for a dining table?' ventured Patrick.

'I don't just do the real McCoy,' snapped James. 'I've got plenty of stripped pine – for them wot want it.'

'Perhaps if you weren't so snotty?' Mickey always found the way his brother was so precious very irritating.

'Look, I don't know. All I know is I'm bloody strapped for cash, with Caroline whelping all over the place and too much competition in Eldenbury and Henry starting school, so that's another ten grand a year to find.'

'What's wrong with the state system?'

'For Christ's sake, do you even have to ask?'

'I was speaking to Guy Portias the other day. From

Eversleigh Manor? His wife swears by the local primary.'
Mickey could never resist the chance to wind James up.
'Wouldn't take her son out when Guy married her, even
when his mother offered to pay the fees for Hazlehurst. If
it's good enough for the Portiases . . .'

'Let's see what happens when they have one of their
own, shall we? Anyway, we digress.'

'Keith, you're very quiet. Any views?'

Keith had indeed been keeping his counsel, which he
had learnt to do whenever the Liddiards were sparring
with each other. But now all eyes were upon him. He
chose his words carefully.

'I think perhaps we all need to have a good think about
where we want to go. Individually. And what Honeycote
Ales means to us. Whether . . .'

As he hesitated, all three of them stared at him in
horror.

'You're saying sell.' Mickey's tone was incredulous. 'A
minute ago you were saying hang on.'

'That was before I realized James wanted out. I can't
afford to buy his share.'

There was a small silence.

'Nor can I,' admitted Mickey.

Patrick heaved a big sigh. 'You don't even have to ask
me.'

Before all hell broke loose, Elspeth ventured in.

'Mickey, there's a phone call for you, from your dentist.
She says it's urgent.'

Mickey looked up, frowning. 'What?'

'She says she's had the X-rays back and she needs to talk
to you.'

Mickey was about to say that the last time he'd looked

his dentist was a bloke, and he hadn't had an X-ray for over two years. But suddenly an image popped into his mind, of a pair of wicked green eyes and a mouth curved into a smile. And he heard a voice. 'If ever I need to speak to you at the office,' it said, 'I'll pretend to be your dentist. I'll say I've had your X-rays back and you need urgent attention.'

'She says it's urgent.' Elspeth was insistent.

'Of course. If you'll excuse me. I won't be a moment.'

Mickey got to his feet and left the room.

Kay Oakley. Kay bloody Oakley. What the hell did she want? He hoped it was just a quick fuck because she happened to be in the area, but somehow he had a gut feeling that there was more to it. It had been that sort of day.

Mandy sat in her office chewing the side of her finger, wondering what was going on in the board room. After the euphoria of yesterday, the atmosphere today seemed rather chilled. Both her father and Patrick had been distracted this morning. Keith had whizzed off somewhere and Patrick had spent all morning on the computer, swearing softly as he tried to get the printer to work. It was almost as if the wedding had been forgotten already. She knew she was being a brat, but she felt a bit miffed. But then, that was men for you. They probably wouldn't give the proceedings another thought between now and the time they had to turn up at the church. But Mandy was longing to plot and plan and scheme and dream.

She decided to phone her mother.

Mandy was very fond of Ginny, but discussing your

wedding plans with your father's girlfriend wasn't quite the same. Besides, Kitty and Sasha always got involved, and they did tend to be a bit overpowering, especially Sasha, who was a devotee of every celeb magazine going and had all sorts of over-the-top ideas. No, this was a time when a girl needed her mum.

Somehow, the fact that Sandra was in Puerto Banus and she hadn't seen her for over nine months had made Mandy forget Sandra's shortcomings. She rarely popped back from her sun-drenched villa, so busy was she with setting up her beauty clinics up and down the coast, offering brow-smoothing injections, thread-vein removal and lip-plumping. Absence, as they say, makes the heart grow fonder, and Mandy had conveniently put to the back of her mind that every time she saw Sandra, she set her teeth on edge and couldn't wait for her to go. She longed for the sort of camaraderie the twins had with Ginny, who had a knack of communicating with her daughters on a girly level, but also provided the comfort and reassurance that only a mother can give. As she picked up the phone and dialled, Mandy felt filled with a warm glow at the prospect of a cosy chat.

Moments later, she held the phone away from her ear as her mother gave a blood-curdling shriek of excitement.

'That's it!' shrieked Sandra. 'I'm coming right over.'

'It's OK, Mum. It's all under control. We're not having a big wedding. Just close friends and family. We don't want to go over the top—' Mandy was too discreet to say that actually they were all pretty strapped for cash. There were certain things you didn't reveal to Sandra.

'Amanda. This is what I have been waiting for since the

day you were born. Have you any idea how important a daughter's wedding is to a mother? And you're far too busy to organize everything. You need help.'

Mandy gulped. She hadn't anticipated this level of excitement. But then, you never knew with Sandra. Her reactions usually depended on how bored she was. Clearly, she had nothing else to distract her at the moment. On another day, she might have been utterly dismissive, leaving Mandy feeling lucky to have extracted a promise to attend the wedding.

'This is a stroke of luck! I've just sold off two of the clinics. I was wondering what to do with the cash. Fantastic. This is going to be the wedding of the year. No, the century. No!' Mandy didn't think her mother's voice could go any higher. 'The millennium!'

'Listen, Mum. Honestly. We want to keep it low key.' Why had she opened her mouth?

'There is no point in a low-key wedding. It's a celebration of two people's love for each other. It's a statement!'

Mandy could hear Sandra's nails clicking away on her computer keyboard as she spoke.

'Right. I've found a flight. I'm coming over Friday. Is there a decent hotel near you?'

Mandy knew from experience that absolutely nothing was going to stand in Sandra's way now that the cat was out of the bag. She sighed.

'I can book you into the Honeycote Arms.'

'Has it got a spa?'

'No, Mum. It's the village pub. But it's very comfortable. And the food's fantastic.'

Sandra sounded doubtful.

'Don't worry. I'll find myself somewhere on the

internet. And darling, I'm so utterly thrilled. I'm going to make this a wedding to remember.'

That, thought Mandy ruefully as she hung up, was what she was afraid of.

As he walked down the corridor to take the phone call from Kay in his office, Mickey ran through all the possible reasons she could be calling.

He could hardly remember her contacting him at all when they were having an affair. It was usually he who had picked up the phone and suggested an assignation. As a mistress, she had been pretty undemanding, wanting nothing from him but sex. That Mickey could handle; it was when women got emotionally attached that he started to panic. Kay had been positively detached. Occasionally he had felt almost used. Not that he minded. It had been fun.

Until it had all gone wrong, of course. You couldn't keep an affair quiet for ever in a place like Honeycote. Word had got out, ironically after they had decided to call it a day, and the shit had hit the fan. Lucy had gone running to James for comfort. Mickey, who had been a heavy drinker in those days, had lost the plot completely. Not only had he jeopardized his seemingly perfect marriage, but the bank was threatening to call in the brewery's not insubstantial overdraft. Feeling the pressure, he had hit upon the idea of burning down the brewery and collecting the insurance. Luckily for him – or not so luckily, depending how you looked at it – he'd been so sloshed that he'd crashed into a wall en route to the brewery to carry out his dastardly deed, and had ended up in hospital for weeks. Even now he limped very slightly; and still got blinding headaches when he was tired or stressed. But everything had been all right in the end. There was nothing like being at death's door for bringing out people's forgiveness. There had been touching bedside reconciliations. Mickey had milked his invalidism for all it was worth, hoping that his misdemeanours would be overlooked in the light of his misfortune.

The tactic had worked. Lucy had forgiven him. While he was recuperating, Keith had come to the brewery's rescue. And as far as he knew, Kay had emerged from the scandal unscathed, and had gone to live in Portugal with her husband, Lawrence. Mickey hadn't heard from her from that day to this, and had barely given her a thought. She had been his last dalliance. The accident had frightened him, and made him realize just how special Lucy was. He'd been faithful to her ever since.

So he rather hoped it wasn't sex Kay was after.

He picked up his telephone.

'Mickey Liddiard.'

'Mickey. It's Kay.' He remembered her voice. So clear and concise. And definite. Kay had always known exactly what she wanted. 'I need to see you.'

'Jesus, Kay. This is out of the blue. It's been, what? Nearly five years?'

'Give or take a couple of months,' answered Kay. 'Come to the Honeycote Arms at six o'clock.'

'I don't know if I can. I'll have to check—'

'I'll be expecting you.'

The phone went dead. Mickey couldn't help smiling. That was Kay. Everything always had been non-negotiable. He felt the tiniest little flicker of excitement, then spoke to himself sternly. He wasn't going down that road again, not even if she was lying stretched out on the bed naked with a rose between her teeth.

He worked out he'd just have time for a shower and a change of clothes, if he wound the meeting up and put his skates on. After all, he didn't want her thinking he'd gone to seed.

5

Later that afternoon, Mayday barged into her mother's kitchen through the back door without knocking, eyes blazing. Mason and Ryan watched in amazement, their forks loaded with turkey escalopes, grilled beef tomatoes and potato croquettes, as she laid into Angela, who was unloading the dishwasher.

'How dare you tell Gran she should go into a home?'

Angela stood up, a floral mug in each hand.

'Because I think it's the right thing to do.'

'You just want to shove her in there so you don't have to worry. As if it's you that worries anyway.'

'Don't speak to me like that. I've got your grandmother's best interests at heart.' Angela opened a heavily leaded glass cabinet and replaced her china carefully.

'No, you haven't. Gran would go mad in a home. She'd hate it.'

'Rubbish,' said Angela briskly. 'Everyone thinks that. But after two weeks she'd be acclimatized.'

'Brainwashed, you mean. They give them tablets.'

'You're always full of conspiracy theories.'

'I've got friends that have worked in Coppice House. Trust me. They're doped up to the eyeballs.'

'I can't leave her to look after herself. I'm worried sick about her.'

'Out of sight, out of mind.'

'If she's too stubborn to do the right thing, then it's up to her. I'm not putting my life on hold to look after her.'

'No. Heaven forbid that you might have to do something for someone else.'

'I don't like your tone.'

'I don't like your attitude.'

Mother and daughter glared at each other.

'You look after her, then. I'm quite happy to pay her nursing home fees. But I'm not running over there every two minutes. I've got my own life to get on with. Mason and Ryan need me.'

Mayday rolled her eyes. Her mother said it as if she was hovering over two babies in a pram. Mason and Ryan towered over her already, and they weren't even fully grown.

'Fine,' she replied wearily. 'I can visit Gran every afternoon, when the pub's quiet. And I'll see if I can arrange some home help. And maybe talk her into having Meals on Wheels.'

'Good luck.' Angela deliberately hadn't gone down this route, knowing it was an option, but not the one she wanted.

'How long will it be, I wonder?' Mayday carried on. 'Before you get bored with Mason and Ryan? Because you're really not very good at looking after people when they really need you. First me, and now Gran. I hope for your sake that there isn't such a thing as karma.'

And with that, she was gone. Angela looked over at her two sons, who were gawping at her.

'Don't listen to her,' she told them. 'It's all the drugs she takes. It gives her a warped view of life.'

'Mayday takes drugs? Cool! Can she get me some?' said Mason, who was getting to a tricky age.

Angela scowled, then cleared away her sons' empty plates, scraped clean except for blobs of superfluous brown sauce, and started stacking the empty dishwasher.

Elsie sat down in the Parker Knoll chair that Angela and Roy had bought her for Christmas. She couldn't put it into the reclining position, as she would never be able to get up again – her fingers weren't strong enough to manage the handle – but the chair was comfy nevertheless. She kept her head as still as she could so as not to disturb her hairdo. Mayday had spent hours rolling her hair round the curlers, then drying it and taking them out again. Elsie hadn't wanted to tell her there was no point in her having her hair done, not even for her own self-esteem. She didn't even look in the mirror any more. But she didn't want to hurt Mayday's feelings.

It was her dearest wish to see her granddaughter settled and happy. Mayday might have a wild streak, but Elsie couldn't help feeling that she would take to family life like a duck to water. If only she could find a decent man. What she needed was someone like Bill. A gentleman to the end. But not dull. Strength, that was what you looked for in a partner. Silent strength. She chuckled. They'd have to be strong to manage Mayday. She'd had a string of suitors over the years, whom she treated with equal disregard. Of all of them, there was only one who Elsie thought deserved the time of day. Although he hadn't been a boyfriend, but a friend, and the two of them were close even now. Patrick Liddiard had stood by Mayday through thick and thin, and Elsie thought he was wonderful. So good looking, with that glossy black hair and those blue eyes, like one of the matinee idols of her youth. And incredible manners. Always helping her to her chair, standing up if she came into the room – not like Mason and Ryan. They had no manners at all. They just scoffed the contents of her biscuit tin in front of the telly when they came round, only just about acknowledging her when she took out her purse to give them a bit of pocket money. Patrick was a gentleman. But he belonged to another class. Mixed marriages rarely worked, even in this day and age. Elsie sighed, wishing there was something she could do to iron out this injustice for her beloved granddaughter. She knew there was a bond between Patrick and Mayday; she sensed it whenever she saw them together. But they were almost too close to see it for themselves. Mayday would only tell her not to be so soft if she pointed it out. 'Patrick's my mate,' she would say. 'He's my best friend. You don't marry your best friend.'

But you should, thought Elsie. Bill had been her best friend, after all.

She picked up the remote and pointed it at the television. It was a large one, with outsize buttons, which she prodded until she found the lottery numbers on a news channel. She'd forgotten to check them the day before. She scrabbled about on the glass-topped coffee table for her ticket, then scrutinized the numbers. She often wondered why she bothered, given the odds, but then people did win. Every week. And, as they said, you've got to be in it to win it. Her numbers were a combination of her wedding anniversary, house number and her date of birth.

Nothing startlingly original. The trouble was, once you'd started, you couldn't stop, because what if your numbers came up and you hadn't bought a ticket? So once a week Mayday bought her ticket from the post office, together with a copy of *Woman's Own*, and if Elsie didn't check her numbers regularly it was because she didn't really believe she'd ever win.

Moments later she scrabbled again on her coffee table for her glasses. Was she going mad? Arthritis she could cope with, but not insanity.

When Keith arrived home from the board meeting, Kitty and Mandy were sitting at the kitchen table in front of an enormous pile of wedding magazines, a pair of scissors at the ready. Sasha was swigging from a can of Diet Coke, giving her opinion. Ginny was slicing chicken breasts, grating ginger and chopping garlic in preparation for her easy Thai curry, a blue and white striped apron over her jeans. She came over to give Keith a kiss, holding her mucky hands in the air.

'Supper in half an hour. Bad day, good day?'

'Pass.' Keith gave her a wry grin. Where would he start?

Mandy pulled out a picture and added it to her pile of possibles.

'Um, Dad? You'd better steel yourself for some bad news.'

Keith's heart started pumping. Had the surgery phoned? Or the hospital?

'What?' he asked nervously.

'Mum's coming over for the wedding.'

Keith breathed out a heavy sigh of relief. 'That's all right, love. She is your mother.'

Mandy made a face that Keith recognized meant trouble. 'On Friday.'

'Friday?'

Mandy nodded. 'Someone's got to pick her up from the airport. She wants to be part of the preparations, she said. As the mother of the bride.'

'Well, in that case, thank goodness you're getting married in six weeks, not six months.'

Ginny looked at Keith askance. It wasn't like him to be so acerbic. But then, Ginny hadn't actually met Sandra.

It was only now he had been separated from his wife for nearly five years that Keith wondered how he'd actually put up with her for so long. Of course, with the benefit of hindsight, he realized that Sandra had probably been bored rigid throughout their marriage. He had been brought up to believe that a woman should look after the house and home and the children, and in return he would bring home the bacon. It was a very simple equation that should have worked. Looking back, he had been completely misguided. It wasn't his fault if that was what had been drummed into him. Perhaps the fact they'd only had one child had been partly to blame. There simply hadn't been enough for Sandra to do. No wonder she had looked elsewhere for her amusement in the end. Keith had come home one day to find her disappearing out the front door with a raft of suitcases, accusing him of not paying her enough attention. He'd been aggrieved at first, then relieved. Not long afterwards, he had met Ginny, and the difference was astonishing. If Sandra was a bulldozer, Ginny was an old-fashioned bicycle with a basket on the front. At the thought of Sandra's reappearance, he wiped a bead of sweat from his forehead.

He felt a bit peculiar. Was it stress? Or something more sinister?

'Would you like a drink?' Ginny was looking at him anxiously.

The threat of prostate cancer, a brewery teetering on the verge of bankruptcy, and the imminent arrival of his ex-wife?

'I rather think I would,' said Keith faintly.

Kay spent a long time deciding what to wear for her meeting with Mickey. She knew the value of first impressions, but she wasn't quite sure, on this occasion, what image she was trying to project, if any. In the end, she decided on jeans. She put on enough make-up to hide the shadows under her eyes and liven up her complexion. Her tan had faded pretty quickly. Her hair was a disaster. She hadn't had it cut or coloured since Lawrence died; it was nearly past her shoulders. So she brushed it out and twisted it up into a knot. She looked at her hands ruefully. No nail varnish. She really couldn't be bothered. Her hands had become dry and chapped from the unaccustomed cold weather. She squirted a dollop of hand cream into one palm and smoothed in the soothing lotion.

Her stomach was churning. What the hell was the matter with her? She usually had nerves of steel, but the forest mushrooms on brioche she'd had for lunch felt as if they were about to reappear. It wasn't too late to back out. She and Flora could climb back into her Micra and go back up the motorway to Slough. Her parents had told her repeatedly that they always had a place with them. But how could she spend the next few years in their spare room, on that soulless estate, looking for a way out?

She looked outside. Flora was playing with Poppy, Barney and Suzanna's daughter. They were having a whale of a time on the pub's wooden climbing frame, bossing each other around as only little girls can. As her daughter swung upside down, laughing, Kay saw a vision of the future she wanted for her. A happy English village existence, with a garden, and friends, and if not a pony then at least a puppy or a kitten. That wasn't too much to ask, surely?

Get a grip, Kay told herself firmly. She knew her rights, after all. This was the right thing to do. The only thing to do.

She heard a knock on the bedroom door. She took a deep breath, then strode across the room to open it.

Her stomach turned over when she saw him. He'd got older, of course he had, because at their time of life the years started showing. But age hadn't made him any less handsome. His hair was slightly greyer at the temples, and there were a few more lines around his eyes. But those eyes still shone brilliantly, and the laughter hadn't gone out of them.

'Hello, Kay,' said Mickey, and his voice sounded so warm, so familiar. It was a long time since anyone had been on her side, apart from her parents. Everyone she had come into contact with had been cold and detached, either bristling with officialdom or trying to disown her. Kay put her face in her hands and breathed in deeply to calm herself. She wanted nothing more than to throw herself into Mickey's arms, feel his strength around her and breathe in the Eau Sauvage she had once teased him for wearing because it was old-fashioned.

For heaven's sake, she told herself crossly. It wasn't as

if she'd ever been in love with him. Their affair had been strictly physical; intermittent sex they had both got off on because they both had low boredom thresholds. They'd suited each other perfectly, because in each other they had found a means of getting the thrills they needed whilst knowing the affair would never spiral out of control, because neither of them were romantics. They were never going to invest any real emotion in their relationship and demand anything of each other. If it hadn't been for the fact that Kay had been labouring under one tiny little misapprehension, she wouldn't be here now.

'Am I that hideous to look at?' Mickey joked. 'I haven't aged that much, surely?'

She took her hands away from her face. 'Hi,' she said. 'Sorry. It's just . . . strange seeing you after all this time. Come on in.'

And she stepped aside to let him past.

Mickey hadn't been sure what to expect when he saw Kay. He might have had an affair with her for . . . how long? A year? Eighteen months? In all that time he hadn't kidded himself that he cared about her, or she him. They'd been in it for the frisson that only clandestine sex can give you.

So he was surprised, when he saw her, to feel shock. She looked tiny, vulnerable, her green eyes huge in her face. Kay had always seemed so tough. She was usually done up to the nines, chic and perfectly made-up. Today she had on jeans, loafers and a white shirt; none of her trademark gold jewellery, only a trace of mascara. Her blonde hair was loosely pinned up in a slide, dark roots evident.

He followed her into the room. She smiled at him rather wanly.

'I'm not sure how to tell you this. It's probably going to come as a shock.'

Oh no, thought Mickey. AIDS. That was why she was so thin. And he definitely hadn't ever used a condom with her. He knew that, because he'd never used a condom in his life. He thought quickly. If she'd infected him, surely he'd be ill by now?

'Don't worry,' she was saying softly. 'It's actually quite a nice surprise. At least, I think so.'

She beckoned him over to the window. Outside, Suzanna's daughter Poppy was playing on the pub climbing frame with another little girl.

'That's Flora,' said Kay simply. 'The one in the denim dress.'

'Yours?' asked Mickey.

'And yours.'

There was a stunned silence. Then Mickey began to laugh. 'Don't wind me up.'

The expression on Kay's face stopped him in his tracks. She wasn't joking.

'Do the maths, Mickey. We were never very careful, were we? I thought I couldn't have children, remember? So I told you not to worry.'

Mickey nodded. Even he, with his tendency to be swept away by the occasion, had queried the wisdom of unprotected sex, but Kay had assured him, with rather a wry smile, that there was no chance she could get pregnant. He'd believed her. Why wouldn't he?

'It turned out not to be me who was infertile,' she informed him. 'It was Lawrence all along.'

Mickey swallowed, thinking of all the times he had ravished her with gay abandon. Talk about Russian bloody roulette.

'I found out soon enough, when I told him I was pregnant. He showed me the piece of paper from the consultant that told him he would never father a child in a million years.' A trace of bitterness crept into her voice. 'Something he omitted to tell me during our marriage. It seemed he was happy to let me take the blame for the fact we couldn't have children.'

Mickey was struggling to take it all in. Even now, he remembered Lawrence, drunk at the Liddiard dinner table that Christmas, crowing that his wife was having an abortion. Mickey had never forgotten the shocked expression on Lucy's face, and his own sneaking suspicion that the child might be his. He'd heard no more, so he'd thought he'd got away with it.

'So it was obvious that the baby wasn't his. He kicked me out on the spot. I was going to get rid of it.' Kay looked defiant for a moment. 'But I couldn't. It was too late. By the time I got to a doctor, I was twenty-four weeks gone. Thank God . . .'

She looked out of the window at Flora, her defiance subsiding.

'So what did you do?' Mickey asked softly. He felt sick. Sick that he hadn't tried to contact her at the time. Sick that all he had felt was relief that she had allegedly dealt with the inconvenience. He was a selfish bastard, he told himself.

'I went to my parents in Slough. Bless them. I couldn't tell them all the sordid details. They just looked after me, unconditionally. Like parents are supposed to.' Her smile was bleak. 'Mum came with me to the hospital while I had Flora. Then they helped me buy a little house, made sure we had everything we needed . . .'

'Kay. I had no idea.'

She looked at him evenly and he squirmed. Had he suspected, he wondered now? He couldn't be sure. It had been all too easy to put Kay to the back of his mind, with everything else that had happened.

'No,' she said with a sigh. 'Of course you didn't. Nobody did.'

'But . . . you and Lawrence? You got back together?'

She nodded. Mickey realized she was struggling to finish her story. Tough, defiant Kay was crumbling in front of him.

'He felt so guilty. About lying to me all those years. I'd never bothered to go and see a specialist because I'd just assumed . . . and to be honest, back then I wasn't all that worried. Kids didn't seem important. I can't believe I thought it didn't matter.'

Her gaze wandered outside to Flora for a moment.

'Anyway, Lawrence tracked me down, eventually. He told me he . . . couldn't live without me, even though I'd been unfaithful. He fell in love with Flora at first sight. He brought her up as his own.'

Kay found her eyes were filling up with tears. She'd been determined not to cry. This was supposed to be a business meeting, not emotional blackmail. But repeating the story to Mickey made her remember just how special Lawrence had been in the end. She turned away for a moment, blinking hard, until she'd composed herself.

'So where is he now?' asked Mickey.

'He . . . died.'

'Jesus.'

'Or, to put it more precisely, he was killed. In a car accident. At least, that's what it was made to look like.'

Mickey looked at her sharply. Kay shrugged.

'I can't prove anything. But it looked rather suspicious to me. He was in with some pretty ruthless people. He didn't like the way they were doing business. Anyway, whether they actually bumped him off or not, they came out of the whole thing quids-in and I was left without a penny.'

'Kay . . . this all sounds like madness. Like some crazy film.'

'Tell me about it. And I'm not holding out for a happy ending. I'm widowed. Penniless. Homeless. With a child to look after. But . . . it's up to me to do the best I can for me and Flora.'

She met his gaze directly. 'Which is where you come in.'

'Ah.' Mickey suddenly felt foolish. How could he have flattered himself that she might be after his body? 'You want money.'

She winced. She had come here determined to be businesslike. Yet when Mickey put it so baldly it sounded awful.

'What I want is a stable, happy life for my little girl. But my hands are tied, Mickey. I don't know where to begin, what to do, how the hell to get us out of this mess. And I absolutely promise you, if it wasn't for Flora . . .'

She trailed away, realizing that a tone of desperation had crept into her voice. She hadn't meant to make this an emotional plea. She'd thought about it long and hard, and decided that tugging on Mickey's heart strings was a cheap

132

trick. She'd wanted to make this a straightforward transaction. She had to pull herself together. She wouldn't get through this if she fell victim to self-pity. She hated people who whinged and moaned about their circumstances.

'I've worked it out,' said Kay, producing a piece of paper. 'I thought a lump sum would probably be easiest. Then I wouldn't have to keep bothering you. I haven't been greedy. I've rounded it off to make it easier.'

Mickey looked at the sum, written in black letters. The figures swam in front of his eyes.

'Half a million quid?'

'I'm sure if I went through the Child Support Agency, or got a lawyer, they'd ask you for more.'

'Half a million?'

'I won't ask you for anything else. That's it.'

Mickey raised an eyebrow. It was all he could manage. He was quite literally speechless. Kay couldn't help smothering a smile. She remembered now that Mickey never was really in touch with the real world.

'I've worked it out on a rough payment of three hundred pounds a week, for eighteen years. Plus quarter of a million for a roof over our heads and school fees.'

'Kay . . . I just haven't got this kind of money.'

'Not cash, no. I can't imagine you have. But you've got plenty of assets.'

Mickey let out a heavy sigh. He knew Kay was no fool. She was a businesswoman. She knew what was what. That he might not have liquid cash, but on paper he was minted.

'If it was just me I can assure you I wouldn't humiliate myself like this. But I've got to look after Flora's best interests.'

She looked Mickey in the eye. 'All I've got is the clothes we are standing up in. And the car my father bought me. That's it.'

'What are you living on?'

'At the moment? The proceeds from my engagement ring.'

Mickey felt sick. His knee-jerk reaction was that he wanted a drink.

'She's how old? Nearly five?'

'Yes. So obviously I need to get things sorted as quickly as I can. Work out where we are going to live, so I can get her into a good school.'

Mickey's heart sank. He knew Kay's idea of a good school wouldn't be the local primary.

'I really need to think things over. This has come as a huge shock.'

Kay managed a rather mirthless smile. 'Don't worry – I wasn't expecting you to hand over a cheque straight away . . .'

Their eyes met.

'And I'll be very discreet. I know you wouldn't want Lucy to know any of this.'

Mickey narrowed his eyes. That sounded like an ill-disguised threat.

'I hope you're not going to use that as a bargaining tool.'

'I don't need to bargain, Mickey. I know my rights. And I know that deep down you're an honourable person. You wouldn't see your own flesh and blood go without.'

Here it comes, thought Mickey. The tight, agonizing steel band round his skull that materialised whenever he was stressed. The one that stopped him being able to think, talk, drive. He groped for the back of a chair and sat down heavily.

'Mickey?'

Kay was surprised to see him quite so affected. He had gone deathly pale. She prayed he wasn't going to keel over completely. That was the last thing she needed – another corpse on her hands. She rushed to fetch him a glass of water.

'Sorry,' she gasped, flustered. 'There wasn't really any way of breaking it to you gently. I mean, you can't half tell someone they've fathered your child.'

Mickey gulped at the water greedily.

Shit, he thought. Another set of school fees. He'd only been ribbing his own brother about school fees earlier. And clothes – he was certain Kay wasn't the type to rush to Primark. Though hang on . . . he was pretty certain Lucy had kept most of Sophie and Georgina's stuff. He remembered her packing it up during her recent clear out—

What was he thinking? He could hardly go home and ask his wife to look out some old clothes for the illegitimate daughter she didn't know he had. Mickey put down the glass of water with a trembling hand.

'How long are you here?' he asked.

Kay shrugged. 'I can't afford to stay much longer,' she replied.

'Don't worry about the bill,' he told her. 'I'll settle that with Barney. Stay as long as you like.'

He shouldn't be saying that. He should be trying to get rid of her as quickly as he could. But Mickey was surprised, very surprised, to find that his overriding emotion was a desire to protect the two of them. His former mistress and his fourth – fourth! – child.

His eyes were drawn to the window, where the light was fading fast. The two little girls had disappeared.

'Suzanna's giving them tea together. Poppy was thrilled to have someone to play with.'

Mickey looked searchingly at Kay. She seemed an entirely different person from the woman he remembered. Less brittle. Softer. Almost . . . fragile. But then, she was a mother now. And a widow. And the way she had spoken about Lawrence, it seemed they had found true love together in the end. All of which combined to give her another dimension, which was rather intriguing.

For a moment he felt the urge to take her in his arms, and tell her it was going to be all right. But he warned himself to keep her at a distance. She'd just asked him for half a million quid, after all, so there must be plenty of the old resilient Kay in there. He mustn't get swept away on a tide of emotion, seduced by the romance of the situation. He must let his head make the decisions, not his heart. Which meant suppressing the overwhelming desire he had to meet Flora. Once he did that, then he knew all reason would go out of the window. He was pretty sure Kay wasn't lying, or acting, or exaggerating any of the facts she had presented him with. But she knew damn well she had the ultimate weapon.

He forced a businesslike briskness into his tone that he wasn't feeling, fighting all his instincts, because his duty was to protect his wife, his family and his business, not his former lover and their illegitimate daughter. Who might, after all, not be his.

6

When Mickey got home that evening, he really had meant to tell Lucy everything.

Five years ago, when his affair with Kay had come out, he'd had a major wake-up call about the way he was leading his life. He'd realized that he was a lucky bastard who didn't deserve his family or his legacy, and had resolved to be a dutiful father and husband from there on in. And he'd done pretty well, considering. Gone was the dissolute philandering booze hound. Now he worked hard, was thoroughly attentive to and grateful for Lucy, and had cut back hugely on his drinking, so it was merely social rather than something on which he depended to get him through the day. He'd learnt to open bills when they arrived, and even pay them. And he had to admit, life was easier for it, if a little predictable.

So when Kay dropped her bombshell, Mickey resolved to bring it out into the open. Marriage was about sharing, after all. And as he drove back the short distance from the Honeycote Arms, still reeling with shock, he came to the conclusion that he wasn't actually guilty of anything. Just because Kay had got pregnant as a result of their affair it didn't make his original misdemeanour any greater. A shag was a shag was a shag, whatever the outcome, and he'd already been hung for that. And forgiven. So in theory he should be able to come clean to Lucy about Flora's existence without any reprisal. As he drove through the pillars and up the drive, he decided they would get through this by sticking together.

There was, however, another car at the front of the house as he pulled up, a sleek navy blue sports car that was coiled like a panther ready to spring. Shit. Bertie Meredith. Fond as Mickey was of Bertie, he wanted his wife to himself. And Bertie meant several glasses of wine and supper. There was no chance of getting rid of him before ten o'clock at the earliest. Since Bertie's girlfriend Erica had gone back to Zimbabwe to run her father's game reserve – less dangerous than living with Bertie – he had been in need of constant entertaining.

Mickey climbed wearily out of his car. His head was still throbbing, and his bad leg felt stiff, making him feel his age. Actually, no, older. He wasn't even fifty yet, but as he limped to the front door he felt positively geriatric. It was astonishing how quickly middle age came upon you when in your head you were still a young buck with the sap rising. He pushed open the door, smelt the delicious waft of Lucy's cooking from the kitchen, heard the sound of carefree chatter and James Blunt droning out of the new speakers. He stood for a moment, wishing desperately that he could saunter into the kitchen and enjoy his simple surroundings with a clear conscience. But somehow he suspected life was never going to be quite the same again.

Just as he guessed, Bertie was lolling at the head of the table, impossibly long legs stuck out in front of him, glass in hand, while Lucy stood chopping flat-leaf parsley with a mezzaluna. She looked up as Mickey came in.

'Darling. I've asked Bertie to stay for supper. You look shattered. Was the meeting bloody?'

'Worse than you can ever imagine.' Mickey's tone was dry, although only he was privy to the joke.

'Oh dear.' Lucy looked anxious.

'Have a glass of wine.' Bertie waggled the bottle at him. 'It's only Viognier, but quite a good one.'

For a moment, Mickey hesitated. He didn't want to have the conversation later with a drink inside him. But if he had nothing, they would think it was odd. He'd just have one. He got himself a glass from the cupboard.

'Top up?' He proffered the bottle to Bertie, who nodded.

'Thanks. I was just admiring your wife's new kitchen. Oh, and by the way. I hear congratulations are in order.' Bertie looked at him meaningfully.

Mickey started. Had word got out already? He was under the impression that Kay hadn't told anyone else. But perhaps he'd been seen at the pub, and someone had put two and two together. Barney, perhaps? Though he was usually pretty discreet.

'What?' he asked nervously.

'Patrick and Mandy. Wedding bells?' Bertie waved his glass around in an expansive gesture.

'Oh. Yes, of course! Fabulous news, isn't it?' Mickey poured himself a hefty slug of Viognier and took a gulp. 'We're really looking forward to it. Aren't we, Lucy?'

Lucy turned from the chopping board, her eyes sparkling.

'Bertie's been an absolute star. He's going to lend me loads of stuff for the garden. Furniture, and statues, and pots.'

'Great.'

'And he can get all the accessories at trade prices. Candles. And lights. And extra plants.'

'That's very kind of you, Bertie. Thanks.'

'No problem. I've told Lucy to come over and choose whatever she wants and I'll get the lads to bring it over in the truck.'

Bertie had a reclamation yard, dealing in antique garden furniture and statuary, but times being what they were, had to resort to a bit of retail as well, just to keep the cash-flow going. He wasn't as much of a snob as James about the antiques trade, which meant he did rather better. Mickey often thought James could take a leaf out of Bertie's book. Where business was concerned, anyway. Not in his personal life. Bertie was nicknamed Tall, Dark and Hands, because of his looks and inability to keep his mitts off anything female, whether she was spoken for or not. Mickey was just about sure that he'd stopped making passes at Lucy after all these years – she kept a special wooden spoon in a pot by the Aga for thwacking him when he got out of hand.

'You do realize that this will be the twenty-seventh wedding I've been to in my life. Not counting my own aborted attempt.' Bertie sounded rueful. 'I'm beginning to wonder if I'll ever make it up the aisle. Is there someone out there for me, Lucy?'

'You'll have to change your ways.' Lucy was always firm with him. Firm but kind. Dealing with Bertie was like dealing with a recalcitrant horse.

'Come on. What's wrong with me? I'm not bad looking.' This was an understatement. But you only had to look at him to know he was a rogue. 'I've got plenty of dosh, and a nice house.'

'Actually, your house is the best thing about you.'

Bertie looked hurt. 'I'm kind. And generous.'

Lucy laughed. 'And modest?'

'I'm just pointing out my attributes. I wouldn't say it to anyone. Only you.'

'Bertie, you don't want to get married. Otherwise you would be.'

'To tell you the truth, I've been giving it a lot of thought lately.' Bertie adopted a rather pained expression. 'I don't want to die a lonely old man. I want a wife. And a family.'

Lucy's eyes widened.

'Steady on.'

'It's what it's all about though, isn't it? Don't you think, Mickey?'

'What? Sorry, I was drifting.'

'Bertie's having a moment. He thinks he's missing out,' Lucy explained.

'Children. Life is nothing without children.'

'Um . . . No. Yes. No.' Mickey floundered, not sure what he was supposed to say.

'Actually, you're right. Life's bloody awful without them in the house. I can't stand it without Patrick and Sophie and Georgina. It's horrible,' said Lucy.

'Ah, well,' said Bertie. 'It's up to me, then. To get myself a pretty little wife and have a clutch of children I can dump on you. So I can take her off to Capri or Sardinia or Cap Ferrat for a long weekend.'

Lucy clapped her hands in delight. 'I'd love that!' she cried. 'I wanted another baby but Mickey said I was mad.'

'Did you?' Mickey looked at her, horrified. 'Did I?'

'Yes. Remember? Just before you went off for the snip. You couldn't get to the clinic fast enough.' She turned to

Bertie, eyes shining. 'I'll look after all your babies for you, darling. So hurry up.'

As Lucy drained the pasta in the sink, Mickey busied himself finding plates and cutlery so he wouldn't have to speak as he digested this latest piece of information. Lucy had wanted another baby? Somehow he'd missed that. Obviously they'd talked when he'd decided to go for the vasectomy, and although she had been a bit wistful, he hadn't appreciated that she'd expressed a real desire. Though perhaps she hadn't. Perhaps she was just rewriting history. People did that, didn't they? But then, he wouldn't have put it past himself to ignore what she'd been saying. He did that all the time. Shut his ears to things he didn't want to hear.

He hadn't been able to shut his ears to Kay. He couldn't gloss over that bombshell. A long-lost daughter wasn't like a bill that you could shove to the back of the drawer. And the implications were far, far greater. If Flora was five, that was another thirteen years of responsibility. Well, more than that, because you didn't cut kids off at eighteen, not if Sophie and Georgina were anything to go by. Patrick was pretty self-sufficient and paid his own way, but the girls were always tapping him up for funds. And could he resist them? No . . .

Another daughter. Another little girl. Never mind what Lucy was going to say. What about Sophie and Georgina? Sophie would be a walkover, but Georgie could be very judgemental and unforgiving. And she was a bit of a daddy's girl. How would she take to a half-sister being dropped like a cuckoo into the nest? And Patrick! Mickey had always worried that he felt a bit of an outsider, because he was only a half-brother to Sophie and Georgina,

and a stepson to Lucy. Even though Lucy had been absolutely wonderful to Patrick, treating him as her own,
and far better than bloody Carola, his real mother. When
Mickey had wrestled Patrick from Carola's clutches and
fought her tooth and claw for custody, the little boy had
barely any clothes and no toys at all, because Carola didn't
believe in them. Lucy had soon rectified that.

Darling Lucy. The angel he didn't deserve. Mickey slid
another shot of wine into his glass. She didn't deserve to
have another of his spawn dumped on her this late in
life, especially when she'd just expressed a desire for one
of her own. It would rub salt into the wound, to have
Kay flaunting Flora. Not that she'd do that deliberately,
Mickey felt sure. Kay had changed; there had been a softness and vulnerability to her that had shocked him. The
tough, ruthless, rather self-centred Kay had gone. Her
only motive was to do what was best for her child. She
wouldn't use Flora as a weapon, or rub Lucy's nose in it.

But there was the nasty question of half a million quid
that wasn't going to go away. Mickey knew Kay had been
serious about that. His stomach churned as the full impli-
cation hit him. Where the fuck was he going to get that
amount from? He'd been so absorbed in the mere fact of
Flora's presence on this planet that he'd overlooked this
minor detail. Could he remortgage the house? Honeycote
House must be worth over a million. But no building
society in their right mind would give him a half-million-
pound mortgage at his age.

'Mickey!' Lucy was calling him, holding a vast bowl of
steaming seafood linguine. 'Can you get something to put
this on?'

'Sorry. I was miles away.'

As they sat down to eat, Mickey eyed his supper with distaste. Usually it was his favourite: big fat juicy tiger prawns in a creamy sauce livened up with a slug of Limoncello. But his appetite, not entirely surprisingly, had vanished. He managed to pick through it, sustained by several more glasses of wine. By the time Bertie left, Mickey was half cut. The Viognier had done the trick, blotting out the finer details of his meeting earlier and numbing his emotions. He couldn't bring it up with Lucy now. He'd be slurring his words, getting everything muddled. Anyway, he reasoned through the fug, it was probably best to sleep on it. See how an illegitimate daughter and a demand for a king's ransom seemed in the morning.

Kay lay in the middle of the bed in the Honeycote Arms, knowing that she should be grateful for the luxury of goose down after her mother's stretchy brushed cotton sheets, but completely unable to sleep. She thought about burrowing in her handbag for the sleeping tablets the doctor had given her, but she didn't want to be a zombie when Flora woke up the next morning. The little girl was snuggled up beside her, her curls spread out on the pillow. She always slept like a top, even with the bedside lamp still on and the telly burbling away in the background.

Kay thought she'd reached rock bottom just after Lawrence's funeral. But now she felt lower than ever. Coming back was a huge mistake. The Honeycote Arms, with its chic-but-low-key designer comfort, its almost tangible Englishness, made her feel homesick – but the irony was she didn't have a home. This was just a temporary haven, even if Mickey had offered to foot the bill. She couldn't stay here forever.

Having Mickey in her room, so solid, so real, so normal, had brought home to her just how desperate her situation was. How on earth could she have thought that throwing herself on his mercy was going to be an easy way out? She could picture Mickey now, sitting with Lucy in the kitchen at Honeycote House. She and Lawrence had been there a few times, for drinks parties and post-hunt suppers, because the Liddiards were madly social and seemed to invite all and sundry back to their house at the drop of a hat. At the time, Kay had felt no envy. She, after all, had lived at Barton Court, which was practically a stately home, and was pristine, perfect, almost like a museum. But now she realized Honeycote House was perfection. A warm, slightly shambolic family home, bursting with life and love and laughter. Kay had almost looked down on it – everything covered in dog hairs and the cupboard doors falling off. Now, she'd give anything for a place like that.

She remembered thinking nothing of her affair with Mickey. As far as she had been concerned, it was insignificant, just a bit of titillation for the two of them. She'd never considered Lucy's finer feelings either; after all, if Lucy was so bloody perfect, Mickey wouldn't be so horny all the time. She had not considered the truth: that the more sex men had, the more they wanted. She had felt all-powerful, knowing she was fucking him, knowing that if she crooked her finger, he would come running. Now, looking back, she just felt cheap. Worse than a hooker, because she hadn't even been paid. She despised herself for it. And she despised Mickey. How could he have sacrificed everything that he had? Everything that Kay realized now was important.

Everything that she was never going to have. She had

no husband, no house, no money. Though she hoped she had gone some way towards rectifying the last two. Kay knew she had pulled out the pin and lobbed a live grenade into Mickey's life but actually, she didn't care. He deserved to face the consequences of his actions. Even if Lucy didn't. But Kay wasn't going to analyse that too closely. If it was a toss-up between protecting Lucy and protecting her daughter, Flora won hands down.

For a moment, she wondered what Lawrence would say if he knew what she was doing. He'd probably be furious that she had gone back to the past and got herself embroiled with the Liddiards again. Was it betraying him, to revert to the biological father for support, when Lawrence had loved Flora so unconditionally? He'd never thought much of Mickey, primarily because he was a lousy businessman. Lawrence had always said Honeycote Ales was a potential gold-mine, and that Mickey was a fool. So Kay doubted that he would be impressed by her actions.

But then, he was the one who'd got himself killed and left them with no money. What the hell was she supposed to do? Kay felt the tears rising, and before she could stop them she was sobbing uncontrollably. Seeing Mickey had brought the past rushing back and reminded her of all her mistakes. It was all her fault that they were here now. And she still didn't know if what she was doing was for the best. Should she have kept Pandora's box shut, stayed with her parents, relied on state handouts, got some pathetic little job in Slough and scratted around for the rest of her life?

It was too late now.

Flora sat up next to her.

'What is it, Mummy? Is it Daddy?' She felt the little

girl's arms go round her neck, and her soft cheek on hers. 'It's OK. He's with the angels, remember?'

'Thank you, sweetheart.'

Kay swallowed down her sobs, hoping Flora was right. She really did. At least if that was the case, one of them was being looked after.

7

Mayday was used to PC Robert Dunne popping in for a coffee every now and again. Patrolling the streets of Eldenbury wasn't an unduly stressful beat, except for the odd spate of shoplifting and the occasional drunk, so he quite often came in for a chat and a gossip, giving her useful snippets of local information: who'd been banged up in the cells overnight for being over the limit, who was going to be up before the beak for petty theft or driving without insurance, and who'd been having a domestic.

So when Rob came into the hotel lobby at midday on Tuesday and asked to see her in private, Mayday was puzzled by his formality. Perhaps one of the staff had been up to no good. Pilfering from the bedrooms? Or dealing drugs?

She led him into her office and shut the door. He stood in the centre of the room, feeling awkward. He was tall, Rob, as tall as you wanted a policeman to be, but with a gentle manner that belied his toughness. He looked at her solemnly, his brown eyes with their unexpectedly long lashes filled with concern.

'I'm very sorry, Mayday. It's your gran.'

Mayday gave a half smile. 'What on earth's she done?'

She couldn't imagine what Elsie would get up to that would involve the police.

Rob gave an awkward cough. 'I'm afraid she's . . . passed away.'

He was used to being the bearer of bad tidings. It was one of the downsides of the job. But he particularly hated it when he knew the person he was informing. Especially when it was someone he liked. And he had a lot of time for Mayday. She always made him feel important, even though he was just a lowly PC. And it wasn't because she was sucking up to him because he was a copper. Mayday was the genuine article.

All the colour had drained from her face and Rob rushed to get her a chair. He hadn't told her the bad bit yet.

'What happened? Who found her? I only saw her last night. She was fine.' Mayday sank into the chair.

'I'm really sorry, Mayday.' Why couldn't he think of something more original to say? 'It looks as if she took her own life.'

'Gran? She can't have. She wouldn't . . .'

Rob cleared his throat to make way for his explanation. 'There was an empty bottle of pills by her chair.'

'Who found her?'

'The neighbour was worried because she didn't pull her curtains or take in her milk. She called us out.'

Mayday seemed to shrink before his eyes. She went from being the larger-than-life extrovert character that he so admired to a helpless young girl. Mayday, who could stop a bar brawl with a single bellow, who threw out diffi- cult customers without batting an eyelid and who he had seen shamelessly pinching his chief inspector's bottom at the station's Christmas party, slumped in her chair and began to sob quietly. Somehow Rob had expected her to take it in her stride. He waited awkwardly, knowing from experience it was best to allow people to have a few moments to let bad news sink in.

'I suppose my mother's been told,' she finally managed, through gritted teeth. 'I suppose she's already rifling through her drawers looking for bundles of hidden cash.'

Rob's eyes widened in shock. Angela had indeed been informed, and was at the scene.

'Yes. Your mother's at the house now. She's called the undertaker.'

Mayday stood up, gathering herself together and wiping away her tears.

'Would you mind driving me out there, Rob?' she asked. 'I've got to make sure everything's done properly for Gran. My mother won't have the first idea what she'd want.'

Rob readily agreed. He would gladly have driven Mayday to the ends of the earth if she'd asked him. 'The patrol car's outside.'

Mayday managed a smile. 'That'll give everyone something to talk about.'

Rob stood aside to let her through the door, touching her arm in sympathy as she went past. She had spirit, Mayday. Cracking jokes even in her darkest hour. You had to admire her.

When Rob and Mayday arrived at Elsie's house, they found Angela in the kitchen. She looked dreadful. She'd been working at the kennels when she was informed, and was wearing a rather tight baby-pink velour tracksuit that had originally been expensive but had been relegated when she spilt bleach down the zip-up top, which didn't quite cover her stomach. Rob was shocked to see she had a pierced belly button, rather inappropriate for a woman of her age, he thought. Tears and mascara were tracking through the thick foundation on her face; her hair was dishevelled, and the glue where her extensions were attached was showing in several places.

As soon as she saw her daughter, she went for her.

'I blame you for this, you know that!' Angela shrieked at Mayday, her eyes wild.

Mayday gazed at her coolly. 'Why?' she asked. 'It wasn't me who tried to force her into a home.'

'You came round here last night. You must have said something that tipped her over the edge.'

'What? Like "Don't worry, Gran, you don't have to go into a home. I'll look after you." That sort of thing?' Mayday's voice was level but deadly.

'She was quite happy when I left her.'

'I brought her some food. And did her hair for her. I left her watching *Emmerdale*—'

'So why did she swallow a bottle of painkillers?' Angela's voice went up an octave.

'Now let's just calm down,' said Rob nervously. 'I don't think there's any point in trying to apportion blame at this stage.'

Angela gave him an evil glare.

'At what stage do you suggest, then?' she demanded.

Rob stepped back. He knew Angela's type. Nasty. Best to stay out of arm's reach.

'Can I see her?' Mayday asked with a quiet dignity that made him feel proud.

'Yes. Might as well have a look at your handiwork,' snapped her mother.

'She's in the lounge,' said Rob. 'We're just waiting for the undertaker to arrive.'

He put a protective hand on Mayday's shoulder as she walked towards the living room. Angela followed, her diamanté flip-flops slapping on the quarry tiles, and he resisted the urge to tell her to keep her nose out. He wanted Mayday to have peace and quiet when she paid her respects, but he didn't want to antagonize her mother, so he said nothing. He was on hand to intervene if things got out of control.

Elsie looked as if she was sleeping. Sat back in her chair with her eyes closed, her hair still in the curls Mayday had set less than twenty-four hours ago. The most remarkable thing was that her face seemed ten years younger, presumably because she was no longer in pain.

Mayday swallowed down a lump that rose in her throat. She couldn't have done any more for her. She knew that. She'd left no stone unturned in her quest to alleviate her agony. She'd been to the GP with her on countless occasions, and raged about the futility of it. She'd tried to arrange for a home help, but had been rebuffed – and she couldn't blame her grandmother for not wanting the indignity of a stranger in her house. She'd tried to get her to try acupuncture, but Elsie didn't hold with it. She'd looked at diet, but to no avail. Elsie was matter of fact about her fate.

'Look, love, I'm crippled with it and that's the end of it. You can't fight Mother Nature when she's made up her mind.'

All that was left was to be able to make her life as

comfortable as possible. She'd bought her an electric blanket, to warm her aching bones. Twice a week she brought her food from the hotel. On a Friday afternoon she cleaned the house from top to bottom, changed the bed linen (she suspected that Elsie had been having accidents at night, unable to face the arduous journey to the bathroom, but she never mentioned it). She'd bought her the remote for the television with extra large buttons, so she could negotiate the channels. And a walkabout phone so she could clip it to her belt, instead of having to try and rush to answer it.

'After everything we did,' Angela's voice wavered. 'You can't do enough for some people. It's a wicked thing to do, take your own life. What about the people you leave behind? I don't think I'll ever get over this.'

'I'm sure you will, when you get the cheque.' Mayday knew she shouldn't have said it, but she couldn't bear the pantomime.

Angela's head whipped round, her face a mask of fury.

'Have some respect, can't you?' she snarled. 'And rest assured there's nothing in the will for you. So all that dancing attendance on your grandmother was a total waste of time.'

Mayday looked at her evenly. 'Funnily enough,' she replied, 'I didn't do it for the money. I did it because Gran looked after me when I needed her.' Despite herself she found her voice rising, furious at her mother's implications. 'I did it because I loved her!'

'Are you saying I didn't love my own mother?' Angela's voice was even more shrill.

'Ladies. Please.' Rob, who'd seen a few spats in his time, was appalled by their behaviour.

Mayday scolded herself silently. The expression on Rob's face was warning enough.

'I'm sorry. I shouldn't have said that.'

Angela pressed her lips together. The last thing she wanted was an apology from Mayday, because it meant that she had to accept it graciously. Her instinct was always to carry on an argument to the bitter end, like a war of attrition, until the other party was worn into the ground.

'We're all upset,' she conceded reluctantly.

Mayday looked at her grandmother again. The baggy blue top and elasticated trousers she was wearing made her want to howl.

'I don't know how long the undertaker's going to be, but I'd like to choose what Gran's going to wear. If nobody minds.'

Angela frowned. This practicality hadn't occurred to her.

'In the coffin, you mean? Won't she just wear what she's got on?'

'No. Gran hated these clothes. She should wear something pretty. Maybe we should get her something new, from one of the department stores in Cheltenham?'

'Are you mad?' Angela looked totally bewildered. 'Mum was never interested in what she wore.'

'How do you know?' demanded Mayday. 'You never took any notice of what she thought of anything. She often pointed things out in magazines that she thought were nice.'

'If it makes you happy.' Angela threw up her hands in despair. 'I'm more worried about where to have the funeral tea. This place isn't big enough.'

'We could have it at the hotel. We can do sandwiches and cakes in the lounge bar. Then everyone can have a drink.'

Angela surveyed her daughter beadily for a moment. The temptation not to be bothered with any of the catering was great, but not as great as the fear that public sympathy might swing towards Mayday if they used the Horse and Groom. She didn't want to be upstaged.

'No. We'll have it at Pantiles.' This was the name of Angela and Roy's ranch-style bungalow. Mayday had pissed herself laughing when someone had once added an extra 's' to the sign on the gates. Although it was quite clear that Angela wasn't pantiless today, as her black g-string was poking out of the top of her tracksuit bottoms. Rob's eyes had goggled when he'd spotted it. 'Roy will do us a bar. The boys can hand round sandwiches.' She clapped a hand to her mouth. 'Mason and Ryan. What do I do about them? Should they go to the funeral? I don't think they should. They're too young to be subjected to a trauma like that.'

Mayday didn't like to say that it would take more than that to traumatize Mason and Ryan. The last time she'd been round, they'd been watching a pirate DVD called *Electric Blue Asian Babes*. But it wasn't up to her. She looked out of the window and saw the undertaker pull up outside.

'I'll go upstairs and have a look in her wardrobe. See what there is.'

'No,' said Angela quickly. 'You're right. We should get her something new.' She burrowed in her bag, pulling out her purse. 'You pop into House of Fraser. Get her something nice. Their spring sale's just started.'

She thrust a wad of cash at Mayday. She didn't want her going upstairs until she'd had a chance to root through Elsie's drawers herself. She was pretty sure there wasn't anything of any great value, but she wanted to be sure.

By lunchtime on Tuesday, Mickey decided that he couldn't get through this latest fracas on his own.

He had had nightmares all night. The worst one being coming last in the Father's Sack Race at sports day, and everyone laughing because he was so old. Lucy woke him at one point, asking what on earth it was he was moaning about in his sleep. He told her it was too much rich seafood, even though he had barely touched his supper.

By the time he and Lucy had got rid of Bertie the night before, it had been too late to start bringing up the ghastly events of the day. Besides, Lucy had been so happy. As they lay in bed she'd burbled on about the wedding, and the email she'd had back from Sophie saying she and Ned would be back from Oz just in time. He couldn't bring himself to burst her bubble.

Come the morning, he was knackered. He scrambled out of bed and into his clothes of the day before, making his escape as quickly as he could, just about managing a cup of tea. He was at the brewery by eight o'clock. He sat in the car park for a while, looking at the familiar buildings clustered around the millpond. It was hard to believe in an hour's time it would spring into life. Sacks of grain would be upended and liquor poured into the huge vat ready for another day's brew, and the air would soon fill with the rich scent of hops and malt. Lorries bearing the Honeycote Ales logo would whiz in and out, ready to take on board their cargo of silver barrels and wend their way across the Cotswold countryside. The walls would ring with shouts and laughter and the sound of the local radio.

Mickey's life had followed this soothing rhythm nearly every day for over thirty years. There were men who had been working here over fifty years, since they'd left school at fourteen or fifteen and were now hovering on the brink of retirement. He had as much responsibility to them as he did to Flora. More, in fact. For most of them, the brewery was their life. Their income, their social structure. It might be a bit of a cliché, but Honeycote Ales was like a big extended family.

He remembered the last time he had faced a similar dilemma, when Graham Cowley from the bank had called him in and told him in no uncertain terms what would happen if he didn't get his act together. He had been so determined to make sure that didn't happen again. He hadn't blotted his copybook at all; his behaviour had been beyond reproach. Although Mickey knew deep down that it was Keith who was in the driving seat, making the important decisions, it was still him who was perceived as the figurehead. He was a Liddiard, after all. It was his great grandfather who had brewed the first drop of Honeycote Ale over a hundred and fifty years ago. The men still looked to him for guidance, advice and reassurance. It was Mickey who was down amongst them, remembering birthdays, enquiring after poorly spouses, sending flowers to the hospital when one of the young lads' wives gave birth, organizing the annual football match between the brewery and the pubs. His role was vital, as it was that sense of camaraderie, of pulling together, of knowing you were being looked after, that made the brewery such a special place. Its employees took huge pride in their work, which was rare enough these days. Mickey had a long list of people waiting for jobs, but as people rarely left voluntarily there were few vacancies.

And that, Mickey knew, was down to him. Keith was good at figures, at deals, at spin. At getting good terms from their suppliers, and good contracts from their customers, and spotting a PR opportunity. But he still didn't know the name of everyone on the floor. The workers liked him and respected him, but he wasn't as approachable as Mickey. He didn't really get his hands dirty – not like Mickey, who jumped in immediately when someone was off sick and took their place without question.

Sitting there, looking at the golden stone of the buildings, he realized he had let them all down. He'd been asked for more money than most of them would see in a lifetime. And he couldn't help feeling aggrieved. This was a crime he had already been hung for, but he couldn't ignore it and walk away. But that, Mickey knew, was life. You could keep your nose to the grindstone and your conscience clear, but you never knew quite what was round the corner. He shut his eyes, which were suddenly heavy with the sleep that had eluded him most of the night.

The next thing he knew, Elspeth was banging on his window, looking concerned. He wound down the window sheepishly.

'Are you all right, Mr Liddiard?' she asked him anxiously, her eyes darting around as if looking for a hosepipe attached to the exhaust.

'Just dropped off for a second,' he replied cheerfully. 'Didn't sleep too well last night. Dodgy prawn.'

He felt guilty blaming Lucy's faultless cooking, but Elspeth was a great one for making mountains out of molehills, and he didn't want her getting any hint that anything was amiss. He followed her, in her prissy floral dress and navy court shoes, into the brewery and promptly shut himself away in his office. He looked at his computer, wondering if the internet might give him some guidance. There must be blokes like him all over the country being hit with requests for money for children they didn't know they had. What should he type in to the search engine? He knew there were a couple of lads at the brewery who were paying maintenance, because it was docked from their pay packets. He felt for them sometimes, because the mothers could be difficult, happy to take their money but not so amenable when it came to visiting rights and access. But he couldn't exactly go and ask them for advice.

By lunchtime, after hours of staring at a blank screen, his head was splitting. Kay hadn't rung to say it was all right, that she'd discovered a secret bank account of Lawrence's and he didn't have to worry. Not that it was just the money. Mickey couldn't get the image of Flora hanging upside down on the climbing frame out of his head – her long brown curls hanging down, the curls that he knew held traces of his DNA.

There was only one person in the world he could share his secret with.

He found Patrick in the main brewery office, which contrasted starkly with the tradition of his own. The walls were painted a bright white, the lights were modern, and there were colourful prints on the walls, glass-topped desks, flat-screen computers and green leafy plants in stainless-steel tubs. This was the hub, where his son kept track of all their tied houses, where Mandy worked on PR and where Elspeth controlled operations.

'Can I have a word?'

'Sure.' Patrick logged off his computer with a click of his mouse and pushed his chair back, looking up at his dad expectantly.

Mickey cleared his throat, looking round the office. As it was lunchtime, there was no one else in, but either Mandy or Elspeth could appear at any moment.

'Do you want to . . . come into my office? It's a bit . . .' Mickey made a face to indicate that the matter was delicate.

'OK.'

Patrick got to his feet, and Mickey felt his heart sink, even though he didn't think it could sink any further. Patrick looked so young. He'd worked his arse off for the brewery over the past few years. Here he was, about to marry his childhood sweetheart, a happy event that should be filling everyone with hope and optimism for the future. But no, along comes his father and pisses all over his strawberry patch. If Mickey could have found someone else to burden with his problem, he would have.

Patrick followed Mickey into his office. Mickey promptly shut the door firmly.

'Must be serious,' observed Patrick. Mickey wasn't usually a closer of doors. He was usually only too eager for any passing distraction.

'That phone call in the middle of our meeting yesterday? It was Kay. Oakley.'

'Bloody hell. Long time no . . .' The look on his father's face made Patrick realize it wasn't a social call. 'What did she want?'

'In a word? Money.'

'Surely she's not blackmailing you? You and Kay were

finished, what – five years ago? She's got no hold over you.'

Mickey sighed.

'Tell me she didn't take pictures?' Bloody Kay, thought Patrick. He thought there was more to her than that.

'There's no easy way to tell you this. There's a child involved. A little girl. Who is, apparently . . .' Mickey paused, not for effect, but because he couldn't quite spit the words out. 'Mine,' he managed at last.

Patrick wasn't easily shocked. In any other circumstances, Mickey would have chuckled to see him so totally floored.

'She was pregnant. That Christmas. If you remember . . . ?'

'Yes. I know. But I thought . . . well, we all thought, didn't we? That it must have been Lawrence's in the end. Even though he denied it at first.' Patrick was struggling to remember the chain of events. Largely because so much had happened, so quickly, that Kay's predicament had taken rather a back seat. She'd left the scene, after all. She and Lawrence had buggered off to Portugal. Out of sight, out of mind. 'So why come running back to you now? I suppose she's up to her old tricks and Lawrence has kicked her out.'

'Lawrence is dead.'

'What?'

'Car crash, apparently. On one of those treacherous cliff roads. She implied it wasn't an accident. That he was involved with some dodgy types.'

'It wouldn't surprise me. He was a bit of a tough nut.'

'A bankrupt tough nut. Apparently.'

Patrick whistled softly. 'That does surprise me.'

'Leaving Kay a penniless widow.'

'Fuck,' said Patrick, getting the picture. 'Fuck.'

'I'm beginning to rather wish I hadn't.' Mickey made a dry attempt at humour.

Patrick didn't need anything spelling out to him. Adrenalin surged through his veins, and he felt his heart start to pound as the instinct to protect his family kicked in straight away.

'You're sure it's yours?' he demanded. 'It seems bloody convenient. You're sure she's not just trying it on?'

'Christ. I don't know. If she says it is, I suppose it is. I can't work it out. You know I'm crap at maths.'

'Well, me too. How old is the kid, exactly?'

'Flora,' said Mickey. 'Her name's Flora.'

Patrick frowned. 'Don't go getting emotionally attached.'

'We're talking about a child here! Possibly mine.'

'You're an idiot. Didn't you use anything? You used to warn me often enough—'

'She told me she couldn't get pregnant!'

Patrick could feel panic claw at his gut. 'You're still supposed to use protection. Haven't you heard of safe sex? Hasn't the message got through to your generation?'

'It would seem not,' Mickey snapped. 'Anyway, I don't think Kay was exactly a high-risk category.'

'That depends on what risk you're taking.'

'There's no need to be a smart arse. I came to you for advice. Not a lecture.'

The two of them fell silent for a moment.

'What have you said to her?'

'Not much. I was too gobsmacked. She told me she'd give me some time to think about it—'

162

'That's kind of her. Considering she'd kept it quiet for so long.'

'I don't think . . .' Mickey started, not sure what he was trying to say. 'I don't think she enjoyed telling me. I think she's desperate. I think this is a last resort.'

Patrick looked at his father pityingly. For all his worldly ways, Mickey had a naïvety that made Patrick want to throttle him sometimes.

'So this is just about money, is it?'

'Child support,' said Mickey. 'Not blackmail. It's money she is entitled to.'

'We'll see,' said Patrick. 'What's she asking for?'

It was such a simple sum. Time and again he'd gone over the calculations in his head and come to the conclusion that, outrageous though it sounded, it wasn't.

'Half . . . five . . . um . . .' No matter which way he said it, it was a small fortune. 'Five hundred grand.'

There was the tiniest twitch in his son's cheek muscle. 'Quite a reasonable opening gambit,' he observed. 'She's obviously not taking the piss completely.'

'Shit. Do you really think she'd get that? In a court of law?'

'Funnily enough, it's not something I've given a lot of thought to. But the papers are always banging on about how much it costs to bring up a child. And we're not exactly paupers, are we? I mean, I know the brewery's struggling. But on paper . . . if our assets were liquid . . . which is what they'd look at . . . I guess. I don't know,' he finished finally. 'But I'm sure Kay does. She'll have done her research.'

Patrick wasn't saying what Mickey wanted to hear. He'd wanted instant reassurance that her claim was ridiculous.

That there was some clause saying that you couldn't just go back to the natural father five years later bleating for money, that there was a time limit and Kay had missed it. By turning to Patrick he'd hoped for some temporary respite, a straw to clutch at. But instead, Patrick was making the situation seem even worse.

'What's Lucy going to say?'

Mickey groaned. 'I don't know. And that's the thing that really worries me, to be honest. She hasn't been herself lately, with Sophie and Georgina gone. She was just starting to perk up, because of the wedding. I just . . . don't know how to break it to her. She'll be devastated.'

Poor Lucy, thought Patrick. Of everyone, she was the one who was going to suffer for this. It was humiliating, everyone knowing your husband had fathered a child by someone else. She didn't deserve the inevitable gossip and speculation. Everyone had always known that Mickey was a bit of a lad and had an eye for the ladies. But living, breathing biological proof of infidelity wasn't funny.

He strode up and down Mickey's office, chewing his knuckle, deep in thought. He cast his mind back to that Christmas, which had brought about so many changes for them all. Some good. Most of them good. Like him getting together with Mandy, and Keith buying into the brewery. And Sophie and Ned finally admitting that they fancied each other like mad. And James proposing to Caroline, though they were looking a bit rocky at the moment. Well, more than a bit, if he was absolutely honest.

Most vividly of all, however, he remembered his own brief fling with Kay. How he'd offered himself up to her as a replacement lover, on condition that she gave up Mickey.

She'd been only too eager to accept the deal. And if he said so himself, he wasn't a bad consolation prize. Patrick took pride in his skills; if he remembered rightly, she'd been pretty appreciative. He'd blown her mind on more than one occasion. And although it hadn't exactly been a chore, for Kay was very attractive, he thought he'd done a pretty noble thing. For he'd felt sure Kay and Mickey's affair was going to end in disaster, and the one person he'd wanted to protect out of all of them was Lucy.

Just as he did now.

'Right,' he said decisively. 'This is what we do. If Kay wants the dosh, she'll have to agree to tell everyone the baby's mine.'

Mickey looked thunderstruck. 'What?'

Patrick shrugged matter-of-factly. 'It's the only solution. It doesn't make me look bad, because if Flora is nearly five the date of conception was obviously before I started going out with Mandy. So the only thing I'm guilty of is having sex with a married woman. I wasn't actually unfaithful to anyone.'

'You would really do that for me?' asked Mickey, incredulous.

'Nope.' Patrick was quite firm. 'But I'd do it for Lucy.'

Mickey tried to take in what his son was suggesting. 'What if Kay doesn't agree?'

'I'm sure Kay won't mind what the story is, as long as she gets the money.'

'I think you're misjudging her.'

Patrick gave a bark of laughter. 'We are talking about the same Kay Oakley?'

'She's changed. You haven't seen her. She's a different person. Almost a shadow of her former self.'

165

'Dad – she's on her uppers. She's going to pull every trick in the book to get your sympathy.'

'You're very cynical for one so young. I'm surprised you want to get married.'

Patrick strode over to the window and looked out at the millpond. The shadow of the brewery tower fell across the dappled water. He wasn't going to say that he was getting married to safeguard all of this. That his impending nuptials were the only means he knew to clinch their security. And even then, their future wasn't certain, because he wasn't sure Keith had the wherewithal to steer them all to safety.

Anyway, it wasn't the only reason. He was getting married because he loved Mandy. Cementing the bond between the Sherwyns and the Liddiards was just the icing on the wedding cake. It was ensuring her security as much as his.

Either way, he didn't want to talk about that now. Kay was the pressing issue.

'Leave Kay to me. I don't trust her not to manipulate you. I'll drive a harder bargain.'

'Patrick. Don't forget. She's our flesh and blood now.'

Patrick rolled his eyes. 'Only now it suits Mrs Oakley. She was quite happy to forget that fact while she was living it up in Portugal, remember? Anyway, we don't actually have proof yet, do we? We've only got her word that it's yours. And if she was bonking you and me and Lawrence around the same time, who's to say there wasn't someone else?'

'She's not stupid. She knows it would only take a simple test to prove it wasn't mine. So it must be mine.' Even

Mickey had worked that one out. 'Let's not go down that road. It would be too tacky for words.'

'I'm just thinking of delaying tactics.'

'Look, Patrick. Forget it. If you're going to be so hard-nosed—'

'Absolutely too right I am. Someone's got to protect our interests. Half a million fucking quid?'

The words rang like a death knell around the office walls. Mickey grimaced.

'Yeah. Never mind who we say the father is. Where are we going to get the money?'

Patrick fell silent. That was the one answer he didn't have. It was all very well playing tough and calling the shots. There was no doubt they were going to have to come up with some sort of cash. And whether it was five hundred thousand, or fifty, or even five, none of them had it.

'I'll go and talk to her,' he said. 'We've got to play for time. I'll ask her if she'd mind waiting until after the wedding. It's only six weeks away. We can give her some money in the meantime. I've got a bit of cash saved up.'

Mickey felt a sudden urge to hug his son. His brave, loyal, unquestioning son, who had done so much for him. Who he didn't deserve. He put his arms round him.

'I've hardly got a thing. Lucy blew a fortune on that bloody kitchen, not that I begrudge it. I've just put a massive deposit on a place for Georgie to rent in Gloucester. And I've promised to pay for Sophie's flight home from Australia—'

What a loser. Expecting his own son to fork out for his indiscretions.

'We've got to think carefully about this, Dad. This is fucking serious. It could affect our decisions about where to go with the brewery. We might not have to give her the whole lot at once, but we're not talking petty cash here.'

And with that, Patrick left the room, leaving Mickey wishing he had never opened his mouth.

Patrick walked back into the main office with his head reeling. But before he'd had time to really absorb the finer details of what his father had told him, Mandy bounced in brandishing a print-out of their wedding invitation. She'd been fiddling with it all morning on the computer.

'What do you think?' she asked. 'I thought we could print it on cream parchment with a sort of rusty brown ink. To make it look old.'

Patrick gave it a cursory glance.

'Fantastic,' he replied, though at this point he couldn't have cared less about the bloody wedding invitations.

'No, really.'

'Really.'

'There must be something you've got to say about it,' Mandy persisted.

'It's perfect. It says everything we need it to say.'

'Do you think it would be naff to have our initials entwined at the top?'

Patrick froze in panic. What was the right answer? He did actually think it would be incredibly naff, for he was all for things being as plain as possible. But he thought Mandy probably wanted him to say it was a lovely idea.

'Sounds a lovely idea,' he said carefully.

Mandy put the invitation down with a sigh. 'You're not interested, are you?'

Oh God. Was this what the next six weeks were going to be like? He might as well be honest.

'If I'm honest, I'm not interested in the invitations. No.'

Mandy looked as if she was about to burst into tears. He took her face in his hands and kissed her gently.

'All I really care about is you and me becoming Mr and Mrs Liddiard. That's what it's about for me. How we do it is . . . almost irrelevant. I'm happy to do it barefoot and go for a McDonald's afterwards.' Mandy opened her mouth to protest in outrage. 'I'm only joking. And I know it's important to you. I completely trust you, Mandy. I know whatever you organize will be fantastic. But I just want to say . . . things are a bit tricky at the brewery at the moment.' Understatement of the century. 'It's not going to make any difference to the wedding, but I have got to concentrate on business for the next couple of weeks. And I'm sorry. But nobody else is going to do it.'

Mandy frowned. 'So don't bother you with the details? Is that what you're saying?'

'Have fun with it. Do whatever you like. And rest assured that I trust you, and I will love whatever you decide. That's why I'm marrying you. Because I trust you!'

He looked at her beseechingly, but could see that his words had done little to placate her.

'But this is the fun bit,' she said. 'I want you to help me. I want us to decide on things together. It's our big day.'

'Let's go out for dinner on Friday,' he offered. 'We'll go through everything. I'll give you my undivided attention. I promise.'

'Mum's arriving on Friday. We're all having dinner at Keeper's Cottage.'

'Oh.' Patrick tried not to look too disgruntled. He found Mandy's mother absolutely terrifying. Ever since the night she had crept into his room and tried to get into bed with him. It took a lot to embarrass Patrick, but the memory of grappling with a drunken Sandra in her slippery satin nightdress still made his cheeks burn.

'What about the guest list?' Mandy persisted. 'We need to get the invitations sent out by the end of the week, so we've got to decide who we're having. And the vicar wants to see us.'

'Let's go to church on Sunday. Have a chat to him then. And we can fine-tune the guest list on Sunday afternoon. Surely the invitations can wait till Monday morning?'

Mandy looked doubtful. 'I know we said keep it small,' she ventured, 'but there's over a hundred already.'

Patrick shrugged.

'In for a penny,' he said.

After all, in the grand scheme of things, a few extra sausage rolls wasn't going to make that much difference.

Somehow he managed to get through the afternoon. Thankfully Keith was out at a meeting, because Patrick didn't think he'd be able to look him in the eye. The information was so loaded, the implications so far-reaching.

If only he had kept quiet his proposal the day before. Somehow it complicated everything. The stakes were so much higher with a wedding on the horizon. He knew it was impossible for Kay to have known about it, but he wouldn't have put it past her to have chosen her moment. She was a tactician, with the ability to prey on weak spots. God knows the Liddiards between them had enough of those.

Try as he might, Patrick couldn't envisage an outcome that wasn't going to cause a lot of people a lot of hurt. He looked around for someone to blame, and every time he came back to himself. He'd done as much damage limitation as he could at the time of Kay's affair with Mickey. He'd always known that it was a loaded gun. Admittedly Kay and Mickey were never going to fall in love and run off into the sunset together – there was nothing romantic about their encounters whatsoever – but their mutually selfish desire for illicit, up-against-the-wall, frantic sex was dangerous. Of all of them, only Patrick had realized at the time just how close they had come to ruin – financial, emotional, marital. And he had worked incredibly hard to deflect that. Not hard enough, it seemed. He should have done the job properly, made sure that the threat of Kay really had gone away, but he had been so relieved by the news that she and Lawrence had left the country that it had never occurred to him that she might reappear one day with the one weapon that no one could argue with.

It was going to be up to him again. Mickey was so clueless, and he had a tendency to panic. He had no idea how to handle the likes of Kay at all. And he was already allowing himself to get emotionally involved. Patrick knew he could trust himself to keep his heart hard. This was, after all, about money and nothing else.

At six o'clock, he managed to make his escape, promising Mandy faithfully that they would sit down later that evening and go through all the wedding details. Then he jumped in his car and made his way up the road to the Honeycote Arms.

He had to get Kay out of the pub, for a start. It was far too close to home. Barney and Suzanna had arrived in the village long after Kay had left, but they might think it strange that Mickey and Patrick were both paying furtive visits to the mysterious blonde visitor. And Mickey had mentioned that Kay's little girl, Flora – his own half sister, Patrick realized, as closely related to him as both Sophie and Georgina – was playing with Poppy. Friendships might be struck up, wine might be drunk, tongues loosened.

He pulled into the car park with its pristine Cotswold chippings, parking in front of a bollard from which swung a black-painted chain. Despite the circumstances he allowed himself a smile. The Honeycote Arms was his pride and joy, and it always gave him a kick when he pulled up outside. He had overseen its transformation from a nondescript village local to a renowned gastro-pub. And unlike many similar ventures, it hadn't opened in a burst of glory and then gone downhill when the managers had lost interest. With Barney and Suzanna at the helm it had gone from strength to strength.

The pub was always buzzing, lunchtimes and evenings, and was popular with locals and tourists alike. They kept ahead of the game by changing the menu frequently but keeping the old favourites, like juicy Aberdeen Angus steak with bearnaise sauce, and fish pie. And so regulars didn't tire of the decor, Suzanna rearranged the furniture to give the place a fresh feel every now and again, adding zebra skin cushions or huge colourful vases or some vibrant paintings to give them something new to look at. She changed the table linen and the floral displays to match the seasons, not in a twee way, but so that every time you went in the atmosphere was slightly different.

Patrick slid in through the front door, quickly glancing into the bar on the way past and noting with pleasure that it was already starting to fill, although it was early. He went up the striped coir runner to the top of the stairs. He knew Kay was in room four. He stood for a moment looking at the door's grey-green paintwork, and the pewter Roman numeral. How strange to think that both their past and their future lurked behind it.

He rapped on the door with a knock that meant business.

He gasped when he saw Kay. He thought Mickey had been exaggerating, but he scarcely recognized her. That brash outer layer had totally evaporated, the brittle glitz that despite himself he had once found attractive. There were lines at the corners of her mouth and eyes that may have been there before, but would have been covered in a careful application of age-defying foundation. Her hair, once immaculate, was long and tousled and unstreaked.

She looked . . . helpless. And startled to see him. He would have expected her hackles to go up immediately, and for her to go on the defensive. But she almost seemed to crumple.

'Patrick.'

There was so much sorrow in her voice. He'd been meaning to lay it on the line straight away, having decided that the only way they were going to get through this was by playing it tough.

He couldn't play it tough with this fragile creature.

'Kay . . . Can I come in?'

She looked uncertainly behind her. 'Flora's just going off to sleep. Can I meet you down in the bar? In ten minutes?'

He was astonished that she was so unsure of herself. He nodded. She gave him a wan smile and shut the door.

Patrick went down to the bar and bought himself a large double Scotch, which he knocked back in one. Then he ordered a bottle of Cloudy Bay and a bowl of olives. He appropriated a pair of armchairs facing each other in a quiet corner. They were low and deep, covered in turquoise and coral striped velvet. He put the wine and nibbles on the low coffee table that separated them. The scene was perfectly set for a romantic assignation.

When Kay came down, she looked a little more like her old self, but not much. She'd put on some pink lipstick and some mascara, and brushed her hair. Patrick found it hard to believe that once he'd slid her out of a skin-tight sequined dress and ravished her in a gazebo. That she'd writhed with delight and dug her nails into him. He stood up politely as she came across to him.

'She's fast asleep,' she said, then gave him an appraising glance. 'You look well.'

He wasn't about to say that she looked dreadful, so he poured her a glass of wine. The glass was so huge, and her wrists so tiny, she seemed barely able to lift it. Harden your heart, he told himself. Kay is perfectly capable of playing us all for fools. He drew an envelope from the inside pocket of his moleskin jacket and chucked it carelessly on the table.

'There's a cheque for five grand in there,' he said curtly. 'It's going to have to last you three months. Because it's going to take at least that long to sort things out. Legally. And financially. And it's all the cash we've got. So take it or leave it.'

She picked it up. 'Thank you,' she said, and he was astonished by the gratitude in her voice. He'd expected a battle, a derisive laugh. But her features had been suffused with relief.

'I hate doing this.' Her voice was almost a whisper, and he had to lean forward to hear what she was saying. 'I would have done anything I could to avoid it. But I didn't have any choice. Flora doesn't deserve what's happened to her. Lawrence was a wonderful father to her. They were everything to each other. Now she's got nothing. Except me. For whatever that's worth.'

She gave a self-deprecating grimace. Patrick was shocked. Kay had never been one for selling herself short. She'd always been bursting with confidence, so incredibly sure of herself. It was one of the things that had made her so sexy. Now she was even less than a shadow of her former self: the bitten nails, that had once been long and shiny red; the flat loafers, when he couldn't remember her in any other than three-inch heels. He'd definitely never seen her in jeans.

Yet there was still something appealing about her . . .

Don't even go there, Patrick, he reminded himself.

'Look,' he said, trying to take an assertive stance, but being as gentle as he could. He didn't want her breaking down in the middle of the pub. 'This couldn't come at a worse time for us. Mandy and I are getting married in six weeks—'

There was a flash of warmth in her smile. 'Oh. Congratulations. I didn't know you were still together.'

'Yes. And I don't want this to spoil the occasion. For Mandy or Lucy or Dad.'

'No. I agree. I don't want to spoil it either. Not at all.'

Kay looked distressed. 'Patrick – just tell me what else I can do. What the hell else am I supposed to do?'

Her eyes were huge as she gulped her wine.

Shit, thought Patrick. He was losing control of the situation. He'd been so sure of what he was going to say, so clear in his mind that he wasn't going to take any crap from Kay Oakley.

'We can't let anyone know this is Dad's child,' he said desperately. 'It would be a disaster. You've got to agree to say that I'm the father. If you want the money without a fight.'

Kay looked at him in amazement. Then gradually a smile crept over her face.

'My God, I'd forgotten what a bloody hero you are,' she said. 'Your father is an incredibly lucky man.'

She tipped another inch of wine into her glass.

'As far as I'm concerned, the paternity issue is strictly between us. I'm never going to say a word to anyone. On paper, I'll say the father is Ronald McDonald, if that's what it takes. But from Flora's point of view, her father is Lawrence, and that's the end of it. She won't ever know the truth.'

'Some people will have to know,' Patrick pointed out. 'Because Dad and I can't magic up the money between us without some sort of explanation. And if there's one thing I've learned in my short little life, it's that it's usually easier to stick to something resembling the truth.'

She sat back, closing her eyes, and he saw dark shadows. A tiny bit of him wanted to scoop her up, put her into bed, smooth her hair . . .

'As long as you understand that my first and only loyalty is to Flora. I'm not doing this so I can go and whoop it up at your expense. Whatever you give me is for her benefit, not mine.'

Somehow, he believed her. Whereas initially he'd had a vision in his head of her gleefully cackling and dashing off to a BMW showroom with their money, now he saw a different picture.

She was getting up. 'I must go and make sure Flora hasn't woken up. She'd panic if I wasn't there.'

Patrick jumped to his feet. 'Kay—' He stopped her as she walked past. He put a hand on each of her arms, feeling the very bones through her shirt. If he squeezed her, she'd snap. 'I don't know what else we can do to help. Can we find you a cottage, or—' He sounded so bloody patronizing. He'd better just shut up.

'I don't know what I'm going to do yet. I'll probably go back to my parents for a week or so while I think about things.'

'Leave your number. You can get me at the brewery.' He pulled one of his business cards out of his pocket. 'And don't worry about the bill here. I'll sort it out with Barney.'

He really had inherited the best bits of his father. They were alike in a lot of ways.

They stood for a moment, no words between them. Former lovers, in a situation so complicated and alien that close physical contact was now almost impossible. Both of them felt the pull for a second, but both resisted. Patrick, because his loyalty was to his own family. And Kay, because she had to protect herself.

As he drove through the narrow back lanes to his cottage, Patrick decided he was going to have to shut his mind to everything that had just happened and focus on the wedding. It wasn't fair to spoil it for Mandy. In fact, he decided, it would be good fun to discuss their plans over a bowl of pasta and a bottle of wine. He felt rotten about dismissing her earlier. She wasn't to know about the can of worms that had just been opened, after all.

As he dropped his car down into second gear to get it up the steep hill that led to Little Orwell, his mobile rang. He glanced at the screen in irritation. It was Mayday, which was odd. She wasn't in the habit of phoning him. Intrigued, he pulled over to the side of the road for a second, letting the engine tick over.

'Hey!'

All he could hear on the other end was a choking sound.

'Mayday?'

'It's Gran,' Mayday sobbed. 'She's killed herself. Oh, Patrick. I just don't know what to do.'

That, thought Patrick, was tonight's plans out of the window.

'Why didn't she say something?' There was desperation in her wail. 'I'd have done anything for her. Anything!'

'Of course you would,' soothed Patrick. 'Where are you?'

'At the hotel. I couldn't stand it at Gran's any longer. My bloody mother's milking it for everything she can get.'

Patrick could believe it. The few times he had run into Angela he couldn't get away fast enough.

'I'll come over as quickly as I can.'

'No. No. You don't have to. I just wanted someone to talk to.' There was a large sniff. 'I think I'll just go to bed.'

'Why did she do it?'

'The arthritis, I suppose. She couldn't stand it any

more. She must have been in such pain. And she never complained. She took all her painkillers in one go.'

'Maybe . . .' Patrick trailed off. He hated platitudes.

'Maybe it's for the best, you mean?' Mayday was always quick to pick up what he was thinking.

What was he supposed to say? 'You know what your gran was like. She knew what she was doing.'

'Yes, but . . .' Mayday's voice cracked. 'Fuck it, Patrick. She was the only person in the world I really cared about.'

He couldn't bear it. He couldn't bear how small she sounded. Feisty, ballsy, crazy, one-off Mayday, who never let anything or anyone get to her.

'Give me half an hour.'

He'd nip home, explain what had happened to Mandy. She'd understand.

'Honestly. Don't worry. I'm fine. I just wanted to ask you a huge favour.'

'Anything.'

'Will you come with me to the funeral?'

Patrick didn't hesitate. 'Of course!'

'I don't trust myself not to punch my mother. I know she'll be weeping and wailing and gnashing her teeth all the way through the service. And she didn't give a toss, Patrick. All the silly bitch will be worried about is getting her hands on the money. I need you with me to stop me throttling her. If you don't mind.'

'Mayday, of course I don't. And any time off you want – don't give the hotel a second thought. I can send someone over to sort it out.'

'I'd rather work. It'll give me something else to think about.'

Patrick could relate to that.

'Well, if you change your mind . . .'

'I probably won't. But thanks. I know you mean it.'

She sounded calmer.

'Go and have a bath and have a whopping brandy sent up from the bar,' Patrick ordered. 'Get a good night's sleep.'

'Yeah.' There was a small pause. 'Thanks, Patrick. You're a real mate.'

Patrick tossed his phone onto the passenger seat and leant back for a moment. He thought about Mayday's granny, who he usually met when he dropped Mayday off after a night out. He remembered eating delicious rhubarb pie in her back garden one Sunday, its crust crisp and glistening with sugar. He'd caught Elsie looking at him with a strange expression, a curious mixture of interest and perspicacity, and the smile she'd given him when he met her gaze had been meaningful. Almost as if she was giving him a clandestine sign of her approval.

It was horrible to think she was dead. He'd known she was poorly, and that Mayday worried about her incessantly. As usual, because it seemed to be his default setting at the moment, he felt guilty, but what more could he have done? Surely it was enough that it was he who had lobbied to make Mayday the manager of the Horse and Groom? That had given her a substantial salary, which in turn she'd been able to use to help her grandmother. How far did paternalism and duty extend? He couldn't add finding a cure for arthritis to his to-do list.

Whatever he did, thought Patrick gloomily, he ended up feeling as if everything was his fault. And who, he wondered, ever worried about him?

*

Half an hour later, Mandy was waving a piece of paper under his nose to try and attract his attention.

'Patrick! You're not listening to a word. Lucy and I think buffet, not sit down, so we don't have to worry about nightmare seating plans. And we're going to get Suzanna to do the food. What do you think?'

He stared back at her rather blankly.

'Mandy, I'm really sorry. I'm going to have to go out.'

'What?'

'Something's come up that I think I should have dealt with.'

'What? What can be so urgent all of a sudden?'

Mandy wasn't the volatile type. She was very even-tempered. But there was a definite flash of irritation in her voice.

'Mayday's granny killed herself last night,' Patrick explained. 'I ought to go and see if she's all right.'

Mandy looked baffled.

'Surely it's too late? Surely she's dead?'

'Not her granny. Mayday.'

'Oh.' Mandy looked down at her lists, crestfallen. 'That's awful. Of course you've got to go.'

'She hasn't really got anybody else to look after her. You know what a total cow her mother is.'

'It's OK. I understand.'

She started tidying away her paperwork. Patrick couldn't imagine how she could possibly have so much already, when he had only proposed to her on Sunday.

'Look,' he said gently. 'I've already told you. Do whatever you think is best. Between you and Lucy, it will be wonderful.'

'You don't get it, do you?' she said sadly. 'It's no fun if you don't join in too.'

He gave her a hug. 'Let me just drive over to the Horse and Groom. Make sure Mayday isn't about to jump out of the window. I really should, as her mate. And her boss.'

'I know you should. I'm not complaining. Honestly.'

He pulled her in close, pressing his lips against her soft, shiny hair. She had every right to complain. Most women, he knew, would have a screaming fit if their fiancé had walked out of planning their wedding to console another woman. But there was more to Mandy than that. She wasn't the clingy, possessive type, and he admired her for it.

'I'll be an hour. Max.'

'No. Make sure she's OK. The wedding's not going anywhere.' She gave him a little mischievous smile. 'I'll save it all for you. Don't think you're going to get out of it that easily.'

'You know I'll be happy with whatever you decide. As long as I don't have Henry stumping up the aisle in velvet knickerbockers with the ring on a tasselled cushion. Or anyone in a nasty shiny hired morning suit with an acrylic cravat. Or a hideous archway made out of balloons . . .'

Patrick had been to enough of Honeycote Ales' employees' weddings to know that all of these things were a possibility. Mandy giggled.

'What about,' she ventured, 'personalised metallic confetti?' Patrick clicked his fingers and pointed at her. 'Spot on.' He scooped up his car keys. 'I'll be as quick as I can.'

Outside, he got back into his car and gave a huge sigh before putting the keys in the ignition. He'd genuinely thought on Sunday that he was taking control of his life.

Now, it seemed that every female he had ever come into contact with was clamouring for his attention. He saw Mandy waving to him from the kitchen window, then draw down the blind. He longed to be back inside with her, laughing over the hideous gimmicks in her wedding magazines. But for the second time that day, he steeled himself for an awkward encounter with a former lover. He was, he decided, coming back as a monk.

8

Friday morning dawned as grey and dreary as only England in late March can muster.

In the Horse and Groom, Mayday woke with a lump of grief in her throat. She'd arranged to have breakfast sent up to her room the night before, but when the knock came on the door, she couldn't bring herself to answer it. She wouldn't be able to speak. She certainly wouldn't be able to eat. She lay there until room service went away, hoping that her staff would get the message that she wanted to be left alone, and that they wouldn't pester her to make sure she was all right. They had been golden all week, all of them, running the hotel like clockwork, with none of the usual spats and quarrels and mini crises.

For several moments she debated not going to the funeral at all. Her grandmother wouldn't know. For all that she pretended to dabble in the mystic arts – one of her party tricks was telling fortunes – Mayday was actually a confirmed atheist and didn't believe in an afterlife. Death was death and that was it, so Elsie would be totally oblivious to her absence, and Mayday didn't care what anyone else might think. She would have preferred to spend the day going for a long walk, alone with her memories. It was only the thought of Angela taking centre stage that forced her out of bed and into the shower.

At Keeper's Cottage, Keith woke with a knot of worry in his stomach. Getting out his cheque book had brought about the desired speed, but now the day of judgement had arrived all too quickly. It seemed there was no perfect timescale where the threat of cancer was involved. On Monday he hadn't been able to bear being at the mercy of the lumbering NHS with its endless waiting lists. Now he wasn't sure if he could cope with the swift efficiency of going private. His biopsy was at midday, which meant by the end of next week he would know his fate. The prospect was so daunting that he hadn't given any thought whatsoever to the fact that he was picking his ex-wife up from the airport afterwards.

Ginny came into the bedroom with a cup of tea. He felt a rush of fondness for her. As far as she knew, he was off to Warwickshire to meet his financial adviser, not to have a needle shoved up his rectum. When he knew that they had something to worry about, that's when he would tell her. There was no need for Ginny to be on tenterhooks waiting for his test results. Besides, the very last person he wanted to find out that he might be ill was Mandy. It would only spoil the run-up to her big day. And Keith knew that the only way to keep a secret was not to burden anyone else with it. Not that he didn't trust Ginny. But she might be tempted to tell Mandy, thinking she was doing the right thing. So he was going to save her from temptation.

He shot into the shower, then went over to his wardrobe. If he was pretending to go to his financial adviser, then he would have to wear a suit, though what he really wanted to wear was comfort clothing. Reassuring clothes that would tell him everything was going to be all right.

Oh God. What if it wasn't? Keith had read all the leaflets. The cancer could be localized in the prostate. Or it could be starting to feel its way out, tentatively exploring the rest of his body. Or it could have hitched a lift in his lymph nodes, or be settling in his bones. Metastasizing. That was the technical term. Could he feel the ache of metastasis?

Of course, it could be nothing . . . a mere plumbing problem. Unattractive as that diagnosis was, he would jump for joy to be told he merely had an uncooperative pecker.

'What should I do for supper tonight?'

Ginny was looking at him anxiously. He tried to focus on what she was saying, but somehow the evening meal paled into insignificance.

'Anything. Sandra isn't interested in food.'

She never had been. All through their marriage, it had been all she could do to get a meal on the table. Sandra had always made it quite clear that she had better things to do than keep house. It was only since living with Ginny that Keith had discovered that food could be a shared pleasure. Not just the eating, but the purchasing and the preparation. But today, he couldn't summon up so much as a flicker of enthusiasm. Usually he would be making all sorts of suggestions, looking up what was in season, in his Nigel Slater Kitchen Diaries, then trotting off to his cellar to find a decent wine to match.

Ginny's face clouded over at his lack of response.

'I wanted to do something special.'

'Honestly. Don't bother. Sandra will be too busy talking about herself to notice what's on her plate.'

He forced himself to go and give Ginny a kiss. Just a perfunctory peck. He didn't want to get too close. If he felt her warmth, her softness, he might be tempted to confess all, so great was his longing for reassurance. He had to keep his distance.

He remembered to grab his briefcase for authenticity.

'Good luck,' said Ginny.

'What?' He looked at her in alarm. Had she guessed? Had he given something away?

She stepped back slightly, startled by his reaction. 'Everyone needs good luck, don't they? When they go to see their financial adviser?'

He managed a grimace. 'I suppose so,' he replied carefully, hating the lie. But it was so much better than the truth. He bolted to the safety of his car, where he could stop the charade. He started up the engine, then wondered exactly what he was going to do for the next three hours. Even if he took the most scenic route possible, the hospital was only just over an hour away.

In Puerto Banus, the sun was out, and Sandra Sherwyn sang happily to herself in her wet room, letting the scalding water trickle over every inch of her body as she examined her precision bikini wax for stray tufts. There were none. Her girls knew better than to leave so much as a millimetre of stubble. Her bush was as well-tended as Wimbledon Centre Court in June. The same went for the rest of her body, which was faultless for a woman of her age. Not that you could rely on other people for maintenance. You had to put the spadework in yourself, which was why she had in front of her an array of loofahs, body brushes, pumice stones and salt scrubs.

An hour later she was exfoliated, moisturized, coiffed, made up and dressed to kill. As a final touch she stepped into a cloud of Marc Jacobs. The droplets settled reverentially upon her shoulders and nestled in her cleavage.

'Alejandro,' she purred at the inert figure in her bed. 'I'm ready for you to take me to the airport. And I don't want any funny business at the check-in. No lingering goodbyes. I know six weeks seems like a long time, but it will fly by, I promise you.'

As Alejandro turned and threw back the sheets, then stretched, for a moment she was tempted to undo all her handiwork, just for the pleasure of feeling that hard cock one more time. He put one hand on it and grinned.

'What do I do with this?'

She raised an eyebrow and smiled. 'Strap it to your leg,' she suggested sweetly. 'Now come on.'

She clapped her hands and he slid out of bed obediently. She swallowed as she watched him pull on his jeans, pushing his erection down as he did up the zip. It seemed a bit of a waste, but there wasn't all that much time to spare. He sauntered across the room to pick up his shirt, and she felt her nipples stiffen as she smelt the sweat on him, sweeter than the most precious cologne. She'd tasted it on her tongue the night before. She'd definitely miss him, she decided, although she'd popped a few things into her suitcase that might make up for his absence.

She wasn't going to miss him for his mind, that was for sure.

'Alejandro!' she reprimanded, as he stood in front of the mirrored wardrobes admiring himself, running his fingers through his shoulder-length hair. Typical Spaniard. He had absolutely no sense of urgency. 'My flight's at twelve. Chop chop.'

At eleven o'clock sharp, Patrick arrived at the Horse and Groom in a dark grey suit, a black tie and a cashmere overcoat, its pockets equipped with everything needed to get through a funeral – a hip-flask, a hefty spliff and a large white handkerchief. His car was pulled up outside on the double yellow lines.

Mayday ran down the main staircase. She was wearing a black mini-dress with a demure white Peter Pan collar, teamed with high shiny black stiletto boots. Her mass of black hair was piled up on top of her head in an elegant beehive. She spotted him at once, and smiled gratefully as she wrapped herself in a floor-length astrakhan coat, pulling up the collar around her face.

He gave her a squeeze. She closed her eyes and allowed herself to enjoy his closeness for a moment.

'Thank you,' she whispered, suddenly wanting to cry. 'I couldn't face it on my own. You know what my family are like, making a drama out of a crisis. I don't trust myself not to slap Mum. She's being completely hysterical. But she hadn't been to see Gran for weeks. Only on Monday, when she told her she should go into a home.'

'It's OK,' Patrick reassured her. He wanted to tell her she looked stunning, but it didn't seem appropriate. They were going to a funeral, not a ball. 'Have you got everything?'

Mayday nodded. He took her arm and led her out to the car. On the front seat was an enormous bunch of daffodils. He picked them up and handed them to her.

'I went to your grandmother's house this morning and picked them from the garden. I thought she'd like them.'

Mayday took the flowers with a trembling hand.

'What a wonderful idea.' She looked at Patrick, her eyes huge with unshed tears. 'Thank you.'

Mayday sat in the front seat, paler than ever, her eyelashes standing out like spiders, her full mouth painted a dark crimson. She looked astonishing. Emma Peel on the Trans-Siberian Express. Anna Karenina meets Edie Sedgwick. She was one on her own, thought Patrick fondly, and he wished he could take away a bit of her pain. As long as he'd known her, Mayday had never asked anything of him. She was a giver, not a taker. She didn't have an ounce of neediness in her. Which was why he was so desperate to do everything he could to support her today. She definitely wouldn't have asked if she hadn't needed him.

They drove through the outskirts of Eldenbury until they pulled up at the crematorium, a forbidding, uninspiring building on the edge of the municipal cemetery. Mayday stared at it.

'I've never been to a funeral.' She looked at him, stricken.

Patrick took the perfectly rolled joint out of his top pocket as reply. They sat for a few minutes, sharing the spliff in silence just as they had shared so many over the years, letting the marijuana soften the harsh edges of their surroundings. As the hearse pulled in through the crematorium gates Patrick stubbed it out discreetly.

Mayday's eyes widened as the enormous black car drew closer with its cargo.

'I don't know if I can handle this,' she said in panic.

'Of course you can,' Patrick reassured her. He picked up her hand, her tiny little white paw, and gave it a squeeze. She leant against him with a sigh.

'What a horrible place to meet your end,' she said sadly. 'There's just nothing about it that gives you any hope, is there?'

Patrick looked at the grey edifice outlined against the grey sky, and imagined the grey smoke that would emanate from the chimney before the morning was out.

'No,' he agreed. 'It's pretty grim.'

His own grandparents were in a pretty little corner of the churchyard in Honeycote, a far more preferable resting place. He'd never met them, for they had died some time before he was born. But he visited their grave nevertheless, when he wanted a moment of quiet contemplation, and sometimes imagined that they gave him advice and guidance from the other side. He often ran his fingers over the raised lead of the Liddiard name. It gave him a sense of pride and comfort.

There was little comfort to be had in the cemetery car park, as they watched the undertakers climb out of the hearse and begin the ritual that provided them with their living. Someone's got to do it, thought Patrick. Just as he provided beer, so they provided ceremony. Gradually the car park began to fill, and people emerged from their cars, dressed in sombre clothing.

'There's a lot of people,' said Mayday in a small voice.

'That's good, isn't it?' said Patrick, rather relieved. He couldn't think of anything worse than a mere half dozen pitching up.

Mayday nodded. 'She had loads of friends. It's only when you see them all together that you realize how many.'

A black Mercedes drew up. Inside Mayday could see her mother. She took in a sharp breath.

'Let's go,' she said. 'I want to get in before her.'

Patrick slipped his arm through hers and led her up the stone steps through the crematorium entrance. He felt Mayday stiffen as she saw the coffin.

'You're OK,' he murmured, leading her past rows of already seated mourners to a row near the front. They sat down, and her hands trembled as she picked up the order of service. Elsie's name and the dates of her birth and death were printed in bold black lettering on the front. She still couldn't believe it, even now.

Heads turned as Angela swept in looking like an extra from a Lynda la Plante two-part special, in a tight black suit with diamanté buttons and a veiled pillbox hat, and flanked by Roy, Mason and Ryan. The undertakers ushered them reverentially to the front row.

Before taking her seat, Angela hesitated in front of the coffin, allowing the church a good view of her profile as she bit her lip and reached out a hand to touch the shining wood. The congregation exchanged pitying glances.

Mayday clenched her jaw. 'Bloody drama queen,' she muttered.

Patrick gave her a warning nudge with his elbow, sensing the antagonism. But then he knew all about antagonistic mothers. He couldn't bear to be in the same room as his own for more than ten minutes, with all her right-on, self-righteous vegan bloody waffle. What his father had ever seen in Carola he never knew. But it was an awful feeling to loathe your own mother, so he was determined to support Mayday and make sure Angela didn't score any points off her.

'Be gracious,' he murmured. 'Don't let her see you're rattled. We can rip her apart afterwards.'

There was something about this hospital, thought Keith, that immediately filled him with confidence. He didn't know whether it was the calibre of the cars in the car park, the fact that he didn't have to scrat around for change to pay and display like you did at the district hospital, or the fact that the reception area was more like a five-star hotel, but he felt reassured by his surroundings. Places like this didn't make mistakes. There was an air of calm, a sense that the staff were in control and efficient, and were here to look after just you, not a million and one other people.

He knew it was morally wrong and that he wasn't necessarily getting better treatment, only faster. But he wasn't in charge of the country, and if he was it wouldn't be in the state it was in, so he wasn't going to apologize to anyone for his decision. At least now he knew, because he was paying, that the consultant wouldn't have his mind on the previous patient, or be looking at the clock, but would give him his undivided attention. He didn't begrudge the money. At the end of the day, if someone was going to be jabbing about in your nether regions, you wanted them to have their mind on the job, and if cash was what it took . . .

He took his place in the waiting room, a copy of *Country Life* on his knee, looking at the tasteful watercolours on the pale yellow walls that a design consultant had chosen as both calming and cheering. Would he feel happier with Ginny at his side, he wondered? He thought not. Other people tended to articulate your fears just as you had managed to assuage them. Anxiety was contagious and put unnecessary strain on a relationship. He was determined to stick to his guns. He would call on Ginny when he knew he needed her.

He had barely had time to start flipping through the tantalizing property section at the beginning of his magazine before he was called through. This was more like it. No interminable waiting. No clock watching. In his GP surgery he had to plough through ancient copies of *The People's Friend*. He jumped to his feet eagerly, and followed the secretary down the plush carpeted hall to Mr Jackson's consulting room.

Mr Jackson himself was calm and matter of fact.

'The most important thing,' Keith told him, 'is that I am on my feet for my daughter's wedding at the beginning of May.'

Mr Jackson nodded gravely. 'I can't make the culture grow any more quickly,' he told him. 'But once we have the results we can act pretty sharpish. And if surgery is necessary . . .'

'Do you think it will be?'

Keith knew it was pointless pushing for an answer, but his need for reassurance was becoming urgent.

'You know I can't answer that yet. But if there is, and it's localized, we can do keyhole surgery. You could be out in a matter of a couple of days. Obviously you'd have to take it easy.'

'But I could walk her up the aisle?'

'Oh yes,' Mr Jackson smiled. 'Now. Are you ready? We'll start off with a little local anaesthetic.'

'How about a lot?' joked Keith, desperately trying to hide the fact that he was utterly terrified.

*

Sandra kicked off her Stephane Kélian mules, stretched her legs out in front of her and accepted a glass of champagne from the pretty stewardess. Some people might think going first class on a flight that barely lasted two hours was a waste of money, but not Sandra. She revelled in the luxury, got a kick out of turning left instead of right, loved the mystery that came from being behind the magic curtain, and relished walking off first to the envious glances of those in economy. She'd earned her extra centimetres of leg room, the undivided attention of the cabin crew and every last drop of champagne.

She tapped her manicured nails on the pile of wedding magazines in front of her. She'd bought five at the airport while she was waiting. Her mouth watered in anticipation. She'd dreamt of nothing else since Mandy had told her the fabulous news, and she was itching to get started on the plans. It was going to be the first chance that she'd had to express herself with her new-found wealth. She'd spent a bit of it on herself, of course, but there was nothing like splashing out on other people. She was going to enjoy it.

The past few years had been hard graft, running the three clinics that she spearheaded herself, then overseeing the franchises so they were run to her exacting standards and kept the customers happy. Sandra was obsessed with customer care. Every woman that walked out of one of her clinics was a living, breathing advert, whether she'd had a simple skin peel or eyebrow pluck, or the full works. Getting them to walk back in through the door on a regular basis was a balancing act. You had to give value for money, make sure that the effect lasted a reasonable amount of time, but was addictive enough to ensure repeat business. Sandra had it down to a fine art. And although she wasn't qualified to wield the needle herself, she knew every single client by name, knew their favourite treatments, their fears, their insecurities.

Four months ago she had taken the decision to sell two of her clinics, and stick to her original purchase. She'd fattened them up to maximum turnover, after all, and there was no improvement to be made that she hadn't already thought of, so as far as Sandra was concerned there was no challenge left. If it was just on tick over, then she might as well stay in one place, kick back and relax. Enjoy life to the full. She was the wrong side of fifty, but looked forty. Even with her enhancements, that wasn't going to last for ever, so she was determined to live it up for the next ten years.

She'd had no shortage of offers. She'd chosen the purchasers carefully, made sure they were serious, sound cash buyers, and the transactions had gone through smoothly. She'd spent the past two months advising them as she handed over the reins. And now she was going to have a much-needed holiday. Six weeks in England, while Marie-Claire held the fort.

Life was good. She was a respected figure, locally. The women were infinitely grateful to her for restoring their youthful good looks. The men were grateful to her for keeping their wives happy, quite content to foot her not insubstantial bills. She had many friends. Constant invitations to restaurants, parties, yachts. Her new villa was a dream. And of course, there was Alejandro. The memory of his burnished skin made her shiver slightly.

Yep. For a disgruntled suburban Solihull housewife with a midlife crisis, she had done pretty well for herself. Where her drive, her stamina, her determination, her guts, and her ability to take risks had come from, she didn't know, for she'd been pretty lazy and unmotivated before she'd discovered her niche. Though to be fair, she'd always been competitive on the golf course. She smiled to herself as she thought of the trophy on the shelf over her enormous inglenook fireplace. That was what had drawn her to Spain in the first place. The golf. If she wasn't so old, she might have thought of turning professional.

The stewardess offered to top up her champagne, and Sandra inclined her head graciously.

'Ooh,' said the stewardess, spying her cache of magazines. 'Who's getting married?'

'My daughter,' said Sandra proudly. 'My little girl.'

'I got married in October,' the girl told her confidentially. 'I got a copy of a Vera Wang dress made in Shanghai. I took them a picture and they made it up for a tenth of the price.'

Sandra just smiled politely. If Mandy wanted Vera Wang, she was going to have the real thing. There was going to be no room for fakes or copies at this wedding.

She opened the top magazine and gave a sigh of delight.

Ginny sat in the kitchen, surrounded by Nigella, Delia and Jamie. The problem was finding a recipe that was simple but nonetheless impressive, and didn't make it look as if you had gone to too much effort. Of course, the person she should ask for advice was Lucy, who consistently produced fabulous meals without turning a hair. But then Lucy was the kind of person who knew exactly what she wanted when she went into the butcher, and had the best cuts brought out for her, while Ginny still wasn't confident about asking the butcher to butterfly a leg of lamb, in case he asked her what she meant. Frankly, she wouldn't have a clue.

Not that she wasn't a good cook, but the sort of cooking Ginny was good at wasn't the sort of meal you served up to impress your husband's ex-wife. Sausage casserole. Tuna bake. Cheesy jacket potatoes. Funnily enough it was Keith who had become the adventurous cook in their house, who came home with haunches of venison and braces of pheasant, and started crushing juniper berries and setting fire to Calvados all over the place. But she'd promised to cook tonight because he was off to see his stockbroker in Warwickshire. And Ginny was worried because he had looked worried.

Keith had been immensely furtive of late. This morning he had been jumpy. Almost snappy, which was very unlike him. Twice she had asked him if he wanted coffee and he had refused impatiently. He'd shot out of the house without touching his breakfast. Perhaps he was twitchy about seeing Sandra. Was it because he was dreading it, Ginny wondered, or was it because he was secretly looking forward to it and was trying to pretend he wasn't?

They had never spoken much about Sandra. She and Mandy kept in touch, of course, but Sandra didn't impinge on them from one year to the next. By comparison, Ginny's ex-husband David had become almost a part of their lives. He often dropped the twins off after they stayed with him in Cheltenham. Inevitably he had his daughter Chelsea in tow, and popped in for coffee, because it killed another hour. Several times Sasha or Kitty had had charge of their little half-sister and brought her back to Keeper's Cottage. Ginny couldn't bring herself to object, because it certainly wasn't Chelsea's fault if her parents were both equally selfish and insensitive. Keith and David often chatted politely as he was arriving or going. They hadn't got to the point of going down to the pub together, but they were quite civil.

How would she get on with Sandra? Now her arrival was imminent, Ginny felt nervous. She had no idea what to expect. She'd once asked Lucy what Sandra was like, and Lucy had crossed her eyes and made a face, which rather indicated that she was hideous. In which case, why was she so intimidated? Sandra was the one who had walked out on Keith and started a new life for herself. Ginny didn't have to impress her.

She slammed her cookery books shut. She'd buy some nibbles from the deli and do her easy Thai chicken curry. They'd already had it this week but everyone loved it and if she added proper fresh coriander and a squeeze of lime juice it would be almost authentic. And she'd go to the new boutique in Eldenbury and treat herself to something to give herself a confidence boost. She'd had a good month and it had been ages since she'd had a splurge. While she was at it she could start looking for an outfit for Mandy's wedding.

As Elsie's coffin slipped behind the red curtains, and a well-worn tape began an unrecognizable dirge, Patrick felt Mayday's grip tighten on his fingers.

'If you want to cry,' he whispered, 'then you should. It doesn't matter.'

Mayday turned and buried her head in his chest. He held on to her tightly, not sure if she was crying or not. As the music ground to a sudden halt, she came up for air, breathing deeply to keep herself calm. A single track of tears had fallen from each eye. Patrick took out his hanky and wiped them gently away.

'You're OK,' he whispered. 'The worst bit's over.'

Afterwards, they walked back to the car holding hands. Mayday watched with narrowed eyes as Roy escorted Angela back to the Mercedes, Mason and Ryan shuffling along behind.

'I don't want to go back to my mum's,' said Mayday defiantly. 'It'll be all she can do not to crack open the champagne. I bet that house is worth the best part of two hundred and fifty thousand now.'

'You've got to go, for your granny's sake. If you don't, your mother will have won.'

Mayday sighed. Patrick was right. Which was why she had asked him to come with her. Mayday knew she could trust him to keep her on the straight and narrow.

In the past couple of years, Eldenbury had gone from being a rather staid Cotswold market town with a plethora of antique shops to a veritable shopper's paradise. There was a deli to rival Fortnum's, a fantastic shoe shop stuffed with jewel-encrusted sandals and a mouth-watering array of pastel loafers, Twig, the to-die-for florist, a hairdresser who could change your life with a single snip of his scissors, and now a wonderful boutique that sold gorgeous clothes with not too terrifying prices.

Ginny stood in the middle of the cavernous changing room and sighed. First she'd tried on a pink linen dress that was far too long. Then a pair of cropped trousers that merely showed off the fact that her legs were like milk bottles. A washed-silk khaki skirt just looked boring even though it had zips and pockets in unusual places. She was on the verge of tears when the assistant held up a cherry-red dress in fine jersey.

'I know it looks nothing on the hanger, but it takes off pounds. And years.'

Reluctantly, Ginny took it off the hanger and slipped it on. She was astonished to discover that the assistant was telling the truth. The dress gave her a subtle cleavage, skimmed her tummy, and was just the right length to make her look a decent height if she wore her black suede boots. It was probably a little more dressy than she had meant to go for, but time was ticking by.

'I'll take it.' She thrust it back at the assistant and went to get dressed again. Then she bought hummus and olives from the deli, a hefty bunch of freesias from Twig that smelt heavenly (she wouldn't tell Sasha where she'd got them from), and a couple of tarts from the bakery. Ginny thought she'd got the amount of effort she was making just right. Enough to be polite, but she wasn't going to stress herself out. Sandra was going to have to accept her as she was.

She was about to get back into her car when she remembered coconut milk. Shit. You couldn't make a Thai chicken curry without it. She thundered back up the high street to the deli again, bursting in through the door with a red face.

'Tell me you do coconut milk,' she pleaded. She really should calm down for a second and make sure there wasn't anything else she'd forgotten. Take a leaf out of Lucy's book, she scolded herself.

'Sorry,' said the man behind the counter. 'We don't stock it, I'm afraid.'

The Spar shop up the road definitely wouldn't. Bugger.

She'd have to call in at the supermarket. That was going to take another twenty minutes out of her schedule. She was never going to get the house in order, prepare the meal and get herself ready in time to look languidly, casually welcoming when Sandra walked in through the door.

Keith did a double take when he saw his ex-wife striding through the arrivals gate at Birmingham Airport. When she'd walked out on him she'd been middle-aged, rather brash, heavy on the make-up and in serious need of a colour consultant, favouring lurid corals, fuchsias and emerald greens.

Standing before him was a different story. Sandra's hair was artfully streaked to ash blonde, in a graduated bob that was long in the front and short at the back with a wispy fringe that framed her face. Her skin was glowing, her eyes wide and bright. She seemed taller. Definitely thinner; much, much thinner. She was wearing a cream trouser suit with a soft lace camisole underneath. She even smelled different; her previous perfume had been cloying and unsubtle. It had stayed on the bedclothes and the furniture long after she had gone. Now she just smelled . . . expensive.

Keith wasn't a fool. He knew that there had been expert hands at work on her transformation, and it hadn't just been brought about through diet, exercise and a decent hairdresser. But he had to admit she looked fantastic.

She smiled. Her teeth had always been rather discoloured, and there had definitely been too many of them. Now they were white and even.

'Hello, Keith.'

The one thing no one had been able to address was

her voice. Strident and grating, it seemed at odds with the vision in front of him. It reminded him, no matter how buffed and polished she looked, this was still Sandra: the pushy, overbearing woman who had walked out on him five years ago because he was boring. Worse, who had walked out on Mandy at a vulnerable age.

She took his hands in hers and surveyed him like an aunt surveying a long lost-nephew. 'How are you?'

Apart from the fact that I've had someone rummaging about in my jacksy all morning? thought Keith. 'Very well,' he replied heartily. 'Very well indeed.'

Sandra put her head to one side. 'Our little girl,' she said dreamily. 'Who would have thought it? It doesn't seem yesterday, does it? Since she popped out.'

Actually, thought Keith, it seemed like several lifetimes. And popped wasn't quite the right word either. Mandy had been breech, and there had been enough blood and screaming to last him a lifetime. It had put him off sex for months.

He took her luggage trolley chivalrously, noting the soft monogrammed white leather of her selection of cases, holdalls and suit carriers.

'How long are you staying, exactly?'

Sandra laughed. 'Don't worry. I'm not staying with you. I've booked myself into Eversleigh Manor.'

Keith raised an eyebrow. Eversleigh Manor was a couple of villages away; the owners did very discreet but expensive bed and breakfast.

'For the weekend?' he asked.

'Not just the weekend! Until after the wedding. I need to be on hand for my daughter.' Sandra dimpled at him. They gave me a good discount for staying so long. I told them they'd hardly know I was there; that I'd be as quiet as a little mouse. Between you and me, I think they were glad of the cash.' This last remark was in a confidential tone. Keith looked at her in disbelief as she prattled on. 'I must say, we should consider the manor for the reception venue. They're moving into weddings. The lady of the house does fantastic cakes.'

Keith was astonished. She knew more about what was happening on his own doorstep than he did.

'I think we've agreed on Honeycote House for the reception,' he ventured.

'Have we?' Sandra arched her brows. 'I don't think anything's set in stone.'

'I think you'll find the invitations have already gone out.'

'I think you'll find they haven't. Mandy promised to wait until I arrived before firming anything up.'

The automatic doors parted and Sandra stepped out into the grey afternoon. She looked up into the sky critically.

'I suppose we're in with a chance with the weather in May,' she commented. 'But I might just mention that I have several friends with sumptuous hotels in Puerto Banus who'd be very happy to do Patrick and Mandy a deal.'

At Pantiles, Angela was playing the dutiful grieving daughter very well, shaking hands with friends of Elsie and murmuring thanks for their condolences. Mason and Ryan hovered uncertainly with plates of egg sandwiches, obviously desperate to get to the Xbox on the huge plasma screen in the corner of the front room, but even they knew that wouldn't be appropriate. Roy was passing out cups of tea and tins of Boddingtons and glasses of sherry, very sensibly keeping his head down.

Patrick and Mayday stood by the fireplace, surrounded by Mason and Ryan's motocross trophies.

'I want to propose a toast to Gran.' Mayday looked determined. 'That service was so impersonal. It could have been anyone's funeral.'

Patrick looked at her sternly. 'It's a lovely idea. But don't say anything you might regret,' he said. 'I know it's tempting, and your mother needs a good slap, but be gracious. For your grandmother's sake.'

Mayday looked at him for a moment, scowling, then her face softened and she grinned.

'You're right, you bastard. As usual.'

Mayday stepped forward into the room.

'Ladies and gentlemen . . .'

Angela's head whipped round, her features set in a mask of suspicion. Mayday smiled serenely once she knew she had the room's attention.

'All of us in here knew my grandmother. Elsie. So I just wanted to take a few seconds to remember who she was and what she was about. You will all know that she was the most thoughtful, considerate, unselfish and giving person on the planet.' With a masterful effort, Mayday managed not to look sideways at her mother as she said this. 'It's obvious now that she was in a tremendous amount of pain. And it's typical of her that none of us knew how much. She never complained. I just hope they're looking after her up there, my brave little Gran. Though if I know her, she'll be making the angels a cup of tea and passing round the custard creams.'

There was a ripple of laughter combined with a certain amount of surreptitious eye-wiping. Mayday had managed to make her little speech sound touching rather than mawkish, which made it all the more moving.

'So please raise your glasses – or your teacups, which as we all know was her preferred tipple – and join me in a toast. To Elsie.'

There was a resounding echo as everyone repeated her words, and a smattering of applause. Angela kept her smile fixed firmly to her face as she moved over to her daughter. Patrick moved forward to Mayday's other side.

'By the way . . .' Angela reached into her handbag. 'Your grandmother did leave you something after all. It seems very appropriate, in the light of your speech. So you might as well have it now.'

She held out a stout little brown teapot, the one that had sat on Elsie's range for as long as anyone could remember. Mayday took it wordlessly. Angela smiled, and the gleam of triumph was quite evident in her eye. All those hours you spent with her, she seemed to be saying, and all you got was a teapot.

'Have you got something we could wrap it up in?' Patrick asked politely. 'It would be an awful shame to break it.'

Angela scuttled off and came back with some bubble-wrap and a plastic carrier bag.

'I hope you think of her whenever you use it,' she said, in a quavering voice.

Mayday couldn't bring herself to reply.

By half six Ginny felt confident and had regained the ground she had lost. The Thai curry was bubbling away nicely, the wine was chilling, the table was laid, the freesias were in a vase on the breakfast bar. She sat down with the latest Zadie Smith, hoping to look engrossed when the visitor arrived, although she had seriously struggled through the first few pages.

Sasha came in and stopped in her tracks. She looked Ginny up and down in dismay. 'Mum. What are you wearing?'

'Don't you like it?'

'Whoever told you red was your colour?' Sasha had never been one to mince her words. 'You look like a beef tomato.'

Ginny felt her chin start to tremble.

'The assistant said it was slimming.'

Sasha's face said it all.

Ginny fled up the stairs, tears stinging her eyes. She ripped off the dress and hurled it onto the floor. She felt rising panic as she heard Keith's car in the drive. She tugged on her jeans, all her false confidence evaporating. She'd bolstered herself up with ridiculous props – expensive flowers, an extravagant outfit, a book she knew she was never going to get through – but the truth could not be disguised.

'Mum, I didn't mean to be mean—'

'I know you didn't. I'd rather you were honest.' Ginny hastily buttoned up a pale blue linen shirt and tucked it into her trousers.

'I just think you should be yourself. You don't need to try and impress Mandy's mum.'

'I wasn't trying to impress her. I just felt like wearing something new.'

'It's a lovely dress. But . . .'

'What?'

'It makes you look as if you're trying too hard.'

Ginny sighed. Exactly what she hadn't wanted.

'You're right. Best just stick to the usual boring frumpy stuff. No point in giving her the wrong impression.'

'Mum. You're gorgeous as you are.'

Sasha put her arms round her mother and gave her a squeeze. Ginny smiled wanly. So gorgeous Keith couldn't wait to scuttle out of bed in the morning. So gorgeous he pretended to be asleep at night. Sandra was going to know the truth: that her ex had landed himself a podgy, middle-aged frump who didn't have a clue how to dress and couldn't cook for toffee either.

She put on her boring brown loafers.

'Stop,' said Sasha. 'Put those boots back on.'

'I can't walk in them.'

'You don't need to.'

Ginny was used to obeying her daughters, so she pulled on her boots. Sasha undid two buttons on Ginny's shirt and pulled it out of her waistband. Then she rushed out of the room and came back in with a chunky necklace made of several strands of brightly coloured beads. She put it on round Ginny's neck.

'There,' she said, satisfied. 'That looks really cool. But not like you've rushed out and bought a new dress to impress your husband's ex.'

Ginny winced. Sasha had always had an uncanny knack of hitting the nail on the head. She forced herself to look in the mirror. Her daughter was right. The necklace gave her a lift, an edge, the heels gave her height. She managed a smile.

'Where would I be without you?' she asked.

Sasha looked distastefully at the discarded dress.

'You are so taking that back tomorrow,' she said. Ginny laughed shakily and put it back on the hanger.

'Come on,' said Sasha. 'Let's go and meet the she-devil.'

Even though he knew he was due for supper at Keeper's Cottage, Patrick felt duty bound to escort Mayday up to her room after the funeral. He was fairly certain it wouldn't matter if he was late, though Keith would probably be desperate for an ally. Between Sandra and Mandy and the twins, all the talk would be of the wedding.

Mayday's rooms were at the top of the hotel – a large living and sleeping area, with the bathroom off. She'd had it redecorated since the last time he'd been in here, and again it hit him just how Mayday had changed. Gone were the wine-dark walls, the smell of incense, the swathes of Indian material, the crazy ornaments. Instead the walls were a deep sea green, at the windows were fluttering gold organza curtains; on one wall was an enormous canvas smothered in lilies, flanked by two verdigris candelabra. The wall facing boasted a Venetian mirror which had the effect of doubling the room's size. There was still a strong sense of theatre, for Mayday loved the dramatic. But she was undergoing a metamorphosis, from a young girl who needed to make a statement by shouting it loud, to a woman who just left a whisper, but whose memory somehow stayed even longer.

He threw himself into a large battered leather armchair by the window, watching as Mayday slung her astrakhan coat onto a tailor's dummy she had fished out of a skip. He realized he hadn't mentioned the wedding to her yet. He watched as she unzipped her boots, kicked them off, then flopped onto her bed, sinking down onto the silk eiderdown with a sigh.

'By the way,' said Patrick, 'I forgot to tell you. Mandy and I are getting married.'

Mayday lay still, staring at the ceiling. She shouldn't care. But she did. She felt as if she were falling from a great height. Her throat tightened; she could barely speak.

'Oh,' she managed. 'When?'

'Second weekend in May.'

'That's . . . only a few weeks away.'

'I know. We decided there was no point in wasting any time.'

'What's the hurry?'

Mayday sat up, her legs curled under her, her beehive coming unravelled.

Patrick shrugged. 'Keith's getting cold feet about Honeycote Ales. I'm worried he's going to sell his share. But he won't if I marry Mandy. So we might as well get on with it.'

'That's an awful reason to get married. That's so cynical. That's a bloody business arrangement—'

Patrick held up a hand. 'Hang on. It's not as if I don't love her. We were always going to get married.'

'Were you?' Mayday looked at him, her eyes like saucers. 'Were you really? Because you've never told me that.'

'We live together. We love each other.' Patrick was aware that his voice didn't sound as confident as it should.

'Marriage is for ever, Patrick.'

'I know that.'

'You're not doing this for you. You're doing it for Honeycote Ales. Like everything you do.'

'Is that so wrong?'

'It is if you're sentencing yourself to a marriage you don't believe in.'

'Trust me, Mayday. I believe in it. Mandy and I will be very happy.'

Mayday reached up and pulled out the rest of the pins in her hair. It tumbled down past her shoulders, wild and unkempt. Her face looked very small amongst the tresses as she surveyed him mournfully.

'I hope you will.'

'Hey.' Patrick came over to the bed and sat beside her. He curled an arm round her shoulders, and sensed her tense slightly. 'It's not going to change anything. We'll always be mates, you and me.'

Mayday buried her head in his chest. 'Not if you're married we won't.' Her voice was muffled.

'Why not? What difference does it make?'

'Women don't like their husbands having . . . close female friends.'

'You don't count, Mayday.'

'Don't I?' she said sadly.

He held her face in his hands. 'You've been my best friend for ever. And you always will be. I tell you everything.' For a moment he was tempted to confide in her, and tell her about Kay. He thought it might be interesting to get another woman's perspective on it. But today wasn't about him and his problems. Mayday had just buried her grandmother. He had to make sure she was all right. He pulled her to him and gave her a tight squeeze. 'And I'll always be there for you. Whenever you want me.'

Mayday gave the merest shadow of a smile. 'I know you

will. I'll be there for you too. Sorry. I didn't mean to spoil it for you. It was a bit of a shock, that's all.'

Patrick glanced at the clock on the wall. He was going to be late. 'Look, I'm due for supper with Mandy's mother any minute. Are you going to be OK on your own here? The staff know you're back – make sure they look after you.'

'I'll be fine. I'm going to have something to eat and get an early night.'

Mayday jumped off the bed. Suddenly she wanted him out of her room as quickly as possible.

'In fact, I'm going to have a bath now, then get some chicken and chips sent up. Thanks for today, Patrick. You were great.'

She gave him a quick peck on the cheek, then walked over to the bathroom. She leaned against the door frame. In her little black dress, her feet bare, her hair tumbling wild to her waist, she looked like a wraith from a fairy tale.

'You'd better go, or you'll be late. And you don't want to incur the wrath of your future mother-in-law.'

When Patrick had gone, Mayday threw herself back onto the bed and sobbed into her pillow for a good five minutes. Then she sat up. What on earth had got into her? She had never sobbed about anyone, ever.

She told herself not to be silly. She was grieving for her grandmother, not Patrick. It was just that his revelation had shocked her, and triggered her outburst. Life was going to be strange without him, for she and Patrick were soul mates. Kindred spirits. She trusted him implicitly, understood him. And they'd carried that trust into bed with them. Mayday always took things further with Patrick than with anyone. She couldn't help smiling at the memory of the things they had got up to over the years before Mandy. She liked to surprise him. And sometimes he surprised her, which nobody else ever did.

Somehow, knowing that he was moving on to the next phase of his life made her realize just how empty her future was. She was twenty-eight years old. She was the manager of a hotel. Where now? Was she going to live over the shop for the rest of her life? She could conceivably move on, to another hotel – bigger, smarter, somewhere more exotic. But why would she want to? She was Eldenbury born and bred. She was comfortable here.

She wanted a man. A man she could respect. A man whose babies she could have. And she knew in her heart of hearts that Patrick was the one. She was never going to find anyone who lived up to him.

Mayday flopped back onto the pillows with a groan as she realized. She, Mayday Perkins, untameable wild spirit, flouter of conventions and shunner of tradition, was in love with Patrick Liddiard.

As he drove towards Kiplington, Patrick reflected that Mayday had seemed rather upset by his revelation, which wasn't what he'd expected. But then, she was probably overwrought. It had been a long and emotional day. Besides, she was probably right – in a way it was the end of an era, his getting married. Their friendship wouldn't be quite the same ever again. But Mayday would get over it. She didn't really need him. She had rafts of admirers, some secret, some overt. The county was stuffed with men who would leap chivalrously to escort her to social events, pull strings, do her favours. She often received flowers and love tokens. She had a special power that was bewitching. There would be plenty of people waiting to step into his shoes. Mayday, decided Patrick as he turned into the drive of Keeper's Cottage, was the least of his problems.

Mandy came out of the house to greet him.

'Was it awful?' she asked anxiously.

'Pretty grim,' he admitted, clambering out of the car. 'How's your mum?'

Mandy put her head to one side as she considered her reply.

'On top form.' She smiled. 'She can't wait to see you.'

Patrick slung his arm around her shoulder as they went inside, grateful for her uncomplicated warmth.

'I love you,' he said suddenly. 'And thanks.'

Mandy looked at him.

'What for?'

'Understanding. About Mayday. A lot of girls wouldn't take kindly to their fiancé scarpering off with another woman for the day.'

'You were at a funeral.'

'Yes. But all the same.'

Mandy looked at him quizzically.

'I trust you,' she said. 'So there's no problem.'

'Of course there isn't.'

Although that depended on your definition of problem, he thought darkly.

In the kitchen, everyone was sitting round the table dipping strips of toasted pitta bread into blobs of hummus, music blaring, and several empty bottles on the table already.

A woman leapt to her feet and threw her arms around

him. He blinked. Was this really Sandra? In his head, he'd imagined that she'd put on weight, would be tanned and leathery and dressed in the lurid, spangly excess that was the uniform of Spanish ex-pats. This woman was slender and elegant. Except for the hefty diamond watch, she was almost restrained in her dress.

He kissed her cheek obediently, astonished by its dewy softness. She squeezed his arms.

'Patrick. You gorgeous, gorgeous thing. I thought you were saving yourself for me.'

Despite himself, he gave her a wink.

'Well, I knew I wasn't in with a chance, so I thought I'd go for second best.'

He couldn't believe he could manage such light-hearted jesting, after the afternoon he'd had.

'You look fantastic,' he told Sandra politely, and she dragged him into the seat next to her.

Ginny looked miserably into her saucepan. Why was Thai fragrant rice so bloody fickle? It was sitting there in a glutinous, congealed mess.

'The rice is a bit . . . stodgy,' she announced.

'Never mind!' fluted Sandra. 'I never touch carbs after five p.m. Terribly bloating. Don't you find?'

She smiled brightly at Ginny, who held the saucepan in front of her stomach to disguise her spare tyre.

'So,' Sandra continued. 'The wedding of the year. Have we decided on a theme yet?'

'Theme?' Mandy's face screwed up in puzzlement.

'I suppose given the location you're going for Rustic Romantic rather than Urban Chic or Tropical Paradise. Though I have spotted a place where you can get potted palm trees if you fancy going for a Hint of Hawaii.'

'Actually,' said Patrick, 'I think the theme we're going for is plain old happy ever after.'

Sandra clapped her hands.

'Fairytale Fantasy!' she crowed. 'Katie Price, eat your heart out. I happen to know where you can hire that pumpkin coach. And it's not as expensive as you might think.'

Six pairs of eyes looked at her in disbelief.

Sandra picked up her glass. 'You're right,' she said. 'I don't want anyone accusing my daughter of copying a jumped-up Page Three girl. We can do far, far better than that.'

Patrick and Mandy exchanged glances.

'Help!' she mouthed at him frantically, and he gave her a wink. Sandra would calm down in a couple of days, he was sure.

Two hours later, Sandra sat back in the front seat and shut her eyes. Patrick had very kindly offered to drive her back to Eversleigh Manor in Keith's car. They sped through the inky-black, winding lanes, music playing softly on the sound system, just loud enough to stop the silence being an awkward one.

She looked sideways at her daughter's fiancé and felt a burst of pride. She couldn't have chosen any better for Mandy. Patrick was chivalrous and charming, but without ever being arrogant or slimy, which Sandra knew was rare indeed. And he was quite stunning. Her mouth watered as she looked at his profile. The cheekbones, the dark brows, the hair that fell across one eye. She couldn't help but feel a twinge of envy. He'd be masterful in bed, she was certain. She felt her pulse quicken at the thought.

The image reminded her of Alejandro. She hoped he'd remembered to water her hanging baskets. She was no fool, Sandra. She knew he would have shipped in some doe-eyed creature the minute he got back from dropping her at the airport; that they would be making the most of her luxurious villa, making love in her seven-foot bed, her wet room, by her infinity pool, feeding each other peaches from the tree and pizza from the carton. She couldn't buy Alejandro outright. Only his body, to maintain her house and grounds and satisfy her sexual urges. Not his mind or his soul. She was paying for his services. She didn't kid herself for a moment that he had any genuine feelings for her.

Until now, it hadn't bothered her. She was a successful woman. She had everything she wanted: a luxurious, five-star lifestyle. She made sure she enjoyed herself. And it was on her terms. If she didn't want Alejandro in her bed for some reason, she sent him home at the end of the day, because it was nice occasionally to slob out and read magazines and not have someone cluttering up your headspace. The arrangement had suited Sandra perfectly.

But tonight had brought something home to her. Seeing Keith at the head of the table, holding court, quietly reigning over the laughter and the chat, had shocked her. It was only to be expected that Mandy should adore him. But the twins were obviously incredibly fond of him too. And Ginny clearly couldn't do enough for him. Even Patrick was deferential, and Sandra didn't think one earned Patrick's deference easily. Yes, Keith was a different man. King in his own home. And Sandra couldn't help feeling piqued.

What nettled her even more was the way Ginny so subtly made it clear this was her domain, and that she wasn't threatened by Sandra's presence. She hadn't dressed up; she'd only been wearing jeans that she'd obviously had on all day. She'd made a bit of an effort for supper, but hadn't pushed the boat out – the starters and the desserts were bought in, and she made no attempt to hide the fact. She'd obviously been reading a novel just before Sandra arrived, not rushing round making sure everything was perfect.

Yes, thought Sandra, superficially she'd been made very welcome, but it was quite clear that she was an outsider. And she couldn't help feeling bitter. Keith was her husband, albeit ex. Mandy was her daughter. She shouldn't feel out of place. They were her family, not Ginny's. She was the mother of the bride.

She was bloody well going to restate her position.

Sandra gripped the handle of her handbag until her knuckles were nearly as white as the soft leather. She'd known she was ready for a life change. A fresh challenge. And deep in her heart of hearts, she wanted a companion. Not a toyboy who was one step up from a gigolo but someone who really cared. She didn't want to start again from scratch, either – hurl herself into the hideous mêlée that was singles clubs, dating agencies and lonely hearts columns.

Why bother with that when she had her own husband who would do very nicely indeed, thank you? Never mind that he was an ex. Or that he had a live-in lover. Sandra was very good at seeing past minor details. As far as she was concerned, Ginny was a very minor detail indeed.

*

Mayday sat on the floor of her room wearing an old Nirvana T-shirt, drinking the rest of a bottle of Jack Daniels mixed with coke. It was probably a mistake, hitting the bottle after the day she'd had. But hell, it was doing the trick. After one, she felt her shoulders relax. After two, the hazy images of the crematorium slid away. After three, she'd forgotten the smirk on her mother's face and felt as if she was wrapped in a cocoon. Everything became slightly warm and fuzzy.

After six, she began to weep.

After seven, she defiantly drank the rest of the bottle down in one and slung it across the room.

By now, she was angry. With everyone. Not just her mother. With the doctors who couldn't do anything, who had constantly fobbed them off with painkillers that were ineffectual – at least, until you took the whole lot. With herself, for not seeing Elsie's despair, for not reading the signs, for not doing enough. With bloody Patrick, for going off and getting married just when she needed him most.

But most of all with her grandmother, for leaving her alone. For abandoning her so that she felt vulnerable. And leaving her a teapot . . .

What the hell was she supposed to do with a teapot? How was that supposed to give her comfort and support during the coming years? All it did was remind her that her grandmother wasn't there any more, make her aware that she wasn't as strong and independent as she thought, and remind her that having Patrick beside her today made her crave him, desperately. That was why people got married; for the comfort she had drawn from his presence; the wonderful feeling that someone was there who cared and would do anything in their power to protect you.

Mayday lurched across the room and picked up the offending receptacle from her dressing table. Patrick had unwrapped it carefully for her, not understanding that receiving nothing would have been better than this. Humiliation burned in her gullet as she remembered her mother's self-satisfaction. She could imagine them all now, sitting round the table at Pantiles, planning what to do with their inheritance. A Caribbean cruise, a hot-tub on the terrace, proper central heating in the dog kennels so they could charge their unsuspecting clients even more . . .

Mayday tried to be good and appreciate it. She tried not to resent the fact that her mother was walking off with a hefty windfall and would be crowing about it for weeks. She tried to tell herself that the teapot was symbolic, that to have it in her possession imbued her with the caring, nurturing qualities that her grandmother had possessed. But it stuck in her craw.

She picked up the teapot and hurled it across the room. The smash was satisfyingly dramatic. But as the teapot bounced off the wall in a thousand pieces, Mayday suddenly felt sick. Even through her bourbon blur, she knew she was going to regret her actions, and that no amount of careful gluing was going to restore it.

She sank to the ground, sobbing, desolation and regret washing over her. The room was starting to spin. She knew she couldn't stop it, no matter how hard she tried to fix her mind to the task. She had drunk too much. Normally, she knew exactly when to stop. After all these years, she knew how to control alcohol and get the good times without the bad times. But very occasionally she forgot that you had to keep one step ahead of the demon, that it could get you when you were weak, when your defences were down. Yep, JD was laughing tonight. He'd got the better of her all right.

The teapot lay there, its insides exposed, the china stained black with years of tannin. She gazed at it dully as it suddenly glided across the room, then returned to its rightful place as she refocused her eyes with a masterful effort. Amidst the shiny brown shards was a piece of paper. Mayday frowned and sat up. She wiped away the tears and snot, and grabbed it. Elsie must have left her a note. Perhaps some explanation for what she had done. Something that would give her hope, perhaps? Respite from her grief and guilt. She unravelled it hastily.

It was a rolled-up lottery ticket. Last week's. She remembered bringing it to Elsie last Friday. She bought her one every week without fail. Mayday scrutinised it for clues, but there was nothing written on it, no explanation, nothing to indicate that it had any significance. Elsie probably wanted her to continue doing her numbers, through some misguided superstition. But privately Mayday thought doing the lottery was for losers. She had no intention of carrying it on. She scrumpled the piece of paper up and let it fall amongst the shards of china, then curled up on the floor. Within seconds, she was asleep.

9

On Saturday morning, Mickey found Lucy in hysterics in the kitchen. He felt a momentary panic before realizing that the tears rolling down her cheeks were from laughter.

'She's even worse than I remembered,' gasped Lucy, wiping her eyes with one of her brand-new French linen tea towels. 'I don't think I can cope.'

'Who?' demanded Mickey.

'Mandy's mother. Sandra. She's come for a "soyt" visit.' Mickey looked blank. 'A site visit, to you and me.'

As if on cue, Sandra swept into the kitchen. She threw her arms open wide, a vision in wide-legged white linen trousers and a gilt-buttoned cardigan, a jaunty red scarf tied round her neck. Considering it was bitterly cold outside and they were landlocked, the nautical look was somewhat incongruous.

'Mickey! Congratulations! I can't wait! We'll soon be related. Isn't it marvellous?'

'Fantastic,' Mickey murmured in agreement as he returned her embrace reluctantly. He knew that the last time he'd seen Sandra he'd been a borderline alcoholic, but this woman looked markedly different from the one he remembered.

'I was thinking about a spiegeltent. The top paddock next to the orchard would be perfect.'

'A seagull tent?' repeated Mickey rather stupidly. 'I thought doves were the thing at weddings.'

Sandra looked at him as if he was a dunce. 'Spiegeltent,' she repeated patiently. 'It's a magnificent mirrored marquee. Absolutely spectacular. Everybody who's anybody has one.'

Mickey looked at Lucy. 'I thought we were using the beer tent. From the point to point?'

'Well, we were. But . . .'

She looked uncertainly over at Sandra, who wrinkled her nose.

'I don't think a beer tent really gives quite the sense of occasion.'

'It's only something to bung up in the paddock in case it tips down,' Mickey pointed out. 'And it's free.'

'Don't worry about money,' said Sandra, holding up a perfectly manicured hand. 'I'm taking care of everything. It's my gift to the happy couple.'

'Oh.'

'I don't want you to worry about a thing. I've had a little windfall, and I can't think of anything better to spend it on than Patrick and Mandy's wedding.'

'Well,' said Lucy. 'That's very sweet of you. But I tell you what. Just so we don't start treading on each other's toes, why don't I take care of the arrangements for the daytime, and you can take charge of the evening? That's when people are going to want to let their hair down, after all.'

Sandra looked quite pleased with this arrangement.

'What a good idea. That way we don't have to keep

swapping notes.' In her hands she was clasping a white leatherbound folder with the words 'Wedding Planner' tooled on the front in gold. She laid it reverently on the kitchen table and took out a pen, scribbling furiously. 'Don't give the evening do another thought. The only thing we need to confer about is numbers.'

She clapped the planner shut in satisfaction. 'I need to check access. And power. We'll need generators, I think. We can't run everything off a plug in the stable yard.' She smiled and swept out again.

Lucy feigned wiping her brow in relief.

'Thank God. I couldn't bear it. She was starting to bang on about ice sculptures and chocolate fountains. If that's what she wants she can have it in her bloody spiegeltent. Just as long as no one thinks it was anything to do with me.'

Mickey looked at his wife admiringly. Lucy had a trick of getting her own way, very subtly. Almost letting people think that her ideas were their ideas. Christ, he loved her. His stomach twitched with anxiety. Patrick would be meeting up with Kay about now. They had decided it was best if Patrick dealt with her. If anyone saw Mickey with her, after all, tongues might wag.

'I've never seen that in real life before,' Lucy was saying.

'Sorry?'

'Top to toe Chanel. Every single thing she's got on. Top, trousers, shoes, belt, earrings . . .'

'Do we care?'

'No. But someone should tell her. You don't dress from head to foot in the same designer. It's incredibly naff.'

Mickey gave Lucy a quizzical look. 'It's not like you to be bitchy.'

Lucy sighed. 'Maybe I'm just jealous. I bet she'll wear Chanel to the wedding.'

'You can too, surely? If you want to.'

'We can't afford it. Not after everything I've spent on this kitchen.'

'Another couple of hundred isn't going to make much difference.'

'Couple of hundred?' echoed Lucy. 'Ha ha ha.'

Mickey grabbed her by the arms. 'Seriously,' he said fiercely. 'I want you to have whatever outfit you want. Just bung it on the credit card. We'll deal with it.'

Lucy looked at her husband warily. Was this guilt talking? It usually was with Mickey. The minute he started chucking money about was when the alarm bells started to go off. She racked her memory for clues. For signs. For giveaways. Nothing sprang to mind.

'I better make everyone some lunch,' she said finally, and wandered off to the fridge to see what delights it held. She still got a kick out of its pristine white interior and all the cunning little accessories – the can-holder, the chilled water dispenser, the wine rack. As she gazed at the contents, half of her was calculating whether she had enough tomatoes to do a *pissaladière*, while the other half wondered if she should be on her guard. It was all too easy to be distracted by the wedding. Was there something else going on?

Bi-polar March had done its usual trick of starting off the day sunny and optimistic, then having a mood swing. The wind was driving across the wildlife park, miserable for its inmates, who were used to warmer climes. Kay gazed rather blankly at the three rhinos. They were quite charmless, she decided. They looked like enormous overweight women from behind, with their lumpy bumpy thick white legs and hefty bottoms. They had no redeeming features, not like hippos, who seemed cuddly in comparison, though the keeper had assured them that a riled hippo was not something to be messed with. She shivered, unaccustomed to the chill. Thanks to the fickle weather, she'd had to buy herself and Flora a new quilted jacket each from the saddlers in Eldenbury, which had eaten into her budget considerably.

She and Flora had spent the past week drifting from one tourist attraction to the next. They'd been on a steam railway, to a quaint model village, a teddy bear museum, and now today the wildlife park – all things that Kay had never visited in the time she'd lived in Honeycote. But why would she have? They weren't places you'd go to without children. In those days, she had wafted from hairdresser to restaurant to boutique, and then back to the hairdresser, little realizing there was another world out there.

To her surprise, she'd enjoyed every moment of her discovery, relishing the time spent with her daughter. She even thought she might have put back on a bit of the weight she had lost, courtesy of a surfeit of cream teas and chips. It was rather like being on holiday. It was certainly a distraction from the fact that she had absolutely no idea what the future held for her. If the Liddiards decided not to play ball, she was stuffed. She was bluffing, after all. She had no intention of degrading herself and dragging them through the courts for money.

She had come to one conclusion, however. She was going to do everything in her power to make sure she and

Flora stayed in the area. The countryside was absolutely ravishing, waking up after the long winter, all buds and birdsong, the white lambs frolicking in the fields mirrored by fluffy clouds bouncing across the blue skies. Today might be a reminder of how ornery the English weather could be, but she knew it could change; that tomorrow she might wake up to a gentle sun coaxing out even more greenery. Besides, she liked the uncertainty. Portugal had been so relentlessly, reliably fine; it was like living with an eternal optimist. In the end, it got on your nerves.

It wasn't just the scenery that was luring her. She'd been into Eldenbury several times, and really did feel as if she was coming home to somewhere she belonged. It was so reassuringly familiar; even the sneaky car-parking space that she'd always used up by the library was still there. She realized with shame that when she and Lawrence had lived there, she had rather looked down on the little town, dismissing it as provincial and slow and slightly backward, always eschewing it in favour of Cheltenham or Bath or London. But she had changed. She had mellowed. She didn't need glitz and glamour; she wanted a cosy, comfortable environment. And anyway, Eldenbury had blossomed in the time she had been away. Still very much the traditional Cotswold market town on the surface, it now harboured a few surprises when you dug a little deeper. So if you fancied a pair of sexy shoes or some exotic bath oil, you could find them amidst the rather more prosaic ironmonger, bookmakers and newspaper shops. It was an eclectic mix of the utilitarian and the exotic, and Kay thought it would suit her exactly. It was the perfect small pond in which to bring up her daughter.

She saw Patrick coming along the path that led to the

rhino enclosure, and allowed herself a smile at how out of place he looked, with his black cashmere sweater over a pristine white T-shirt. For a moment she allowed herself to imagine that he was hers; that he had come to join her and Flora and was going to whisk them off to the café for lunch. And later they would go back home, to a dear little cottage, and have a delicious supper together—

Kay snapped herself out of her fantasy. Why was she torturing herself? Patrick wasn't hers. This was a clandestine meeting set up to discuss a sordid situation, and Patrick would be going back to his beautiful fiancée as soon as he could make his escape. Besides, Kay didn't want him. Not really – he was far too young. After everything she'd been through, his youth sat uneasily next to her. Five years ago, the difference had been invigorating. Now it was just . . . depressing.

Flora ran up and stopped several paces from them, eyeing Patrick warily.

'Darling,' said Kay. 'This is one of Mummy's friends. From when she used to live in Honeycote.'

Flora moved closer. She was a pretty little thing, with dark curls and a snub nose and freckles. Patrick tried very hard not to scrutinize her for Liddiard traits, but there was certainly no trace of Lawrence whatsoever. He gave her an easy smile. A few years ago he wouldn't have had a clue what to say to a four-year-old girl, but Caroline and James descended on them all so frequently that Patrick was now quite at home with small children.

'Have you seen the white tiger?' he asked. 'I've come all this way specially.'

Flora nodded her head solemnly. 'He's not white at all. He's jolly dirty.'

'Oh,' said Patrick, feigning disappointment.

'But he's still nice,' said Flora. 'Come on. I'll show you.'

She ran off down the path, and Patrick and Kay fell into step alongside each other.

'We're having a board meeting on Tuesday,' Patrick informed her. 'I expect we'll end up having to sell.'

He tried not to sound too bitter, because it wasn't just Kay's fault that this was a probability, but she was forcing their hand rather.

'As I said,' Kay countered, 'if I could find any other way out of my predicament, I would.'

'I understand. I'd do anything to protect my family. As you know.' He gave her a sidelong glance. 'I've found you somewhere to stay in the meantime. It's the landlord's accommodation at the Peacock Inn. We've had to close the pub, because it's subsiding. But the flat's perfectly safe; it's over the garage at the back. It's sitting there empty. We can't put a proper tenant in there because we don't know if we're going to sell the pub, or do it up. But if you want it . . .' He trailed off for a moment. It sounded so feudal, offering her a place to live that would keep her safely out of the way, but close enough to keep an eye on her. He wasn't sure how she would take his offer.

She was surprisingly grateful. 'It sounds perfect.'

Patrick shrugged. 'It's warm, at least. And Flora can play in the garden. But be careful of the river.' He shoved his hands in his pocket and pulled out a bunch of keys. 'You know where the Peacock is? Just outside Blockford, on the back road to Eldenbury. I went in and put the heating on, and checked all the appliances. The decor's pretty grim, I'm afraid . . .'

'But beggars can't be choosers?' Kay knew her remark

was barbed, but she took the key off him. 'Thank you.'

They'd reached the white tiger's lair. The beast lay there, staring balefully, quite unapologetic about the fact that his coat wasn't Persil white, but rather tobacco stained.

'See?' Flora pointed, indignant.

'You're right,' said Patrick. 'He's not white. He's yellow. They should call him the yellow tiger.'

Flora put her hands on her hips. 'I think we should ask for our money back, Mummy.'

Kay exchanged a wry glance with Patrick. 'She's her father's daughter all right.' She laughed, and stopped short.

Patrick gazed into the middle distance, wondering why this observation annoyed him so much. If Kay was demanding money from Mickey, and they were falling over themselves to help her out of her predicament, then he rather wished she wouldn't refer to Lawrence as Flora's father.

Kay sensed his disapproval. 'Sorry,' she said. 'Shit. What a mess this all is.'

'Perhaps you and Dad should have thought about that five years ago.'

Kay touched his sleeve. 'You're so fantastically good at being judgmental, Patrick. You must have a very clear conscience.'

Her tone was light, but the remark was extremely loaded.

'Actually, I have.'

'So it's just been you and Mandy. For five years?'

Patrick turned to her with a scowl. 'It's none of your business, but since you ask – yes.'

'Very impressive.'

'Not really. I'd have thought it was quite normal.'

Kay's lips twitched. 'You can't tell me you've always been a saint, Patrick. How else did you get to be such a tiger in the sack?'

Her eyes were mocking him, but Patrick stared her out, triumphing inwardly when she blushed and looked away. 'Pure animal instinct, Kay. Right. I'd better go.'

'Come and have a cup of coffee,' she pleaded. 'Or a sandwich.'

'I can't. I'm meeting Mandy and her mum at Honeycote House. Wedding plans . . .'

Kay was appalled to find tears suddenly springing up in her eyes. Of course he couldn't wait to get away from her and go and join Mandy, who Kay remembered as quite stunning. But she just wanted to sit down for five minutes with another human being; someone who knew her. And chat. Not about anything in particular. She clenched her teeth together to stop herself from begging him for his company.

'Anyway,' said Patrick. 'I think it's best if I keep away from Flora for the time being. We don't want her confused.'

He gave her the most fleeting of kisses on the cheek and walked away.

Kay watched him go, feeling as if she had been punched in the guts. She deserved his froideur, his immovability. She'd been a bitch, questioning him like that, even if she didn't quite believe his reply. She took in a deep breath, to staunch the flood of hysteria that sometimes threatened to overwhelm her.

Patrick was right. She and Mickey should have thought about what they had been doing. But had she been so wicked? Had she done something so evil? People were unfaithful every day of the week. And they got away with it. What was it she had done to deserve the grief and the hopelessness and the terror that was rising up in her gullet even now? It was almost like drowning.

It was only the feeling of Flora's little hand in hers that managed to calm her. For a moment she had been tempted to scale the fence and throw herself at the tiger's mercy; he'd make pretty short work of her, she was sure. She'd be a mere canapé.

'Hot chocolate?' She managed to find her voice, and it was steady.

'Where did that man go?' demanded Flora. 'He was nice. I wanted to show him the cheetahs.'

Mayday woke up on her bedroom floor at midday, shivering. She gazed at the carpet, knowing that as soon as she moved the pain would kick in. She wouldn't know the extent of the damage until she became vertical, so she lay as still as she could while she gathered her thoughts, trying to work out the reason she had got herself into such a disgraceful condition.

The first thing she remembered was Elsie's funeral. Her grandmother had been laid to rest yesterday. It was final. Mayday thought that was a pretty good reason for getting slaughtered. But what had happened? Had she got drunk at the wake and been carried home? She thought not. She scrabbled about in her memory bank. Patrick had come with her to the crematorium. And her mother's house afterwards. He wouldn't have let her get in a state like that. He'd have looked after her; he was—

Shit. Mayday remembered the second blow of the day.

Patrick was getting married. In less than six weeks. His marriage would mark the end of their friendship. Had she presumed that they would just drift on for ever, kindred spirits who shared an impenetrable closeness that was never questioned by either of them? No wonder she had wanted to drown her sorrows.

She managed to raise herself up to a sitting position. She felt a tight band around the back of her head and an overwhelming desire to vomit. Which was hardly surprising; she could see the offending empty bottle in the corner of the room. Had she sobbed on Patrick's shoulder? Drunkenly pleaded with him not to go ahead with his nuptials? She hoped very hard that she hadn't. Mayday spent her life keeping her counsel and trying not to show her true feelings. It was the one reason why her mother enraged her so much, because Angela could always provoke her into showing her cards. She prayed that Patrick had gone before she had lost all reason.

She was trawling around in her brain, trying to remember when he had gone, when the image of a lottery ticket glided past. She grabbed on to the memory. Why had there been a lottery ticket? She looked gingerly for clues. There was the broken teapot. That's right; the lottery ticket had been inside.

She moved her gaze slowly round the room, and saw it scrumpled up in the corner. She gazed at it, breaking out into a sweat, her very pores oozing Jack Daniels. A wave of nausea swept through her; even her bones felt sick. Keep it in or let it out? Mayday thought she was better off trying to get rid of it. Less work for her liver.

Ten minutes later, her hair sticking to her face, her forehead soaked in perspiration, she thought she'd probably disposed of the last of her bender. She tried a tentative glass of water, praying that it would stay down and she could start to rehydrate. The last time she'd had a really shocking hangover, Elsie had brought her toast and tea in bed and had mopped her brow. She hadn't been disapproving at all. Her grandmother was the least judgmental person she knew. Correction. Had known.

Mayday remembered someone telling her the best hangover cure was a bowl of rice with seaweed and soy sauce. The rice soaked up all the toxins while the seaweed and sauce replaced the minerals. She got to the phone and managed to croak out her order. She didn't bother with the seaweed. That was pushing it in the Cotswolds.

'Can you bring me up a bowl of plain rice? And a bottle of soy sauce?'

Astonishingly, it did the trick. Mayday wouldn't have thought she could keep anything down, but it made her feel a little bit stronger. She lay on the bed for twenty minutes while she assessed her recovery. She felt well enough to manage a shower. She stood in the scalding water for ten minutes, dousing away every last alcohol-soaked bead of sweat.

She looked pale and red-eyed, but at least she was vertical. She did her hair in two long plaits, pulling on a black military-style button-through dress and a pair of old boots. Then she looked again at the ticket.

What was the significance? Why had her grandmother left it rolled up in the spout? She supposed she should check the numbers, just in case. She walked carefully over to her laptop, which was linked into the hotel's computer system. It seemed to take hours to boot up. She fumbled with the mouse, peering at the letters on the ticket that gave her the lottery's web address. They swam around, swapping with each other, but eventually she managed to pin them down.

She checked and re-checked, but even in her inebriated condition there was no denying it. The numbers matched. The piece of paper in her hands was worth a cool five million, four hundred and eighty-three thousand, six hundred and ninety-four pounds.

And twenty-three pence.

Patrick came back to Honeycote House to find Mandy, Sandra and Lucy poring over a plan of the house and gardens and adjoining fields spread out on the kitchen table amidst the remains of lunch.

'I thought we could put some tents up in the bottom paddock,' said Lucy, wielding a black felt tip. 'For anyone who doesn't want to drive home. A bit like Glastonbury. We can do bacon rolls the next morning.'

Patrick raised an eyebrow. 'I thought we were just doing tea on the lawn.'

'The thing is,' Lucy pointed out, 'if you're going to go to any bother, you might as well go the whole hog. And if everyone's made an effort to dress up, they'll be a bit cheesed off if all they get is a cup of tea and a cucumber sandwich.'

'I don't want to go on about it,' said Sandra. 'But money is no object.'

'It's not about money,' said Lucy firmly. 'It's about giving a sense of occasion. We can do that without breaking the bank.'

Patrick cut himself a slice of tomato tart and peered over Mandy's shoulder. 'It looks like a military operation.'

'It is, let me assure you.' Sandra's voice was stern. 'And don't worry, you'll be getting your orders.'

Patrick winced.

'Don't worry.' Lucy hugged him. 'All you have to do is turn up. We're taking care of everything.'

Patrick caught Mandy's eye and she gave him rather a despairing glance, rolling her eyes towards her mother and shrugging her shoulders as if to say 'What can you do?' He cut another slice of tart and wandered off to find his father.

Mickey was in the pantry mixing up a jug of Pimm's. He didn't look up. He was too busy chopping mint, which he threw in on top of the mound of cucumber and orange slices already swimming in the amber liquid. Patrick marvelled that his father could be so preoccupied by a simple task when their whole existence was in jeopardy. But then that was Mickey: master of the displacement activity. Patrick envied him the trait.

Mickey filled up the rest of the jug with lemonade, judging the right amount with an expert's eye. 'I'm trying to perfect the recipe,' he said. 'I thought we could have Pimm's when we get back from the church. If we go straight onto champagne everyone'll keel over. And it'll be refreshing if it's a hot day—'

'Everybody's obsessed with this bloody wedding,' Patrick complained. 'The only ones who aren't are me and Mandy.'

'Shut up and try this.' Mickey poured him a glass, then looked towards the door to see if there was anyone on the horizon. 'How was Kay?'

'Bitter,' pronounced Patrick.

'I'll stick some more lemonade in.'

236

'Not the Pimm's. Kay, you idiot. She was . . . edgy.'

'Bound to be. Did you give her the keys to the Peacock?'

'Yeah. She seemed pleased.'

'I hope you told her it's the best we could do.'

Patrick nodded. 'She understands. I don't think she was expecting us to conjure up a bijoux thatched cottage straight away.'

Mickey grimaced. They both knew that the Peacock was only a stopgap, but did Patrick have to keep hammering it home?

'The kid's sweet, by the way.' Patrick looked at his father for a reaction.

Mickey stayed stony-faced. 'I don't need to know that. I'm just worried about the money. I've been thinking,' he went on, sotto voce. 'Sandra's obviously rolling in it. Why don't we . . . we could . . . how about . . . ?' He trailed off rather lamely, then rallied. 'I thought we could tap her up for a few quid. Well, more than a few.'

One look from his son gave him the answer. 'You have absolutely got to be joking. There is no way I want to be beholden to that woman. She'd have us by the balls for the rest of our lives. It's bad enough that she's subsidizing the wedding—'

'Well, that's up to her.' Mickey was indignant. 'There's no need for any of it, if you ask me. But I just thought . . . we could say it was a loan. For a new plant for the brewery or something. She wouldn't miss it.'

'No way. We're going to find our own way out of this mess.'

Mickey sighed. It was hard dealing with Patrick when he took the moral high ground. He personally didn't have any problem whatsoever with divesting Sandra of the cash she was so quick to tell them she had. But Patrick wasn't playing ball.

'Fine. Well, we better go and see Robert Gibson on Monday, then. See exactly where we stand.'

'Why does he need to know?'

'He's our solicitor. It's what he's there for. To protect our interests.'

'I don't want everyone knowing our business.'

'Robert's not going to tell anyone, is he?'

Mickey knew only too well how discreet Robert was. He'd confided in him on several occasions. And Robert was wise. He might only be a small-town solicitor, but it was surprising what he came up against. The Liddiards' sordid little secret was a mere drop in the ocean compared to some of the scandal Robert had dealt with.

Patrick scowled. 'Robert can't make Kay and Flora vanish off the face of the earth, can he? Even if he can come up with some legal loophole that gets us out of it, we're morally obliged to help them.'

Mickey put his hands up. 'I know, I know. I'm not trying to wriggle out of it. I just want to know what's . . . normal in these circumstances.'

'Normal?' Patrick looked at him witheringly. 'There's nothing normal about it, Dad.' He drained his Pimm's and banged the empty glass down on the work surface. 'Too much lemonade, if anything. And not enough mint.'

Kay stood in the middle of the flat, utterly dismayed. Flat was a misnomer. It was more of a bedsit, with a small kitchenette leading off the living area, a windowless shower room no bigger than a cupboard and a bedroom that was entirely taken up by a double bed, with no room for a bedside table let alone a wardrobe or a chest of drawers. But it wasn't the size that bothered her so much as the smell. Damp mixed with something that smelled like leaking gas, as well as rancid cooking fat, stale cigarettes and some sort of ghastly rose-scented air freshener that someone, presumably Patrick, had squirted round in a vain attempt to cover it all up.

She walked into the kitchenette. The lino on the kitchen floor was peeling. Last year's calendar hung from a drawing pin. The window was filthy, smeared in grease.

'Is this our new house?' Flora looked extremely doubtful.

'Um . . . it's just somewhere to stay. For the time being.'

She couldn't cave in now, even though she felt cold panic closing round her chest. Her mobile rang. She stared at it.

'Mummy! Your phone!'

She picked it up cautiously. 'Hello?'

'Is it OK?' Patrick sounded worried. 'I know it's a bit grim, but I didn't really have the chance to do anything about it. I'll come over tomorrow and help you clear it out. I'll bring over some bedlinen and crockery and things. And a telly.'

'It's a dump,' Kay agreed. 'But it'll have to do. Where else can I go?'

She walked through the living area. The cheap rubber-backed carpet was splattered with stains of indeterminate origin – curry, coffee, vomit? A bare light bulb hung from the centre of the room, swinging as ominously as a hangman's noose. The walls were covered in blown vinyl that someone had tried to paint over with a sickly green.

'I can send someone round in the week to paint it out,'

Patrick offered. 'But you'll have to make yourself scarce while they do it.'

Kay stopped by the window. Outside she could see the pub garden: a soft green lawn dropping down to a river bank, sprinkled with daffodils. It was quite stunning, but all she could feel was despair. Yet again she was being reminded that she was a shameful secret. Even a poor relation would have been allowed to stay on site while the place was redecorated. But not Kay and her illegitimate brat.

'Do you know what, Patrick?' she asked softly. 'Don't worry. I'll bloody well do it myself.'

She put down the phone and turned to Flora, who was looking at her uncertainly.

'Let's go down to the river,' she said, holding out her hand. 'I bet there'll be ducks.'

Patrick switched off his phone and shoved it in the glove compartment. He didn't want it trilling unexpectedly, in case it was Kay calling with a litany of complaints. Although in a funny way he trusted her not to cause trouble. Well, any more trouble . . .

He knew he was allowing himself to get sucked into her predicament. But what sort of a person would he be if he didn't care? Kay had once been his lover, and Flora was his own flesh and blood. It was his duty to look after them.

Of course, strictly speaking it should be Mickey doing the worrying and the running around. But Patrick didn't trust his father to cope first-hand with this delicate situation. He'd either upset Kay, or fall in love with her – either way he wouldn't be able to keep her presence a secret because he was a blundering fool incapable of covering his tracks. So it was up to Patrick to sort it, on top of everything else.

He walked into the kitchen at Little Orwell Cottage. It was tiny, but idyllic, with its pale green Shaker cabinets and limestone floor. He and Mandy did their best to keep clutter to a minimum, because the last thing either of them wanted to do at the weekends was tidy the house. As a result Patrick sometimes thought the cottage felt unlived in, after the chaos he was used to at Honeycote House. But in other ways it was an antidote to the turmoil of the brewery and his family, a sanctuary that was always reliably just as it had been left. He never came back to find uninvited guests or impromptu parties or blazing rows. Patrick needed that little bit of calm in his life. He was particularly grateful for it now. He found the little table in the kitchen laid for the two of them; he could make out two thick steaks waiting on the side in their greaseproof paper, and smell potatoes baking.

'Hello?' he called out tentatively.

Mandy bounded into the kitchen, throwing her arms around his neck.

'I'm so glad you're back,' she cried. 'I just want you to myself tonight. My mother is driving me nuts. And please – can we talk about anything but weddings?'

Patrick hugged her to him. She'd obviously just come out of the shower and she smelled delicious, of some tropical paradise – passionflower and coconut and melon. It reminded him of one thing they hadn't discussed yet.

'Anything but,' he agreed. 'Although, I did wonder – maybe we should think about our honeymoon?'

Mandy giggled, releasing him from her grasp.

'I'm surprised Mum hasn't organized that for us as well.' She went over to the fridge, and pulled out a bottle of white wine. 'I can't believe it. She's been here less than twenty-four hours and she's completely taken over. I thought Lucy was going to wig.'

Patrick took the bottle from her and opened it with the state-of-the-art corkscrew he'd had attached to the work surface. They might have kept gadgets to a minimum, but some things were absolutely essential.

'Don't panic. In a few weeks' time it'll all be over and we can just be plain old Mr and Mrs Liddiard. And you'll probably be bored rigid. Stuck with me for the rest of your life.'

'No, I won't.' Mandy was emphatic as she took her glass of wine from him. 'It sounds like heaven.'

She went over to the cooker and put a heavy-bottomed skillet on to heat.

'By the way, how's Mayday?'

Patrick realized with shame that he hadn't given his friend a thought all day. How long would it have taken him to pop into the Horse and Groom and check up on her? He couldn't admit to Mandy that he'd forgotten.

'She's OK,' he said carefully. 'A bit tied up with all the red tape. There's a lot to organize.'

'Poor thing.' Mandy slipped the steaks into the pan, where they gave a satisfying sizzle.

'Yeah.'

Patrick looked over at his soon-to-be-wife as she moved around the kitchen. He wondered what she would say if she knew the truth about the family she was marrying into.

Hopefully, once the Kay problem was sorted, that would be it. They could embark on their married life with a clean slate. No more skeletons, no more illegitimate relatives, no more blackmail.

Later, after supper and a second bottle of wine, as they made love on the living-room floor, oblivious to the thriller on the television that had failed to grab their attention, Patrick felt in his heart that it was all going to be all right. None of what was happening was of his making. He had a clear conscience. He could only do his best. And he loved Mandy – no one could take her away from him. Even if the brewery collapsed, and Kay did her worst and destroyed his family, he and Mandy would still have each other.

Shock, it seemed, was an even more effective hangover cure than rice and soy sauce.

Mayday sat in the chair that Patrick had sat in the afternoon before, staring at the red numbers, her head totally clear.

She was a millionaire. A multi-millionaire.

She'd phoned the lottery hotline earlier that day to check the numbers. They had confirmed the amount and were sending someone down with the cheque. A woman who was specially trained to deal with lottery winners, who could put her in contact with financial advisors, legal advisors, anything Mayday wanted. Yeah, she thought cynically. They'll all be queuing up to give me bloody advice and get their hands on my money.

They'd asked her if she wanted any publicity.

'Absolutely, definitely one hundred per cent not,' she'd replied.

The last thing she wanted was for her mother to find out.

For now she understood. Her grandmother had found the means to protect her from beyond the grave. She'd hidden the ticket in the symbolic teapot, knowing this was the one way that Angela wouldn't get her hands on it. And knowing that Mayday would be financially secure had given Elsie the courage to take her own life. This knowledge made Mayday feel overwhelmed with yet more grief. Yet, she told herself, the money would have gone no way towards relieving Elsie's pain. She owed it to her grandmother to enjoy it. Spend it wisely.

There was, of course, one person she was desperate to call and share the news with. But she couldn't pick up the phone to him. Not now. To protect herself, Mayday knew she had to keep Patrick at arm's length.

Subconsciously, she'd always known that she and Patrick had no future together. Hadn't she said as much to him the very first night they met? She was, after all, no better than hired help, even though she was no longer a mere barmaid, but management. Mayday was no fool. She knew these things still mattered. That Patrick Liddiard marrying Mayday Perkins, the scrubber from the council estate at the wrong end of the village, would have sent shockwaves through Eldenbury society.

She remembered his twenty-first birthday party. He'd given her a smart, engraved invitation, and she'd laughed. The parties she went to didn't merit official invitations. He was adamant that she should come. She could remember her dilemma even now. She hadn't wanted to stand out at the party. She'd wanted to belong. She'd wanted to be one of those shiny-haired, white-teethed beauties in their strapless silk ballgowns, careless and confident, still stunning even when they were cross-eyed with too much punch. But she couldn't wave a magic wand and become one of them. She didn't have the genes or the bloodline. So she'd turned up at midnight in a PVC minidress that was laced down the front, and bondage boots. And even though she had been the object of much admiration, even though legions of drunken boys were fighting for her attention, even though Mr Liddiard himself had dropped an admiring kiss on her shoulder, she knew it was only because she was a novelty. She knew that because the girls snubbed her. She could sense them whispering behind her back, scandalized by her outfit. And the mothers visibly shuddered, grateful that their daughters didn't dress like that, and praying that their sons didn't get off with her. She would never, ever belong. She was rough trade, and it had left a lasting bitter taste in her mouth.

It was ironic, she thought, that it would be scandalous for Patrick to marry her for love, yet somehow it was OK for him to marry Mandy for money. For Mandy had passed the unwritten test. Mandy was acceptable, even if her money was slightly shiny and new, because she had been to the same school as Patrick's sister, Sophie, and had thereby been elevated up the class system.

Mayday knew Patrick as well as she knew herself. He could protest all he liked, but she knew his forthcoming marriage was primarily a political move, not one motivated by passion. Yes, he was probably fond of Mandy in his own way, but he was very measured when he spoke about her. His eyes didn't sparkle. It depressed Mayday to think of him chained to someone he didn't really love, all because of that bloody brewery.

He was obsessed with Honeycote Ales. None of the other Liddiards seemed to care much; they just saw it as a meal ticket. But Patrick took such pride. Only he seemed to appreciate the value of their heritage, the fact they had brewed beer for the locals for nearly two centuries, that they were an intrinsic part of the geography and history and economy and had a reputation to uphold. It was a point of honour for him to keep the flag flying. Mayday knew that the brewery would only collapse over his dead body; that he would fight tooth and claw to keep it afloat and preserve the integrity of the Liddiard name. She thought about all the times he had confided in her, about the fire in his belly and the passion in his eyes. She was privy to all the secrets, the strategies, the bank balance, for he trusted her implicitly. Sometimes, it was as if he was describing an illicit affair to her, asking her advice about what he should do. Now, as she sat scrutinizing the ticket that was to change her life, it occurred to Mayday that Honeycote Ales was Patrick's real love. Why else would he be prepared to sacrifice himself?

In which case . . .

She looked down at the red numbers. She held the key to his happiness in her own hands. How far would all this money go at Honeycote Ales? Quite a long way, she imagined. The brewery could be completely refurbished. Several of the pubs could be transformed. The Horse and Groom could have a long awaited makeover. Mayday's mouth watered as she imagined it becoming the ultimate Cotswold townhouse hotel.

What should she do? Was it too late to stop the proceedings? She calculated that it had been a week since Patrick had proposed to Mandy. Surely not too many arrangements had been made? Surely he could extricate himself discreetly? Of course there would be uproar initially, but when things had died down, when Mandy's wounds had been licked and she was back on her feet . . . then Mayday could come out of the woodwork. It didn't matter how long it took. She'd wait a lifetime if she had to.

Mayday let the precious slip of paper flutter to the floor. She must still be drunk. She couldn't phone up and stop the wedding just because she'd come into a load of cash. She would only be doing what she had derided; luring him with her money. She didn't want to buy Patrick Liddiard.

No, decided Mayday. If she was going to have Patrick, it would be because he had decided, of his own volition, that Mayday Perkins was the woman for him.

10

On Tuesday afternoon, Patrick sat under the 'Thank you for not smoking' sign that Elspeth had carefully laminated and put up in the boardroom, and lit his fourth Marlboro. He'd ditched the Lights in favour of full strength. When it was all over, then he'd give up, he decided, but at the moment, nicotine was keeping body and soul together.

Mickey and Patrick had had to come clean, for they had no way of getting access to the kind of money they needed without the board's cooperation. And so Patrick had just undergone the most humiliating ten minutes of his life, even though what he had revealed to a shocked Keith and a knowing James was not strictly true. But he and Mickey had decided it was best to stick to their story: that Flora had been fathered by Patrick, for by making Patrick culpable there was less potential flak. James was Patrick's godfather and was duly protective of him, whereas there had always been an antagonistic undercurrent between him and Mickey, and Mickey didn't trust him not to blab to Lucy if they told him the truth. But James would keep quiet to protect Patrick. As would Keith.

Mickey stood up to take centre stage.

'So,' he said rather grimly. 'It looks as if we have reached something of an impasse. We – Patrick and I, for I'm not going to let him face this one out on his own – have a huge financial commitment that we can't honour with things as they stand. James has stated his financial position quite clearly. And Keith . . . ?'

He looked over to Keith, who was looking rather sad. He coughed, and twisted the signet ring on his little finger as he spoke.

'I'd love to be able to pull a magic rabbit out of the hat and tell everyone it is going to be all right,' he said slowly. 'But I can't. I've reached a time in my life when I don't feel, for various reasons, that I can rise to this challenge. Ten years ago I would have wanted to fight, to have made some compromises, raised some money, taken some risks. But I think, given our collective situations, that would be suicide. The stakes are too high and we don't have the expertise. This is not a cottage industry that can bumble along with the family at the helm any longer. I think we are in danger of jeopardizing everything if we don't recognize that. I think the brave and the right decision would be to sell.'

As he gave Honeycote Ales the death sentence, Keith felt sick. There was no way he could give them any other verdict, given that his own future was so uncertain. How could he make them promises? He might be dead by the end of the year. At least this way everyone would come away with some profit.

'Thank you for your honesty, Keith.' Mickey looked around at everyone else gravely. 'I think the next move is for me to talk to the bank, and ask Robert Gibson to start drawing up some guidelines for a prospective purchaser. Obviously, we want a place for Patrick, so that he can stay on as a consultant for at least five years. I can spend the next few months training him up, teaching him the mysterious ways of the master brewer. Letting him in to the closely guarded secrets of Honeycote Ales . . .'

Mickey managed a smile. He kept the recipes for each of their individual brews – the proportions of hops, malt and liquor and the addition of any extra ingredients – that had been handed down since the brewery's inception. But even as he spoke those words a cold chill settled over the table. A new buyer might not give a fig for their magical formulae. Honeycote Ale could become a weak, gassy, forgettable brew cooked up in some faceless factory unit. But they couldn't afford to protect their heritage and keep the name synonymous with quality and tradition. They didn't have that luxury. All they could hope was that a prospective purchaser would buy for the right reasons.

'The most important thing,' Mickey went on, 'is that what has gone on in here stays inside these four walls. If we are to get our best price, we mustn't let any interested parties know how vulnerable we are. Apart from the bank and Robert, no one else must know. Especially not Mandy or Lucy or Ginny or Caroline.'

'How very sexist,' drawled James. 'Personally, I like to share everything with my wife.'

'Except the washing up,' shot back Mickey. 'And the childcare.'

James met his gaze evenly, then slowly raised an eyebrow before looking away. Mickey felt his stomach turn over. He felt sure his brother was telling him that he knew everything; that he wasn't fooled by Patrick's charade for a single moment.

Patrick put his head in his hands. He hated it when the

stress of a situation caused Mickey and James to snipe.

Keith felt the need to take control yet again.

'Mickey's right, I'm afraid.' He spoke adamantly. 'This is a delicate situation. If word gets out we'll be instantly devalued, which could cost us our profit. We need to put up a united front, and give the impression that we are quitting whilst we are ahead, rather than giving up. Is that quite clear to everyone?'

This short speech reminded everyone why they had been so grateful to have Keith on board. He was so focused. He could assess a business situation and encapsulate it into just a few words. He looked around the table, and everyone nodded.

'Good,' he said. 'We're all agreed, then. As of three o'clock this afternoon, Honeycote Ales is open to offers.'

After the meeting, Keith felt an overwhelming sense of relief. For him, it was one more decision that had been taken out of his hands. Although he loved the brewery deeply, he didn't have the same loyalty ingrained since birth that the Liddiards had. And somehow the thought of getting rid of it relieved him of a burden. Either way, it made perfect sense. If he was going to die, then he wasn't going to be of much use. And if he was going to live, then frankly that's exactly what he wanted to do. Live a little. Go and see all those far-flung places he had never visited because he had grafted all his life. Go to Glyndebourne. Go fly fishing in Scotland. He still had another agonizing week before the results of his biopsy, which would tell him if he definitely had cancer, and if so what grade it was. But either way, he had decided that things had to change.

As he left the building, he found Patrick hovering nervously by his car. He looked incredibly young, as if he was waiting for his exam results.

'I just wanted to say I'm very sorry about everything,' he said. 'And I want you to know that I still worship your daughter. But if you think in any way that I'm not fit to marry her . . .'

Keith frowned, and for a moment Patrick thought he was going to say that was exactly what he was thinking.

'I think what you did was very brave. And I shall be proud to call you my son-in-law. Very proud indeed.'

He put a hand on Patrick's shoulder, then turned and got into his car rather quickly and drove off, because he had felt a momentary panic that Patrick was going to pull out of the wedding through some sort of misguided sense of honour. And that was the very last thing he wanted. While his own future was so uncertain, he wanted Mandy's to be set in stone. If he had to leave this world, he would only be happy knowing she was safe in Patrick's hands. He wouldn't trust anyone else with her. Patrick might have made a terrible mistake, but at least he was man enough to face the consequences. And Keith admired him for that. There were very few people left happy to take responsibility for their actions.

His daughter was marrying a gentleman. That was all he needed to know.

Mandy tried on the twelfth dress of the afternoon and sighed. It was sheer lace, with a high halter neck and a full-length skirt that was slashed to the thigh.

'Oh wow,' sighed Sasha. 'That looks amazing.'

'No way,' said Kitty. 'It's far too glitzy for a country wedding.'

Sasha rolled her eyes in exasperation. 'Well, let's just put her in a boring taffeta meringue, then.'

'Why not let Mandy make up her mind?' Ginny chided her squabbling daughters gently. They often lost sight of the point – in this case the fact that it was Mandy's wedding.

She was looking at her reflection critically.

'It's a fantastic dress. If it was green, or black, or red, I'd wear it to a party, no problem. But . . .' She wrinkled her nose, not quite sure what was wrong with it. The infuriating thing was that every single dress she'd tried so far had looked fantastic on, but none of them had felt quite right.

'For my money,' interjected Sandra, safe in the knowledge that it was her money, 'none of these are special enough. I want my daughter to feel special.'

Lucy looked at the price tag and said nothing. For two and a half grand, she'd want to feel more than special.

There were six of them in the changing room. Seven, if you included the assistant hovering by the white velvet curtain that separated them from the rest of the shop. The room was large and airy, strung with white chandeliers that threw a flattering light onto giant scrolled mirrors which allowed the future bride to see herself from all angles. There were two dear little white velvet sofas for mothers and bridesmaids to sit on and give constructive comments. But there weren't usually five people giving advice. Five people with very different opinions.

The assistant gave an inward sigh and smiled brightly. 'Perhaps a glass of wine?' she suggested. 'Perhaps everyone needs to relax?'

Sandra gave her a withering glare. 'I don't think it's a good idea to choose your wedding dress drunk.' She turned back to her daughter. 'Mandy, I think we need to focus. You need to narrow it down. Are you going streamlined and sophisticated? Ruffled and romantic? Or . . . what?'

Mandy struggled out of the skin-tight lace and emerged red-faced. She stood in the middle of the changing room in a white bra and minuscule thong, quite unselfconscious. But distressed nevertheless.

'None of it feels like me.'

'You've just got to keep trying. What about this?'

Sandra plucked a heavily beaded camisole with a plethora of chiffon ruffles off the rail of dresses that hadn't yet been tried. Lucy could see that Mandy was blinking back tears of frustration. Or perhaps exhaustion. This was the fourth shop they had been in.

'Perhaps we should just leave Kitty and Mandy to get on with it?' she suggested. 'I think we've got a case of too many cooks.'

Mandy looked at Lucy gratefully. Sandra turned and gazed at her with a mixture of aggrievement and scorn.

'I am not missing out on my only daughter choosing her wedding dress,' she stated.

'No. Of course not. Sorry,' said Lucy, realizing she'd put her foot in it. 'In that case, why don't Ginny and I go and have a cup of tea? There's that little patisserie we passed earlier.'

'Good idea,' said Ginny, whose head was throbbing. Why on earth had she agreed to come on this outing? Mandy didn't need her. But the twins had been adamant, and she was supposed to be looking for wedding outfits for herself. 'Come on, Sasha. You can come too.'

Sasha looked mutinous. 'I'm supposed to be taking the photos,' she hissed.

This was a covert operation. Kitty was going to copy whichever design Mandy ultimately chose. It had been agreed that Sasha would take surreptitious snaps on her mobile so they could compare the different dresses when they got home.

Lucy looked at Ginny and nodded towards the door. 'Looks like it's just us, then.'

As Lucy and Ginny left, Mandy turned back to the assistant.

'Actually,' she said. 'I think you're right. A glass of wine for everyone would be perfect.'

She caught her mother's disapproving eye and smiled sweetly.

'After all, this is supposed to be fun.' She flopped onto the white sofa in her underwear and shut her eyes. 'I think I might just wear jeans,' she declared.

'Over my dead body,' snorted Sandra.

Behind her, Sasha mimed stabbing her in the back. Mandy shut her eyes, not sure if she wanted to laugh or cry. No one had told her that choosing a wedding dress would be such hard work.

Ginny and Lucy made their way down the street and into the tiny patisserie they'd passed earlier, flopping into their seats and ordering tea and cakes, which arrived mercifully quickly. As she picked up the teapot and poured, Lucy looked at Ginny.

'Ginny . . . I don't like to say this. But you don't seem yourself.'

Ginny grabbed her teacup and drank so she didn't have to answer straight away, scalding her mouth in the process. What on earth was she supposed to say?

'What . . . what do you mean?' she stammered.

'I don't know, exactly. You just seem a bit . . . subdued.' Lucy helped herself to a macaroon and bit into it thoughtfully.

Ginny scooped two spoons of sugar into her tea. It was one of the wonderful things about Lucy; the way she noticed things other people missed, the way she could pick up on your mood. Only today Ginny wished fervently that Lucy hadn't picked up on the fact that she was feeling rather vulnerable. She couldn't bear to talk about it.

She couldn't, absolutely couldn't, bring herself to tell Lucy Liddiard that she and Keith hadn't had sex for more than three months. She would never understand. Lucy was the sexiest woman alive, in a very understated way. She was sitting there, with her glowing skin, her hair escaping from the slide that pinned it up, in her short-sleeved cashmere top and skinny jeans and ballet flats, not looking a day older than the incipient bride. Ginny was certain that the Liddiards were probably at it seven nights a week, because what man would be able to keep their hands off Lucy? Whereas Keith seemed to be able to restrain himself from her only too well. And she knew why. Keith had gone off her because she had gone to seed, was always tired and, although she knew she shouldn't, wore big baggy knickers from Tesco because they were so much more comfortable.

She'd tried her best last night. She'd specifically put on a strappy nightdress instead of her usual pyjamas, and had playfully suggested a massage. She had caught a fleeting look of horror on his face before he had blustered a polite refusal and gone scurrying off to his laptop. Mortified, she'd taken off the nightdress and consigned it to the laundry basket. He'd crept into the bedroom an hour or so later. She had pretended to be asleep, and she could almost feel the relief emanating from him.

But she couldn't bear the humiliation of admitting this to Lucy. So she stirred the sugar into her teacup, took a bite of macaroon, and gave Lucy a bunch of reasons for not being herself that were all true, but weren't the actual truth.

'I think I'm just tired. It's all a bit of a strain. I suppose I'm just not sure of my role in all of this. I'm not the mother of the bride, but I feel I should be supporting Mandy as Keith's . . . well, whatever.' She was blustering, casting round for convincing reasons for her lacklustre countenance. 'And I've been working too hard. Business is booming, but it's still at that stage where I have to be hands on – I'm not confident enough to delegate yet. And I find Sandra . . . Well, it's just a bit awkward.'

She was trying to be tactful, because she didn't want to sound like a bitch. Lucy put a hand over hers and leant forward with a mischievous smile.

'You don't have to say anything. I think you're a saint. Just hold on to the fact that when the wedding is over she'll be gone.'

Ginny managed a smile. 'I'm sure her heart's in the right place.'

Lucy narrowed her eyes. 'I wouldn't be so sure. I'm sure Sandra's jolly nice as long as she's getting her own way. That's why I split the wedding down the middle. I don't want to fall out with her, but I know there is no way on God's earth we will agree on anything.'

Ginny nodded agreement, thinking that you couldn't get two people less alike than Sandra and Lucy.

'She's not at all what I expected, you know,' she said suddenly. 'I didn't expect her to be so . . . glamorous.'

Lucy rolled her eyes and waved her fingers in the air with a snipping motion.

'Darling, if we spent as much as she had on plastic surgery . . . And anyway, you're far more gorgeous. I know Keith thinks so.' She frowned. 'You don't feel threatened, do you? Because you shouldn't.'

'No, no, no. Of course I don't feel threatened.' Ginny laughed, thinking she sounded slightly hysterical. 'It's just a bit strange, that's all.'

'Good. Then let's finish our tea and go up the road to Liberty. We're supposed to be looking for outfits for ourselves too, remember?'

Ginny finished her tea with a sinking heart. The last thing she wanted to do was try on outfits, especially after the fiasco with the red jersey dress. The assistant in Eldenbury had been very snippy when she'd taken it back the next day.

'You liked it enough when you tried it on in here,' she had said accusingly. Ginny had longed to retort that as it was obvious she didn't have a clue what suited her, the assistant had been criminally irresponsible to sell the dress to her in the first place. But she hadn't; she had just stood there helpless with tears stinging her eyes while the assistant had stroppily re-credited her bank card. There was no way she could ever go back there now, so she had to try and choose something today, because she wouldn't be able to afford another day off now for weeks. But what a nightmare, having Lucy as a shopping buddy. Not because she would be horrible – far from it – but because Lucy would look good in a sack.

Before they could make their escape, however, Sandra swept in with the twins and Mandy in tow.

'We're going to Liberty,' she announced. 'I am convinced that Vera Wang is the only way forward. And by the way—'

She fell into a vacant chair, looking round at her expectant audience.

'The hen night.' She smiled triumphantly. 'I've had the most fantastic idea.'

Mickey left the meeting with a sour taste in his mouth. He felt thoroughly disgusted with himself. He'd sold his family business down the river because of a moment's indiscretion. And sat back and watched his son take the rap for it. What a wanker.

He went into his office and began sketching out a draft contract to take in to Robert Gibson. Every point he made was like a dart piercing his heart. Seeing it in black and white made him sink deeper and deeper into gloom. He struggled manfully through until the clock in the corner struck six, when he glugged down two measures of brandy. For the last few years he had kept his office a booze-free zone, but in view of recent events he had sneaked a bottle of Courvoisier in. He was monitoring his drinking, trying to be careful not to go down that road again, but there was no denying it was a comfort.

This evening it didn't seem to help, however. The sense of self-loathing and shame almost seemed to increase with every drop he swallowed. Mickey slammed his glass down on his desk. Why should he have to suffer this? He wasn't the only guilty party, after all. And what say had he ever had in the decision-making process? It was Kay who had told him she couldn't get pregnant. Kay who had chosen not to tell him about Flora and then come out of the woodwork when it suited her . . .

He phoned Lucy and left a message to tell her he wouldn't be home until late – the girls wouldn't be back from their shopping trip yet anyway. Then he scooped up his car keys and strode out to the car park. He jumped into the driving seat, accelerated up the steep drive that led out of the brewery, shot out onto the road and belted out of the village.

He hadn't calmed down by the time he reached the Peacock Inn. If anything, he was more incensed. He unlocked the door of the flat and strode in without knocking. Kay was in the kitchen, and looked up in alarm.

'Mickey? You frightened me to death. How did you get in?'

Mickey dangled a key in front of her.

'You could have knocked. I might have been . . .'

She trailed off. Mickey leant against the doorjamb, staring at her. 'You'll be glad to know the board agreed this afternoon to sell off Honeycote Ales. You've successfully brought about its demise, after a hundred and fifty years. But don't worry – the cheque will be in the post.'

She went rather pale. 'I didn't know you'd have to sell. I thought you could . . . borrow it or something.'

'It's not really a bona fide reason for a loan, is it, paying off your mistress? I think we'd have had trouble raising the money.'

Mickey knew his words were harsher than she deserved. Kay's eyes were huge.

'I'm sorry,' she stammered.

'Only for as long as it takes you to fuck off with my hard-earned. Tell me, Kay: would you ever have told me, if Lawrence hadn't pegged it? Probably not. It might have jeopardized your life of luxury, after all. Far more important to hang on to the villa and the pool and the yacht—'

'We didn't have a yacht,' retorted Kay. 'And anyway, when did you ever care about me? You knew Lawrence threw me out that Christmas. You knew I was pregnant. And surely it occurred to you that the baby might be yours?' She looked at him accusingly. 'But did you try and get in touch? No. You just thought "Thank God she's gone." Didn't you?'

Damn. She'd been so determined not to throw this accusation at him, knowing it wouldn't help her cause. But she felt entitled to defend herself.

Mickey felt the brandy rise up in his gullet. 'I did try to phone,' he stammered.

'Not hard enough. I was terrified.' Kay was into her stride now, filled with righteous indignation. 'I would have given anything for just a single word of reassurance from one of you Liddiards. But none of you could wait to see the back of me. In the end, it was only Lawrence who was man enough to find me. He stood by me. And he loved Flora. From the moment he set eyes on her.'

Kay was trembling. All the colour had drained from her face. She grabbed onto the kitchen work surface for support as she felt her knees about to buckle underneath her. Mickey stepped forward and caught her just in time.

'I'm sorry,' he said gruffly. 'I've behaved appallingly. Yet again. It was a bit of a tough day, that's all. I shouldn't have taken it out on you.'

Kay was taking in big shuddering breaths. 'Why did he have to go and die? None of this would have happened . . .'

'Shhh.' Mickey stroked her hair until he could feel her relax. They stood together, very still, for a few moments.

'What's going on?' demanded a small voice.

Mickey and Kay sprang apart. Flora stood in the doorway looking indignant, wearing a white cotton nightdress sprigged with roses, her teddy slung over her shoulder.

'This is . . . Mr Liddiard. He's the landlord.' Kay was satisfied that this wasn't a lie. 'He's come to see if there's anything we need.'

Flora surveyed Mickey as a headmistress might a new pupil on the first day of term. 'This place is a dump,' she informed him. 'If it wasn't for the ducks, we'd be off.'

Kay clamped a hand over her mouth, suddenly desperate not to laugh, where only a moment ago she'd been on the brink of falling apart. But that was the beauty of children: they could bring you back to your senses in a second.

Mickey was flabbergasted. Standing before him was a hybrid of his three children. The wide eyes and the flowing curly hair belonged to Sophie. The righteous indignation was pure Georgina. And the urge to protect was Patrick. Mickey wouldn't dare put a foot wrong with the redoubtable Flora in the room.

'Darling, go back to bed,' said Kay. 'Mr Liddiard and I have a few things to discuss. I'll come and tuck you up in a minute.'

Flora looked Mickey up and down. He felt himself shrivel under her gaze.

'Goodnight,' she said, rather primly, and turned on her heel.

When she'd gone he turned to Kay, who was still trying not to laugh.

'She's . . . quite a character,' he said weakly.

'It's not surprising, is it?' Kay replied. 'Look at the parents.'

Mickey suddenly had the sense that things had taken a wrong turn. He should never have come here. He was on very dangerous ground indeed. There were feelings stirring inside him that he couldn't control. He had to get out before he started compromising himself, making foolish promises he couldn't keep.

As he made his escape, it was all he could do not to rush back in and look at Flora. Yet again, he cursed himself for drinking. If he hadn't been half-cut, he wouldn't have come looking for Kay. And if he hadn't come looking for Kay . . .

As he drove back to Honeycote House, all he could see was that little face, those accusing eyes, that determined tilt to the chin. Pride and curiosity surged up inside him in equal measure. He longed to turn around, drive back to the Peacock, scoop them both up and bring them home. He felt an overwhelming sense of shame that the two of them were locked away in that hovel, even though he knew Patrick was on top of it, and was making sure they had everything they needed.

Mickey just about managed to keep the car pointed towards Honeycote. He mustn't crumble now. It was only a matter of time before he would have the means to give Kay what she wanted. If he gave in before then, all hell would break loose. He gritted his teeth and clutched the steering wheel, telling himself to focus on the wedding. It was the least he could do for Patrick, who had gone beyond the bounds of loyalty yet again.

After all, if his son deserved anything, it was a happy wedding day.

Kay sat on the sofa in the living room, gazing at the screen of the small portable television Patrick had brought over, but not taking anything in. She was still in turmoil from Mickey's interruption. The encounter had unleashed a torrent of emotions in her. She'd gone from wanting to punch him in the face to longing for the comfort of his arms around her. She couldn't help wondering where things would have led if Flora hadn't walked in on them. He'd left the scene of the crime pretty quickly, as if he couldn't face the physical evidence of his guilt. Bastard. Coward. But then, that was Mickey all over and always had been.

For a moment she felt tempted to grab her car keys, drive over to Honeycote House and confront him in the comfort of his own kitchen. She wasn't going to be his dirty little secret any more. But she couldn't face the fall-out. More than anything, she couldn't bear the thought of Lucy. Lucy was always so calm, so dignified. She would never in a million years get herself into a predicament like Kay's. And Kay didn't need to be made to feel any more worthless than she already did.

She told herself to sit tight and be patient. She tried to visualize herself in a year's time, when she had her money. She pictured a tiny cottage on the edge of a village. A coat rail in the hall with Flora's school blazer hanging on it, and a pair of red wellies underneath. A rabbit hutch in the garden. A friend round for tea, with Marmite sandwiches and Jaffa cakes. Simple things.

Surely none of it was too much to ask.

'Look,' Kitty was saying firmly to Mandy. 'Forget all the crap we've seen today. It was all over-designed, tarty rubbish made for people with no imagination. I think I know what you like. I've seen every outfit you possess. I understand your personality. I know the sort of wedding you're having. Let me do some simple sketches.'

They were all having a debrief back in the kitchen at Keeper's Cottage – everyone except Lucy who'd gone back to Honeycote House.

Mandy nodded gratefully. Her head was whirling.

'I didn't think it would be so difficult. It's not as if I even care that much. I mean, I want to look nice, obviously. But I want to feel myself.'

'My point exactly,' said Kitty. 'None of those dresses was made with you in mind.'

'Let's see what Kitty comes up with.' Sandra looked extremely dubious. 'But for my money you looked like an angel in the Collette Dinnigan.'

'I don't want to look like an angel,' said Mandy. 'I want to look like me.'

'Trust me.' Kitty grinned. 'I'm a fashion student.'

Sandra looked rather dubiously at Kitty, who was wearing a pinstripe waistcoat over tweed shorts and footless leopardskin tights, then opened up her white leather wedding planner with a flourish. Mandy peered inside her mother's folder. It was bulging with brochures, quotations, catalogues, swatches of material and snippets of ribbon.

'Mum, what is all this?'

Sandra snapped the folder shut. 'Never you mind.'

'No, seriously. What have you got planned?'

'What haven't I got planned?' Sandra's eyes were twinkling. 'Don't you worry. It'll be all right on the night.'

'We are just having a disco and a pig roast?' Mandy suddenly felt very nervous. 'That's what we agreed.'

She thought she and Patrick had been quite firm about not going over the top. In the end, they had decided to invite everyone from the brewery to the evening do. There had been certain key members of staff who they wanted to invite, but it was hard to know where to have the cut-off point without causing dissension amongst the troops, so the most diplomatic solution was to ask them all. But she thought they had made it quite clear to Sandra that they wanted something down to earth. Anything too flash would be sending out the wrong message.

Perhaps they hadn't been clear enough.

'You are keeping it simple?' Mandy persisted.

'I'm just arranging a couple of little surprises.'

'Like what?'

Sandra gave a tinkling laugh. 'Don't panic. There's not a lot I can arrange anyway at such short notice. Just a few little embellishments to make it a night to remember.'

Mandy knew that if she protested, her mother would dig her feet in further. So she decided to keep quiet. After all, how bad could it be? At least the wedding breakfast was safe in Lucy's hands. She trusted her future mother-in-law implicitly. Anyway by seven o'clock, when the evening guests arrived, everyone would be completely sloshed.

Just then Sandra's mobile trilled. She leapt on it and walked across the room.

'Hello?' Her face broke into a smile as she listened. 'Oh, that's absolutely marvellous. I knew you'd swing it for me. I'll pop you a deposit in the post straight away.'

She snapped her phone shut. Everyone looked at her expectantly. She closed her folder and zipped it up defiantly.

'You're not getting anything out of me. You'll all have to wait.'

When Keith came in ten minutes later, he was hugely relieved to find the kitchen full, the wine open, and everyone chattering nineteen to the dozen. He had been dreading finding Ginny on her own, because he couldn't have kept quiet about what had gone on at the brewery that afternoon. It was killing him as it was, keeping quiet. The temptation to give in and spill the beans was enormous. But it wouldn't be fair. He couldn't burden her with it all. Keith simply didn't believe that problems were halved by sharing them. To his mind, they were doubled. So the fact that he clearly wasn't going to get a word in edgeways in his own house was, for once, a huge bonus.

'Dad!' Mandy jumped up, clearly pleased to see him. She pulled out a chair and poured him a glass of wine. 'We've got so much to tell you.'

'How was the wedding-dress hunt?'

'Disastrous. But Kitty's got a plan. And Mum's had the most brilliant idea.'

Keith looked at Sandra warily. She was looking particularly smug.

'The hen weekend,' she said dramatically. 'I've arranged for them all to go to the villa. The weekend before the wedding. Puerto Banus is becoming a very popular hen-night destination. They'll have a wonderful time. They'll all be able to top up their tans, get a bit of rest and relaxation before the big day. And it's a fantastic night spot. Bars, clubs, restaurants, millionaires . . .'

'Bring them on!' cheered Sasha.

'That sounds a very good idea.' He looked around the table. 'So who's going?'

'Everyone, I hope,' said Sandra.

'Not me,' protested Ginny. 'I'm far too old to go on a hen weekend.'

'No you're not!' protested Mandy. 'You've got to come. You need a break. Doesn't she, Dad?'

'Yes,' agreed Keith. 'I think a weekend in the sun is probably just what she needs.'

He smiled over at Ginny, but she flushed and looked away. He remembered the night before with shame. She'd been so sweet. He'd longed to follow her upstairs, but the prospect of his humiliation had been too much to bear. It wasn't long now, he told himself. He would soon know his fate.

'Can I ask Caroline as well?' Mandy had a flashback of her soon-to-be sister-in-law looking exhausted the weekend before. 'Caroline's a real party animal given half the chance.'

'Good idea,' said Sasha. 'Get her away from that arrogant pig of a husband.'

'Sasha!' chided Ginny automatically.

Sandra beamed. 'You can ask whoever you like. There are five double bedrooms in the villa. The more the merrier, as far as I'm concerned. And you'll have Alejandro to look after you.'

'Who's Alejandro?' everyone chorused.

'Alejandro,' replied Sandra, 'is my man that does. Everything.'

She smiled, giving herself a private recollection of exactly what.

'Everything,' she repeated. 'He'll make sure it's a hen weekend never to be forgotten.'

Later, as Ginny took a load of pizzas out of the freezer and chopped up a salad, she felt overwhelmingly depressed. Keith could barely look her in the eye any longer. He'd deliberately – or at least she felt sure it was deliberate – sat at the other end of the table. And he'd been so adamant that she should go on the hen weekend, when they could have taken advantage of the girls being away to spend some time together. But he'd gone straight on line and booked all their flights. And paid for them. Ginny knew she should be grateful, but she felt as if she was being shunted out of the way.

Lucy wasn't coming. They'd phoned her and asked, but she'd protested that as it was the last weekend before the wedding she would take the chance to get the house and grounds into shape. Caroline had been asked too, but wasn't sure. She'd never left Percy for any length of time, and James wasn't exactly keen on the idea. But they could work on her.

She poured oil and vinegar into the dressing jar and gave it a good shake. She shouldn't be ungrateful. Maybe a break was what she needed. Some time out to get her head around things. And she'd be glad of some sun. At least if she was a bit brown, she wouldn't look so blobby in whatever outfit she finally managed to get herself into. Maybe she'd try and talk to Keith before she went. Screw up her courage and see what was the matter. If he wanted rid of her, she'd rather know. She'd still have her girls, after all. In fact, the way things were going it looked as if she'd have Kitty and Sasha for the rest of her life.

II

Death, Mayday had decided, brought out the best in some people.

It had been an extraordinary few days. Coupled with still grieving for her grandmother was the curious notion of knowing she was rich beyond her wildest dreams. The cheque had been lodged. The money was hers. But still she hadn't touched it. Everything she thought of to buy seemed pointless. And so she carried on at work as if nothing had happened, even though she was entitled to time off for compassionate leave. What was she supposed to do? Sit up in her bedroom snivelling? Instead, she spent a satisfying day with the chef deciding what would go on the summer menu. And another day composing a letter to send to all the customers on their database, urging them to look ahead and book an autumn break. She'd walked around on automatic pilot, feeling nothing, because her grief cancelled out her euphoria. But the one thing she had appreciated was how kind people had been.

In particular, the staff. They were still being brilliant, keeping on top of any obstreperous guests and resolving any problems that came to the fore without running to her in a panic. The hotel consequently ran like clockwork, which just went to show that they could do it when they wanted to.

And then there was Rob Dunne. Rob had been in every day since her grandmother had died. It had almost become a ritual, to the point when she made sure there was fresh coffee in the pot just after ten, and had a plate of short-bread sent out from the kitchen. She'd usually been up for several hours by then, as she liked to tackle the paperwork before guests started checking out, so she was ready for a break when he ambled in, his cheery face beaming. She fed him biscuits, and he fed her gossip about suspected cockfighting, a shoplifting ring consisting entirely of pre-pubescent girls, rumours of an illegal rave. Torrid tales of the underbelly of Eldenbury life kept her entertained, and helped her forget about the fact that her mother hadn't checked up on her once.

She knew Angela was all right, because she'd seen Roy once or twice in the high street and he'd told her she was bearing up under the strain. It had been all Mayday could do not to laugh in his face, because the only strain for Angela was probably the wait for probate until she could sell Elsie's house. But she didn't, because she liked Roy, and he had to live with Angela, poor bugger.

Mayday also knew it wouldn't be long before she saw Patrick again, because they never went for more than a few days without seeing each other, whether it was busi-ness or just a quiet drink. And she wasn't entirely sure how she was going to feel when she saw him. So when Patrick walked into the bar that evening, she felt as if she'd taken a huge hit of amyl nitrate. Her pulse rate tripled, her heart pounded, the blood rushed to her head. She could feel her face burn and her pupils dilate. He kissed her cheek and asked how she was, running an affectionate hand down her arm and looking at her with such concern. She muttered a reply and asked him if he wanted a drink.

'Definitely,' he confided, then glanced around to see if there was anyone in earshot as she went behind the bar to serve him. 'I can tell you, but keep it quiet. I don't want the staff getting worried. We're selling the brewery. Lock, stock and barrel. Ha ha.'

He laughed dryly at his own pun. Mayday looked at him aghast as she handed him a glass of Shiraz.

'But why? You can't! I mean, I know things are rocky. But . . .'

'The whole thing's a fucking disaster. James is practically bankrupt and wants out. Keith's windy about something; I'm not sure what, but he's definitely lost his nerve. And as for Dad . . .' Patrick rolled his eyes up to heaven. 'He's surpassed himself this time.'

'How?' Mayday was curious. She knew Mickey was no angel; Patrick had often asked for her advice about his wayward father. But she thought he'd calmed down since his accident.

Patrick was silent for a moment. He knew he shouldn't divulge the truth, but he would trust Mayday to the ends of the earth. And, frankly, he wanted someone to share the burden with. Someone who wasn't directly involved. Mayday wouldn't be judgmental. She'd take it all in her stride.

'You remember Kay Oakley? From Barton Court?'

Mayday made a face. 'The stuck-up blonde who thought she was God's gift to everything in trousers?'

Patrick smiled. Mayday had a way of putting her finger on the button.

'You've got it. Anyway, she's tipped up with her daughter. And no prizes for guessing who the father is.'

He gave a wry grin, and Mayday's eyes widened.

'Not you?'

'No, no. Not me.' Patrick assured her hastily. 'Dad.'

Mayday thought back for a moment. 'But weren't you . . . ?'

She clearly remembered Patrick admitting an affair with Kay.

'Yes. But she's definitely not mine. I'm not as dim as Dad. I managed to use some protection for a start. Anyway, Kay wants serious money. Money we ain't got. So . . .'

'You've got to sell? Just like that? Who to? And what happens to everyone?'

'Don't worry. We're going to be very careful who we sell to. And there's going to be some sort of deal in place where I stay on as a consultant. So don't worry. You'll be safe.'

He was so reassuring, and Mayday felt her heart melt. She immediately wanted to tell him that he didn't have to worry. Not about her, at any rate. But she couldn't.

'But after everything you've done,' she protested. 'Marrying Mandy, I mean. To keep the brewery on its feet. I thought that was going to solve everything.'

Patrick looked at her, his smile rather fixed. 'I keep telling you, I'm not just marrying Mandy to save the brewery,' he said. 'That would be plain mercenary.' He lit a cigarette. 'I'm rather grateful for the wedding, actually,' he reflected. 'At least it's given everyone something else to think about. We're not going to tell them until after it's all over, anyway. We don't want to spoil it.'

'But what about you?' Mayday persisted. 'Everything's spoiled for you, isn't it? You love Honeycote Ales.'

Patrick flicked his ash and shrugged. 'To be honest, it's a millstone. I'll be glad to get rid of the responsibility. I'll still be involved, but I can clock in and out like everyone else and forget it when I get home.'

Mayday looked at him. He'd smoked his cigarette in sixty seconds flat. He was knocking back his wine as if it was going out of fashion. His hair was tousled from running his hand through it every other second. His skin was pale; his dark brow furrowed. Who was he trying to kid?

'The thing is,' he was saying, 'it's not going to happen overnight. Dad's talking to Robert Gibson. He's asking him to put feelers out. Discreetly.'

'It's the end of an era, though, isn't it?'

Patrick didn't reply for a moment. Mayday could see the tension in his jaw. She sensed the disappointment emanating from him; sensed that he felt he had failed. Himself, his family, his employees. His ancestors.

'I'd like to think of it as a new beginning,' he said with determination. 'Anyway, you don't want to hear my shit. Have you been all right? I've been thinking about you. I'm really sorry I haven't been in sooner.'

Mayday fiddled with a beer mat. 'I just feel . . . empty, really,' she admitted. 'Like there's no point. I used to go over to Gran's two or three times a week. I keep thinking there's something I should be doing, then remembering I don't have to any more.' She stopped, not wanting to sound self-pitying. 'Maybe I just need a crazy weekend away somewhere.'

Patrick stubbed out his cigarette. 'Then let's do it.'

Mayday looked puzzled. 'What do you mean?'

'I'm supposed to have a stag weekend, aren't I? Well, I can't think of anyone I'd rather spend it with. I'm definitely not letting bloody Ned organize anything. But we could go somewhere. You and me.'

'We can't,' said Mayday doubtfully. 'Can we?'

'I don't see why not. Apparently the girls are all going to Puerto Banus to let their hair down at Sandra's villa.' Mandy had texted him with the news earlier. 'So why can't I go somewhere? London. Let's go to London. I need some new shoes and a haircut.'

Mayday stared at him. He must be drunk. He'd probably change his mind once he'd sobered up. And she wasn't sure whether to agree. Even though there was nothing she wanted to do more in the whole world.

'Anyway,' Patrick was saying. 'I trust you. I trust you not to strip me naked and tie me to a lamp post.' He looked at her and laughed. 'I think.'

Mayday chuckled. 'You might enjoy it,' she teased. 'I'll book us somewhere to stay, shall I?' She looked at him doubtfully. 'Two rooms?'

'Just one room,' said Patrick, chucking back the rest of his wine. 'It's OK. No one will know. And it's only us. I mean, how long have we been mates?'

12

T he words had been sticking in Ginny's throat since she had woken at half past six. She had been lying there trying to get them out. But she was afraid. Afraid of what the answer might be. She couldn't go on like this, though. It was up to her to break the deadlock. She shut her eyes, swallowed, then spoke. It came out in an ineffectual croak.

'Shall we have the day off together?'

There. She'd done it.

Keith was silent for a moment. How tempting it would be to capitulate, to go out in the car somewhere nice for lunch, to tell her the truth, to hear her words of comfort. But he had promised himself to stay strong. He didn't need to offload this crisis. There was, after all, absolutely nothing she could say to alleviate his worry. She wasn't a surgeon, or an oncologist, or a clairvoyant.

'Out of the question,' he said gruffly, and threw back the duvet.

Ginny bit her lip and shuffled back down under the covers. What on earth had happened to him? She knew that when you moved in with someone the gloss usually wore off after a while as their true personality emerged. But they had lived together for some time now, and Keith had proved himself to be very even-tempered, easygoing and generous of spirit. Where had this terse, withdrawn character come from? Was this the real him? Because if so he had done a very good job of hiding the truth until now.

Maybe that was why his wife had left him. She had always assumed it was Sandra who had been the guilty party, but perhaps she had felt as cut off and isolated as Ginny did now. Perhaps she had felt her husband had become a stranger?

She decided to persevere.

'I just thought perhaps we should . . . talk?'

'About what?' Keith turned to look at her en route to the shower. His face was expressionless.

Ginny shrugged. 'It's just . . . we don't seem to have time for each other any more.'

Keith stood still. He could feel his heart pounding inside. Should he come clean?

No, he told himself. The last thing he wanted, if the news was bad, was for poor Ginny to feel obliged to stick by him, to nurse him through the inevitable horrors that would in the end lead to death. She didn't deserve that. She was still young; she deserved happiness after everything that bastard dentist had put her through. And that didn't mean becoming Keith Sherwyn's nursemaid.

He knew she'd be wonderful. He knew she'd be endlessly patient, and kind, and comforting. But he didn't want that for her. It would be so much easier for her if he ended their relationship. He wouldn't tell her why, because she would insist on staying with him to the bitter end. And if he did break it off, it would be easier for her if he kept himself detached. Not unpleasant, because Keith didn't have it in him to be nasty. But distant.

'It's a very nice idea,' he said carefully. 'But I've got an important meeting today. Maybe some other time.'

Important meeting. Hah! That was an understatement. To be told whether you were going to live or die. It didn't get much more important than that.

When Keith had gone Ginny flipped back the duvet as if to get out of bed, then lay there staring dully at the ceiling. She felt no incentive to get up whatsoever. In some ways, this was almost worse than when David had left her. At least then she had had something to rail against. She'd been able to console herself with the fact that his desertion was totally unjust. She'd been able to focus her resentment on Faith, the ghastly hygienist he'd run off with. But this miserable co-existence was more insidious. There was nothing that she could put her finger on. It was dull, grey, frustrating, and it made her feel more insecure. At least when your husband left you there was a sense of a new beginning. It had been a challenge. A tough one, but Ginny now felt she was a better person for it.

Keith obviously didn't. What was the matter? Was he bored? Did she grate on his nerves? Did he yearn for young flesh? Did he wish she wasn't a success? Would he prefer her to stay at home? Did he, in fact, resent the fact that her business was booming, growing faster than she could keep up with, while Honeycote Ales was obviously foundering? Men's egos were fragile, she knew that. Did he feel as if his nose was being rubbed in it? Did he feel inadequate? A failure?

All these questions and many more ran through Ginny's mind. What they needed was a good heart to heart. She should book them a weekend away, so he could forget about the brewery, she could forget about Mrs Tiggywinkle's, and they could both forget about the bloody wedding. Not that she resented the wedding for a moment. She was thrilled for Mandy, whom she adored. But it did seem to have everyone running round like headless chickens.

In the end, Ginny forced herself out of bed. She had three more clients to do quotes for, and she needed to recruit a couple of extra cleaners. Shake a leg, she told herself. She had a fantastic reputation for reliability and value and great service. She couldn't sacrifice that just because she was having a few personal problems.

Besides, her business might be all she was left with, if things got really grim.

So. There it was in all its glory. His tumour. Mr Jackson showed it to him on the scan. It was quite extraordinary, thought Keith, to think that this innocuous little blob could eventually kill him if it wasn't dealt with.

It was grade two. Which made it sound like a listed building, but in fact meant that, for the time being, it was contained in the prostate. And his Gleason factor, the score by which the aggressiveness of the cancer was rated, was six. Which was, apparently, good. Good, Keith couldn't help thinking, would have been no cancer at all. But Mr Jackson seemed positively optimistic.

'This means it's not going to grow quickly. On the other hand, you are relatively young for a prostate cancer diagnosis. So rather than monitor the disease, I would recommend a radical prostatectomy. In other words, we whip it out. Thereby eradicating the problem. With any luck.'

'I see,' said Keith slowly, not sure what to think.

'Because I do keyhole surgery, it would be a relatively simple procedure. You'd be up and about pretty quickly.'

'Would I need chemo afterwards?'

'We'd need to check that it is definitely contained within the prostate. But if that is the case, you wouldn't need any further treatment. As for side effects,' Mr Jackson gave a rueful smile. 'There is, of course, a possibility of incontinence and erectile dysfunction.'

'No change there then,' said Keith gloomily.

'We have simple procedures to help overcome that. My recovery rate is second to none. And if the worst comes to the worst, there are drugs.'

'You mean Viagra?' Keith felt hot with humiliation. This was all too horrible for words. Never mind, he told himself. He'd just go without, rather than face the embarrassment.

'You may find that your lack of performance up until now has been a consequence of the tumour. In which case, once we remove it, you'll be as right as rain.'

'And if we don't remove it?'

'It's cancerous, Mr Sherwyn. We would have to monitor it regularly. And you'd probably end up having surgery eventually anyway, with the added possibility of chemo.'

'You're saying go for the operation.'

'It's your decision, obviously. But just let me say that these are the operations I like. We know exactly what we're up against. Straightforward in and out. Bish bash bosh. Job done.'

Keith wished he had his confidence. He didn't feel bullish. He just felt frightened. He knew cancer was malicious and devious; that it could pull the unexpected out of the bag no matter how experienced the consultant. That was why millions and millions were spent on research every year. Because no one really understood. No one could give a cast-iron one hundred per cent guarantee.

'So,' said Mr Jackson. 'How's your diary looking?'

Keith blinked. It was almost as if they were arranging a game of golf.

'How long do I need to stay in?'

'We're going for keyhole surgery. So two nights max. As long as you've got someone to look after you at home.'

Keith glossed over that one. He didn't mention that no one at home knew anything yet. And looking at his diary, they still needn't know anything. If he could fix his operation around the hen weekend . . . The girls were off on the Thursday and back on Tuesday. He'd be on his feet by then. And if they suspected anything, he had it all worked out. He'd say he'd nipped in for a quick hernia operation; that the consultant had fitted him in at the last minute.

Mr Jackson seemed to think that was perfect timing.

'Come in on the Friday night. We operate first thing on Saturday. You can be home on Monday morning, all being well.'

'What do you mean, all being well?' Keith looked anxious. 'What might go wrong?'

Mr Jackson gave him what he thought was a reassuring smile. 'Some people don't react well to anaesthetic. Or you might get a little infection. I don't mean anything sinister by that.' He paused. 'Though of course, we never know exactly what we're going to find.'

Keith tried to calm himself by taking deep breaths. He didn't want to lose it in front of his consultant. His heart was tap-dancing all over the place, and he could feel beads of perspiration pop out on his forehead.

'So what do I do in the meantime?'

'Carry on as normal. Your prognosis is good, Mr Sherwyn. We've caught the thing early, we're on top of it. Just relax.'

Easy for you to say, thought Keith, his hand trembling as he blocked the days for his operation out in his Filofax.

People always felt very at home in Robert Gibson's office because he kept it very comfortable, with the minimum of officialdom or paperwork on display. With its dark red walls and paintings of racehorses and the incredibly comfortable leather button-back chairs, his clients often didn't want to leave. For Robert provided them a safe haven. Added to which, he was quite the most unshockable, non-judgemental person most people ever had the fortune to meet, with twinkling brown eyes and a schoolboy sense of humour that was rather endearing. He was strangely old-fashioned in his dress, but those who knew him well knew that was a cover-up, that his tweed jackets and checked shirts and knitted ties belied his shrewdness. It suited Robert if people thought he was a bit of a bumpkin, because it meant they trusted him. The solicitor at the other end of town wore Italian suits and spent half his time in London and no one told him anything.

Robert had been intrigued to see Mayday Perkins' name in the appointments diary. What on earth did she want? It wasn't as if she didn't have plenty of opportunity to speak to him, for he came into the Horse and Groom every evening at thirty-five minutes past five – his office closed at half past and it took him precisely five minutes to walk along the high street. He always had a pint of Honeycote Ale, which he made last twenty minutes while he sat in contented contemplation munching his complimentary bowl of smoked almonds. And he would chat to Mayday, who loved this time of the day best – the quietish lull that was somehow full of expectation, just before the bar and the dining room started to fill. She often came and joined him for a cocktail, which Robert always insisted on buying even though she could have helped herself for nothing. He relished that twenty minutes because it belonged to him – not his clients and not his needy and rather grasping wife Fleur – and never did he resent spending those precious moments with Mayday for company. She charmed him. She was quirky, witty and gorgeous; voluptuous and earthy, a combination which Robert found quite beguiling. So unlike his wife Fleur, who was brittle and superficial. They were almost the antithesis of each other.

And here she was, in front of him, in a white dress that seemed to be on inside out because the seams were all showing, and a black bra underneath, and her hair tumbling everywhere. He looked at her from behind his half-moon glasses and gave her a broad beam.

'How can I help you, m'dear?' He always called her that. In fact, he called everything female and under sixty 'm'dear', except his own wife.

Mayday had thought very long and hard about it and decided that of all the people she knew, she trusted Robert Gibson the most, and that he would probably give her very good advice. Everyone who was anyone in and around Eldenbury used him. He was trusted and respected.

'I wondered . . . if you could give some advice about something. I'm really not sure what to do.'

His face clouded over. 'Are you in some sort of trouble?'

'Not exactly.' Mayday bit her lip. 'Although I'm starting to think it's a bit of a nuisance. I haven't told anyone yet. You'll be the first. And I don't want it getting out.'

'I'm privy to more secrets than you could possibly imagine. I wouldn't be a very good solicitor if I went blabbing to all and sundry. Nothing you tell me goes beyond these four walls.'

'I'm sure you wouldn't. I'm sorry. I didn't mean . . .' Mayday was flustered, worrying that she'd offended him. But he gave her another kindly smile.

'It's all right. Just rest assured that nothing you tell me will go any further.'

She took a deep breath.

'I've won the lottery.' She laughed, realizing it was the first time she'd actually spoken those words. 'Over five million.'

Robert spluttered. He'd thought perhaps she'd been cited in a divorce case, or possibly wanted to write her will.

'How the dickens have you managed to keep that quiet? Most women would be running up and down the high street blaring it out to the world and his wife.'

Mayday looked fierce. 'I don't want anyone knowing. Not yet. Especially not my mother.'

Robert nodded understandingly. 'I think you're very wise. Lottery wins are notorious for bringing out the worst in people. They can often be a curse rather than a blessing.' He looked at her gravely. 'But you're right to confide in me. We should make sure you're being looked after properly and investing it wisely. I know they have people that do all of that, but if you want me to make some recommendations . . .'

'Actually, it's not so much that. I've had an idea of what I'd like to do with it. Or some of it. And I want to know how to go about it.'

'Well, don't open a florist, whatever you do.'

Mayday giggled. Twig was very successful on the surface, but Fleur was incapable of keeping to a budget and spent her profits before she'd made them. Robert had often confided in Mayday rather ruefully about his spendthrift wife. She leant forward.

'I want to buy into Honeycote Ales.'

Robert's eyebrows shot up to the ceiling. It hadn't been a week since Mickey had sat in that very chair, gloomily revealing to him that they were going to have to sell. Coincidence? Robert didn't think so. He knew Mayday had her wits about her. And that she was quite close to Patrick. He'd seen them chatting in the bar on more than one occasion, and he could read body language. They were very comfortable with each other. Did she have inside knowledge? Robert decided to play his cards very close to his chest. He didn't want to betray the Liddiards' confidence, any more than he would dream of betraying Mayday's. He'd simply play devil's advocate.

He steepled his fingers. 'Honeycote Ales?'

Mayday gave him a knowing smile.

'We can play I-know-that-you-know-that-I-know. Or we can cut to the chase. I know they're looking for a buyer. I also know they've got a string of conditions attached that no potential purchaser would even begin to honour, so they're on a wild goose chase.'

Robert stayed silent. This was true. Mickey had been through the wish list with him earlier in the week, and it had been all Robert could do not to tell him to dream on.

'I know the brewery's weaknesses. I know its strengths. And while I sympathise with the Liddiard ideals in principal, I think the whole thing needs shaking up. More to the point, it needs cash if it's going to survive.' She spread out her hands. 'Which is where I come in.'

Robert had to force himself to shut his mouth, which he had felt dropping open in astonishment. He let her carry on.

'I don't want to buy a fuck-off house and a holiday villa and a Ferrari with my winnings. Well, maybe just a small Ferrari.' She flashed him an impish grin. 'But I don't want to fritter the rest away. I want to invest in something that will give my life some meaning. I've worked for Honeycote Ales since I was seventeen. I love the Horse and Groom. I know it's tragic, but it is actually my life. So it makes perfect sense to me, to put my winnings into the company I love. And I'm pretty sure with the right team behind me I could make it work.'

Robert nodded, very carefully, taking in everything she had said.

'So what do you want me to do?'

'I want you to approach them for me. Tell them you've got an interested investor. Show them my ideas. I'm working on a proposal. It'll be ready by the end of the week.' She paused. 'But I don't want you to tell them it's me.'

'They will want to meet you. You'll have to come clean eventually.'

'Yes,' said Mayday. 'But by then they'll want me so much it won't matter.'

Robert looked impressed. 'You're a shrewd one, aren't you? I'm envious, I must say. I've always thought it would be fun to run a brewery.'

Mayday put her head to one side and surveyed him. He felt himself go warm under her gaze.

'Come in with me,' she suggested.

Robert shot her a quizzical glance. 'Me?'

'You'd give me some credibility. After all, I'm only a jumped up barmaid at the end of the day. They might take me more seriously if I had you as a partner.'

For a wild moment, Robert was tempted. But he knew he'd be going in for all the wrong reasons. Mayday was totally bewitching. He wasn't even sure he should be acting for her. He pulled himself together.

'Somehow I don't think Fleur would like it. And I've got enough to do running this place. But thank you. I'm very flattered.'

'But you will speak to them?'

'Of course. Although we need to do our groundwork first. Bring in your proposal and we'll go through it. Then we need to talk about price, terms, timescale . . . It's not just a question of writing a cheque. We need to protect your interests.'

Robert's professional side suddenly took over. He remembered the finer details of Mickey's meeting with him. There were definitely murky goings-on with the Liddiards, and while he couldn't betray his client confidentiality, he didn't want Mayday swooping in and eradicating their problems just because she'd struck lucky. At which point it occurred to him that he really shouldn't be representing both parties.

He knew which client he'd rather keep.

But it didn't matter at this early stage. Initially, he'd merely be effecting an introduction. He felt a frisson of excitement. He loved days like this. Days that threw up the unexpected, not the usual tedious conveyancing and alimony squabbles that made up much of the small-town solicitor's workload.

'And now, m'dear, I insist on offering you a glass of champagne to celebrate your win.'

Robert kept a supply of bubbles in his fridge for when his clients closed deals or exchanged contracts or finalized their divorces.

Five minutes later they clinked glasses.

'I must say,' said Robert, 'I don't want to count our chickens, but I am rather pleased. I had visions of Honeycote Ales being bought out by some ghastly asset stripper.'

'Who says I'm not an asset stripper?' Mayday shot back, her eyes full of mischief.

Afterwards, Robert sat back in his chair with his hands clasped behind his head. That was the beauty of living in Eldenbury. Sometimes things just fell into place. He couldn't think of anything more pleasing than Mayday at the helm of Honeycote Ales. For a moment he wondered about her and Patrick, then remembered Mickey had told him Patrick was about to get married. Pity, thought Robert, who was an unashamed romantic. That would have been the perfect ending.

13

Mandy spent all week trying to persuade Caroline to come on her hen weekend, but without success. 'I need an ally,' she begged. 'I can't cope with the twins on my own. You know what they're like.'

Kitty and Sasha, even if they did have wildly different dress sense, attracted much attention on a night out, identical twins apparently being the stuff of every male's fantasy, and Mandy didn't want to be left standing like a spare part. And Caroline was a notorious party animal, or at least she had been pre-children. She was the first on the dance-floor and the last to drop. Mandy knew she would have the time of her life, given the chance.

But at the moment she felt too exhausted to even contemplate Mandy's offer.

'I'm in bed by nine every night,' Caroline protested. 'You don't want me around. I'd be a complete yawn. Plus I've got nothing to wear. I can't go clubbing in a sick-stained sweat-shirt.'

In the end, Mandy asked Lucy to try and persuade her. 'She needs a break. And she'd enjoy it once she got there. She'd get a bit of sun and a bit of fun.'

Lucy agreed to do her best to talk Caroline round. When she walked into her kitchen, however, she was shocked by what she found and immediately felt riddled with guilt. She knew Caroline had been struggling with the three little ones, but she'd been so wrapped up in the wedding and its preparations that she hadn't found the time before now to drop in and see how she was coping. Now, the scene that greeted her made her stomach curdle.

Constance was wandering around with just a top on. Lucy could see her potty by the back door, but judging by the wet patches on the floor she hadn't made it. Henry was slumped in a beanbag eating handfuls of Cheerios out of the box and watching a video turned up to full volume. Percy was sitting in his highchair surveying it all like a baby king, still in his babygro, gnawing on a dessert spoon which he occasionally gagged on, then withdrew. When Lucy picked him up, she realized that half his weight came from the fact that his nappy hadn't been changed for hours – it swelled out around him like a life belt. The breakfast things were still everywhere – bowls of mush and bits of banana and crusts of bread on every available surface.

Caroline was nowhere to be seen.

'Where's Mummy?' asked Lucy, panicking inwardly but trying to seem calm.

Henry shrugged and stuffed another handful of Cheerios in his mouth.

Carrying Percy, Lucy walked through the house cautiously. She found Caroline in the living room, fast asleep in front of the television. She started awake when Lucy called her.

'I wasn't asleep,' she protested. She looked dreadful. She was wearing an old maternity skirt and a baggy peasant blouse. The elasticated sleeves were digging cruelly into the flesh at the top of her arms, and she had no bra on. Her hair was lank, her skin mottled, her eyes dark and bruised-looking. Lucy didn't think she'd had a bath or a shower for some time. She looked about ten years older than the last time Lucy had seen her, and she hadn't been looking her best then.

'Caroline, those children were all alone in the kitchen. Percy was in his high chair. Anything could have happened to them. What if they'd opened the back door, or if one of them had got a knife?' It wasn't in Lucy's nature to lecture, but she was deeply shocked. Surely it went against any maternal instinct to leave your children unsupervised?

Caroline just stared at her blankly. She was catatonic with tiredness, Lucy realized.

'I'm going to take Percy and Connie upstairs and give them a quick bath. Then I'll give you a hand in the kitchen. Then we need to talk.'

She was just turning to go when Caroline's voice rasped out.

'It's all your fault.'

'Mine?'

'It's all very well you walking in here and giving me a lecture. But you're the one who told me to have him. Remember?'

True enough, it was Lucy Caroline had turned to when she'd found out she was accidentally pregnant yet again, just three months after giving birth to Constance. She'd sat in the kitchen at Honeycote House, pale with shock.

'I know it's an awful thing to say, but do you think I should get rid of it?' she'd asked. 'It's early days – I'd only need to take a pill. It wouldn't be like a real . . .' She hadn't even been able to bring herself to say the word.

Now, Lucy felt the need to defend the advice she had given Caroline at the time. 'All I said was I think you'd regret it if you had an abortion.'

'Not as much as I regret this!' Caroline snarled, and Lucy jumped back, frightened. Caroline's face was contorted with fury, eyes blazing out from a bloated, reddened mass of features. She looked insane. Totally unrecognizable.

'I know why you did it!' Caroline's voice was a mixture of hoarse and shrill. 'You told me to have it so I'd turn into a wreck and then you could have James.'

'Caroline—' Lucy tried in vain to interject.

'Look at me!' Her voice went up another octave, her eyes bulging with the strain. 'James won't go near me. And I'm not surprised. Are you? Who'd want to touch me – a big, fat minging blob?'

Percy started wailing.

'Shut up! Shut up! SHUT UP!' Caroline clamped her hands over her ears, then dissolved into sobs.

Lucy's first instinct was to phone James. He was Caroline's husband, after all. This was his responsibility. But something inside told her that James was probably half the problem, and what Caroline needed was some good sound advice, some practical help and a decent night's sleep. None of which James was likely to give her.

'What do you want, anyway?' Caroline managed to demand through her tears. 'Have you come to crow? Mrs Fucking Perfect?'

Lucy flinched. Maybe she should leave. Caroline was being unbelievably hostile. She probably wouldn't take kindly to Lucy trying to help, not if she saw her as the enemy. But Lucy didn't have it in her to walk out on someone who was in such a state. Caroline clearly didn't know what she was saying. So she stood her ground.

'I came to persuade you to go on the hen weekend,' she said calmly. 'The girls are all desperate for you to go.'

Caroline looked at her sullenly, her eyes pink and piggy. 'Yeah, right. They'd seriously want to be seen with me.'

'They do. They asked me to come and ask you. And I think you should go. You need a break.'

Caroline's sigh seemed to come from the very depths of her soul. 'You can say that again.' She raked her fingers through her hair, pulling it back into a pony tail, twisting the curls round each other. Her hair was so greasy it stuck in place. 'But it's out of the question. James won't let me go.'

'Don't be ridiculous.'

'He won't. He can't manage the kids. I'm still up and down all night with Percy. James wouldn't cope.'

Lucy was astonished. How could fiery, assertive Caroline let James walk all over her like that? She couldn't believe how diminished the girl was. Once, Lucy had almost been intimidated by her. Caroline had been a force to be reckoned with: a ruthless career girl, assertive, extrovert and confident. Now she was a shadow of her former self. Not even a shadow. It was astonishing what hormones could do.

Hormones, combined with sleep deprivation and drudgery. If anyone needed five days in Puerto Banus, sleeping and eating and soaking up the sun, it was Caroline.

'Right,' Lucy said firmly. 'This is the plan. Percy is coming home with me. Give me two nights, and I promise you he will sleep through. But first, you're going to go and have a long hot bath while I get the kids dressed. Then we're going to get this place cleaned up.'

Caroline blinked slowly, not sure if she was believing what she heard. 'You'd really do that for me?'

'Of course. What else have I got to do with my time? Go on. Go and have a really good long soak.'

She turned Percy round to face her and met his baleful eye. 'You, young man, are coming with me and we are going to have no nonsense.' She was rewarded with a huge toothless grin that made her heart melt. She tutted. 'You have got no idea how much trouble you've caused, have you?'

Percy carried on beaming. Caroline wiped her eyes.

'I love him so much,' she said in a voice that was tight with tears. 'But it's so bloody hard . . .'

Lucy wasn't sure if she was talking about James or Percy. But she didn't ask.

Upstairs was no better than the kitchen. Toys and clothes were strewn along the corridor, the beds were unmade, the linen badly in need of changing. The children's bathroom was thick with grime, wee all over the loo, footprints all over the floor, grubby towels chucked everywhere. Lucy ran a bath and stuck Percy and Constance in together, then tackled what she could whilst keeping them in view. She coerced Henry into picking up all the toys – she had to resort to bribing him with a fifty-pence piece, which made her realize he was in danger of turning into a grasping little horror, but he managed it in the end.

Thankfully, by the time Percy was dried and dressed in a fresh new outfit, he was ready for his morning nap, which enabled Lucy to stick Constance in front of the telly, stick on a wash, and get all the breakfast things into the dishwasher by the time a subdued but slightly more presentable Caroline appeared.

'I'm sorry,' she said, and dissolved into tears again. 'What a card-carrying bitch. I just feel so . . .' She couldn't even find the words. 'I feel like a total failure. I feel as if everyone hates me. James. And the children. I can't help feeling they'd be better off without me.'

Lucy put her arms round her and held her tight as she cried and cried.

'It's going to be OK,' she soothed. 'We'll get it sorted. I promise.'

Mickey got the shock of his life when he got home that evening to find Lucy dancing round the kitchen to Van Morrison with a beaming Percy on her shoulder.

'Meet the lodger,' she said happily.

'What?'

'I'm baby-whispering,' she explained. 'I'm training Percy to sleep. It should only take two nights. You don't mind?'

Mickey was speechless. Lucy went over to the Aga to stir her white sauce. Percy stared at him over her shoulder, his fist in his mouth, his expression saying firmly, 'Hands off, she's mine'.

'Caroline's in a terrible state,' Lucy told him. 'She hasn't had a proper night's sleep since Percy was born. She's practically psychotic, poor thing. I had to go and see your brother. Tell him in no uncertain terms that she needs a break.'

'I bet he loved you for that.'

'I don't know what he's thinking of. The poor girl's on her knees. And he just sits in that shop of his drinking coffee and flicking through *Country Life*. I'm sure he doesn't sell any furniture.'

Lucy looked at Mickey fiercely, as if he was somehow to blame. He decided it was best to keep quiet. He didn't want to give Lucy any hint that James was in financial straits, because she might start looking at the bigger picture.

'Never mind,' he said cheerfully. 'It'll be nice to have a house guest. We'll sort you out, young man.'

He tickled Percy under the chin and was met with an unblinking stare, as if the little boy was telling him he knew exactly what his game was.

As Lucy shifted Percy onto the other shoulder and flung some chopped parsley into her sauce, Mickey remembered how easy she had always made it all look. The kitchen had always been full of children in various stages of development, but it had never stopped her doing anything. She'd always been able to give them her undivided attention but get on with life. The mistress of multi-tasking. And she'd always looked stunning. Never tired or drawn or grubby. She was a natural mother and homemaker, wife and hostess. Perfect, in other words, thought Mickey ruefully. Which was why she'd found life so hard recently. With all the children effectively gone, her role had been totally diminished. Now, with Percy in one hand and a wooden spoon in the other, she was herself again. Juggling effortlessly.

He felt sick.

How did life do that? He had just allowed himself to feel a modicum of relief. Robert Gibson had called to say he knew of someone who was seriously interested in the brewery. A cash buyer. He was going to send over their proposal the following week. Mickey had pictured a big fat cheque, a proportion of which he could use to pay off the big, fat skeleton in his cupboard. He'd be free at last.

'What do you think, Micks?' Lucy was saying. 'I'm still not too old. Madonna did it. Cherie Blair did it. What do you think, Percy? Do you fancy a little cousin to play with?'

Mickey prayed Lucy was only flirting with the idea. She didn't really mean it, surely? But how the hell would she feel if she knew that he already had what she was clearly longing for? Another child, who was living less than five miles down the road. Mickey shivered as he realized how easy it would be for Lucy to bump into Kay and Flora, but he could hardly tell them not to go out. He knew Kay was doing her best to keep a low profile, because she didn't want their deal to go sour. But it could happen.

He'd get on the phone to Robert straight away. Tell him to hurry up the deal. They'd negotiate down on price if they had to, just to get it in the bag as quickly as possible. Then he could pay Kay off. And there was going to be an important condition. That she moved as far away from Honeycote as possible.

14

M andy stood on the doorstep of Little Orwell Cottage. Beside her was a bulging weekend bag, filled with most of her summer wardrobe: little dresses and jewelled flip-flops, several swimsuits and bikinis, wispy chiffon kaftans – enough to cover every eventuality on a sun-drenched hen weekend. She scanned the road anxiously, waiting for Caroline's car to appear over the brow of the hill, hoping that for once her future sister-in-law would be punctual.

Half of her was excited about the trip, but the other half felt quite ill at the thought that, when she came back, her wedding would be only a few days away, even though Lucy and Sandra had taken over the preparations for the reception entirely. It was stressful enough worrying about all the other details – flowers, bridesmaids, hymns, present lists – not to mention the dilemma of her appearance.

She had tried on her wedding outfit the night before, in total secrecy, with just Kitty. They had made sure that everyone else was out, because the last thing they needed was interference. And it had been perfect – there were just a few little alterations to be made, but Kitty could do that when they got back from Spain.

'Just don't eat or drink too much,' she warned. 'I can take it in, but I can't let it out.'

So the dress was wonderful. But there was still hair, make-up, jewellery, shoes and underwear to coordinate. She'd booked an entire day at the Barton Court spa on Thursday – manicure, pedicure, bikini and leg wax, eyebrow threading, eyelash extensions . . . Mandy sighed. There was no excuse for looking less than perfect these days.

Patrick came out of the house and slid his arms round her waist.

'Now I hope you're going to behave,' he said. 'I've heard about these hen weekends.'

'Course I will.' She grinned. 'I just want to get some sun, and have a good night out on the town. What are you going to do?'

'I might go to London on Saturday. Do some shopping. I want a new shirt and some decent shoes.'

He couldn't quite look her in the eyes as he spoke. She peered at him, concerned.

'Are you all right?' she asked. 'Only you seem very quiet these days. You haven't really been yourself.' She bit her lip anxiously. 'You're not having second thoughts, are you? Only if you are, just say . . .'

Patrick felt an utter heel that she should think that. He knew he'd been subdued and preoccupied, but he couldn't tell her why. Or maybe he should? She was going to be his wife. There should be no secrets. But it wouldn't be fair to James and Mickey. They'd all agreed to keep the deal quiet for the time being.

'To be honest,' he said, 'the wedding's the only thing that's keeping me going at the moment.'

Her face lit up with relief, and she flung her arms around him. 'I can't wait to be Mr and Mrs Liddiard!'

'I wish it was just us going away for the weekend,' he murmured into her neck.

'I could say I was ill,' she suggested huskily. 'We could book into a hotel somewhere . . .'

Patrick gently disengaged himself from her embrace as Caroline's car appeared on the horizon.

'You can't let the others down,' he said. 'Have a fantastic time and I'll see you when I get back.'

At Keeper's Cottage, Sandra had arrived to wave everyone off. The girls were still upstairs bickering over what clothes to take. Ginny was packed and ready, so she made Sandra coffee. They sat rather awkwardly in the kitchen. At least, Ginny felt rather awkward. Sandra seemed quite at home, radiant in a yellow shift dress that showed off her toned arms, courtesy of fifty lengths of her pool every morning. Ginny was glad she was wearing a cardigan that covered up her bingo wings.

Sandra beamed brightly over the top of her coffee cup. 'I just wanted to say, Ginny. If you wanted a little bit of a . . . lift for the big day?'

'Lift?' Ginny was baffled. Was Sandra offering her drugs?

'As stepmother of the bride. You know . . . all eyes upon you. You might be glad of a little bit of a boost.' Sandra smiled kindly. 'It's quite painless. And any untoward swelling will have gone down by next Saturday.'

Ginny stared at her. Then the penny dropped. 'You're saying I need . . . work?'

Sandra sighed. 'Why has it become such a dirty word?

And why is it such a stigma? Why are women so afraid to give themselves a little helping hand? We can't turn back the years, but we can stop the ageing process in its tracks—'

'I'm perfectly happy with my face as it is, actually,' retorted Ginny. 'I think a few lines here and there give it character.'

Sandra considered Ginny's statement. As her breath went in her eyebrows went up in disbelief. 'Well, you're one of the lucky ones. Not everyone is so confident at our time of life.'

Our time of life? thought Ginny indignantly. She was a good ten years younger than Sandra, who was giving her a rather patronizing smile, as if to imply that one day she would come to her senses and realize she was a wrinkled old bag.

'I've had grown women weeping with gratitude in my clinic,' Sandra informed her. She passed a hand over her own skin, rather lovingly. 'It's life-changing, Ginny. I don't want to force you into anything, of course. But if, while you're over there, you feel tempted, just pick up the phone to the clinic. Marie-Claire will look after you. Complimentary, of course.'

She dived into her handbag and handed Ginny a brochure.

'Take a look through. There's always lip-plumping. For the bee-stung look.' She cocked her head to one side and surveyed Ginny critically. 'You're a very pretty woman. Giving nature a little nudge is nothing to be ashamed of. I like to think of it as enhancing. Enhancing one's attributes.' She picked up her coffee cup. 'It's so hard to be a woman these days. We have to be all things to all people.

In the kitchen, in the boardroom, in the bedroom . . . There's nothing wrong with asking for a little help.'

Ginny set her own cup down on the table, rather too hard.

'I'm just going to go to the loo,' she said with gritted teeth. She couldn't bear to sit in the room with the woman a minute longer. She fled up to her bedroom and sat on the bed, clutching the brochure. What a cow! But out of the corner of her eye, she caught sight of herself in the mirror, and a little bit of her wondered if Sandra was right. When she looked at her reflection these days she didn't like what she saw. There was a dullness to her skin. And her eyelids did look a bit droopy. The skin under her jawline wasn't as taut as it could be. Her blonde hair was going darker, which meant the threads of grey that had started appearing shone out along her parting.

She sighed. It was downhill all the way now. Watching the twins blossom and bloom and sparkle brought it home all the more. Their skin was soft, with a sheen to it that no amount of jabs or infilling could bring. They had a shine to their hair that Ginny knew no masks or conditioners could bring to hers. They had a lustre, a brightness, a glow. And she had to admit she was jealous. No, not jealous, for she didn't begrudge her daughters their beauty, not for an instant. Envious? What was the point of envy? It just made you bitter and twisted. Surely it was better to accept that your time was over and embrace the signs of ageing? Not like the likes of Sandra, who were in desperate denial, fighting it to the bitter end.

Though she couldn't deny that Sandra did look good. In a line-up, it might be hard to tell which of them was the older. OK, so that look wasn't what she would go for herself – it was far too glamorous and high-maintenance – but Sandra was definitely eye-catching: her brow smooth, the skin taut across her cheekbones and jawline. Eyes bright and dewy. Hair sleek and glossy. Nails beautifully polished. Ginny looked down at her own hands. They were dry and chapped, the nails ragged. She often had to stand in when her girls were off sick, and she didn't bother with rubber gloves when she cleaned. And now she was paying the price.

Oh dear, she thought. She had committed the cardinal sin in this image-conscious era. She had Let Herself Go. She probably wasn't eating as well as she should at the moment, which meant that she had lost weight in the past couple of weeks, but at her age, ironically, weight loss was ageing. Losing that subcutaneous fat added years. Throw in the greying hair, the unkempt hands, the fact that she never wore anything but jeans and it was no wonder Keith couldn't muster up enthusiasm for any bedroom action.

Ginny wondered sadly whether a woman was ever allowed to be comfortable in her own skin. When you were young and in your teens, you wanted to look older. In your twenties, you didn't appreciate your relative youth – Kitty and Sasha, who were in their prime, were riddled with neuroses and insecurities about their looks. Then the baby-rearing years passed in a blur of stretch marks and spare tyres and hair loss. When you'd just about got over that, and were clawing back your confidence and self-esteem, then your husband left you for a younger model, sending you spiralling back down to square one.

Ginny thought there had been a small window when she had felt sexy and confident, just after she'd moved to Honeycote and first met Keith. She remembered one particular day, when her ex-husband David had turned up to moan about his lot, and she'd caught him looking at her rather longingly. She'd felt invincible that day. She'd got over her divorce and got herself a new man. She knew her eyes had been sparkling, that her bum had looked fantastic in her new jeans, that her choppy bob had made her look, in a good light, a tiny bit like Meg Ryan.

She didn't feel like Meg Ryan any more. Not at all. She fingered Sandra's brochure thoughtfully. Maybe she needed to get a grip on herself. Keith had been rather gruff in his goodbye this morning. There had been a moment when she sensed he wanted to say something important to her, but he hadn't. He'd told her to enjoy herself and scuttled off to the brewery.

Ginny sighed. If he was going to tell her it wasn't working, that it was all over, he would probably wait till after the wedding. Maybe she had some time to pull herself together. Or maybe she was a lost cause . . . ?

'Mum! Caroline's here!' Kitty was shouting up the stairs.

She wished fervently she wasn't going. She was going to look ridiculous, trailing round Puerto Banus after Mandy and the twins – even Caroline had fifteen years on her. She would look like some ageing chaperone, dogging their every footstep in case they fell into temptation. She imagined them being ushered into a pulsating, glittering nightclub and the bouncer putting up his hand to stop her, denying her entry on the grounds of lack of youth, lack of beauty. As she pictured the humiliation, her guts twisted inside her. It wasn't too late to pull out. She'd tell them she had a stomach upset.

'Come on, Mum!' Kitty was at the door, jumping up

and down with excitement. 'We're going to miss the plane if we don't hurry.'

Ginny sighed. There wasn't time to demur. Not now. Maybe a break was what she needed. It would give her a few days to look at herself, examine her life, try and put her relationship with Keith into perspective. She tucked Sandra's brochure into her handbag and picked up her case with a sigh. It contained a couple of linen skirts, some T-shirts and a cotton dress. A frumpy middle-aged woman's wardrobe. But then, that's what she was.

As Caroline's car disappeared out of the drive twenty minutes later, Sandra slipped into the driving seat of the Audi cabriolet she had hired for the duration of her visit and allowed herself a little pat on the back for a job well done.

She'd been as subtle as she could. Just sown those few tiny seeds of doubt. Ginny could protest all she liked that she was happy with the way she looked, but Sandra knew there wasn't a woman on the planet who didn't have reservations about her appearance.

No, Ginny would definitely be ripe for plucking. And Alejandro was just the man for the job. He could do more for a woman's self-esteem than any top cosmetic surgeon. After all, wasn't she testament to that herself?

She picked up her mobile phone and dialled the villa. When he answered, she allowed herself to imagine his bare torso, those sinewed arms, and her mouth watered.

'Alejandro. The girls are on their way. Now, don't forget, I want you to treat them all like princesses. Do you understand? I don't want them to lift a finger. You're to prepare all their meals. And clear up. Make their beds every day. And I want those bathrooms gleaming. If they want driving anywhere, you drop whatever you're doing. Do you get the picture?'

Sandra knew she could afford to talk to him like that, for she paid him extremely well to loll about in her house and water her peach trees while she was absent.

'Sure. No problem,' he replied easily. 'Everything is ready. The beds are all made. The refrigerator is full. There are fresh flowers. I have thought of everything.'

'Good. And Alejandro – there is just one more task. For which you will be . . . generously rewarded. But I will need evidence. Photographic evidence . . .'

And she outlined her instructions with precision.

The next phone call she made was to her ex-husband. For this she had a change of tone. Honeyed rather than assertive.

'Keith. It's Sandra. I wondered if we could have dinner tonight?'

'Dinner? You and me?'

He sounded very unsure. She pretended to sound anxious.

'It's just that I'd really appreciate your advice. There are a few . . . financial issues I want to discuss. I want to make sure that what I've decided is the best thing for Mandy.'

She knew that would swing it. Playing the helpless female usually worked. And Mandy was Keith's weak spot. She always had been.

'OK,' he sounded reluctant, but at least he had agreed.

'I'll book a table at the Lygon Arms.'

'The Lygon Arms?' Keith sounded startled. The hotel was definitely a special occasion venue; a five-star landmark in the picturesque village of Broadway.

'I think we should treat ourselves. Anyway, I've always

307

wanted to go there, and it's no fun eating on your own. I'll meet you there at eight.'

She rang off happily, slipping her phone back into the depths of her handbag. As she started up the ignition, she eyed Keeper's Cottage critically. It was certainly very pretty, and Keith and Mandy had done it out very tastefully. But it had no presence. It wasn't really a statement. Nevertheless, she had no doubt that it would sell quickly. As would her villa. Stick the value of the two together and they could probably afford something pretty spectacular – perhaps not a manor, but one of those substantial, sprawling country houses that the Cotswolds did so well. Like Honeycote House, she thought, but with heating that worked and windows that weren't about to fall out.

She remembered the first time she had stepped over the threshold at Honeycote House, when she had come to collect Mandy one weekend during a trip back from Spain. She had been rather intimidated by them all at the time. The Liddiards en masse were daunting even to the most socially confident. Sandra had done her best to be the life and soul of the party nevertheless, but had only succeeded in feeling loud and brash, especially in contrast to the graceful and dainty Lucy. She knew there had been glances exchanged behind her back, and a sigh of relief when she had left. And on the few occasions she had met them subsequently, she had definitely felt a fish out of water.

But she had changed. Then she had been a nobody; a dull housewife with a penchant for gin. Now Sandra Sherwyn was a force to be reckoned with. She was a successful entrepreneur, she could probably put her hands on more ready cash than all of the Liddiards put together, she looked fantastic and she was in total control of her life. She was in a position to wake up in the morning and do whatever she wanted. Have whatever she wanted. Success breeds confidence. She was living proof of that. Yes, decided Sandra. She was ready. She knew that with Keith by her side it would only be a matter of time before she was queen of the local scene.

Spain had been fantastic. Spain had given her the best years of her life so far. But it had been a lonely journey. She had worked tirelessly. Even when she was supposedly off duty she was networking, circulating, winning people over, spreading the word. It had paid off. But now it was time to kick back and enjoy the fruits of her labour. She wanted companionship, a social life, a home . . . not a sterile symbol of her success. No matter how stunning her villa was, it had never felt cosy, inviting, welcoming, relaxing. Spectacular and luxurious, maybe. But it could have belonged to anyone. She'd bought it fully decorated and furnished. There wasn't an iota of individuality within its walls.

And when she had her home, she wanted to sit at the head of her table, as guests, family and friends came and went, ate her food, drank her wine, danced to her music. She wanted people to fall over themselves to be invited into her inner circle. And she couldn't do that alone. She knew that to be a social success you had to be part of a couple. And Keith already had his foot in the door. He had a wide circle of friends, and an even wider circle of acquaintances. He had respect and credibility. The template was there. She just had to build on it.

Sandra started up the car and headed out of Kiplington towards Eldenbury. She'd phone the Lygon Arms to book a table, then buy a local paper and skim through the property section over a cup of coffee somewhere. She might be moving a bit too fast, but Sandra enjoyed anticipation. Looking forward to something was often more pleasurable than the reality. She adored plotting and scheming and planning, moving the chess pieces of life around to make sure she had checkmate every time.

While she was at the Lygon Arms later, she mused, she might just ask them about weddings. She was thinking of a nice quiet civil ceremony followed by lunch. Second time around it was better to be discreet. Especially when you were marrying your own ex-husband.

Later that afternoon, the hen party tumbled out of the MPV they'd hired at the airport, travel weary but full of excitement.

Sandra's villa was quite breathtaking. It was perched on a hillside with staggering sea views to one side and mountains to the other. There were gasps of delight at the lush greenery, the rambling terrace, the scent of the flowers, the glimpse of the azure blue swimming pool that winked in the sunlight.

Open-mouthed, they ventured inside.

The accommodation was palatial, centred around a large open-plan area with a vaulted ceiling, hung with a wrought-iron chandelier the size of a wagon wheel. To one side was a kitchen in a dark, warm, rustic wood set against bright blue and yellow ceramic tiles. A long table with benches down each side denoted the dining area, while the living room was marked out by three sofas at right angles to each other, carved out of wood and filled with dark blue linen cushions. On the wall was a flat-screen television and discreetly mounted speakers. Modern sea-scapes adorned the walls. There was little clutter, just a glass bowl filled with lemons, a vase of fresh flowers, and a couple of chunky wooden candle-sticks. It was almost like a luxury hotel.

'Bloody hell, Mandy. You never told us it was like this. This is film star stuff,' said Sasha accusingly.

Mandy herself was looking staggered. 'This is new. She bought it a few months ago, after she sold the clinics. She just had an apartment before. Nice, but nothing special. I'd got no idea.'

Suddenly the French windows that looked out onto the terrace opened, and a figure stepped into the room.

'Fuck!' whispered Kitty in awe.

The intruder was tall and lean. His hair was dark, but streaked fair in places by the sun and the sea. Loose, it would have curled down to just above his shoulders, but he'd caught it up in a leather thong, thereby showing off his razor-sharp cheekbones and his slanting eyes, as black as coal and fringed by Bambi eyelashes. A faint line of black stubble on his top lip and chin outlined his mouth. He wore nothing but a pair of faded jeans, slung low on his hips and held up by a battered leather belt with an elaborate buckle in the shape of a skull and crossbones.

'Ladies. You are a little earlier than I expected. The traffic from the airport must have been good.' He smiled in delight, his eyes lighting up, showing even white teeth. He indicated his bare torso. 'I apologize. I meant to dress for you. Excuse me.'

'Please. Don't worry.' Ginny spoke for all of them, the only one able to find her voice. 'You must be Alejandro.'

'And you must be Ginny.' He pronounced it 'genie' as he descended on her with his hand outstretched. 'Sandra told me you would be in charge.'

'For my sins,' replied Ginny, taking his hand with a blush and suddenly thinking of several other sins.

'I am here to do for you whatever you want. Sandra has said I must tend to your every need.'

'You're going to be jolly worn out by the end of the weekend, then,' said Caroline cheerfully. Whether it was being free from the tyranny of her husband and children, three gin and tonics on the plane, or the sight of Alejandro, it wasn't clear, but she seemed to have perked up immeasurably.

'I'll bring in your cases. Then I'll show you your rooms. And then I make cocktails on the terrace.' He turned to Mandy. 'This must be the beautiful bride-to-be.'

He took her hand and kissed it. Mandy visibly melted. The others all waited their turn, hearts thumping, as he correctly guessed who each one was, even divining which twin was which, then went outside to retrieve their luggage from the car. Five pairs of eyes watched his retreating muscular back with longing.

'How did he know who we all were?' wondered Sasha.

'Sandra will have described us. I'll be the fat, ginger one,' said Caroline.

'She never said he was a sex god,' breathed Kitty. 'I thought he was going to be some lecherous old man who'd ogle us by the pool.'

'He's totally divine,' giggled Ginny. 'He should come with a health warning.'

'First one to shag him gets fifty quid.' Caroline loved a bet. And a challenge.

'Dream on,' said Sasha. 'I bet he's got a girlfriend that looks like Penelope Cruz tucked away somewhere.'

There was a collective sigh as they individually realized they didn't have a hope.

'Come on,' said Ginny. 'Let's choose our rooms and go for a swim. I don't want to waste a moment.'

She suddenly felt the need to cool down. Was it a hot flush? That was all she needed. To be menopausal on top of everything else. Although now she was here she felt a bit better. You couldn't help but feel light-hearted in this wondrous setting. No wonder Sandra was so upbeat and optimistic. Never mind the cosmetic surgery – the sunshine alone made you feel ten years younger.

Alejandro prepared them the most delicious evening meal. The table was covered with colourful plates made from local pottery, piled high with *jamón* Serrano, gleaming black olives, tomato salad, chunks of manchego cheese, marinated red peppers, and his speciality, patatas bravas – wedges of potato cooked in paprika, and dunked into bowls of garlic mayonnaise.

'I hope nobody wants a snog later,' said Caroline, happily scooping up glistening blobs of mayo.

Thanks to Lucy's divine intervention, Percy was now sleeping from seven at night till seven the next, and it had made all the difference. Now she was able to get a decent night's sleep, Caroline felt able to cope. She'd even managed to get organized enough to book Percy and Constance into the crèche at the leisure centre in Eldenbury and start swimming. She'd dropped five pounds in just a fortnight, because she no longer needed to keep her energy levels up by stuffing biscuits and the children's tea.

She'd already decided to hit the shops the next day and buy Lucy something to say thank you. God knows how long she would have carried on in her postnatal fug. It was only now she felt almost back to normal that she realized how dangerously low she had felt, and she was grateful to her sister-in-law. Especially after she had been so foul and practically accused her of trying to seduce James. But luckily Lucy didn't bear grudges.

Caroline took a slurp of wine and giggled to herself as she imagined James coping with the dreaded bedtime ritual. Henry was pretty savage by the end of the day, and Constance never missed an opportunity to be unco-operative if she sensed someone was at the end of their tether. James was used to walking in the door at seven and helping himself to a drink while he listened to *The Archers* and read the paper at the kitchen table, oblivious to the mayhem going on upstairs while his wife administered baths, bottles and bedtime stories. Caroline relished the image of him withstanding Henry's pleas for yet another Thomas the Tank Engine adventure, as Constance repeatedly threw her rag doll out of bed and demanded its retrieval.

There had been a moment the day before when she had nearly bottled out of going, but Lucy had soon put her straight.

'James will survive. It'll do him good. And anyway, what can go wrong? He can always ring me if he really comes unstuck.'

Caroline had left the fridge bulging with food, and several lists, timetables and menus stuck to the wall next to it. All James had to do was follow her instructions. And now she was determined to make the most of her few days of freedom. She was determined not to feel guilty, or worry about what was going on at home.

'So, Alejandro,' she purred, piling another helping of Serrano ham onto her plate. 'Where's the action round here?'

Alejandro was in the kitchen making *crema Catalana* – the Spanish equivalent of crème brulée, served in individual terracotta dishes. He had a flat metal disc on a long handle which was heated up then applied to a layer of sugar sprinkled on top of the custard, whereupon it melted into a hard layer of toffee. He looked up from his task with a reassuring smile.

'Don't worry. I will get you all the best tables, into all the best clubs.'

'Good,' said Caroline, licking her fingers. 'This is my first taste of freedom for nearly five years. I want to make the most of it.'

Ginny shot her a worried glance. She knew Caroline had once had a bit of a reputation, and that she was hard to control when she'd had a few. What if she went off the rails over the weekend? The Liddiards would never forgive her—

With a start she realized Alejandro was filling up her cava glass and pressing it into her hand.

'Relax,' he urged her, and looked deep into her eyes. Colouring furiously, she managed to smile back and lifted the glass obediently to her lips. He was right. Why should she worry? Caroline was old enough to look after herself. Why did she always feel the need to cluck around everyone, Ginny wondered.

'Shopping tomorrow,' Sasha was declaring. 'I need an outfit for the evening do.'

'Aren't you going to wear your bridesmaid's dress?' demanded Kitty, a little hurt. She'd spent the past week up until midnight making the outfits, since Mandy had rather belatedly decided that she wanted the twins and Sophie and Georgina to escort her down the aisle as well as Constance.

'There is no way I'm going to strut my stuff in white organza.' Sasha was adamant.

'Oh God,' groaned Caroline, suddenly brought back down to earth. 'I've got to find something too.' She poked at her middle.

'Join the club,' said Ginny gloomily.

'You know what?' said Alejandro, bearing a tray full of completed desserts. 'You will all look gorgeous, whatever you wear.'

Five pairs of eyes looked at him doubtfully as he handed out the calorie-laden pots of sin.

'That's not going to help the cause, is it?' observed Caroline.

They all picked up their spoons regardless, unable to resist temptation. It was going to be that sort of weekend.

Sandra arrived at the Lygon Arms nice and early. The famous hotel was the perfect combination of ancient and luxurious. A sprawling Cotswold coaching inn whose frontage took up the centre of the chocolate box village of Broadway, it was all flagstone floors and inglenooks and oil paintings. England at its best. As the chill of the night air took hold, fires were being lit while guests put the finishing touches to their appearance before coming down for pre-dinner drinks. Ice buckets were filled, the chefs furiously chopped vegetables and reduced sauces, and the last of the stiff linen napkins were put onto the tables with pride.

Sandra embarked on her search for the perfect spot for her encounter with Keith. The bar, she decided, was cosy, but not intimate enough. She prowled around until she found a little cubby hole off the foyer, furnished with a couple of deep sofas where guests could take coffee and read the paper. She ordered a bottle of Dom Perignon to be brought there, then sank into the sofa nearest the window. She decided against kicking off her boots and tucking her legs underneath her. That was a bit too relaxed. That could come later.

She'd stage-managed the whole evening very carefully. The champagne to start with, and a little plate of appetizers, to give them enough time to unwind and relax together. It was vital that she should put Keith at his ease as soon as possible. Then a delicious dinner in a table tucked away in the dining room, before retreating for coffee and brandies on this very sofa, by which time the lights would be dimmed and the fire lit. By then, Keith would have drunk far too much to drive home. She'd make sure his glass was kept topped up. When it came time for him to go, she would express concern. It shouldn't be too hard to persuade him upstairs, even if it was just on the pretext of another coffee to sober him up. She'd booked the room. Well, a suite, actually. With a sumptuous four-poster bed and a palatial bathroom . . .

She could hear herself making light of it even now.

'It's not as if we haven't shared a room before. We've got nothing to hide from each other.'

Of course, once he was in situ, then she could move in. It wouldn't take much. She could remember his weaknesses. And she'd learnt an awful lot since then, courtesy of Alejandro.

She popped her glass on the arm of the sofa, selected a magazine and pretended to be thoroughly engrossed while she waited. But despite her carapace of confidence she found it hard to concentrate. She took another sip of her drink, disconcerted to find that she cared so much. After all, she'd trained herself to be impenetrable over the past few years.

She hadn't realized quite how much the evening's outcome mattered.

Keith walked into the foyer of the Lygon Arms at two minutes past eight. He'd passed it on countless occasions, but had never actually been in, and he was charmed by what he found. It was understated and gracious, with a roaring log fire, stone walls, tapestries and a large table scattered with glamorous international magazines. It had the hushed air of genteel luxury; the rooms smelled of beeswax and lilies and wood-smoke. He worried that he might be underdressed in just a casual jacket, that he should have put a suit on, but the other guests he spied looked to be smart but casual. It was a country hotel, after all, not overly formal. But special nevertheless.

Keith realized that he couldn't remember the last time he and Ginny had gone somewhere like this to eat. They always ended up at the Chinese in Eldenbury or the Honeycote Arms. A sudden vision of her popped into his head, and he felt filled with remorse. He hadn't been able to face saying goodbye properly this morning. He'd made his escape while she was in the shower. How cowardly could you get? He knew they'd arrived safely, because

Mandy had phoned, but he'd made no effort to contact Ginny and make sure she was all right.

It wasn't long to go now, he told himself. By this time tomorrow he would know his fate. And when it was all over – if it was all over, and he got the all clear – then he could make it up to her. He'd bring her here, in fact. Pamper her, give her some space from the twins, give themselves some time to rediscover what they were all about. They were going to do a lot more of that, Keith decided.

He found Sandra in a little snug, sitting on a sofa engrossed in a magazine. She stood up with a welcoming smile, dressed in a grey cowl-neck sweater dress and shiny brown leather boots, several strands of pearls strung round her neck. She looked very much at home, as if this was where she belonged, and Keith was once again amazed at how she had changed. Five years ago she would have stuck out like a sore thumb, wearing something garish and inappropriate and commenting in a loud voice on her surroundings and the other guests.

'Isn't it perfect here?' She gave him a kiss on each cheek. 'I'm thinking of taking up full-time residency.'

Keith settled down in an armchair adjacent to the sofa she was occupying. It was deep and comfortable, and as she handed him a glass of champagne he felt himself relax. Strange though the situation was, this had been the right thing to do. Otherwise he would have found himself alone in a spookily empty Keeper's Cottage with only the television to keep his mind off the horrors of the weekend ahead. He took a tentative sip. He mustn't drink too much before his operation. He wanted to be as fit as possible.

'The girls all arrived safely,' Sandra told him. 'I've got

Alejandro keeping an eye so they don't get into mischief.'

'The whole thing is very generous of you.'

She batted his comment away.

'No point in the villa sitting empty.' She peered at him. 'You should have a few days there yourself. You look as if you could do with some sun.'

Keith smiled gingerly.

The waiter arrived with two leatherbound menus, and handed them one each. 'Let me tell you the chef's special,' he said.

'I hope he is,' quipped Sandra, with a girlish giggle. 'I've seen the prices.'

She was fizzing inside. This was going to be a wonderful evening; she could feel it in her bones.

Keith escorted Sandra into the dining room with its huge vaulted ceiling and coats of arms on the wall. They were shown to a discreet table tucked away in the corner. Throughout the first two courses, they chatted, politeness gradually warming up into animation as a couple of glasses of excellent Riesling slipped down. Sandra was very amusing about the acquisition and subsequent sale of her clinics, describing how as a panic-stricken middle-aged woman she knew exactly how to prey on the vanity of the inhabitants of the Costa del Sol. Keith had to admire her.

'Of course, I've kept the flagship,' she told him. 'It virtually runs itself. So now I'm looking to invest over here. Of course, there's not so much sun, so there aren't as many wrinkles. But there's still a huge market. And the more people who succumb, the worse the ones who haven't look.'

'But not everyone can afford it,' Keith pointed out.

'Don't worry. I'm looking into payment plans. Low-interest loans. And of course the half-price introductory offer.'

'I'm not sure if I approve.' Keith somehow felt it was wrong, exploiting women's vanity when the ageing process was inevitable.

'If I don't do it, somebody else will.' Sandra speared her Gressingham duck with vigour. 'And at least I make sure my staff are properly trained. There are a lot of cowboys out there. My standards are the very highest.'

If the way she looked was anything to go by, thought Keith, then she wasn't lying. 'I must say,' he admitted, 'I admire you. I would never have guessed you had it in you.'

'The overweight, gin-swilling Solihull housewife?'

He hesitated. It was all right for her to say it, but not him. She grinned.

'It's all right. I know that's what I was.'

She put down her fork, suddenly serious.

'Keith – I think I owe you an apology.'

She put a hand on his. Keith swallowed nervously, feeling it would be rude to snatch it away. He felt as if he was being pinned to the table.

'What on earth for?'

'I treated you really badly. It's taken me this long to realize. At the time, of course, I thought I was right.'

'I'm not following you.'

'When I left you. It was stupid. Cruel. Selfish. And you had done absolutely nothing to deserve it.'

'Oh.' Keith was surprised. He remembered only too well the barbed remarks she had slung at him on departure. About him being boring, married to his work, not having time for her. He had been hurt and bewildered. He had only ever tried to do his best for Sandra and Mandy. Sandra had been vociferous in her complaints at the time, so he was astonished that she was now admitting culpability.

'I've had some time to think about it. And I want to explain,' she was saying. 'Not so that you can excuse me, because it was inexcusable. But I think you deserve an explanation.'

'OK . . .' Keith agreed cautiously, wondering what on earth was going to come out of the woodwork. He managed to extricate his hand from under hers in order to pick up his glass.

'The long and the short of it is . . . I was bored. Out of my skull. Now that I'm fulfilled, now that I have challenges to face, risks to take and rewards to reap, it's crystal clear. I had no real role in life. Nothing to get my teeth into, or to give me my own identity. You were so busy with work, Mandy was off at boarding school, and I was beside myself with the tedium of it all.' She leaned in. 'I don't blame you for one minute, Keith. You had a business to keep afloat. It wasn't your responsibility to make sure I had something to fill my days. It never occurred to me to find a job or start a little business. And I'm afraid that I mistook having affairs as the way out of my rut. I felt flattered. I felt alive. I thought fantastic! I can leave boring old Solihull and my boring old husband behind and be a new person.'

She broke off. She seemed to be struggling to find the next words.

'But you are a new person,' Keith prompted her. 'Look at you. You're incredible.'

'Yes,' she said softly, and to his surprise he saw a tear hovering in the corner of one eye. She blinked rapidly to suppress it. 'Most people would think I've got everything. The world at my feet. But there's one thing I don't have.'

She looked up. Her eyes were filled with tears now, shiny bright. Her mouth trembled.

'You,' she said simply, then looked away as if the pain was too much. Keith watched in astonishment as she wiped her eyes with her napkin.

'Me?' he exclaimed, flabbergasted. 'But . . . I thought . . . I would have thought . . . Sandra, look at you. You're an incredibly glamorous and successful woman. You could have anyone you wanted.'

'Except the one I really want.' She had composed herself now. She managed a smile. 'I bitterly regret it, Keith. I never fell in love with anybody else. I've only ever loved you. But it's taken me five years to see what I lost, through my own stupidity.'

She took hold of his hands across the table, and looked deep into his eyes. Keith could only think of one way out.

'I've got cancer.'

Sandra was shocked into silence for a good ten seconds. Her mouth dropped open, and she gaped like a goldfish.

'Cancer?' she stammered. 'What of? And how long? Have you had it, I mean. Not how long have you got. My God, Keith . . .' She took a slug of burgundy. All the colour had drained from her face.

'It's OK,' Keith said calmly. 'It might not be as bad as it sounds. It's cancer of the prostate. It's very common, and treatable if caught early enough.'

And he went on to explain his diagnosis. And his

prognosis. And tell her he was due to go in for his prostatectomy the very next day.

'With any luck, I should be out by Monday. And no
one need ever know there was anything wrong.'

'But I did!' said Sandra triumphantly. 'You see. I knew
there was something wrong, didn't I?'

Then she grabbed hold of both his hands.

'You poor, poor darling. Don't tell me you've been
keeping this all to yourself?'

'Well, yes—'

'But you can't go through all that worry on your own!'

'I have. I didn't want to burden anyone else. How
could I tell Mandy, when she's about to get married? And
Ginny . . .'

He fell silent. His reasons for keeping it quiet from
Ginny were so complicated. To explain it to Sandra would
mean voicing the one fear he had never spoken of: that he
might not make it. Keeping his distance from Ginny was
his way of protecting her.

Sandra pursed her lips. 'What kind of a relationship is
that, when you can't share the lows as well as the highs?'

'There just didn't seem any point in worrying Ginny till
I knew there was something to worry about.'

Sandra shook her head in disbelief. 'I can't believe that
she didn't sense something was wrong. If I could see it,
why couldn't she?'

Keith shrugged awkwardly. He felt very uncomfortable
with his relationship being analysed like this. But perhaps
that had always been his problem; an inability to bring
unpleasant things out into the open, at least when they
concerned him. It was odd – he found himself able to discuss the twins with Ginny, or her ex-husband, and offer

very practical advice. But when it came to Keith Sherwyn, he was a closed book.

'I know it seems odd,' he went on to defend his decision. 'But I felt the fewer people who knew about it the better. I didn't want to spoil the wedding. Surely you understand that?'

Thoroughly shaken by Keith's revelation, Sandra excused herself and went into the ladies. Her hands were trembling slightly with the shock as she re-applied her lipstick in the mirror.

She would have to completely rethink her strategy. Obviously it was quite out of the question to lure Keith upstairs. Sex was going to be the last thing on his mind right now. Christ, how horrible. Cancer. She felt very frightened all of a sudden. In all her meticulous planning, she hadn't seen this one coming, and she felt her confidence draining away. Even she couldn't outmanoeuvre the big C. Keith's future was out of her hands. Some greater being than Sandra had already decided what was going to happen. But maybe she could still use the situation to her advantage. He would be feeling vulnerable. Frightened. Poor, brave Keith. There weren't many people who would suffer in silence like he had.

Well, Sandra would look after him. She could do tender loving care. At least she thought she could. She'd never done it before, but if that's what it took . . . And one thing was for sure – he wasn't going to get any from Ginny. While the cat was away . . .

She clicked the lid back on her lipstick, fluffed up her hair, and practised a look of loving concern in the mirror. Loving, with a hint of anguish.

'Are you all right?'

She hadn't noticed another guest coming out of a cubicle to wash her hands.

'Yes, thank you,' snapped Sandra.

'Sorry. You looked as if you were in pain.'

'I've never felt better.' And she snatched up her bag and walked out of the cloakroom.

By the time pudding was cleared away and they had nibbled half-heartedly at some local cheeses, Keith found he had completely unburdened himself to Sandra. It was such a relief to be able to share his problems with someone. And in order to deflect her attention away from his impending operation, he told her about the problems at the brewery. He left out the more confidential and lurid details about illegitimate children and demands for large sums of money, but confided in her that they were having to sell.

'I don't have the strength or the enthusiasm to carry on any more,' he admitted sadly. 'And if my illness does prove serious, I'll be better off without it. At least this way I can come out with a share of the profits from the sale.'

'If there are any profits,' Sandra pointed out. 'No one in their right mind would pay top dollar for it in its current state, by the sound of things.'

'Actually, we've already had an offer.'

'How much?'

'Well, an expression of interest,' he corrected himself. 'And we haven't negotiated a figure yet,' he said carefully. 'But they've given us a very interesting proposal outlining what they'd like to do.'

'If they can get it at a knock-down price.' Sandra didn't see the point in beating about the bush.

Keith clutched the stem of his brandy glass, wondering if Sandra was right. He'd been so preoccupied he hadn't really focused on Honeycote Ales recently. He'd just been relieved there might be a taker. The prospective purchaser probably was toying with them, teasing them, tantalizing them, all the time ready to pounce and screw them right down, knowing that Honeycote Ales needed them more than they needed Honeycote Ales.

Sandra was staring rather intently at her oat cake. She seemed lost in thought.

'Sandra?'

She looked up, frowning. 'Really, all you need is someone who will buy out Mickey and James.'

'And me,' Keith reminded her. 'I want out too.'

'No, you don't.' Sandra shook her head in disagreement. 'You only think you do because of what you're going through at the moment. You love that brewery. So really, what we're looking at is finding someone who'll buy out the Liddiard brothers, then invest enough to get the brewery back on its feet. In order to make it work for you and Patrick and Mandy. The Sherwyn-Liddiard dynasty,' she finished with a flourish.

'I suppose so.'

Sandra felt a flutter of excitement in her stomach. She couldn't believe the way everything had fallen into her lap this evening. Not that she would have wished cancer on Keith, she told herself hastily, but she had a feeling that he was going to be all right. With this latest news, however, not only did she have an emotional hold on him, but possibly a financial one as well.

She picked up her glass.

'It's almost as if it's meant to be,' she said dreamily.

'With Patrick and Mandy marrying next weekend, I can't think of a more wonderful wedding present.'

Keith didn't know if it was the rich food, the stress, the brandy, or the implications of what she had just said, but he definitely felt the room start to spin.

'What?'

'Honeycote Ales,' she finished triumphantly. 'A bit difficult to wrap, maybe. But a damn sight more useful than a four-slice toaster.'

It took all of Alejandro's powers of persuasion to stop Ginny from helping with the washing up, once everyone had eaten their fill.

'But you prepared everything!' she protested.

'It's my job. And you are on holiday.' Alejandro steered her firmly towards the sofa, where the others were already installed in front of the plasma television.

'Don't complain, Mum. Make the most of it.' Sasha was flipping through the channels with the remote.

'It just seems rude.' Ginny sat down reluctantly, piqued that nobody else seemed to have any problem with him doing the donkey work. Kitty was sitting at Caroline's feet, painting her toe nails – 'I can't reach them myself,' Caroline had complained – while Mandy was flicking through the last of the magazines they had bought on the plane. Eventually, though, she began to relax and became absorbed in the Harrison Ford movie Sasha had settled on.

When the last plate had been put away, Alejandro came over. 'Anybody wants to come for a drink?'

'It's a bit late, isn't it?' said Ginny, looking at her watch. It was gone half eleven.

Alejandro laughed. 'Everybody in Puerto Banus is just starting to come out to play.'

The girls debated his proposition for a moment, but the general consensus was they were all exhausted after the journey and would make an early night of it.

'We need our beauty sleep,' explained Sasha. 'We're going to need it for all those millionaires tomorrow night.'

'Then I will see you at breakfast. Do you have any special requests? I usually do Señora Sherwyn coffee and rolls.'

'Fresh mango would be nice, if you can get hold of it,' said Sasha airily.

'Sasha!'

'Only kidding, Mum!'

Alejandro had slipped out into the night and got on his moped. It had been an interesting evening, he thought. They were all so attractive, but different. Even the twins. Kitty might be quieter than her sister, but was possibly the wilder deep down, while Sasha was all talk, he suspected. The redhead, Caroline, wouldn't need much encouragement, but would be trouble afterwards; an emotional time bomb. The bride-to-be was untouchable, beautiful but untouchable – definitely a one-man woman. And what a lucky man. And as for Ginny. She was adorable, but she didn't know it. She was tense, unable to relax, and gravely lacking in confidence – all common enough problems at her age, when insecurity and self-doubt seemed to rampage out of all proportion. If he was to carry out his instructions, Alejandro decided, he needed help. It would take weeks to wear her down of her own accord, even with his powers of persuasion.

He wove the bike through the back streets, parked and slipped in through a tiny doorway that led into a crowded bar. It was a far cry from the glamorous establishments that lined the marina; this was a seedy joint, generally filled with the workers who toiled behind the scenes creating the ritzy façade that kept the tourists happy. Fishermen, boat-builders, waiters. It wasn't his usual choice of venue, but tonight he needed to find someone in particular.

He pushed his way through the sweaty throng and found Raoul in his usual place, looking fat and happy. As well he might. Business was booming. He had a huge network out there working on his behalf, suave and well-dressed, able to get past the bouncers and security staff, for nobody in their right minds would let the rancid, long-haired Raoul into their establishment. Not that he cared a jot. The way things were going, he'd be able to buy the whole of the marina before long.

Raoul looked askance at his friend when he joined him at the bar. The two of them had been at school together and were still firm friends, even though Alejandro disapproved of Raoul and Raoul thought Alejandro was a fool, dancing attendance on rich older women for a pittance. He'd often tried to recruit him to work the clubs – with looks like that Alejandro would make them both a fortune. But Alejandro steadfastly refused to get involved in the drug business. So Raoul was bemused by his request.

'What's the story, then?'

'Hen weekend at the villa.'

Raoul nodded sagely. The hen and stag scene in Puerto Banus had been largely responsible for his rise in profit. 'You want to keep the ladies happy, huh?'

Alejandro smiled thinly. The less said, the better.

Raoul rummaged in his inside pocket. He didn't usually keep stuff on him, just enough for personal use. But Alejandro wasn't asking for much.

'You wanna ask me over to enjoy the party?'

'I don't think so, Raoul. No offence.'

Raoul laughed until his cheeks wobbled, then pulled out a little plastic bag.

'Enjoy, my friend. And don't forget – you wanna join me in the business, we can clean up . . .'

Alejandro took his booty. 'Thanks. But no thanks.'

He made himself scarce as quickly as he could. He hated that bar. It reminded him of the squalor and the poverty he had come from. He was working so hard to get out. He'd been saving for three years for a deposit on his own apartment, away from his mother. Somewhere he could take his girlfriend, instead of squatting at Señora Sherwyn's when she wasn't there. And the money Sandra had offered him for this weekend's task was going to help him reach his target.

Alejandro threw the little bag up in the air with glee, then tucked it into his jacket pocket. The last thousand euros were in sight. He was going to have his own space at last.

15

S andra rose at six on Saturday morning. It had been gone midnight by the time she and Keith had said their rather solemn goodbyes the night before. Her plans might have changed somewhat in the light of his revelation, but they were watertight nevertheless. Never let it be said that Sandra Sherwyn couldn't think on her feet, she thought, as she swept around the twenty-four-hour supermarket just outside Eldenbury.

Her heart had gone out to Keith as he had driven off from the Lygon Arms. He looked so vulnerable, alone at the wheel, his head silhouetted in the street lights. How awful for him, to be going back to an empty house knowing what was to come the next day. She couldn't bear to imagine how he would feel when he woke, which was why she was now determined to get to Keeper's Cottage as soon as possible. She didn't want him to be alone any longer than he had to. Swiftly, she bought an Ian Rankin paperback, a Sudoku puzzle book, a new sponge bag filled with men's toiletries, several bottles of elderflower cordial and a bag of the barley sugar sweets she knew were his favourite. Little things to show she cared. Little things that Ginny should be buying, she thought triumphantly, as she paid for the goods and hurried back to her car.

She was at Keeper's Cottage by ten to seven. She knew Keith was leaving at half past, in order to be at the hospital by quarter to nine.

'I'm only staying for a couple of nights.' Keith looked at her booty, alarmed. 'At least I hope so.'

'You want to have everything at your fingertips, just in case.'

Sandra tucked her thoughtful extras into his overnight bag, then busied herself tidying the kitchen. She couldn't make him breakfast, as he was to have nil by mouth in anticipation of the anaesthetic, but she wanted to make herself useful. And she couldn't bear to sit down with him and just wait. She flipped on the television, ostensibly to catch the headlines, but actually to fill the silence that otherwise she would feel obliged to fill with inane chatter.

Keith looked at the clock, trying to remember the time difference between Kiplington and the Costa del Sol, but his brain felt like mush.

'I'm wondering if perhaps I should phone Ginny after all,' he said.

'It's too late now,' Sandra told him, peeling off her rubber gloves with a snap. 'You'll just ruin the weekend for her. And Mandy. Come on, let's pack up the car.'

She led him out to her Audi.

'It's OK. I can drive myself,' Keith protested.

'No, you can't. What about when you come out? You'll be in no fit state.'

Sandra flipped open the boot and slung his overnight bag inside.

'I hadn't thought of that,' he admitted.

'It seems to me you haven't thought anything through very much,' chided Sandra. 'It's lucky I'm here to help.'

Keith had to admit that he was grateful for her presence. He had only just got to sleep when he woke at five with a sudden start and a heavy heart, too frightened to go back to sleep in case he overslept. The hands of the clock seemed to be made of lead, and he had nothing to think about but his own fate. What was going to happen? What would they find? Would he come round to find Mr Jackson looking down at him sorrowfully? Or would he not come round at all? Would he have a violent reaction to the anaesthetic or the latex on the surgeon's gloves or would his body reject any blood given to him if he needed a transfusion? He didn't allow himself to imagine a happy outcome, as he felt it was bad luck. Although some would tell him that positive thinking and visualization would bring about the desired result, Keith didn't subscribe to that school of thought. He shied away from counting his chickens. After all, if he expected the worst, he couldn't be disappointed.

His head was throbbing with tension by the time he got into the passenger seat. As Sandra slipped in beside him, she gave him a reassuring pat on the arm.

'You're in the best possible hands, remember,' she told him. 'And they've caught it early. There's no reason why you shouldn't make a full recovery. The tumour's contained in the prostate; it's not aggressive . . .' She repeated everything he'd told her back to him, spreading out her hands to indicate there was only one conclusion, then gave him a sympathetic smile. 'I understand. It must be awful. I had a lump once . . . I didn't sleep for weeks.'

'Did you?' Keith looked at her, horrified.

'It was benign. Just a bit of fatty tissue. But the waiting was terrible.'

Keith stared at her. To think she had been through the same thing, but hadn't had any choice about whether to share her agony.

'I'm so sorry.'

'Don't worry about it. I'm fine now.'

'No. I mean, I'm sorry about us. You shouldn't have had to go through that on your own.'

'It was my own fault, wasn't it?'

'I don't know,' said Keith slowly. 'Was it? Surely I should have seen that you were unhappy. Unfulfilled. Maybe I was just burying myself in my work because I didn't want to face the truth?'

It had been worrying about the past which had kept him awake till dawn. For all those years he had blamed Sandra for the breakdown of their marriage, but after last night he was able to see it all from a different angle. There had been so much misunderstanding, so many assumptions, and now it was too late to go back and address what had gone wrong. He had shut her out of his life. Just as he was now shutting Ginny out. He had become cold and distant because he hadn't known how else to behave. Of course Sandra had left him.

The two of them gazed at each other.

'We never talked about it,' said Keith. 'Not properly.'

'I didn't exactly give you the chance.'

Keith felt choked. Suddenly there didn't seem to be enough air in the car for both of them. He put a hand to his collar, trying to loosen his tie. He couldn't find the right words for what he wanted to say. Anyway, it was far too late for reconciliation. In a few hours' time he might be lying on the mortuary slab. He felt a bead of sweat trickle down the back of his neck.

'Would it be all right if we had the roof down?' he finally managed.

Patrick stepped onto the station platform at Eldenbury, trying his best to look inconspicuous. It was unlikely that he would see anyone he knew getting onto the train to Paddington, but sod's law said there would be some cheery soul who would come bounding up to him. That was the problem with being born, brought up and having a family business in a small town. Everybody knew you. Everybody thought they owned you. It was on a par with celebritydom; you lived in a goldfish bowl. Not that it really mattered. He and Mayday had both agreed that being seen on a train together could be passed off as co-incidence, whereas driving in a car would not.

He saw her sitting on a bench at the far end of the platform. She was wearing a bottle-green crushed velvet frock coat with high heeled leopard-skin boots and not, as far as he could see, much else. He sauntered over to her casually, so that any onlooker would not suspect they had arranged to meet.

'Hi.'

She looked up. Her eyes glittered green to match her coat, and Patrick remembered her disconcerting penchant for coloured contact lenses. It had confused him on more than one occasion. Her mass of hair was in a loose pony-tail tied to one side.

'You look gorgeous,' he said, because she did.

'I got us first-class tickets,' she grinned in reply. 'You can upgrade for a fiver at weekends.'

The train rumbled in. Patrick followed her on board. The first-class carriage they chose was virtually empty;

just one whiskery gentleman and a businesslike woman, neither of whom they recognized. As the train drew out, Patrick stretched his legs out, relaxed and grinned. He was determined to enjoy the weekend. It would be an escape from the nightmares of the past few weeks. Not the wedding preparations as such, for he was looking forward to that, but all the other clandestine stuff. Kay – although she had kept her head down, she played on Patrick's conscience. And the brewery. Although the way things were looking, that particular cloud seemed to have a silver lining.

The proposal they'd had from the potential investor looked amazing. The plans were ambitious but realistic, outlined in an achievable time-frame that made the most of what they already had. In other words, it built upon Honeycote Ales' strength whilst bringing in innovations that had made Patrick's heart beat with excitement. Whoever the investor was, they had respect for what already existed, but enough flair and imagination to take the company to another level.

But he wasn't going to spend the weekend thinking about whether they could strike a deal, and what it meant for everyone. This was his time. His much deserved first and last moment of freedom. He looked over at Mayday, her hands curled round a cup of cappuccino, gazing out of the window. She looked rather pensive, and Patrick wondered if she was thinking about her grandmother. She deserved a break too – she hadn't taken any compassionate leave after the funeral. He was going to make sure they both enjoyed themselves.

Mayday watched the telegraph poles slipping past outside. She had resisted the temptation to buy a copy of the *Financial Times* to read on the train. That might have aroused Patrick's suspicions. She'd been devouring it over the past few weeks, scouring its pages for ideas, picking up key phrases and concepts that would underpin the proposal she and Robert had worked on together, holed up in his office until the small hours. Mayday's only worry was that Robert's wife Fleur might get suspicious about what they were up to and come in screaming like a banshee. Robert, however, was very philosophical about the possibility.

'We're not guilty of anything, are we?' he pointed out quite reasonably. 'We're working.'

He seemed happy to give her his advice for nothing. She could have afforded to pay him whatever he asked, but he was so enchanted by the prospect of her buying into Honeycote Ales that he wanted to make sure she presented herself to best effect. To Robert it was like a fairytale. He liked and admired both Mayday and the Liddiards, and was firmly convinced that they would flourish together. So he'd given her the benefit of his experience and advice quite willingly – gleefully, in fact. He'd even contacted a friend of his who was a venture capitalist and asked him to look over their business plan, and it had been given the seal of approval.

Her core idea was to develop the brewery itself. Mayday knew that the building was under-utilized; that there were rooms lying empty and outbuildings that had fallen into disuse. Her plan was to convert the superfluous accommodation into a one-stop food emporium encompassing an organic butcher, a greengrocer, a cheesemonger and a bakery as well as a comprehensive deli. With readily available parking and the lure of a café, it would be like a mini shopping village, and she knew there would be hordes of wealthy people happy to spend a morning topping up their fridges and larders with the best local produce. The area was full of foodies who snipped recipes out of the weekend supplements, and subsequently charged around looking for smoked pimenton and pomegranate molasses. Besides, it had become such a nightmare to park in Eldenbury, customers would prefer to go a little out of their way if they could be sure of a pleasant experience. And it would be a lure for tourists too, who would be able to take a bit of the Cotswolds home to their kitchens. With careful planning and some judicious building work, the brewery could still run in tandem with the new concept. If necessary, the brewery offices could be housed in a separate building in order to maximize the retail space. And Robert had suggested that they might be able to get a grant to fund a visitors' centre: several breweries around the country exploited their heritage in this way.

As for the tied houses, Mayday had divided them up into three categories to focus their development. Indulge took its inspiration from the Honeycote Arms; gastro-pubs with fine wine lists which attracted wealthy, aspirational diners. Relax represented the more traditional hostelries whose facilities would be developed to attract locals and families – darts, dominoes, skittles, playgardens, children's menus. And finally Escape, spearheaded by the Horse and Groom, where the accommodation would be invested in for the tourist trade.

She wanted to establish Honeycote as a brand, a trademark that was quintessentially English, representative of the unique and breathtaking area it was based in, exploiting its qualities, its produce, and its traditions while making the most of twenty-first century trends. As landlady of the Horse and Groom, she understood the demographics of the indigenous population as well as the needs of the tourists. Her plans served them equally well. Robert had been impressed. She had been unashamed when she told him she had kept his wife's floristry business under careful scrutiny – she had watched Twig flourish with interest, and it had told her that there were lots of people with a huge disposable income in the area who wanted to make their lives more pleasurable. You only had to walk in there on a Friday afternoon and see the ranks of hand-tied arrangements waiting to be delivered to homes round the county ready for the weekend.

If the experience had taught Mayday anything, it was that even if she didn't get her chance with Honeycote Ales, she couldn't stand still. She had the bit between her teeth; she was desperate for a challenge. And she knew she understood the basic principles of business. As she and Robert worked through their plan that became more and more apparent. She could see pitfalls a mile off, find solutions to problems, and if it was clear an idea wouldn't work she was able to drop it rather than cling onto it stubbornly. Her time at the hotel had been a perfect blueprint, after all. She had never been afraid to introduce innovations and new ways of doing things. And she'd turned over the biggest profit for the brewery the year before. OK, so the Horse and Groom was their biggest tied house, but it would have been very easy to make a loss. If that didn't prove her credentials, then nothing did.

She was absolutely dying to discuss all her ideas with Patrick. But he hadn't given any hint of what was happening, so she had to keep quiet – any clue that she knew and she would give away her identity. Besides, this weekend wasn't about Honeycote Ales. It was about them. Patrick and Mayday. And whether they had any future together. It was exactly a week before the wedding. This was her final chance.

At last, the train insinuated its way into the station, and they joined the queue for a cab. Mayday gave the driver the address of the hotel. Ten minutes later, they pulled up outside Claridge's.

'What are we doing here?' Patrick frowned. He'd expected some faceless chain hotel with anonymous bedrooms.

Mayday looked rather bashful. 'I've got a confession to make.'

Patrick looked at her suspiciously. It was very unlike Mayday to be coy. She was always totally upfront.

She gave him a rather tentative smile. 'My gran left me some money.'

Time stood still for a moment while Mayday made up her mind whether to tell him the truth. Once the secret was out, there was no going back. She'd told herself all along that she didn't want to buy him. She didn't want his attitude tainted by the lure of filthy lucre. Yet she longed to give him a taste of the life he could have with her. Pulling up at Claridge's was only the beginning.

Perhaps she could give him the taste without the whole truth.

Half the truth. She'd tell him half.

'Not a fortune. Just enough to have a bit of fun with. So I booked us in here.' She hugged him in excitement. 'I've got us a suite. On the top floor.'

'Mayday, you shouldn't have done that. You should

have spent it on yourself.' Patrick felt mortified. After the horrible time she'd had recently, Mayday deserved a treat.

'This is on myself. I've always wanted to stay at a posh hotel, only there's no point in me coming on my own. It would be miserable. With you it'll be fun.' She flashed him one of her conspiratorial smiles. 'Anyway, I'm planning to go wild in Harvey Nichols this afternoon. Come on.'

He couldn't argue, as she grabbed him by the hand and pulled him into the foyer. Patrick was aware that the tophatted doormen were looking at him askance. But he smiled to himself and followed her.

'Mr and Mrs Perkins?' the receptionist was saying.

Mayday looked at Patrick, not sure what to say. He gave a nod.

'That's right,' he said, slipping an arm round Mayday's waist. It would be far too complicated to explain that in fact this was his stag night. A little thrill went through him. He didn't think he'd ever done this before, checked into a grand hotel under an alias. As the porter swept up their minimal luggage, Patrick took Mayday's hand and followed him to the lift.

Inside, he stared at their reflection surreptitiously while Mayday chattered to the porter. More than ten years, they went back together. He supposed that this would be the last time. Mayday was right. If you were married, you couldn't have a close relationship with another female. Even platonic. And to be honest, platonic and Mayday were mutually exclusive. Just looking at her now made him want to take her in his arms, with her husky voice, her wicked laugh, her dancing eyes. But he wasn't going to do that. It wouldn't be fair. After all, hadn't he learned the lesson from his own father that you can't have your cake and eat it?

Keith sat in his private room in his hospital gown. There was five minutes to go before they took him down to theatre. He was astonished to find that instead of the sick panic he had felt for the past few weeks, he felt rather calm. In fact, he was almost looking forward to his operation. There was something rather reassuring about the momentum of the admission procedure, the way everything had been taken out of his hands, the way everyone seemed to know exactly what they were doing. It was far away from the experience he had imagined, the one you read about in the papers. He had envisaged lost medical notes, interminable waits and staff contradicting each other, culminating in someone whipping out a kidney instead of his prostate. But that, he supposed ruefully, was the benefit you got from writing out a cheque.

Sandra was sitting in the chair next to his bed, reading the *Daily Telegraph*. Most surprising of all, she had added to his sense of serenity. Her brisk, businesslike manner made it impossible for him to fret; she simply wouldn't allow it. His heart had sunk at first when she had appeared at Keeper's Cottage earlier that morning, and he had rued his weakness in telling her about his illness – he had kept his trap shut for so long, only to cave in at the eleventh hour. But now he was enormously grateful for her presence. She seemed able to second guess his every anxiety and put it to rest. She had already demanded a precis of his predicament from Mr Jackson.

'I want to hear it from the horse's mouth. Something might have been lost in translation.'

Mr Jackson had obliged, with good humour. No doubt he was used to dealing with the likes of Sandra on a daily basis. Then she had proceeded to demand a change of room: one with a tranquil view of the sloping lawns at the back rather than the car park.

'We don't want to look at all the other patients coming and going, thank you very much,' she told the receptionist.

Then she had ticked off his lunch requirements for the following day.

'Roast chicken, I think, don't you? Lamb can be a bit fatty. But you'll need something decent – it'll be your first proper meal for more than twenty-four hours. Then apple crumble. Cream or custard?'

There was quite simply no question that he wouldn't be here.

Keith felt treacherous thinking it, but he couldn't help feeling that Ginny would not have instilled the same confidence in him. She would never demand an audience with the consultant, or get his room changed. She would be anxious, awkward, and he would be able to see only too clearly the fear in her eyes. He was, he realized, grateful for her absence.

He looked over at his ex-wife and felt a sudden rush of gratitude for her strength, realizing that he had never really appreciated it. He had never asked her for support during their marriage. He had forged his own way, kept his worries to himself, made all the decisions unaided. What might have happened to them if he had been less insular? If they had been a partnership instead of two separate entities drifting off in different directions?

Then again, maybe Sandra had only become the success she was because they had separated. Maybe being alone was what had given her the drive. Keith reflected that he would never know what might have become of them. It was too late for regret. Far too late. He might not even have the chance to eat the lunch she had chosen for him, let alone atone for his mistakes.

But he couldn't go down to theatre without saying something.

'Sandra?'

She looked up from the paper with a smile.

'I just wanted to say . . .' What did he want to say? Not too much. It wouldn't be fair, if he didn't survive, to start unburdening his feelings now, when there wasn't enough time.

'You don't have to say anything.' Her voice was gentle, and full of understanding.

'Yes, I do,' insisted Keith. 'I wanted to say . . . thank you.'

That was enough. He didn't have to be specific. He could have just meant thank you for the books and the barley sugar. But he hoped she understood that in amongst those two words were a hundred others.

'We're ready for you, Mr Sherwyn.' A nurse swept in, followed by a hospital porter.

Sandra jumped up, took his face in her hands and kissed him.

'I'll see you in a couple of hours,' she said, gazing into his eyes.

Keith felt his heart turn over. He couldn't be sure why. Whether it was because he was about to be wheeled off to meet his fate at the hands of Mr Jackson, or because he had a glimpse of the past, the chirpy, upbeat girl he had married all those years ago.

'I . . .' The words stuck in his throat. 'I'll see you later.'
'I'll be here,' she promised.

Sandra sat back down to wait. The paper lay at her feet, discarded. It had been a mere prop. Only now could she afford to let her façade slip. She felt quite nauseous with anxiety. It had taken her so long to realize what she wanted, and now he might be taken away from her. A trifle self-consciously, she clasped her hands together in prayer. She couldn't remember the last time she had done this, but surely it was worth putting in a call to the powers that be?

'Dear God,' she murmured, 'please let him be all right.'

In downtown Puerto Banus, the marina shone and sparkled and the sunlight bounced off the gleaming white yachts that rose and fell gently in the water. Everywhere there were tanned bodies, crisp linen, elegant high heels, diamanté-studded sunglasses, the wink and glitter of diamonds, shining manes of hair, wrists bearing serious watches. The air was warm and filled with a thousand scents, fresh coffee, foreign cigarettes, frying garlic – the smell of luxury, pleasure and money all mingled into one.

The hen party had spent the morning oohing and aahing. The shops were cruelly tantalizing, displaying clothes and shoes and handbags that almost made them weep with desire. Versace, Herme's, Chanel, Ralph Lauren: it was like the pages of the glossiest magazine come to life. They were now having lunch ahead of an afternoon's shopping in Zara, Mango and El Corte Inglés, where they would buy pale imitations of the clothes they had been drooling over.

They sat outside at a pavement café, munching on char-grilled squid and people-watching, making up stories for the glamorous couples that passed by their table.

'This is the life,' breathed Sasha. 'I could live here happily.'

'You'd soon get bored,' her mother told her.

'You've got to be joking!' Sasha looked back at her, incredulous. 'This is heaven.'

Ginny had to admit that the glitzy setting did suit her daughter, and that their table was getting admiring glances from male passers-by. Yet again she felt like the elderly chaperone. She didn't want to put off any potential suitors. She didn't want to cramp their style.

She knew she shouldn't have come. She should have stayed at home and built bridges with Keith. They could have gone to Stratford together: they still had to choose a wedding present for Mandy and Patrick. She wondered what he was up to. She pulled her phone out to give him a ring, then remembered that she hadn't done whatever complicated thing it was that meant she could make international calls. In fact, her phone probably didn't work abroad at all. It was old-fashioned and out of date. Just like she was. She tossed it back into her bag.

'I think I'll go back to the villa and have a siesta,' she said, 'if we're going to be out until all hours this evening.'

The truth was she didn't fancy trailing in and out of the shops with them all. She would either be called upon to give the twins superfluous reassurance or money, both of which she felt ill-inclined to bestow when they needed neither – they would each look stunning in a bin bag and she knew perfectly well David had slipped them a wad of cash before they went away.

'Aren't you going to come shopping?' Kitty looked concerned.

'To be honest, I'd rather lie by the pool and read.' Ginny spied a taxi and waved her hand in the air.

Half an hour later, she was stretched out on a teak sun lounger by Sandra's pool, but she couldn't relax. What was the matter with her? She sighed. She needed to get a grip. She couldn't put a damper on everything for the rest of her life. There was quite a bit of it left, after all. She shifted onto her stomach, trying to get comfortable. The problem was she wasn't happy in her own skin any more. She didn't feel as if she belonged. She was the first to acknowledge that she wasn't in the first flush of youth, but why did she feel the need to melt into the background all the time? It didn't happen to everyone when they hit middle age, after all. Look at Lucy Liddiard: still confident, gorgeous, stylish – Lucy would be happy to be out with the girls, shopping and lunching and giggling. As would Sandra . . . Sandra, who was the wrong side of fifty and positively radiant. Ginny just felt grey and lifeless and boring.

As she lay there debating her dilemma, becoming increasingly miserable, Sandra's advice – to 'give nature a helping hand' – kept coming back to her. Gradually it dawned on Ginny that perhaps there was something in it. According to the papers and magazines, everyone was doing it. And if it made you happier with yourself, then why not? She burrowed in her handbag for Sandra's brochure, which she'd meant to bin at the first opportunity. She leafed through it carefully, looking at the photographs, reading the testimonials. Maybe Sandra was right? She should give it a go. And if she didn't like it, if it didn't do

348

anything for her, she needn't bother again. On the other hand, if it was a miracle, then she'd be stuck with top-ups every six months for the rest of her life. But then, she was earning money, proper money. Why shouldn't she spend it on something that made her feel better?

Gingerly, she picked up the phone and dialled the clinic.

'Mrs Sherwyn told me to expect your call,' the efficient manageress informed her, and Ginny felt a flash of annoyance. Then she thought, bugger it.

'Yes,' she replied crisply. 'I'd like to book some treatments, please.'

Ten minutes later she put the phone down. Marie-Claire had agreed to block out two hours of her time on Monday in order to have a proper consultation and then proceed with whatever treatment they decided Ginny needed. She'd been very reassuring.

Ginny stretched in satisfaction, yawned, and picked up her Jilly Cooper, having long given up on Zadie Smith. Some time later, she awoke to find Alejandro standing over her. She sat up, hastily covering herself with a towel.

'I've come to prepare some tapas before you go out tonight,' he smiled. 'To line the stomachs. It will be late before you eat.'

Ginny looked at her watch. She'd been asleep nearly two hours. 'The girls should be back any minute.'

Alejandro spied the brochure on the table beside her. He picked it up, frowning. 'You don't need this.'

'I so do,' she laughed in reply, sounding like one of her daughters.

'You want to look like Mrs Sherwyn and her friends?' he demanded. 'They all look the same.'

He affected a rather surprised look with a pronounced pout, and Ginny collapsed into giggles.

'Sandra looks bloody fantastic,' she told him. 'I don't care what anyone says. I'm going to give it a go.'

Alejandro shook his head sadly. 'Crazy.'

He dropped the brochure back on the table distastefully and walked away. Ginny shut her eyes. She wasn't going to argue. How would someone like him have any idea what it was like, to feel long past your sell-by date?

Patrick wasn't a great one for shopping. He and Mayday had agreed to go their separate ways and meet up at tea time. He headed for Jermyn Street, and had done everything he needed after one hour. He bought himself a pair of Oliver Sweeney Chelsea boots, highly polished with a lime-green lining. They would go perfectly with his morning suit but he'd be able to wear them with anything afterwards. And he topped up on some new shirts from Thomas Pink. With at least another hour to kill, he treated himself to a new haircut and a wet shave at Trumpers. He sat in a mahogany-lined cubicle, while the barber worked up a lather of soap on his skin with a badger brush and set to with a terrifyingly sharp razor. Afterwards, he felt as if the top layer of his skin had been taken off, but he couldn't deny that his complexion looked about ten years younger. And his hair was cut to perfection; layered short into the neck but keeping the fringe and top long. Another week would take the newness off it. He gave his reflection a rueful grin. He would do.

He made his way over to Knightsbridge and found Mayday in Harvey Nichols, burdened down with carrier bags.

'Have you spent all your money?' he asked.

She smiled, thinking that it would take more than an afternoon to get rid of her prize money. Though she hadn't done badly. She'd booked a personal shopper, and been surprised to find how much she had enjoyed them bringing her outfit after outfit that fitted the brief she'd given. For the first time in her life she experienced the cut, the fabric, the finish and the detail that went with designer clothing, and was amazed to find how much she relished it. She had always enjoyed expressing herself through what she wore, but this lifted dressing up to another level. And the assistants had loved attending to her, with her rock-chick looks, her wild hair, and her attitude that meant she could get away with outfits that most customers shied away from. She had come out of the dressing room elated, her bags stuffed with Temperley, Sass & Bide, Stella McCartney, Matthew Williamson and Alexander McQueen. Not to mention a raft of boots and shoes.

There was just one more detail to complete the makeover.

'I want some new perfume,' she announced. 'I've worn the same thing for years and years. I want a change. Choose something for me, Patrick.'

Patrick was unnerved by the challenge. Mayday had smelt the same for as long as he could remember: Thierry Mugler's Angel, with its heavy, seductive scent of vanilla. Patrick couldn't imagine her smelling of anything else. But he liked the idea of choosing a new perfume for her, as if he was in some way branding her. She led him through to the cosmetics hall, where the search began in earnest. They worked their way through the different counters, spritzing clouds of cologne and eau de toilette onto little strips of cardboard, breathing in the myriad fragrances: musk, pepper, amber, jasmine, bergamot, mimosa, lily of the valley, honeysuckle, ginger, ylang ylang, basil, sandalwood, patchouli, orange blossom. There was a concoction for every type of woman, from sophisticated to youthful to carefree to wanton. Patrick needed something that captured a mass of contradictions.

In the end, he chose from Annick Goutal. The subtlety of her fragrances seemed to evoke rather than dictate emotion, with a haunting after-effect. Mayday's heart was thumping as he dabbed his final choice behind her ears, on her wrists, and on the beating pulse in her neck. The smell of Turkish rose enveloped her, making her feel quite giddy as the words on the bottle repeated themselves to her over and over again.

Was this a message from him to her? Or was it just a coincidence? He was probably blissfully unaware of the irony.

Ce Soir ou Jamais.

Tonight or never.

By the time the girls came back, Ginny realized she'd made a terrible mistake. Falling asleep in the Mediterranean sun had been asking for trouble, even though she had slathered herself with sun cream. She was burnt to a crisp, her head was throbbing and she felt sick.

'I'll have to give this evening a miss,' she announced in the kitchen glumly, sitting on a barstool with her head in her hands.

The others groaned in protest. But she stood her ground.

'Honestly. I feel dreadful. And I don't want to start bleating that I want to go home at eleven o'clock.'

'Alejandro! Tell her she's got to come.'

Alejandro paused in the middle of slicing up the tortilla he had made to keep them going. He looked at Ginny and frowned. 'You've made the tourist's worst mistake,' he chided. 'You underestimate the strength of the sun.' He held a hand over her bright red chest. 'I can feel the heat from here.'

If Ginny could have gone any redder, she would have.

'I'm staying here,' she insisted. 'No one wants to see Lobsterwoman out on the town. Anyway, you'll have more fun if I'm not in tow.'

'Just come for the meal. It won't be the same without you,' Mandy begged.

Ginny had been so sweet and supportive to her over the years, and had made her dad so happy. Mandy was mortified to think she might feel surplus to requirements. Besides, she didn't want things to get too wild, and without Ginny there to keep the others in check she might lose control. She wasn't too worried about Kitty, but Sasha and Caroline were equally unmanageable when their blood was up.

Ginny, however, could not be persuaded.

Alejandro nodded his approval.

'I think you are very wise to stay behind.' He pulled a sharp knife from the drawer and started hacking up lemons, squeezing the juice into a tall glass jug. 'Go and get ready, girls. You haven't got that long to make yourselves beautiful.'

And he ducked as an indignant Sasha threw a lemon at his head.

*

Two hours later, the four girls lined up in front of Ginny for inspection. They each looked stunning and totally different. Mandy, cool and sharp in embroidered white linen trousers and a turquoise crocheted vest. Kitty, bohemian in a pink baby-doll dress emblazoned with skulls. Sasha, glitzy in a backless mini sheath. And Caroline, voluptuous in a bias cut Missoni-style striped halter neck that displayed her staggering cleavage. The sun had kissed them all. They were golden and glowing, filled with champagne bubbles and laughter.

Then Sasha and Kitty produced a customised tiara for Mandy – a concoction of tulle, pearls and twinkly fairy-lights to show she was the bride-to-be.

'It's got to be done, Mandy. Every girl has to be humiliated on her hen night,' Sasha told her. 'Just be grateful that it's not a hat with condoms swinging from the brim.'

Mandy gave in with good grace, then got her own back by producing sparkly hot-pink Stetsons for them all to wear as members of her hen party.

'I knew there was no way you'd let me get away with it,' she grinned at the twins. 'And I wasn't going to be the only one to stand out in the crowd.'

'You won't stand out in Puerto Banus,' Alejandro assured them. He was used to seeing hordes of strangely dressed girls prowling the streets. By the end of the night they were usually incoherent and legless – he had often found half-dressed fairies and fallen angels slumped in the gutter, their shoes in their hands. He just hoped this lot had more self-control, but in case they didn't he had already warned his network of friends to look out for them, and make sure they didn't get into any trouble. Puerto

Banus might be a party town, but it sometimes ended in tears.

'I will drive the girls to the restaurant,' said Alejandro. 'And you, Ginny – you must drink some of my lemonade and take one of these. It will settle your stomach and clear your head.'

Alejandro handed her a glass filled with lemonade and a tablet.

'Then go to sleep. Just for an hour. I will wake you when I come back. You will be better, I promise.'

Sasha giggled. 'I don't know if we should trust Mum and Alejandro alone together.'

Ginny rolled her eyes. The prospect of the two of them getting up to anything was utterly preposterous.

'Have a fantastic evening,' she urged, kissing each of them. 'I am watching Keanu Reeves on Sky and going to bed early. See you at dawn.'

As soon as they had gone, she flopped onto the sofa with a sigh of relief. The last thing she had wanted was to dress up and spend the evening drinking in hot, sweaty, crowded bars full of beautiful young people. She flicked on the television, then swallowed the pill Alejandro had given her, enjoying the tart coolness of the lemonade as it slid down her throat. She shut her eyes, deciding she would have a nap for half an hour until he came back. Then she'd have a quick supper and an early night so she could make the most of the next day, when hopefully the effects of too much sun would have worn off.

Alejandro couldn't help grinning as he drove along the coast road and dropped down towards the marina. The sun was still shining, the windows were down, the music

355

was blaring and the girls sang along. As they hit the streets, he got envious glances from passers-by – and whistles and waves that the girls returned. They had only shared one bottle of champagne between them before going out, but he did wonder if they'd had anything else, their spirits were so high.

The thought led him to a fleeting moment of guilt. Should he have given Ginny that tablet? Surely one little pill wouldn't hurt. If he didn't drop one himself he could keep an eye on her. It would make the job so much easier, after all. It would be like plucking one of the ripe peaches off the tree in the garden. Otherwise it could be tricky. Alejandro knew he was irresistible to most women, but Ginny had an aura of anxiety and uncertainty that he knew from experience was inhibiting. It might take him days to break through her shield. Whereas his little white dove would have her cooing and billing. She would enjoy it.

After all, it wasn't called Ecstasy for nothing.

Alejandro pulled up outside the bar he had chosen for them to start their evening. There was a cocktail lounge and a restaurant serving proper Spanish food, not the ersatz crap that so many establishments now churned out for the tourists. His friend Pedro, the doorman, came rushing forward to open the doors for the girls, and they emerged like superstars.

'Come in with us,' Kitty begged Alejandro. 'Come and have a drink.'

'No, no, no – it's a girl's night.'

'You can be a token hen,' insisted Sasha. 'We're not sexist.'

But Alejandro stuck to his guns.

'You're crazy,' observed Pedro, amazed Alejandro was passing up the chance to chaperone them.

'Gotta work. But look after them for me.'

'Don't worry. I won't take my eyes off them.'

Pedro watched admiringly as the bride and her cowgirl cohorts filed into the bar. Alejandro gave him the thumbs up then got back into his car. For a while he sat there, wondering if what he was about to do was the right thing. Then he thought of the money. Sighing, he switched on the ignition. That was the thing about life. It was always money dictating to you in the end. Making you do things you didn't want to do. Turning you into a person you didn't want to be. Even Raoul, slimy though he was, probably didn't want to be a drug dealer deep down. They were all in the same trap.

Patrick decided to go for a walk while Mayday got ready for dinner.

He didn't want to invade her space. He knew from Mandy that girls spent a long time agonizing about their toilette. Besides, he felt a little bit awkward. He would never have worried before, but he sensed a change in her that was unfamiliar. A curious mixture of both vulnerability and confidence. She carried herself differently, somehow. She was more subtle, more mysterious. Womanly, Patrick decided. Yet there was an underlying fragility to her that unnerved him. Mayday had always been so robust. He decided that she was probably still raw from her grandmother's death. He could almost pinpoint the change in her to the day of the funeral. The problem was he wasn't quite sure how to handle this new Mayday. The old one had been so easy: up front, no strings. Patrick could have left her behind with no conscience. But suddenly . . .

When they'd got back from shopping, he'd watched as she'd laid her purchases out on the bed, admiring them, stroking the rich fabrics. She was wearing the scent he had chosen. The smell got right inside his head, intoxicating him, as it occurred to him that he would never see her wear half of these clothes. Who would get the benefit? Who would watch her drop them to the ground? He knew Mayday had no shortage of admirers. It had never bothered him before. Now, Patrick realized with unease that he was jealous. Jealous of those unknown suitors, those rivals for her affection, the fact that someone else might undo her buttons, peel off her stockings . . .

Shit. This had been a mistake. As soon as they had pulled up at Claridge's he should have put his foot down. It wasn't what he'd envisaged at all. He'd just anticipated a bit of malarkey with an old mate. Now, here he was, burning with feelings that had ignited when he least expected it. This was turning into something special. Something meaningful.

A week before his own wedding.

He left the hotel and walked briskly around the block. A gentle evening sun was shining, and the city was starting to fill up as people drove in for their Saturday night's entertainment. Sleek cars glided by, some with tinted windows, some with chauffeurs, and Patrick couldn't help but be curious as to how the passengers had reached their position in life. He wandered down Bond Street, eyeing window after window of exquisite luggage, ice-white diamonds, gilt-framed masterpieces – everything so ridiculously out of reach that the journey couldn't fail to make one feel depressed and deprived, unless one had the strength of mind to realize that it was all meaningless rubbish, and that those who could afford to shop here were not necessarily happier than anyone else.

Mandy, he knew, would be in seventh heaven. She'd be pressing her nose against the glass, admiring the shoes, the dresses, the jewels. She adored her labels, and drooled over them in her fashion magazines every month. But to her credit, she had it in perspective. She'd focus on her key purchases, the one item of the season that she couldn't live without – a handbag, a pair of shoes, a trench-coat – and would save up for it. And once she'd acquired it, she appreciated it and looked after it. She never made mistakes, or rushed on to the next purchase, but artfully managed to mix her prestige pieces with high-street basics. As a result, she always looked a million dollars. Patrick wondered fondly what she was wearing tonight . . .

By the time he returned to the entrance of Claridge's, he chided himself for being distracted by Mayday. He was about to marry the woman he loved, for heaven's sake. He was just being a typical bloke, unable to resist what was underneath his nose. He should just walk away, but he couldn't now – that would be impossibly rude, when she'd spent her grandmother's bequest on the room. They'd have a nice dinner together, then he'd plead exhaustion and crash out. He could make his escape early the next day. She wouldn't be offended. Mayday wasn't like that.

Keith opened his eyes and saw Sandra's face above his, wet with tears.

What did this mean? Was he dead? Was she standing

over his corpse? Why else would she be crying? It took a lot to make Sandra break down.

Behind her he could discern a shadowy figure. Mr Jackson. Had he come to apologize for cocking it up? Was he going to explain what had gone wrong? Or was he about to announce the time of death, glancing up at the clock like a character from a hospital drama?

Keith wanted to speak but his throat felt raw and his head felt a bit swimmy. Why didn't someone tell him what was going on? Though he supposed if he was dead there would be no point in telling him anything.

Sandra reached out and took his hand. She lifted it to her cheek and he could feel her warm tears. Then she kissed his fingers.

That was it. He'd definitely gone over to the other side. Sandra wasn't one for showing her emotions in front of men in white coats.

Bugger. He'd left so much undone. The wedding was going to be spoilt. And what the hell was Ginny going to say? He should have given her a hint that something was wrong. It was going to be a terrible shock. He hoped that Sandra would be tactful.

'Mr Sherwyn.' Mr Jackson's voice boomed out, making him jump. 'Good news. Good news. Everything came out as clean as a whistle. Of course we need to drop it over to the lab just to make sure, but I'm very pleased.'

Keith's eyes swivelled round. He was in a bed. Not on a slab. In a room. Not a mortuary.

Heavenly relief slipped through his veins. He smiled up at Sandra, who was now weeping openly.

'I love you,' she sobbed.

Keith summoned up all his strength. 'I love you too,'

he replied, then shut his eyes, drifting off into a dreamless sleep.

Sandra dropped his hand.

'It might take him a while to recover consciousness properly,' said Mr Jackson.

'No problem,' said Sandra happily. 'As long as everything's all right.'

'I'm quite confident your husband's going to make an excellent recovery.'

'Marvellous.' Sandra smiled, not bothering to correct his misunderstanding.

'Although it might be a while before he's back in full working order.'

'Never mind that,' Sandra twinkled, 'I'm a very patient woman, Mr Jackson. Very patient indeed.'

16

When Patrick met Mayday in the bar, he had to look twice to make sure it was her.

She was usually shielded by her wild mane of hair, but tonight it was smoothed into a sleek chignon, and he could see that her face was perfectly heart-shaped, punctuated by delicately arched eyebrows. Her eyes were painted with a glimmering pewter; her lips glistened with her trademark dark red. Her dress was a long sleeved pale-pink shift trimmed with black velvet that was saved from being demure by fishnet tights and towering stilettos.

She looked utterly ravishing. The crazy rock chick wild child had been groomed and tamed to produce a tantalizingly exotic young woman. Of course the money helped. The dress was Temperley, the shoes Rupert Sanderson. Furthermore, her art deco earrings were vintage Cartier, and upstairs in her suitcase was the necklace that went with it, but Mayday had decided that would overpower the outfit.

As Patrick led her through the tables after the waiter, he could feel every pair of eyes in the room feasting upon her, with varying degrees of lust or envy depending on the sex or inclination of the owner. It was clear everyone was wondering who she was. As she slid into her chair she cast a demure gaze around the room, and everyone looked away. Claridge's wasn't the place to be seen gawping.

They drank a bottle of Perrier Jouet champagne while they looked at the menu.

'I could get used to this,' said Patrick.

Mayday looked at him solemnly. 'This is our farewell dinner,' she reminded him.

'Actually,' said Patrick, 'I don't think we've ever been out for dinner before. Not just you and me.'

There had been crazy nights out. Many of them. But nothing like this – one to one, with no distraction but the occasional obsequious waiter. For a moment Patrick wondered if he should have done a bunk earlier, but assured himself he was doing nothing wrong. Most men behaved far worse on their stag nights. He was just having a meal out with his oldest friend, who happened to be a girl. And he was certain the twins and Mandy would be doing their fair share of drinking and flirting in Puerto Banus. That was the whole point of stag and hen nights, wasn't it? Getting it out of your system . . .

The hen party was sitting at their table in the cavernous restaurant, surrounded by glittering silver pillars and palm trees that reached the ceiling while huge plasma screens played Lionel Richie videos. The noise was ear-splitting. Everyone who was anyone on the Costa del Sol was out in force, swigging cocktails as the waiters rushed round filling up their glasses as quickly as they finished their drinks.

At the head of the table, resplendent in her head-dress, Mandy looked round at her friends and smiled. It didn't get better than this: to be dressed up to the nines, in a glamorous restaurant with your best mates, in a glorious sun-drenched hotspot, with handsome men falling over themselves to get your attention. Since they had arrived at their table, three bottles of Bollinger had been sent over by admirers.

'It's over a hundred pounds a bottle,' she'd protested, looking at the menu.

'More fool them,' Caroline had announced, unashamedly knocking it back.

Mandy was a little bit dubious, feeling it was unfair to drink the champagne when they were already spoken for.

'It gives out the wrong message,' she objected. 'It implies we're available.'

'Well, we are,' Sasha pointed out. 'Me and Kitty are.'

'So am I. For one night only.' Caroline was defiant.

'What do you mean?' demanded Mandy, shocked.

'I mean that if I get an offer, I won't turn it down.'

'But . . . what about James?'

'He won't know.'

Mandy felt her cheeks flush, then decided that Caroline was just trying to shock her. She always got controversial when she'd had a bit to drink. For a moment she felt uncomfortable. The rules were obviously different in here. Filled with well-heeled and dazzling people out for a thrill, it had the air of an upmarket pick-up joint. She felt a flutter of panic, and wished Patrick was with her. Then she told herself to relax. It was her night. She was supposed to enjoy herself, and she didn't have to do anything she didn't want to.

Caroline leant forward, Bollinger spilling out of her glass.

'James hasn't touched me for months. I haven't had an orgasm since Percy was born.'

'Too much information, Caroline,' sang out Sasha.

'I just want to know that I'm still in full working order.'

'Well, you don't need somebody else to tell you that, do you?'

Caroline re-filled her glass. 'I want to be sure that it's not me. That I'm not so unattractive that no one wants to touch me with a bargepole. You've got no idea what it's like.'

For a moment, it looked as if she was about to burst into tears. Then she caught the eye of a dark-haired man in a white linen shirt three tables away. He lifted his glass to her and she raised hers in return.

Mandy hid a smile. Caroline was incorrigible, but if it made her feel better about herself, she supposed there was no harm in it. She looked round for the waiter and signalled for him to bring them some more bread. They needed something to soak up the alcohol while they were waiting for their food.

She had a feeling it was going to be a long night.

Ginny emerged from her sleep to feel a finger trailing itself along her forearm. She opened her eyes to find Alejandro looking down at her. Dusk had fallen while he'd been gone. The room was filled with candles, pulsating with a warm glow.

'How do you feel?'

Ginny smiled, a slow, sleepy smile that came from deep inside her. She stretched luxuriously. Her sleep had refreshed and relaxed her. She felt filled with energy and yet languid, almost liquid; her veins thrumming with a low-voltage buzzing sensation.

'Amazing,' she breathed. 'So much better.'

'Good.' Alejandro nodded approvingly.

Ginny looked around her. Everything was just perfect. The room. The light. The music. She could hear droplets of sound falling all around her, golden notes that melted into the candlelight then flickered on her skin. As she moved it was like swimming through the air. She was graceful, supple, sinuous. Everything she touched felt soft, like swansdown.

'So now it's just us.'

His voice snaked through her, rich and dark, exploring every corner of her being. She shivered with the delight, looking into his eyes. She felt as if he was her guardian angel, sent here to protect her. Protect her, and so much more. She wanted to experience him, and she sensed he wanted that too. The force hung in the air between them, a two-way mirror shimmering with lust.

'Dance with me,' he said.

She held up her hands, and he slipped each of his fingers between hers until they were inextricably entwined. He pulled her to her feet and she moved closer to him. They were barely an inch apart. She could feel his breath on her cheek like the gentlest caress, and her breasts against his chest, and each of their hearts beating, synchronizing, pulsating in time with the music. They swayed to the rhythm, and Ginny felt filled with an overwhelming desire for this being, knowing that he felt it too. He was smiling at her with his eyes and his mouth, his beautiful mouth. She wondered how it tasted, and she reached out her tongue, tracing the outline of his lips wondrously. He tasted just as she imagined, marshmallow sweet.

They dropped down onto the rug as their hands began to explore, and it felt as if his fingers were melting into her skin. Soft strokes that sent a silver ripple through her veins. Her clothes fell away, superfluous, abandoned, discarded, for she longed to feel his naked warmth. And suddenly there he was against her.

How long it lasted she didn't know. But they explored every inch of each other, swimming in a luscious, spun-sugar vortex. She felt him inside her, and he became part of her, and she wanted to be him as their limbs melted and they remoulded into one.

And not once did the encounter seem ridiculous. She felt neither self-conscious nor anxious nor guilty. Not even when he took out his phone to record their union on his camera.

'I need some pictures,' he said hoarsely. 'To remind me of us. In two days you will be gone, and I will have nothing of you.'

To Ginny it seemed perfectly natural to capture the moment; a celluloid memory of their combined ecstasy. So she smiled at the tiny lens, lying back on the rug with her arms above her head. She felt foxy, abandoned, and completely undone . . .

Patrick and Mayday both agreed that their meal at Claridge's was the most heavenly either of them had ever eaten. They began with celeriac risotto with pine nuts, followed by West Country pork cooked in honey and cloves, then shared a caramelized apple tarte tatin with cinnamon ice cream. As Mayday scraped the last of the dessert up with her spoon, she sighed in satisfaction.

'That was amazing.'

Patrick raised his glass. 'Well, a toast to your grandmother for letting us enjoy it.'

For a moment, Mayday wanted to reveal that she could eat here every week for the rest of her life if she wanted. And that Patrick could join her. But she didn't.

'She'd have been horrified by the prices,' she pointed out. 'She used to think the price of Sunday lunch at the Horse and Groom was scandalous.'

'What do you want to do now?' asked Patrick. 'Go clubbing? Find a casino? Or a little bar?'

Somehow, the thought of hitting the bright lights didn't really appeal. Once she would have been eager to dance until dawn, but suddenly she felt drained.

'I'm tired, to be honest,' she said carefully. 'All that shopping . . . We could get an early-ish night.'

She couldn't look Patrick in the eye.

'I must admit, I'm pretty knackered,' he agreed. 'It's been a mad few weeks. Let's make the most of the luxury.'

They settled the bill, then made their way out of the restaurant, across the black and white marble of the reception hall and into the lift. They travelled up in silence, studiously avoiding each other's reflection in the mirrored walls.

A few minutes later, they were in their suite, standing next to the bed, awkward. They had never been awkward with each other before, but the room that had seemed so palatial earlier on now seemed tiny. Claustrophobic.

'I've had a wonderful evening,' said Patrick finally. 'Thank you.'

He pulled her to him and kissed her cheek, holding her in the crook of one arm. She stood very still. It would be so easy to slip both arms round her now, push her back onto the bed and enjoy what he knew would be at least an hour of teasing and tantalizing. And no doubt some sort of surprise. Mayday was anything but predictable in bed. But he wasn't going to take her, like some cheap tart on a stag night. He couldn't do it. It would diminish their friendship, which he valued above all else.

'Night night,' he whispered, wanting to say so much more but not knowing where to start.

She stayed motionless for a moment. All he could feel was the slight rise and fall of her chest as she breathed in and out.

'Night night,' she replied, then slid out of his clasp and walked into the bathroom.

Ten minutes later, they climbed carefully into the enormous bed, falling back on to the soft pillows and shutting their eyes tight, each hoping that sleep would come upon them quickly.

The Crescendo was supposed to be the most exclusive night-spot on the coast. Its walls were made of Perspex cubes which changed colour gradually, from tangerine to violet to turquoise, interspersed with tanks of multi-coloured tropical fish – one could only hope the glass was soundproof, as the music was deafening. On the dance floor, scantily clad girls were writhing to the throb of the beat.

In the middle of the mêlée was Caroline, arms above her head, her smile stretching from ear to ear. Every pair of male eyes was fixated on her cleavage, and the way her dress clung to her voluptuous hips. It didn't seem to matter that she was carrying a little too much weight. She was womanhood personified; ripe and full of promise. Every other female paled into insignificance next to her.

And she was revelling in the limelight; dancing, laughing, talking, flirting . . .

Mandy watched anxiously as she left the dance floor, holding the hand of the man in the white linen shirt who had caught her attention in the restaurant. He had sent a message over to their table, inviting them into this apparently exclusive establishment, and they had enjoyed walking past the queue of hopefuls outside and being ushered in without question. Philippe Romaine was a mover and a shaker in Puerto Banus. He had one of the biggest yachts in the marina. And he only had eyes for Caroline.

'What do we do about her?' Mandy shouted in Sasha's ear.

'Leave her be. She's having fun,' said Sasha. 'You know, I reckon most of these girls are hookers.' She looked disparagingly at a pneumatic blonde in a tutu, mesh vest top, lace stockings and thigh length boots – all in white, which set off her caramel tan. 'Shall we go?'

Even the twins couldn't keep up with the air of debauchery. Everyone was on the pull or on the game. And the drinks were nearly twenty quid each.

'We can't just leave her.'

'She's not going to come with us,' replied Sasha airily. 'She's old enough to know what she's doing.'

'But she's married!' wailed Mandy. 'To my future uncle-in-law! What about the children?'

'She's just having a laugh. She hasn't started divorce proceedings.' Kitty was a touch more consoling than her sister. But she still didn't seem to think the fact that Caroline had got off with a mystery millionaire was terribly shocking.

'Mickey and Lucy will never forgive me. Or Patrick.'

'Mandy – it's not your fault. If it's anyone's fault it's James's, for not paying her enough attention.'

The three of them looked over at Caroline, who was now whispering in Philippe's ear, her arm snaked around his neck.

'It's going to end in tears,' said Mandy.

'No, it's not,' Sasha contradicted. 'It'll do her the world of good. I wish I'd pulled a diamond broker, I can tell you.'

Mandy sighed, realizing that there was no way she was going to get Caroline out of the nightclub short of pulling her out by the hair.

'I'll tell her we're going.'

She marched over to Caroline. 'If you want to come with us, we're going now.'

Caroline fixed her with a look which dared Mandy not to spoil her fun. 'I'm going back to Philippe's yacht for a night-cap.'

'If you're sure,' said Mandy. She turned to Philippe. 'Fuck her over,' she said. 'And you'll be sleeping with the fishes. I'll personally make sure of it.'

She gave the sweetest of smiles that left him quite clear she wasn't joking, then walked off.

Philippe looked at Caroline. 'Your friend is scary.'

'My friend is wonderful,' she corrected him. 'And she meant everything she said. Now come on, show us the colour of this yacht. I'm starting to think you might be having me on.'

He wasn't. Caroline held onto Philippe's linen-clad arm as they walked along the pontoon. People were still out on their decks, drinking, music playing, and many of them gave Philippe a wave of greeting as he walked past. Finally they came to a halt.

'Here we are,' he said, holding out a hand to help her on board.

A few minutes later, Caroline was sitting on deck herself, a heavy tumbler of Hennessy in her hand.

'So, how do I know you really are a diamond broker?' she demanded. The thrill of the chase and too much alcohol was making her confrontational. Besides, she had a perfectly good point. 'How do I know you're not just a deck-hand, looking after this boat for someone else?'

Philippe chuckled softly. She was a feisty one all right. That's what had attracted him. He was so used to women hanging on his every word, in awe of his wealth and position. It was refreshing to be with someone who was so clearly unimpressed. She was no pushover, lying there amongst the plump cushions on the banquette that ran along the deck, almost as if she owned the place.

'Wait there,' he instructed, and Caroline raised a provocative eyebrow. She looked so inviting, those red curls falling onto her bare shoulders, those incredible breasts.

He knew just the piece. His mouth watered as he imagined the jewels against her bare skin. She would look spectacular in just that and nothing else.

Moments later he hurried back carrying a black velvet-lined box. He opened it reverentially. Inside lay a diamond necklace that even the uninitiated could recognize as real, so authoritative was its glitter.

'Bloody hell,' breathed Caroline. 'It's not exactly Accessorize, is it?'

'It's worth nearly as much as this boat,' answered Philippe proudly. 'Lift up your hair.'

Caroline obeyed. She shivered slightly as his hands slid the necklace around her neck and did up the clasp. As her hair fell back down, so the jewels fell against her collarbone, cold and heavy.

Philippe raked his eyes over her, and nodded in approval.

'Fantastic,' he pronounced. 'Not all women could wear a piece like that. But you have the presence to carry it off.'

'The boobs, you mean,' Caroline laughed, in no doubt as to what it was that was enthralling him. Men were such simple creatures when it came down to it. Even James, with his seemingly erudite ways, was just a boob man at heart.

'Show me.' Philippe's voice was hoarse.

Caroline lifted her arms behind her neck and undid the clip that was holding her dress up, letting it drop to her waist. The diamonds glittered between her breasts. She tossed back her hair and threw back her shoulders. She felt like a goddess. She was in total control. She knew whatever she asked for now she could have. She lay back down in a Rubenesque pose, resting her head in one hand.

'What now?' she asked, her eyes sparkling as brightly as the diamonds.

Philippe gazed at her in awe. He couldn't take her up on deck. Philippe wasn't an exhibitionist, although he suspected Caroline might be. No, he would take her in his cabin, where he would be in control. But first, it needed champagne, candlelight, soft music. The atmosphere had to be just right. He might not be an exhibitionist, but he was definitely a perfectionist. He disappeared below deck again.

'Five minutes,' he called up the stairs behind him.

The night air had suddenly turned cold, and the breeze was dissipating the effects of the night's drinking. Caroline sat up, shivering, her brandy untouched. As the evening's alcohol melted away, reality crept in.

She was sitting on a million-pound yacht, with a diamond broker who was gagging for it, about to commit adultery. And once she'd done that, Caroline knew there'd be no going back. She'd no longer be in control. She would have broken the rules, and as a result would have no bargaining power. She wouldn't have a leg to stand on. And confident as she was of Philippe's admiration for her, she wasn't sure how far that admiration would go in the cold light of day.

Besides, what was she going to do? Run off with him leaving Henry, Constance and Percy to fend for themselves? Of course not. No matter what happened, she had to get back on that plane with the others, back to the children, back to James. Back to reality.

She got to her feet, retying her dress around her neck.

She'd set out to prove something to herself that evening. And she had done it. She had proved that Caroline Liddiard was still sexy and desirable. That she wasn't just an overweight, downtrodden hausfrau, but an attractive woman who could pull if she had to. And she had!

Yes. The old Caroline was still there. She realized it was up to her to find the old James and rekindle their marriage. James had made her feel passionate and abandoned once. And she had set his pulse racing too, once upon a time. What they needed was some time alone together, to rediscover each other, for her to dress up and for him to wind down. A weekend in the sun, with nothing to worry about except exactly which restaurant to go to for dinner.

Lucy would have the children for them, she felt pretty sure. She'd organize it as soon as they got back. Sometime after the wedding. They'd get that out of the way first.

Caroline picked up her shoes and tiptoed across the deck. She didn't feel too guilty about Philippe. She was sure they were queuing up for him. No doubt he had a different girl in every port. He was probably changing his sheets even now, eradicating the evidence of his previous conquest.

As she crept along the pontoon, Caroline breathed a shaky sigh of relief. She'd had a lucky escape. She told herself she was her own worst enemy. Once she had a drink inside her, she didn't know when to draw the line. Thank goodness she had come to her senses just in time.

Mayday stood at the window, peering between the thick, interlined curtains, looking out on to the London street. Despite the lateness of the hour, cabs were still gliding past and the occasional siren could be heard. A gentle rain had started to fall. A cluster of revellers began to run for shelter.

She felt overwhelmingly alone.

Why on earth had she tortured herself like this? What the hell had she hoped for? She had set herself up for the biggest disappointment of her life, and the emptiness inside her was unbearable. Worse than the feeling when she'd seen her grandmother's coffin slide behind the curtains at the crematorium.

She had everything. Everything and nothing.

As she stood there, looking out at the city, Mayday thought that what she probably needed was a change. She'd never really stepped out of her tiny little world, and that was why she was vulnerable. She shouldn't be trying to cling on to the one thing she knew and understood. She should strike out, have an adventure, come to the big city and widen her horizons. With the money she had, she could have a fabulous time. She could buy a penthouse apartment, start a business. It probably wouldn't be long before she met someone who would help her forget . . .

She felt a hand on her shoulder and nearly leapt out of her skin.

She turned.

Patrick was gazing at her, those eyes she knew so well scanning her countenance. He reached out a hand to touch her cheek, then gently moved his thumb across her mouth. She could feel tears welling up and shut her eyes to staunch the flow and block out the vision of his face, so familiar and yet so far out of reach. Oh God, he was kissing her. Proper kisses. Soft and gentle, like no kiss they had ever shared before. And suddenly she was in his arms and she was pulling him closer and closer and it was almost like dying, because every time they had ever been together flashed before her, but never had it been like this. It had never been like this with anyone. And Mayday knew, as she fell into a deep tunnel filled with silver stars, that it would never be like this again . . .

17

Honeycote House didn't know what had hit it. For the past three days it had been undergoing a complete makeover in anticipation of the following weekend's celebrations, and even though it was now Sunday it was clear it wasn't over yet. Mickey and Lucy had attacked the house and grounds with vigour, enlisting help from the various gardeners, odd-job men and decorators they had employed over the years. All the paddocks and lawns had been mown to perfection, the hedges clipped with precision, the flower beds weeded and their edges cut. Lucy had gone mad with a paintbrush: everything that stood still long enough was given a touch up, including the front door and the outside loo in the stableyard, where she'd even put on a new wooden seat that didn't wobble precariously when you sat on it. Every tub was planted up with white pansies. A lorry arrived with tons of pale yellow Cotswold chippings for the drive – it took them three hours to rake it all evenly, but when they had finished they wondered why they had never bothered before.

Mickey and Lucy had fallen into bed exhausted on Saturday night, but found they both woke up early on Sunday raring to go as soon as the sun rose, filling the sky with a golden May glow that was impossible to ignore.

'It's amazing what a difference all this has made,' Lucy observed, as they perused their handiwork of the day before, cups of coffee in hand. 'Really, we've been total slobs all these years.'

'There's nothing wrong with a bit of decaying decadence,' countered Mickey. Much as he appreciated the way the house and grounds were looking, he didn't want some sort of precedent being set. The Liddiards had never been the type to spend the weekends mowing the lawn and washing their cars. There was too much fun to be had.

Lucy poked him playfully in the ribs. 'I think that's rather glamorizing the fact that actually you can't be arsed.'

They spent the morning clearing out one of the stables to use as storage for the drinks. In the loose box next door, Pudding the pony was booting the door with his foot, indignant at having been locked in. He couldn't be trusted not to escape and eat all the newly potted bedding plants.

'Pudding!' Lucy chided him. 'You know, Mickey, I've been thinking . . .'

Mickey looked away, knowing from experience that any brainwave women had at the eleventh hour was bound to involve stress or money. Or both.

'What?'

'It's silly keeping Pudding here. We're never going to use him again.'

'You don't mean sell him?' Mickey looked outraged. All the children had learnt to ride on Pudding who, despite his frisky demeanour, was nudging thirty. 'He's part of the family.'

'Exactly. So we should give him to James and Caroline.

He'd be perfect for Henry and Constance. He could live in their orchard.'

'I suppose he'd have more fun if he was ridden,' Mickey admitted.

Lucy wiped her hands on her jeans and rearranged the tendrils of hair that had come loose. 'I want to put another coat of paint on the front door, then I promised to pop over and see how James is coping without Caroline. I'll run it past him.'

Mickey nodded. 'I'll sweep out the rest of the yard and get the hanging baskets up.'

Lucy gave him a hug. 'Do you know what? I've really enjoyed doing this. It's therapeutic, somehow.'

'Bloody hard work, if you ask me,' grumbled Mickey. 'Let's go to the pub for lunch.'

'It's a deal,' said Lucy happily.

Mickey watched her go. In some ways she was right. The hard physical work of the weekend had taken his mind off things. But every now and then reality swooped in and punched him in the stomach, almost taking his breath away.

In a week's time, this would be the setting for a joyous family occasion, with feasting, merriment and celebration. But it would be a total pantomime, with none of the guests knowing the truth behind the scenery and the masks. It was going to be a pretty convincing charade. Mickey had almost fooled himself that everything was going to be all right. And Lucy was entirely taken in. She didn't suspect a thing. In fact, she was the happiest he had seen her in a long time.

Mickey felt his mood plummet and the gloom take hold.

Pudding kicked on his door. He wanted to get out.

'I know exactly how you feel, mate,' said Mickey.

A couple of miles away, his brother James stared gloomily down into his coffee cup, trying to assemble his thoughts over the thundering noise of the television, and came to the conclusion that he was a complete arsehole.

He didn't like the person he had become any more than anyone else did. Caustic, ungiving, arrogant. But he was petrified. The bills flooded in week after week, and there just wasn't the income stream to cover it. He'd lost his touch. His private client base had dwindled to nothing – not necessarily through any fault of his own, as some of them had died, others moved abroad. But he had done little to replenish them and now he was paying the price. It was becoming more and more difficult to lure customers through the door of the antique shop. Too much competition, the internet, the fashion for sleek, modern designs – there were a hundred reasons why.

Before, he would have had time to get out and about and network amongst his contacts, pump them for information and ideas, maybe even pinch a few clients off someone else. But he was being pulled in too many different directions. As soon as five o'clock came he was keenly aware that he was expected home. He couldn't go out for a quiet supper with the local auctioneer, or a dealer down from London, or slip up to town during the big antique fairs to get the lowdown and the gossip. He wasn't a free agent any longer. He was a married man with three children.

In theory, he should be happy to go home at the allotted hour. But his vision of marriage and fatherhood was so far removed from what greeted him when he walked over the threshold that he had come to resent his curfew. The chaos of the children's tea was still all over the kitchen when he came in, the children were grizzling and Caroline was at her wit's end. He supposed these days it was unreasonable to expect to find three bathed and fed infants waiting eagerly for their hard-working father to bestow a kiss on each of their brows before being stuffed into sweet-smelling beds and falling asleep at half past six. It was gone eight before Caroline finally came down to the kitchen and started their supper.

Now, he realized after just twenty-four hours what hard work it was for her. Thank God Lucy had sorted out Percy for them. James had been shattered last night when he had finally got the children into bed after a day of internecine riots, tantrums and occasional bouts of vomiting, but at least he had been able to get a full eight hours sleep before they woke again. Poor Caroline had been dealing with this on major sleep deprivation until recently. James felt cowed by his discovery. And not a little ashamed. He had been so wrapped up in his own tale of woe that he had dismissed her plight as self-induced and exaggerated.

They were, he realized, in a mess. Financial, emotional, physical, practical. And he was buggered if he could see a way out. For a start, he couldn't bring himself to admit to failure. He just couldn't open his mouth and tell Caroline they were practically on the breadline, that he hadn't broken even for months, and that next month's mortgage payment was looking decidedly dodgy. He'd already worked out that he could take a mortgage holiday, but that was the start of a slippery slope. It was just a delaying tactic. Though perhaps by the time the month after was due they would know what was happening to the brewery. That was the straw he was clutching at. Getting rid of his shares would bring them some respite. Another few months at Lyttleton House, at least. And perhaps by then a miracle would have happened. Some television reality show would have made antiques all the rage. Proper antiques, not the car boot tat that was so prevalent. People were always coming into the shop with bits of old rubbish wrapped up in the *Daily Mirror*, wanting a valuation. Perhaps a television director would wander in one day – the Cotswolds was always full of media types on weekend breaks – and spot James's star quality. He would be cast as an expert, become a celebrity in his own right . . .

James sighed. There was no point in fantasizing. It was quite simple. He shouldn't have bought such a big house. But he wanted his family to be brought up in the same surroundings he'd enjoyed. Lyttleton wasn't quite as large as Honeycote House, but it had come at a price. A price he was paying every month, and it was hurting. He cursed his aspirations, his snobbery and his pride. He would rather die than downsize. The humiliation would be unbearable. And how could he do it to his wife and children?

There was a roar of outrage from the living room as the latest video came to an end. He got up wearily to put on another one. He'd always been rather sniffy about the children being plonked in front of the television, but now he understood.

When he came back into the kitchen, Lucy was letting herself in the back door.

'I've had a brainwave,' she said brightly. 'I wondered if you would like Pudding?'

'Pudding?' James was puzzled. It was only just after breakfast.

Lucy laughed. 'Pudding the pony,' she explained. 'Connie's just about big enough to be led on him. I thought it would do Caroline good, to get back with horses. And the exercise would—'

'I can't afford to keep a fucking pony, Lucy.' James sat down rather heavily.

Lucy helped herself to a coffee from the extortionately expensive Italian cappuccino machine James had bought, unable to stand a moment longer the freeze-dried coffee granules that Caroline provided.

'He only eats a few pony nuts and a bit of hay.'

'Wormers, vet bills, shoeing, insurance? And Connie would need a new hat and a back protector . . .'

Lucy looked crestfallen at his lack of enthusiasm. 'We can sort out hats—'

'Lucy. Don't you get it?' The warning tone in James's voice silenced her. He put his head in his hands. 'Oh God. What a mess.'

Lucy came and sat next to him, sliding an arm round his shoulders. He shrugged her away. When he looked up, his face was bleak, devoid of any hope. It frightened her.

'What is it, James?'

'I don't know what to do, Lucy. I don't know where to turn.'

'What's the matter? I mean, I know you and Caroline haven't been very happy lately.'

'That's an understatement.' He sighed. 'It's everything.

Business is bad. And we aren't getting on. We never seem to have any fun. It's just a constant battle from dawn till dusk. And I can't afford to get us out of the mire. We both desperately need a holiday. But I'm . . . practically broke, Lucy. And I don't know what to do.'

'Have you talked to Caroline?'

'God, no. She's got enough to worry about. And we can't exchange two words without it turning into a full-scale row.'

'Well, I think you should. If you're being beastly—'

'Beastly?' James gave a bark of sardonic laughter. It was typical of Lucy to use a word like that. Caroline would use more succinct, four letter words to describe him, he was sure.

'You are being beastly, James. I've seen how you treat her.' Lucy fixed him with a stern stare. 'I think if you both went at this as a team, instead of fighting like cats and dogs, you might have a chance. But you're at each other's throats. Constantly.'

'There's just no respite. This bloody house is chaos. I can't handle it.'

'For heaven's sake, James. I think you're expecting too much.'

'Too much?' James exploded. 'You always seemed to manage.' He pointed around the kitchen. 'You'd never let your house get into a state like this. There were never Cheerios down the back of the sofa and potties full of wee ready to trip over. You never ran out of bog roll. You never gave Mickey macaroni cheese made with a shop-bought sauce three nights running. You didn't look like a bag lady . . .'

He trailed off miserably.

As he spoke, it struck him that Lucy was the root of his problems. Lucy was the dream woman against whom he had compared his own wife. He remembered when Sophie, Georgina and Patrick were little. Honeycote House always had an underlying air of calm, even though there was always something going on. Lucy seemed to juggle parties and fun while always making sure the children were clean and fed and in bed at a decent hour. His enduring memory was of the three children in their pyjamas eating boiled eggs at the kitchen table while Lucy prepared a supper party for twelve. An hour later she would reappear looking impossibly glamorous, the children tucked up in bed, ready to greet her guests with a smile and a tray of home-made canapes. There was no way on God's earth Caroline could pull that off. It was all she could do to get their own supper on the table, and that was usually inedible.

Lucy was an angel. Mickey didn't deserve her. And James's feelings for her were as strong as ever. She only had to crook her finger and he would come running.

She was talking to him now. That low, gentle voice that he loved.

'I think you've got a rather romanticized view of things,' she said quietly. 'And it wasn't quite the same for me as it is for Caroline. For a start, I didn't give birth to three children in quick succession. Patrick's not actually mine, remember. He was nearly at school by the time I married Mickey and had Sophie and Georgina. And I can assure you, there were days when I looked pretty dreadful. It wasn't easy. Besides, I'm not a career girl like Caroline. I was quite happy to keep house and look after the children. I expect Caroline's frustrated.'

'Don't I know it. She keeps ramming it down my throat.'

'Then talk to her. Talk to her about the business. See if you can come up with a plan of action between you. She's probably got some fantastic ideas, but if you don't give her the opportunity, if you don't tell her there's a problem, then she can't help.'

James tried to look convinced by Lucy's argument. He knew she was talking sense.

'Remember the girl you married, James. Caroline had a high-powered job when you met. She was incredibly successful. You've got to try and find that person and make her your ally. Not push her away.'

'She pushes me away.' James remembered the few times he had endeavoured to reach out to Caroline in bed, and her outright rejection. He could feel her recoil whenever he touched her.

'All marriages have their rough patches. You've just got to decide to make it work, and accept that you can't necessarily have things as you'd like them. Then try and enjoy what's good.'

'Easy to say.'

'You have to. Look at me and Mickey. Our marriage hasn't always been a bed of roses. But we got through it. Look at us now.' She beamed. 'We've had a fantastic weekend, just working on the house, getting ready for the wedding. Teamwork. That's what it's about.'

For James, time stood still. He stared at Lucy, standing with her back to the sink, in her jeans and an old Sloppy Joe sweat-shirt splattered in paint, her hands curled round her mug. Here she was, lecturing him in his own kitchen about how to run his marriage, holding herself up as an example, when she had no idea of the truth. She was totally deluded. Teamwork?

He had one second to decide whether to disabuse her. To tell her that her perfect marriage was a sham. For James hadn't been fooled by Patrick's charade for one moment. His brother hadn't been able to meet his eye at the board meeting, when Patrick had confessed all. You didn't grow up with someone and not learn to recognize signs of guilt. Kay's illegitimate brat belonged to Mickey, and he was about to sell off his share of the brewery to pay for it. And Lucy didn't have a clue.

If James told her the truth, he would be there to pick up the pieces. Just like he had been last time, when she had originally found out about Mickey's affair with Kay. He remembered making love to her when she'd come to him for comfort, knowing she was vulnerable but unable to resist making his dream come true.

He gazed at her. Even in her scruffiest clothes, she was stunning. She should be his. He had the key.

But it wouldn't work this time around either, for he knew that he had shown his true colours. In treating Caroline the way he had, Lucy had lost all respect for him. She would never want him now. He had seen the look of disgust in her eyes on more than one occasion. And she had made it clear to him what she thought of him, that Sunday they had all gone round for Mickey's birthday. By telling her Mickey's secret, he would only prove that he was not worthy, for he wouldn't be doing it for the right reasons, but purely selfish ones.

He had a split second to make up his mind. Whether to blow everything apart. Or to put his obsession with Lucy to rest, and find a way to resuscitate his marriage.

He took a deep breath. 'Do you think it's too late for me and Caroline?' he asked her.

'Of course not,' said Lucy stoutly. 'You've just got to get your act together. Having kids is hard, James, but I can assure you, it goes all too quickly. Before you know it, they've gone. They're getting married. The house is empty. And it's shit.'

James swallowed. He could see the glimmer of a tear in her eye.

'I'm just saying enjoy them,' she croaked. 'They're beautiful. And so is Caroline.' She stood up. 'I've got to go. I want to put another coat of paint on the front door before lunch.'

She put her cup in the sink and walked over to the door. She was so perfect. So fucking unbelievably perfect. She should have been his. But she wasn't.

'Thanks, Lucy,' he managed, raising a weary hand in farewell. And when she'd gone, he put his head in his arms.

A moment later, Henry came tearing in, skidding across the floor.

'Dad, we're bored. And Percy's puked. Can we go somewhere? '

James's initial reaction was to refuse, to snarl at Henry to bugger off and leave him alone. But something in what Lucy had said sank in. Maybe he should try taking her advice.

'Oh dear, poor old Percy. Let's get a cloth, shall we?' he said cheerfully, standing up. 'And where would you like to go?'

'Birdland!' yelled Henry.

Great, thought James. Penguins, peacocks, pelicans. Fucking marvellous.

'What a good idea.'

While Lucy went to see James, Mickey swept the whole of the stableyard until it was clean enough to eat his lunch off. He stopped for a breather, leaning over the stable door, staring at Pudding. He could feel his chest tighten, and a sharp pain under his ribs. It was difficult to breathe. He hoped he wasn't having a heart attack. Not now. It would ruin the wedding. The sale of the brewery. Kay. Everything. He tried to keep himself calm, but the pain just intensified.

It was the pony that was doing it. Every time he looked at the little creature, he imagined Flora on his back. How the hell could he give him away when his own daughter, his own flesh and blood, would undoubtedly get as much pleasure from him as Sophie and Georgina had? For Flora was as much his as they were.

Mickey knew he couldn't carry on. He couldn't deny Flora's existence any longer. He had to come clean to Lucy. He knew he would never be able to sleep at night if he went ahead with the plan as it was. Even though Kay wasn't pressing him for recognition, it was the honourable thing to do.

Besides, he owed it to Patrick. He couldn't let his son start married life with a slur on his reputation that he wasn't even responsible for. OK, so it hadn't been made common knowledge, but at the end of the day Mickey realized he had used Patrick shamelessly, taken advantage of his sense of honour. He couldn't continue the deception. Even if he lost everything, Mickey decided, then at least he would know he had done the decent thing for once in his life.

Pudding lifted up his chin as high as he could and rested it on the stable door, peering over at him in a quizzical fashion. Mickey took another breath in, and the pain in his chest seemed to dissipate. Maybe he'd just overdone the sweeping.

'Don't give him his nuts yet. He'll guzzle them down. I'll give him a net of hay to be getting on with.' Lucy was back. She was striding across the yard with a smile. 'Puds, you've had a reprieve. It looks like we're stuck with you.'

She scratched the pony between the ears and looked at Mickey ruefully.

'James doesn't want him. He's really on his uppers, apparently. Practically bankrupt. Do you think there's anything we can do to help?'

Poor, sweet, generous, naïve Lucy. She hadn't a clue that the treacherous Liddiard brothers had already conspired to sell their birthright to get them out of their respective holes. Mickey pushed his hair back out of his eyes. He reeked of sweat from the morning's work. He'd go and have a bath, get a bottle of wine out of the fridge, sit Lucy down—

No. That was another of his faults. Procrastination.

'Lucy. I've got something to tell you.'

Her face went pale. 'Don't tell me Sophie's not going to make it back.'

She was living for seeing her eldest daughter again.

'No,' said Mickey hastily. 'Nothing like that.'

'Oh. What, then?'

He could just say that the fridge they were using for

drinks wasn't going to fit into the stable because the extension cable wouldn't reach.

'Kay Oakley. She came to see me. A few weeks ago.'

'I thought the Oakleys had gone to Portugal. Are they back?' Lucy flicked back the stable bolt and went to get Pudding's haynet. 'Why did she want to see you?'

'She's got a daughter. A little girl called Flora. She's . . . she's . . .'

'What?' Lucy paused in the doorway. Pudding nudged her with his nose, reminding her of the task in hand.

'She's mine, Lucy. Flora's mine.'

Lucy said nothing for a moment. She stepped out of the stable and shut the door, still holding the net in her hand.

'How do you know?'

'Well . . . Kay told me.'

'Can she prove it?' The tone of her voice had altered completely. It was flat, hard.

'She doesn't need to prove it. The dates add up. And . . . Lawrence was sterile, apparently.'

'Was?'

'He's dead. He died in a car crash, a few months ago.'

There was a moment as Lucy took in this information. Then she started to laugh. 'For God's sake, Mickey. You haven't fallen for that old trick? Surely you know Kay well enough? She'd say the Pope was the father if she thought she could get something out of it—'

Mickey spoke as gently as he could. 'I've seen the child. I don't need to do a paternity test.'

Lucy stopped laughing. She took in a deep shuddering breath. 'You've seen her?'

'She's beautiful. She's just like Sophie, but with a bit of—'

The words were knocked out of him as Lucy dropped the haynet and punched him in the stomach with all her might. 'You bastard!'

Mickey slumped back against the wall, winded, gasping for air. Lucy stepped forward again, her fists still clenched, and he cowered, appalled by the extent of her rage.

'You complete and utter shit. You knew I wanted another child. And all along you had your own. How could you do that to me, Mickey?'

'Hold on. I didn't know about Flora. Not until—'

'Don't waste your breath lying to me.'

'It's true. Kay came to me for money. Lawrence left her penniless.'

'My heart bleeds.'

'Lucy, we're talking about a little girl. A little five-year-old girl. I can't just cut her out of my life. I've got to support her.'

He'd told her this much. He had to get it all out.

'I'm selling my shares in the brewery. And so is James. We . . . think Keith wants out as well.'

Lucy stepped back, brushing her hair out of her eyes. 'You're selling the brewery?'

'Selling our share. It's probably not as bad as it sounds. We've got someone who's interested in investing. And Patrick will still be on board. We think it's for the best, getting out now.' Mickey spoke as fast as he could in an effort to convince her that the decision made sense. 'The brewery needs heavy investment if it's going to survive, and we don't have the resources—'

'Not if you're having to pay for illegitimate brats. And houses you can't afford. No.'

Mickey flinched. Lucy crossed her arms.

'Well, you've obviously all discussed it. Does Ginny know you're selling? Or Caroline? Or Mandy, for that matter?'

'We . . . didn't want to worry any of you. Until things were definite.'

'How very emancipated of you.'

'Lucy. Please. I've tried to do the right thing. For everyone.'

Mickey had never seen such a terrible expression on Lucy's face. Disappointment, hurt, betrayal. Loathing. Disgust.

She finally spoke. 'Rubbish,' she said bitterly. 'If I know you, you've tried to slither out of it, keep it quiet, get everyone else to cover your back. Anything but face up to reality.'

Mickey felt the words slice through him like the sharpest sabre. Is that really how little she thought of him?

Lucy walked away from him, then broke into a run, disappearing around the side of the house. He heard her car start up, then drive off.

Pudding gave an impatient whinny. He could see the bloody haynet. Mickey picked it up wearily and went to tie it onto the ring.

'OK, Pudding,' he sighed. 'What the hell do I do now?'

James had summoned up all of his courage and taken the children to Birdland. It had taken him an hour and a half to get them dressed and ready and to remember all the stuff he had to take with him, but he had managed it.

As they stood in front of the flamingos, he felt an overwhelming sense of achievement. Henry and Constance were jumping up and down with excitement, Percy was crowing with delight in his pushchair and against his better judgement James had bought them packets of sweets to stuff in on their way round.

He decided that maybe it wasn't so hard to bring himself down to their level. He'd always been rather petrified of taking charge, but when you got down to it their needs were pretty simple. OK, it was exhausting, and the whole nappy thing was pretty grim. But once you'd accepted that you had to do it, it wasn't so bad after all.

He felt rather proud. So proud that he helped himself to a handful of Haribo from Henry's bag and ate them without gagging. He would do chicken nuggets and potato smiley faces for lunch, he decided, instead of the calves' liver and mash he had been quietly determined to make them eat before his conversion.

His phone rang. Maybe it was Caroline. He went to answer it with a smile. She'd be astonished when she found out where they were.

But it was Lucy. She sounded strained.

'James. Where are you?'

'Birdland! We're having a brilliant time. I took your advice—'

She didn't seem interested. 'Did you know? About this child?' she demanded.

James sensed he had to proceed with caution. 'Which child?' he asked lightly.

'How many are there?' said Lucy with a heavy irony. 'Kay Oakley's. The one she's using to wheedle a fortune out of our family.'

'Uuh . . . um,' said James slowly, playing for time, trying to work out what she knew already, and what his story should be. 'You mean . . . Patrick's little indiscretion?' He thought he'd better toe the party line for the time being.

Lucy let out a hiss. 'Is that what you've been told? That it's Patrick's?'

'You mean it isn't?' He was treading very carefully.

'You know it isn't.' Her tone was deadly. 'I don't believe you Liddiard men. Kay Oakley saunters back into your life with her demands and you drop everything and start selling off the family silver.'

'Lucy. We have a duty to the child.'

'What about the duty you have to your own wives and children? You've been sitting there in that boardroom, making decisions that affect us all, without asking us what we think. It's insulting. And chauvinistic. I bet Caroline would have something to say about it if she knew.'

'You're probably right.'

'Is that all you've got to say? You're just going to stand by and watch while everything falls apart?'

James looked up at the pale spring sky. He looked at Constance and Henry peering over the wall at the pelicans. He didn't want to get involved. He shuddered to think that less than two hours ago he might have been up to his neck in it. Common sense, thank God, had prevailed. Now he didn't have time to sort out Lucy's marriage. He had his own to deal with.

'It's not really anything to do with me,' he said mildly.

'How much is she asking for, James?'

'I'm not sure, exactly.'

'You must have some idea.'

'Um . . . I think it was . . . somewhere around . . . half a million. Roughly?'

Lucy uttered an exclamation of disgust and impatience and hung up.

'Dad, can we go and watch the penguins being fed?' pleaded Henry.

'Absolutely,' said James.

Penguins, he decided, were far more important than paternity suits.

18

Keith smiled happily down at his roast chicken. He didn't think he had ever been so pleased to see Sunday lunch in his life. The day before, he hadn't been sure he would even see the choice that Sandra had made for him, let alone feel like eating it. He was starving. He picked up his knife and fork with relish.

OK, so he was in a bit of discomfort. And he wasn't all that keen on tubes and catheters, but he had been assured that they would come out soon. Counteracting that was the relief. It was a wonderful feeling and he revelled in it again and again, enjoying the pleasure those few words gave him: the cancer is no longer within me. He felt he deserved to wallow; after all, he had spent so much time worrying.

With every bite of his meal, he felt strength flowing back into him. Not just physical strength, but mental. He felt ready to take on the world. With his anxiety dispatched into the ether, there was suddenly space in his head for everything he had been neglecting ever since his first trip to see the consultant. Before, he hadn't been able to focus on anything, because the fear had dominated his every waking moment.

There were so many things to think about. The

wedding – he was thrilled to know that he would be able to walk Mandy up the aisle next Saturday, even though he would need to take it easy. But at least he would be able to concentrate on the joy of the occasion, without the dark shadow that had been dogging him.

He must focus on the brewery, too. He had only been able to look through the proposal they had received half-heartedly. Now he would be able to go through it with a fine-tooth comb, and draw up a list of questions to fire at their proposed buyer. He knew it was all too easy to make things look enticing on paper. Words cost nothing, after all.

Most important of all was Ginny. She was due back tomorrow evening. He should do something to welcome her home. Perhaps book a table at the Lygon – he would be able to enjoy it properly this time. And he would tell her everything; ask for her understanding and her forgiveness. He could do that now that he knew he was going to be all right.

He smiled as he put down his knife and fork, then pulled the bowl filled with apple crumble and custard towards him. As he picked up his spoon, he could hear Sandra's voice fluting down the corridor. He closed his eyes, wishing that she wasn't here. For all his buoyant mood, he suddenly felt very tired. Perhaps it was the rather large lunch, or the after-effects of the anaesthetic, but his lids felt heavy.

Sandra swept in.

'I thought I'd let you rest this morning,' she said. 'I went over to Keeper's Cottage to make sure it was spick and span. Changed your sheets. Hoovered round a bit. Scrubbed the bathroom. You want everything pristine for when you go back – we don't want you picking up any infections. And to be honest, it needed doing. I suppose everyone just ran off to the airport without a second thought on Friday.'

Keith felt rather indignant on everyone's behalf. The cottage had been fine when he left. And to be fair, it wasn't as if they knew he was going into hospital.

Sandra sat down on the chair next to his bed.

'I've told Mr Jackson he can pop over to the villa for a week's holiday if he likes. As a thank you.'

'That's very thoughtful of you.'

'Although he'll have to hurry up. I'll be putting it on the market soon.'

'Will you?' Keith looked at her, surprised. 'But you've only just bought it.'

She gave him a look that made his heart sink. A look that was part triumphant, part coy.

'We can really go places, Keith,' she said, her voice simmering with promise. 'We are going to make such a team. We've got the world at our feet.'

'Have we?' Keith wished he hadn't guzzled his lunch so quickly. He felt slightly queasy.

'It's what should have happened at the very start. We should have worked as a team in the first place, instead of driving ourselves apart. We should have moved together, to the Cotswolds. I should have been at your side. I should have supported you. Honeycote Ales wouldn't be in the mess it's in now. But at least it's not too late.'

Keith pushed his bowl to one side, his appetite suddenly vanished. 'Too late?' he faltered. 'For what?'

'Keith . . .' She peered at him from underneath her immaculately coiffed fringe, a smile playing on her lips.

'We're meant to be together. We know that. And what a beautiful, beautiful present for Mandy. Her mum and dad back together. It's almost poetic.' There was a dreamy expression in her eyes.

'Sorry, Sandra . . . I . . .' He was scrabbling for any memory that might give him a clue what she was on about. 'I don't think I understand.'

She looked rather put out by his lack of comprehension.

'Last night. You told me that you loved me.'

'Yes. But there are different sorts of love, Sandra. I meant . . .'

What had he meant? His memory was a bit blurry. Things had been coming back to him in the wrong order all morning, because he had been dozing on and off. He remembered feeling all sorts of things for Sandra the day before. A certain fondness, and appreciation of everything she had done for him. And a definite regret. But not the sort of regret that meant he wanted to start again. Just sorrow that they had caused each other such pain.

All of those things had obviously combined to send out the wrong message. When he had told her he loved her, she had misinterpreted it as a desire for reconciliation. He had meant that he loved her as a friend. Not husband and wife.

Keith shuddered inwardly at the prospect. Sandra might have changed, but not beyond recognition. Her assertiveness, her ability to take control, her steely deter-mination had been just what he'd needed the day before, but he knew it would drive him mad before long. She was incapable of getting anything other than her own way. Sometimes that was a strength. It was undoubtedly what had made her a success in business. But Keith knew he couldn't live with it.

The set of her jaw now, for example. He remembered it from their marriage. It was a look that brooked no argument. So many times he had given in to it, just for a quiet life.

He wasn't going to give in this time. He had to let her down. He would like to do it gently, but the problem was that with Sandra if you did things gently she didn't always get the message.

He summoned up his courage.

'Sandra,' he said firmly. 'We might as well get this straight right now. I'm extremely grateful for your support over the past couple of days. You were a pillar of strength to me in my darkest hour. I will never be able to thank you enough. But there can't be any more between us. Too much time has passed. We can't go backwards. And . . . I love Ginny. Despite what you might think, we are happy together. Any tension between us at the moment is entirely my fault. And I'd like to think it was for a good reason. Now I know I'm all right I can make amends. I'm sorry if I sent out the wrong message to you – I wouldn't want to hurt you for the world.'

He forced himself to look her in the eye. He had to make it absolutely clear. The tiniest chink in his armour and she would be straight in.

'There can be nothing between us. I hope you understand.'

There was a tiny pause. Sandra smiled, stood up and took away his tray. Then she went back to his bedside and smoothed his covers.

'I think you should have a rest,' she said in a soothing

401

voice. 'It's all been rather too much for you. We can talk about things later.'

Despite himself, Keith felt his eyelids go. She was right. It had been a bit much. His speech had been a huge effort. And it would be heavenly to drift off into oblivion, knowing that he wasn't going to jerk awake with anxiety, that everything was all right . . .

As soon as she was satisfied he was asleep, Sandra picked up her mobile and went out into the corridor. She'd tried phoning him three times already this morning, but he hadn't answered. Typical bloody Spaniard. He might cook like an angel and fuck like the devil incarnate, but he had no sense of urgency whatsoever. If she didn't get the evidence in the next twelve hours, it would be too late. She had to strike while Keith was still vulnerable. It wasn't a task she was necessarily going to enjoy, as he would probably be very upset. But she would be there to comfort him. And the ends would justify the means, she was confident of that. It was only right that they should be together again.

'Alejandro,' she barked into the handset as his voicemail clicked in. 'Call me back immediately. I need to know what's going on ASAP . . .'

The sun hung hot and heavy over the deserted swimming pool. Silence reigned inside the cool walls of the villa. Lunchtime came and went, but still the inhabitants slumbered on, much-needed sleep repairing their excesses of the night before.

Ginny was the first to wake. Her mouth felt dry and her head felt . . . where, she wasn't quite sure. As she sat up, her heart crashed about inside her chest. Why was she feeling so unsettled? What had happened? Something. She knew there was something. Crazy images were replaying themselves in her head. Images she could neither believe nor comprehend.

She looked around for clues.

She was quite alone in her bed. The sheets were smooth, unrumpled. There was no evidence of any foul play.

Sex. Filthy, deep down and dirty, sinful sex. That's all she could remember. Her limbs twitched and her flesh trembled as she tried to piece together what had happened, but even as it all came back to her she couldn't believe it. She must have had more sun than she had thought. She must have spent the night hallucinating. She had no idea the sun could do that to you. It was dangerous . . .

The house was as quiet as a grave. She didn't know what time the revellers had finally got in, but if experience was anything to go by they wouldn't be up for hours. She pulled on her dressing gown and ventured out into the cool of the corridor. She followed it down to the living room. There, the scent of the candles hit her, sending her stomach tumbling. She saw the sheepskin rug, and had a flashback of its softness that was so real it took her breath away.

Alejandro. She remembered now. Oh God. Ginny put a hand to her mouth. The memories came back to her, as clear as day. Now she could remember, she could smell him on her. The scent made her feel quite peculiar. She thought she might swoon.

A figure appeared in the room. Kitty, yawning, wrapping herself in a kimono. Her daughter peered at her.

'Mum? What are you laughing at?'

'Nothing.' Her voice sounded strangled. 'Did you have a nice time last night?'

'Great. You'd have hated it. It's lucky you didn't come.'

Oh, but I did, thought Ginny, and wanted to giggle again. She pulled herself together. Why on earth was she laughing? It really wasn't funny. It was tragic. What if someone had caught them? She couldn't remember what time it was when Alejandro finally took his leave, but there was no doubt the girls could have walked in on them at any moment and got the shock of their lives. Him and Ginny rolling round on the carpet like tiger cubs. Not a pretty picture—

Picture. Suddenly she remembered pictures and it didn't seem quite as funny any more.

'Coffee?' she managed to ask. She needed caffeine, something to clear her head. She really did feel most odd.

'Are you sure you're all right? You look really . . .'

'What? Rough?'

'No, actually. Sort of . . . sparkly.'

'Fresh air. Spanish sunshine. Change of scene.' Ginny spoke lightly. She didn't want anyone looking too closely at her.

Kitty shrugged as Sasha came in.

'What, no kitchen staff?' she demanded. 'I was expecting to be hand-fed fresh fruit at the very least.'

'He's allowed a day off, isn't he?' Ginny couldn't bring herself to say his name.

There was a knock at the door.

'That's probably him now. I'll get it.' Sasha wandered over to the door. Ginny's tummy lurched. She wasn't ready to face him yet. She didn't know what to say. Or think. Or do.

But it wasn't Alejandro.

'It's the police,' announced Sasha. 'I think they're after Caroline.'

Two swarthy policemen followed her into the house, brandishing their badges. Sasha looked at Kitty, alarmed.

'Did Caroline come back?'

'Shit.'

The pair of them rushed towards Caroline's room, followed by the policemen.

'Hey!' shouted Ginny in indignation. Did they have a warrant? Did they need one? It probably didn't matter either way. This was Spain. She had a feeling the rules were a bit different over here, if all those Ray Winstone films were to be believed.

Caroline sat up in alarm as the twins burst into her room, followed by two uniformed officers who started gabbling at her in broken English and pointing in excitement at her chest. Realizing she was stark naked, she put her hands over her nipples.

'Does somebody want to tell me what's going on, exactly?'

'Madam, you are under arrest.'

'What on earth for?' she demanded indignantly.

The larger of the two jabbed at her chest again.

Baffled, Caroline looked down, then spotted the source of their excitement.

'Ah,' she said. 'The necklace. Bugger. I'd forgotten all about it.' She shook back her hair and smiled at them sweetly. 'It's OK. It's just a misunderstanding.' She went to take it off, then realized she would be baring her assets once again. 'Um, if one of you would like to take it off, you can take it back to Mr Romaine. Then perhaps I could go back to sleep. This is the first proper lie in I've had for months.'

Sadly, however, it wasn't that simple. The Spanish police had her marked as a professional jewel thief. They ordered her to get dressed, removed the necklace as soon as she was decent, and promptly arrested her. Ginny did her best to negotiate with them, but they were having none of it.

'I think I'd have done a better job of covering my tracks if I did this for a living,' stormed Caroline as they put her into the back of the police car dressed in last night's frock and a pair of trainers. 'I'm not a complete idiot.'

By now Mandy had been woken by the furore and joined them on the front step. The four of them watched helplessly as the police car whisked her off.

'Bastards!' exclaimed Sasha. 'It's a set up. They're as corrupt as anything over here. He was probably using her as a donkey.'

'A what?' Kitty looked at her sister, completely flummoxed.

'You mean a mule,' Ginny corrected her with a sigh. 'I suppose I'd better phone James.'

This was exactly the sort of scenario she had been dreading. And she wasn't feeling up to it at all.

'You can't phone James.' Kitty was horrified at the idea. 'It's not going to look very good, is it? How can we explain what's happened without admitting she copped off with a diamond broker?'

'It might do him good to know he's got competition. And anyway, she didn't sleep with him, did she?' Sasha started laughing. 'Just ran off with the swag.'

'It's not funny,' Ginny reprimanded her. 'She could be in serious trouble.'

'Why don't we call Alejandro?' suggested Mandy.

'No,' said Ginny quickly. 'There's nothing he'll be able to do.'

'At least he can speak Spanish,' Sasha pointed out reasonably.

'I haven't got his number,' Ginny tried as a last resort.

'I have!' cried Kitty. 'He gave it to me in case we got stuck for a taxi last night.'

Ginny bit her lip as Kitty got out her phone. She turned to Mandy. 'Do you know if your mum's got a solicitor over here?'

Mandy shrugged. 'She must have. But I don't know who. Shall I call her?'

Kitty hung up the phone. 'Alejandro says he'll meet us at the police station.'

Hurrah, thought Ginny. A perfect Sunday. Trying to get someone out of a foreign jail when your only ally is the pool-boy you've been rolling round on the carpet with . . .

Despite Ginny's misgivings, Alejandro was an absolute star. He arrived at the station two minutes after they did. By his demeanour, the previous night might never have happened. He gave nothing away, just greeted the girls solemnly and listened to the story.

'There's no way Caroline meant to steal the necklace. I mean, you don't go round wearing the evidence, do you?' Sasha was indignant. 'The bloke's obviously pissed off because he didn't get his leg over, and wants his revenge.'

'Don't worry. I will deal with it.' Alejandro was calm and reassuring. Ginny gave him a grateful smile, then blushed.

They trooped into the station, where Alejandro had several heated conversations with several different police officers, accompanied by much gesticulation and hand gestures that made Ginny quite certain Caroline would never be seen again. On the contrary, it seemed to do the trick, and later that afternoon she was released. In fact, the Spanish police seemed rather relieved to get rid of her. Even though they hadn't been able to understand most of what she was saying, they knew it wasn't complimentary. Eventually, they conceded that perhaps running off with a valuable necklace was an easy mistake to make. It never ceased to amaze them what English girls got up to when they'd had a few drinks. They didn't seem to have any self-control whatsoever. Though it did make the job interesting.

'Thank you,' said Ginny, heartfelt, as they left the station.

'My cousin is a high-up officer in Marbella,' Alejandro explained. 'He could have made life difficult for them.'

He smiled at Ginny and she felt herself turn beetroot. Now the drama was over, she had to confront her demons.

'Last night,' she stammered. 'I should never . . . Please don't say anything. To the others.'

Alejandro put a hand on her arm and she leapt back like a scalded cat.

'Hey,' he said kindly. 'Don't worry.'

For a moment he thought she was going to cry. Her chin trembled. 'I'm sorry,' she said. 'I feel as if I've lost control. Of everything. I was supposed to be in charge . . .'

Alejandro frowned. 'Caroline is grown up. She is responsible for herself. Not you.'

'No.' Ginny shook her head. 'I should have gone with them. Then it would never have happened. And I wouldn't have made a fool of myself . . .'

'You didn't make a fool of yourself,' he said softly.

'I don't usually behave like that.'

He flashed her a wicked grin. 'Well, maybe you should more often.'

Ginny closed her eyes, wondering how on earth she had got herself into this situation.

'Come on, Mum!' Sasha was shouting to her from the car. 'We're all starving. Get a move on!'

Alejandro touched her lightly on the shoulder. She felt her knees go weak.

'Go on,' he said gently. 'I'll see you back at the villa.'

Ginny was torn. Half of her wanted to tell him not to come back, that they could do without him for the next twenty-four hours of their stay. But the other half was desperate for his presence. In the end, she had no choice. The girls would think it strange if she banished him and might start asking awkward questions. Besides, he had bought a huge bag of fresh seafood to make them paella. It would be the most awful waste.

Back at the villa, Alejandro soon had everyone dicing onions, peppers and garlic, peeling king prawns and scrubbing mussels while he cooked an enormous pan full of saffron rice. Once or twice he caught Ginny's eye and she turned pink, unable to stop herself from smiling.

'You know,' he whispered in her ear as she laid the table. 'You look ten years younger than when you arrived.'

The strange thing was it was true. Ginny had looked in the mirror earlier. Her skin seemed to glow, her eyes sparkled, the worry furrow between her brows had gone, and her mouth seemed to smile rather than frown. She thought about the appointment she had booked for tomorrow. At this rate, she wasn't going to need it.

All through the evening, Alejandro could feel his mobile in his pocket, vibrating on silent. He knew exactly who it was trying to contact him. Eventually he took the phone out onto the terrace while the others ate.

'Alejandro!' Sandra's harsh voice grated down the line. 'Where are the bloody photos? For heaven's sake. Don't you understand time is of the essence?'

From the terrace, Alejandro observed Ginny at the end of the table. It had been like watching a flower unfurl. She had positively blossomed. To betray her to Sandra would be like hacking a rose in full bloom from its stem. She would shrivel up with the humiliation. Wither away.

Alejandro weighed up his options. The damning evidence was on the phone he was holding. If he took the cash, there was no denying that it would change his life for the better. Yet he knew that if he did take it, he would be haunted by her. She was so sweet, Ginny. So warm. So caring. Everything, in fact, that Sandra was not.

Could he sacrifice her just for a few hundred euros?

He tried to harden his heart. Another day and Ginny would be on a plane. He'd never see her again. He wouldn't have her on his conscience.

'Hello? Hello? Are you there?' Sandra was getting even more impatient.

'Yes. I'm here.' He made up his mind. 'And I'm sorry, Sandra. I couldn't get the photos. It was impossible.'

Sandra gave a malevolent hiss of disbelief. 'Don't be ridiculous. You can't have tried hard enough.'

'Oh, believe me. I tried very hard. And I'm not very pleased. It's never happened to me before.'

'But it's impossible. How could that . . . lump turn you down?'

It was the description of Ginny as a lump that finally did it.

'Well, she did,' said Alejandro firmly. 'And another thing, Sandra. When you get back, I won't be here.'

'Well, as long as the place is clean and tidy and the fridge is stocked. I suppose you are owed some time off.'

'No. You don't understand. It's not time off. It's goodbye.'

'Goodbye?'

He winced at the volume of the indignant shriek. He smiled.

'Or should I say . . . adios.'

'You needn't think you're getting a penny out of me! You lazy, disloyal piece of Spanish shit. After everything I've done for you!'

Everything she had done for him? Alejandro raised his eyebrows in amused disbelief. He'd given her food fit for the gods and multiple orgasms. Laughing softly, he hung up. It was no skin off his nose. There would be plenty more Sandras around wanting more of the same. He'd be in gainful employment by the end of the week, even without a reference. He was sure of that.

He looked down at the phone in his hand, then scrolled through the menu with his thumb until he found the photos in question. Looking back at them was making him feel horny. It had been some night. He debated keeping them as a memento, then decided it would be all too easy for them to fall into the wrong hands. He hesitated for a second then pressed 'delete', several times in quick succession, until all the evidence was gone.

When he came back inside the others were ribbing Caroline.

'So, what's it worth,' asked Sasha, 'to keep it quiet from James?'

'I'm not guilty of anything!' Caroline insisted. 'It was all perfectly above board.' She grinned at her own pun. 'I didn't go below deck at all.'

'Just think,' sighed Kitty. 'He might have whisked you off on a Mediterranean cruise. Showered you with even more diamonds.'

'Nah. He was bound to be a knob,' Caroline was happily dismissive.

'Anyway, Caroline's married to James,' Mandy reminded them.

'Don't be so old-fashioned, Mandy. Everyone's entitled to a bit of fun every now and then, to remind them what it's all about. Aren't they, Mum?'

Ginny could feel herself turning puce.

'I don't know,' she stammered. 'But it's probably not a good idea.'

'Well, apart from you, of course,' said Kitty kindly. 'Mum would never do anything like that. She's far too sensible.'

Ginny thought she would quite like to slide under the table and die of embarrassment. Alejandro was slicing up a pineapple as if they hadn't had wild animal sex not ten feet away from this very table.

Sandra stood in the hospital corridor, incandescent with fury.

She had no idea of her next move, and she wasn't very good at losing.

Her instinct was to chuck her mobile at the nearest wall and throw an almighty wobbler. That was what she usually did. But there would be nobody there to take any notice. Besides, that was just a cover-up for what she really wanted to do, which was to sit down and weep.

She had to face up to it. She had to acknowledge the fact that she was never going to be truly happy if she carried on behaving the way she had all of her adult life: scheming, manipulating, bullying and having tantrums. She'd come out on top materially by behaving that way. She was worth a bomb. But inside, she was worth nothing. Even Alejandro was desperate to get away from her. Was she that repellent?

Of course she was.

She had tried to get back the man she loved by tricking him, laying traps, pretending to be something she wasn't. And even if she had succeeded, she wouldn't have been able to keep up the pretence for long. Keith would have soon seen her for what she was and always had been. And how many lives would she have ruined into the bargain, just so she could get her own way?

She couldn't face going to say goodnight to him. She was terrified of breaking down, pouring out her heart and confessing all. No, decided Sandra. She would slip away, keep what was left of her dignity intact. Nobody need ever know.

She slipped out into the car park. Tears were streaming down her cheeks. She hoped nobody saw her; they might think that someone had passed away. She hurried to the door of her car. It was tempting to drive straight to the airport and see if she could get on a flight, but she had to stay another week. She would see the wedding through, see Patrick and Mandy married. And then she would take stock. Decide what to do with her life, see if she could find a way to repair the damage. Rebuild herself into the kind of woman who deserved a man like Keith.

A woman like Ginny. A kind, patient, giving, warmhearted woman with the strength to resist flattery and temptation because she believed in love.

19

On Sunday afternoon, Patrick left the train at Eldenbury station and got into his car. He wasn't sure what to do. He didn't fancy going straight home. The cottage would be empty and he would be left alone with his thoughts, which he didn't want as they made him feel too uncomfortable. He wasn't particularly proud of his behaviour.

He decided to drive over to Honeycote House to see how the preparations were going. Lucy would give him supper, he was pretty sure. And tomorrow, after a decent night's sleep, the weekend would be a memory that he could bury. His conscience was only pricking because he was tired and a bit hungover. Misdemeanours always seemed greater when you were under par.

He and Mayday had skirted round each other that morning somewhat awkwardly, having woken up tangled in each other's limbs. Luckily, breakfast arrived not long after, bringing a welcome distraction. It was wheeled in on a trolley, Hollywood movie style. There were silver domes, white plates, exquisitely prepared fruit, a basket of tiny warm croissants and Danish pastries, as well as a dish of bacon and scrambled egg. The two of them shared their meal and pretended to immerse themselves in the Sunday papers.

Each sensed that the other wanted to make their escape, but neither vocalized it. Nor did they talk about what had happened in the early hours. Discussing it would turn it into something it wasn't.

As checking-out time loomed, Mayday announced that she had decided she was going to stay another couple of days.

'I've never spent any time in London,' she said. 'And I want to explore. It's a total change of scene for me. I think it'll take my mind off what's happened recently. Gran dying,' she added hastily in explanation, in case Patrick misunderstood.

Patrick had agreed it was a good idea. He was relieved not to have to sit on the train together, or worry about being seen when they got back to the station.

'Thank you for the most fantastic weekend,' he said, hugging her goodbye as the taxi pulled up to the kerb. 'I'll never forget it.'

He didn't look back as the taxi drove off. He had to look forwards now. It was less than a week to the wedding.

Now, as he drove up the drive to Honeycote House, he was amazed at the transformation. The tyres of his car crunched merrily over the newly laid chippings, and the air was filled with the sweet smell of freshly mown grass. He suddenly felt guilty that he had left Mickey and Lucy with all the preparations while he'd been lording it up in Claridges.

The front door was ajar. It had been repainted in a muted grey-blue. Lucy had pinned up a notice warning of wet paint. He pushed the handle gingerly and walked in, thinking that the house sounded very quiet. Maybe they'd gone off to the pub.

He knew exactly what had happened as soon as he walked into the kitchen. Mickey was sitting there, head in his hands, a bottle of wine on the table in front of him.

Patrick sat down next to him. His father looked at him dully, his eyes red-rimmed. Not from tears, probably, but from drink.

'Lucy knows.'

Patrick sighed. 'I suppose it was too much to expect that it wouldn't get out. Did somebody see Kay?'

'No. I told her.'

Patrick looked at his father, aghast.

'I'm sick of living a lie. I couldn't keep it quiet any longer.'

Patrick ran his fingers through his unfamiliarly short hair, wishing he still had the length to tug at.

'How did she take it?'

Mickey's smile was grim. 'She punched me.'

'Lucy?' Patrick had never known Lucy hurt a fly.

'I've never seen her so upset. Not even when she found out about Kay in the first place.'

'Couldn't you have kept your mouth shut? At least until after the wedding?'

'I'm sorry, Patrick. The last thing I wanted to do was to ruin your day.'

Patrick felt absurdly angry. After everything he had done. After all the sacrifices he had made to keep the Liddiard name intact. He was even marrying Mandy for the family's sake. Well, partly. Not that he would ever admit it, not in a million years, but there had been a split second last night . . . Patrick pushed the thought to the back of his mind. Dwelling on what might have been wasn't going to help.

'For heaven's sake, Dad,' he exploded. 'Everything was in place. We had it all sorted out. Why did you have to go and blow it?'

Mickey reached out automatically to fill up his glass, but the bottle was empty. He slammed it back down on the table, suddenly feeling resentful that the blame was always laid at his door, that he was always the bad guy, the loser. It wasn't his fault. He hadn't bumped off Lawrence Oakley. If anything, he thought he was being rather brave.

He scowled at his son. Perhaps Patrick didn't like him behaving well. Perhaps Patrick had got used to the glory and got rather a thrill from having to make up for his father's deficiencies. Mickey decided he was tired of having to make excuses for his behaviour, and letting other people run rings around him just because he felt eternally guilty. If he was open about what he had done and how he felt, people would have to fall in with him for once. It was a liberating thought.

'I can't keep Flora hidden away for the rest of my life. I just can't.' He was uncharacteristically emphatic. 'Look at the fun you lot had here. In the fields, and the woods, on the ponies. Here, in this kitchen. All the birthdays, all the Christmases, bonfires, barbecues, camping . . .' Memories came flooding back. 'Why should Flora be deprived of the chance to have all of that? She should be allowed the sort of childhood you all had, not an isolated existence. Why can't everybody just see past all of the scandal and make the best of what I agree is the most monumental fuck-up of all time but can't be changed?'

Patrick had never seen his father so impassioned. Mickey's eyes were blazing. He leaned in to his son, and grabbed him by the shirt.

'I fought for you, Patrick. Do you know that? I went through hell, battling against your mother because I believed Honeycote House was where you belonged. I wanted you to have all of this, not some shitty little sub-standard flat in the arse end of London. I didn't give up. I could have done the easy thing and bunged your mother a load of cash to bring you up with. But I didn't. You were my flesh and blood. I brought you back here. So please – don't stand in my way when I want to do the same for Flora. The rules are the same for both of you. She has the same amount of my blood as you do.'

Patrick lit a cigarette, his hand trembling. His father had never spoken to him like that before, and he felt chastened, realizing that in his desperate attempt to save everyone's feelings, perhaps his father's had been left out.

'I'm sorry, Dad,' he managed. 'I didn't mean . . .'

'I know you didn't.' Mickey pulled his son to him for a moment and held him. Patrick suddenly wanted to cry. Everything was unravelling too fast. He felt confused about what was right. What his role was.

Who he loved.

No. He had no room in his head for that one.

'What about Lucy?' he asked. 'Where's she gone?'

'I don't know,' Mickey replied. 'To find James, I expect. He'll be only too thrilled to have her weeping on his shoulder. He's been waiting years for me to slip up again,' he added bitterly.

'Actually,' came a voice, 'I'm here.' They both looked up to see Lucy standing in the doorway, pale-faced but defiant. She walked across the room with her arms folded. She took up her familiar position, her back to the Aga, and shook out her hair.

'I have spoken to James,' she announced. 'I got it all out of him. Eventually.'

She glared at Mickey.

'I don't know why you inspire such loyalty in people. I really don't. And Patrick, don't you ever, ever take the blame for your father again.'

'It was to protect you!' protested Patrick.

'Only because you were all worried about what I might think or do or say.' Lucy was scathing. 'Kay was smart enough to see that. How else did she think she was going to get her hands on half a million quid? Only if you were all running round scared witless of me.'

Mickey and Patrick looked at her warily.

'There's no way I'm going to let Kay Oakley come back here and blackmail us. And ruin Patrick and Mandy's wedding into the bargain.'

'We can't just throw them out onto the street,' Patrick pointed out.

Mickey shot his son a grateful glance.

'Of course we can't,' replied Lucy. 'The child is Mickey's daughter. And none of this is her fault.'

She came and sat down at the table with them. 'I spent the afternoon driving round thinking about what to do. My first reaction was to shoot Kay. After I'd shot you, of course.'

She glared at Mickey, who managed a weak smile.

'But actually, that didn't really solve anything. And it didn't help Flora, who really is the innocent party in all of this. So I started looking at practical solutions. Obviously we haven't got five-hundred-thousand to shell out just like that. Unless you're keeping something else from me?'

'Of course we haven't.' Mickey had managed to find his tongue. 'That's why we were trying to raise the money. By selling our shares . . .'

Lucy picked at a piece of candle wax on the table.

'I know James wants to sell. And maybe Keith too. But I don't see why you should be forced to sell all of your interest, Mickey. Especially not now you've got someone wanting to invest. This could be really exciting. You might have the chance to do things with Honeycote Ales that you've always dreamed of. Why should Kay get in the way of your dreams?' Lucy paused for breath. 'I came up with another idea. Which would mean you wouldn't have to give up the brewery.'

Mickey and Patrick looked at each other.

'Fire away,' said Mickey.

Lucy waved her hand around the room. 'This place is far too big for us now. We've been rattling around for the past six months. So, I thought . . . if Patrick and Mandy moved in here, Kay and Flora could have Little Orwell Cottage to live in for as long as they need to. Without actually giving it to them, of course. It still belongs to Patrick, but at least they've got a roof over their head while she's growing up.'

Mickey frowned. 'What about us?' he demanded. 'Where do we live? Are you suggesting we stay here with Patrick and Mandy? Only that doesn't seem fair on them—'

'No. This is their home. After all, they'll probably be starting a family before long.'

'So we live in a caravan, then? Or go on a cruise?'

'We convert the stable-yard.' Lucy dug in her pocket and spread a piece of paper on the table. On it she'd drawn some rough sketches. 'There's enough space to create a three-bedroom house with a decent-sized kitchen and living room. We should get planning permission without any problem. We can design it exactly as we want it. I think it could be . . . fun.'

There was a stunned silence.

'What if Mandy doesn't want to live here?' Patrick wished he hadn't opened his mouth as Lucy's steely glare slid round to meet his gaze.

'She's got to accept what she's marrying into. And if she doesn't like it, there's still time to cancel the wedding.'

Patrick fell silent. Lucy was right. They were all going to have to cut their cloth.

'As for money,' Lucy went on, 'I suggest you give Kay a job at the brewery. She's a good businesswoman, if I remember. And hard-working. There must be something she can do on the marketing side.' A thought occurred to her. 'Where is she, anyway? Where's she been all this time?'

'She's staying at the Peacock. In the flat.'

Lucy digested this new piece of information. Patrick and Mickey waited tensely for her reaction. How would she feel, knowing her nemesis had been billeted only a few miles away?

'That flat's . . . uninhabitable,' she said finally.

'We made it as comfortable as we could,' replied Patrick.

'You have been busy.' Lucy looked back and forth between the two of them. 'Right. Well, we better phone her. Sit round the table and thrash it all out.'

'Today?' Things were happening too quickly for Mickey.

'The others are back from Puerto Banus on Tuesday morning. Sophie and Ned get in that evening. I think we need everything straight by then. So we can tell everyone what's going on.'

Mickey quailed at the thought of his daughters knowing his sordid past. But he knew Lucy was right. He marvelled at her fighting spirit, her ability to see the bigger picture, her determination to keep everything together for them. Though he doubted he was completely off the hook. Surely in a quieter moment, when they were alone together, there would be recriminations.

Patrick picked up his car keys.

'Come on, Dad. I'll drive you over.'

Mickey was about to protest, but Patrick looked pointedly at the empty bottle on the table.

'Ask her for supper.' Lucy stood up decisively. 'Get her to bring Flora over so we can meet her. She's going to be one of the family from now on.'

At the Peacock, Kay watched from the window as Patrick and Mickey got out of the car and walked across the courtyard to the flat's entrance. She felt a cold chill settle around her heart. They looked so serious. She saw Patrick glance up to the window nervously, and she stood back so he couldn't see her.

For a moment she compared them. Which, she wondered, would she choose now? Mickey, very much the English country gent, distinguished but slightly unkempt, always looking as if he had just jumped off a horse or a woman. Or Patrick, with those Byronic features, haughtier than his father but with that decadent edge. They were so similar, yet so different. As she knew. Her cheeks burned slightly as the memories fast-forwarded through her mind – her and Mickey in the back of a horse box, her and Patrick in a gazebo. Those stolen moments that had such far-reaching consequences for all of them.

Why were they here? Had they come to tell her that they weren't going to play ball? That there wasn't going to be any money? She knew she shouldn't have counted her chickens. She'd been to look at a couple of houses – nothing special, because she would never be able to afford what she wanted. But she longed to be settled and to have a roof over their head that they could call home, so Flora could feel secure and have her things around her.

She'd also made the mistake of booking Flora in for a trial day at Hazlehurst, the little prep school in Eldenbury. They had a place for her in September if she wanted it. And Kay knew that if she wanted anything for her daughter, it was that. She would make every sacrifice and work her fingers to the bone to pay the school fees. But if the Liddiards weren't going to contribute, it was out of the question.

Of course, she'd get money out of them in the end. But it would be a long, drawn-out and humiliating process and she didn't think she had the strength to fight. She felt so weary. Depressed. The doctor had told her it was hardly surprising, and to make sure she looked after herself – eat well, get plenty of fresh air. She got plenty of that all right – the wind whistled through the cracks in the window panes.

She heard the knocker on the flat door go. Flora was colouring quietly in the living room. She rushed into the bathroom to look at her appearance. She'd need at least half an hour to even start to look human. She ran her fingers through her hair to try and give it a semblance of body, then gave up.

Her heart felt heavy as she went to open the door.

'Hey!' said Patrick as soon as he saw the expression on her face. 'It's all right. We've only come to ask you for supper.'

Mickey stepped forward. 'I've told Lucy everything, Kay. I don't want to keep you and Flora a secret. You shouldn't be locked away here. We want you to be . . . part of the family.'

'Oh.' She looked from father to son warily.

'We want to offer you Little Orwell Cottage,' Patrick went on. 'It belongs to me, but it would be perfect for you and Flora.'

Kay blinked. This wasn't what she'd expected. She'd been convinced they were going to try and fob her off somehow.

'Of course, if you don't like it we can think again,' Mickey finished.

Kay couldn't help it. She threw herself on his shoulder and wept. She was tired of being strong and brave. She was tired of doing the maths and coming up with zero on the bank balance. Most of all, she was tired of being alone. But now it seemed as if she might have a future.

'It's OK,' said Mickey, patting her shoulder. 'Everything's going to be all right.'

'Sorry.' Kay pulled herself together, wiping the tears away, thinking that she must now look even worse, if that was possible.

Flora appeared in the doorway, clutching her colouring book.

'I need a purple,' she announced, totally ignoring the visitors. 'And I haven't got one.'

Kay sighed. If only real life was that simple, and all you wanted was a purple. How easy would that be?

Mickey was insistent that she should only come for supper if she felt up to it. He didn't want her to feel intimidated.

'You're joking,' she said. 'I'm desperate for a meal with other human beings. I'd have dinner with Genghis Khan and Hannibal Lecter, given half the chance.'

'Anyway,' said Patrick. 'We're not going to eat her.' Mickey was gazing through the doorway at the little girl, still engrossed in her colouring. 'What do we tell Flora?' he asked.

Kay had liked the idea of moving into Little Orwell Cottage. And she nearly bit Mickey's hand off when he suggested working at the brewery.

'At least I'll have a sympathetic boss,' she managed to joke, 'if Flora gets chicken pox.'

But they hadn't really discussed how to explain everything. Kay sighed.

'Can we cross that bridge another day?' she asked. 'I just don't know. I think she's too little to take much in. Can we just say . . . we're friends? For the time being while she gets to know you?'

Mickey nodded, marvelling yet again at how complicated the situation was. Every time you solved one problem, it threw up another, which was astonishing given the split second it had taken to get into the situation in the first place. With a bit of luck, things would get easier now.

An hour and a half later, Kay's mouth was dry with nerves as she drove towards Honeycote. She'd had a shower, blow-dried her hair properly, put on some make-up. She was wearing a fresh pair of jeans and a cream cotton twin set; comfortable, but low key. She knew Lucy would look stunning. She always did.

Was Lucy Liddiard actually a saint? Kay wondered. How could anybody be quite so good, welcoming her husband's ex-mistress into the family home? Kay hoped sincerely it wasn't some sort of trap. Maybe Lucy planned to push her down the cellar steps, lock her in and keep Flora for her own?

Kay told herself not to be paranoid. Lucy was just being practical and grown-up. As she came to the outskirts of Honeycote, she wondered if she should have stopped off for chocolates or flowers. It seemed rude to turn up empty-handed when Lucy was going to so much trouble at short notice. But the village shop was closed and she wasn't going to turn round and go into Eldenbury just so she could appear with a box of After Eights.

Anyway, she pointed out to herself, they were family now.

As she turned into the drive of Honeycote House, she suddenly felt another flood of nerves. The house looked stunning in the early evening sun and the scent of freshly cut grass evoked a wave of nostalgia.

Lucy appeared on the doorstep. Kay felt her courage leaving her. What if Lucy turned on her?

She wouldn't. She was far too gracious. Kay got out of the car, and busied herself helping Flora get out. Together they walked hand in hand to the front of the house.

'Kay,' said Lucy, and ran down the few steps to greet her. Kay felt her arms around her, her cool cheek against hers.

'I'm so sorry about Lawrence,' Lucy kept her voice low, so Flora wouldn't hear. 'You poor thing . . .'

'Thank you.' Kay had learned to accept condolences automatically and without emotion.

'And is this Flora?' Lucy knelt down and looked into Flora's face with a smile. 'Flora, I'm Lucy.'

Flora gave an uncertain smile, and held on to Kay's hand. Lucy stood up, and ushered them into the house.

'It's only shepherd's pie,' she said. 'Pot luck, I'm afraid. And everything's a bit chaotic, because of the wedding.'

Half an hour later, Kay was eternally grateful for the wedding. It had given them all something neutral to talk about while drinks were prepared and Lucy put the finishing touches to the meal.

'How long's supper?' asked Mickey.

'About ten minutes.'

'Can I take Flora outside? I want to show her something and it will be too dark after we've eaten.'

Kay nodded her consent, and Flora seemed quite happy to trot outside with him.

She was left alone in the kitchen with Lucy, who brought over a thick white envelope and dropped it on the table in front of her. Kay opened it uncertainly. It was an invitation to the wedding, with Kay and Flora written in ink on the dotted line left blank for guests.

'Thank you,' said Kay. 'We'd love to come.'

'Good,' replied Lucy. 'It's up to you what you want to tell people, by the way. We won't say anything unless you want us to.'

She smoothed the mashed potato over the top of the mince. Kay watched her evenly. She'd got the measure of

Lucy now. She was cleverer than the men gave her credit for. Acknowledging Kay's presence and bringing her into the family fold like this was damage limitation at its best. Kay now had absolutely no leverage over any of them. Her power had been diminished. She was no longer a shameful secret to be kept at all costs. There would be no danger of her using emotional blackmail. Lucy had made sure, very subtly, that from now on Kay would have to toe the line and play by their rules.

Frankly, she didn't care. She wasn't going to rock the boat. She had what she wanted. Correction, she had what she was entitled to. It had been a long haul and now, at last, perhaps she could start looking forwards. Any trouble had already been caused.

But she wasn't going to let Lucy intimidate her.

She picked up her wine. 'Anyway,' she said contentedly. 'Cheers.'

And she met Lucy's gaze boldly as they clinked glasses.

Outside, Flora stood open-mouthed in front of Pudding's stable. Pudding peered over the top nosily.

'I really need somebody to ride him,' Mickey was explaining. 'He gets very bored, you see. And my girls are too big for him now. Would you like to come and ride him for me?'

Flora reached out her hand to stroke his nose. 'Is he naughty?' she asked.

'He's very naughty sometimes,' replied Mickey. 'But he needs someone to love him.'

'I love him,' decided Flora. 'Definitely. Will I need a hat?'

'We can sort you out a hat.'

'Lift me.'

Mickey hesitated for a moment, then picked her up and held her so she could peer into the stable. All the memories came flooding back, of warm little bodies in his arms. He blinked back tears. He might not have been a model husband, but he thought he'd been a good father. He'd always had time for his children, played with them, taken them riding, built them dens. He could do it all again for Flora.

He heard footsteps behind him and turned. It was Lucy. His instinct was to put Flora down. He felt guilty.

'It's OK,' said Lucy. 'I don't mind. Not really. Another baby would have been silly.'

They stared at each other while Flora went on patting Pudding's nose, oblivious. 'Supper's ready,' said Lucy eventually.

Mickey let Flora drop back down to the floor. 'You better wash your hands,' he told her.

As Flora trotted back across the yard to the back door, Lucy and Mickey followed. She slipped her hand into his.

'It's going to be fine,' she said definitely. 'Flora will fill in the gap before the grandchildren arrive.'

'Grandchildren?' echoed Mickey, alarmed. 'I'm not sure I'm ready for grandchildren yet . . .'

But it was with a considerably lighter heart that he stepped back into the kitchen.

20

The day of the wedding dawned with a dense, hazy sky that would not reveal whether it hid sunshine or rain. In the kitchen at Honeycote House, Mickey, Bertie and Ned stood next to the radio, waiting for the weather forecast with bated breath. The announcer's dolorous tones informed them that it was going to be dry and sunny, with temperatures in the mid-twenties.

'Thank God for that,' said Mickey fervently.

'Right,' said Ned, rubbing his farmer's hands together. 'Let's get cracking.'

Bertie stretched out his arm for the teapot and lit another cigarette.

'It's barely dawn,' he grumbled. 'I'm not awake yet.'

Mickey grinned. Bertie was rarely up before noon, but he'd hauled himself out from between the sheets and driven over with a truck of furniture pillaged from his own home to supplement the chairs and sofas from Honeycote House. It had been Lucy's idea to 'bring the inside outside', but they could only do it once they were sure it wasn't going to rain.

'It's going to be a scorcher!' Sophie bounded into the kitchen, her curls wilder than ever. 'I can smell it.'

Lucy and Georgina were lugging in tin buckets of

flowers from the scullery where they had been sitting in water overnight.

'We've got four hours,' said Lucy, looking at the kitchen clock. 'I'll do sausage sandwiches at midday, then everyone can go and get themselves ready.'

'We'll never do it!' wailed Georgina.

'Yes, we will,' replied Lucy firmly, brandishing her secateurs. 'And I'd advise you all to get moving before Sandra arrives. Or God knows what she'll have you doing.'

No one needed telling twice. The kitchen emptied rapidly, leaving Lucy alone with Sophie. Together they laid all the flowers out on the kitchen table, ready to arrange.

'Are you OK, Mum?' Sophie asked.

Lucy hesitated. She had felt much, much happier since Ned and Sophie had arrived home on Tuesday night, followed by Georgina on Wednesday. She and Mickey had sat them all down and told them about Kay and Flora. They had been shocked, of course. Georgina had been very indignant, and had spoken about Kay in very disparaging terms. But it was the more sensitive Sophie who had waited until afterwards to come and see Lucy, and make sure that she was all right. She was obviously still concerned.

'Darling, I'm fine,' she reassured her daughter. 'There's nothing I can do about what happened, so we just have to get on with it.' She started snipping the stalks of a sheaf of white tulips. 'And don't worry. We're not going to turf you or Georgina out of your rooms. This is still your home.'

Sophie busied herself with a bundle of freesias. This just wasn't the time to tell Lucy that she and Ned were thinking of emigrating. And anyway, now she was home she wasn't so sure it was a good idea. Australia was paradise, but Honeycote was home, and it always would be.

Mandy had decided to get ready for the wedding at Keeper's Cottage. It didn't seem right to get dressed in the home she shared with Patrick. Besides, the twins were on hand as her stylists, hairdressers and make-up artists. And she wanted to be near her father.

Keith had brought her a cup of tea this morning, and sat on the end of her bed. Even though she'd lived with Patrick all this time, she felt very aware that today marked something momentous, and for a few moments it made her feel very small, and a bit sad. She'd had a little weep on his shoulder, and he'd patted her on the back.

'Hey,' he said. 'There's absolutely nothing to cry about. I promise you that. Today is going to be a very beautiful day.'

Mandy sniffed. 'What's the weather like?'

He drew back the curtain. 'Hazy at the moment. But it's going to be hot, once those clouds have burnt off.'

She managed a smile as Sasha banged on the door and barged in.

'You better get your hair washed,' she ordered, 'or there'll never be time to dry it properly. And don't forget to moisturize or your tan won't take.'

Kitty appeared behind her. 'Your mum's just phoned,' she announced. 'She's bringing over Danish pastries from the deli in Eldenbury. She says she knows you won't eat otherwise.'

Keith knew when he had been outnumbered.

'I am, as they say, out of here,' he chuckled. 'Shout if

you need me for anything. Not that I can imagine I'd be of any use whatsoever.'

He shut the door carefully behind him, not wanting to be party to any of the mysterious female preparations that were, as far as he was concerned, akin to witchcraft.

He'd been allowed out of hospital on Monday afternoon. Sandra had sent a car for him, and had been profusely apologetic at not coming to collect him herself, but she had a crucial meeting to do with the wedding. He was rather relieved, because it meant he had an hour or so to gather his thoughts at home before Ginny got back with the girls.

It had been an agonizing wait before he had been able to get her on her own. The twins had babbled all the way through supper, telling him all the things he wanted to hear and some of the things he didn't.

'And oh my God . . . Sandra's pool-boy housekeeper driver type person Alejandro . . . he was soooo fit. Wasn't he, Mum? We wanted to bring him back home. He could make a fortune around here keeping all those frustrated rich housewives happy. In fact, Mum – that could be our new marketing ploy. Hunky Butlers. What do you think?'

'Very good,' murmured Ginny, clearing away the plates.

Keith thought she seemed tired, but it had probably been exhausting being the only responsible adult. Eventually, Kitty and Sasha had gone upstairs, and he had sat her down in the drawing room and told her the truth.

Now, Keith stepped into the bedroom he had shared with Ginny for the past three years. He thought he could do with a lie down. He still felt tired after the operation – it hit him every now and again. And if he didn't rest it was going to be a long time before he got the chance.

Well into the small hours, he imagined. He'd just have five minutes, he told himself as he lay down on top of the bed. If you didn't actually get under the duvet then it didn't count.

He awoke with a start to find Ginny looking down at him. Keith thought he had never seen her look so beautiful, her eyes shining blue against her Spanish tan – the redness had faded at last to a golden brown. She was dressed just in her underwear – a pale pink silk bra and French knickers. In his head, he wanted her so badly. But his body . . . it was still very early days. The consultant had said it would take time, but now the tumour had been removed, now the pressure was off, he should be back in working order. He just had to be patient.

He lifted a hand to take one of hers, and drew her towards the bed.

They lay in each other's arms for a few moments. Then Keith cleared his throat.

'I was wondering,' he said, 'how you'd feel about . . . us getting married? I know we're not exactly love's young dream. But I'd like to think I was going to spend the rest of my life with you. And it would be nice to make it official.'

Ginny felt her heart contract. When Keith had told her about his tumour, his cancer, his operation, it had been a double-edged sword. She had felt huge relief, that his treatment of her over the past few months had a logical explanation. She had felt regret that he had gone through the whole nightmare on his own, without anyone to confide in or to reassure him. Most of all, she felt guilty that she hadn't had the strength of character to discover what it was that was wrong between them, but had been rather introspective and self-indulgent about it, with almost disastrous consequences. But then, perhaps if Keith had been open with her in the first place, she wouldn't have descended into the maelstrom of self-doubt that had made her succumb to Alejandro's advances.

As she lay there debating Keith's proposal, she told herself that she had to bury what had happened between her and Alejandro. There was no point in bringing it out into the open. It would only cause Keith distress; distress that he certainly didn't need while he was trying to recuperate. And why should she let it stop her and Keith finding happiness together? It had been a moment of weakness brought about by a powerful combination of her insecurity, his irresistibility, and the after-effects of the hot sun. She needn't say anything to anyone. Ever.

And it wasn't as if she and Alejandro would ever have come to anything. She had made it quite clear to him that it was a one-off, and didn't flatter herself that he had been anything other than relieved. At the airport, he had grabbed her by the magazine rack and given her a rather passionate kiss goodbye that had made her quite giddy, but there was never any hint that it had been anything other than a one night stand.

So she needn't say a word.

'I think it's a lovely idea,' she said dreamily. 'But we mustn't say anything today. Today belongs to Mandy and Patrick.'

'It does,' agreed Keith, but he felt filled with a secret delight that he knew would be with him all day long, as he fell to sleep, and when he woke the next morning. A delight that was the perfect antidote to the dread he had been burdened with for so many weeks.

Recovery was just around the corner.

Lucy looked at her dress hanging from the knob of the wardrobe and smiled.

It was perfect. Pale grey silk chiffon with pink polka dots. Sleeveless, with a bow tied under the bodice, and soft pleats falling to the knee. She had grey suede sling-backs, and a huge pink floppy hat to wear with it.

Next to it hung Mickey's morning suit. For once in her life she worried that she might be accused of being naff, for she had found him a grey tie with pink dots that matched her dress almost exactly. But somehow she felt the urge to demonstrate that they belonged together.

She blew on her nails to dry off the pale pink varnish. Along the corridor she could hear Sophie and Georgina arguing over the hair straighteners, and the thud of music, and she smiled. Outside the gravel crunched as a van arrived. Lucy peeped out of the window and saw Suzanna and Barney Blake arrive with the food. She gave a wave, but knew they would get on with the task in hand, unloading everything into the fridges in the kitchen and the stable yard.

Sandra yodelled up the stairs to her. 'I'm off now! See you at the church!'

Lucy still had no idea what Sandra had planned for the evening. She'd seen two big lorries drive down to the bottom paddock the night before, but it was screened by a small copse which prevented anyone from seeing what was going on, and so it remained a mystery. At seven o'clock that evening, the guests were going to be allowed down through the trees to discover what delights awaited.

Mickey came into the bedroom with a bottle of champagne and two glasses. 'Shall we have a quiet toast?'

Lucy nodded in agreement. She thought a glass of champagne was just what she needed – a few bubbles in her veins to give her a lift, for it had been a hard morning's work. She stood up and took the glass off Mickey gingerly in case her nails were still wet.

'To us,' he proclaimed. 'I'm so proud of you, you know. I don't deserve you. But I bloody love you.'

She chinked her glass against his gently. 'I love you too,' she said. 'And I'm proud of us. You and me and Patrick. And the girls.' She swallowed. 'Nothing is ever going to get in the way of us.'

As they drank to each other, she wondered how many more weddings there would be at Honeycote House in their lifetime.

Kay surveyed herself critically in the mirror.

She had to be very, very careful today. This was her first excursion into the public eye. Was the dress too much of a statement? It was a pale gold silk shift dress with a single strap going over one shoulder. It wasn't tarty, because it wasn't tight, or short, falling just below the knee. But it was very eye-catching, and obviously very expensive. She felt determined to wear it. She'd never worn it before, as she'd bought it just before Lawrence died and hadn't yet had a suitable occasion. And it was so very definitely, mouth-wateringly her. For the first time in months, Kay felt like her old self again. She'd become so tired of her recent persona, the Kay who was in mourning, who was at other people's mercy, whose personality and spirit had seemed to vanish into the ether along with her husband's soul. But this dress restored her former spirit. She managed a flirtatious grin in the mirror, and almost laughed out loud.

She bloody well would wear it. OK, so she'd have to tone it down. She resisted the killer heels the dress cried out for, and went for mid-height court shoes. She put on discreet jewellery instead of the bling her gut told her to wear. And instead of big hair, dramatic eyes and red lipstick, she did the natural look, with her hair just softly tousled. She'd let the dress speak for itself. And just in case anyone thought it was too much for church, she slung the matching fringed silk shawl around her shoulders.

It was stunning. But no one could actually accuse her of attempting to take centre stage, she was certain. She picked up her bag and her car keys, ready to go. She was incredibly nervous, but at the same time excited. She had nothing to be ashamed of. Anyone who wanted to look down on her wouldn't be worth knowing. But there was still the fear of some whispered disparaging remark, an accusing finger, a titter. She was going to have to be bloody strong. Which was why she needed her armour. Kay wouldn't have felt strong in a demure linen suit. But in her fabulous fuck-off frock, she was ready to do battle.

She held out her hand to Flora, who was in a yellow gingham dress, her curls captured in a French plait tied with a matching ribbon. Flora would be OK. Poppy from the Honeycote Arms was going to be at the wedding, because her mother was doing the food. And then there were the cousins. Proper cousins. Kay felt a little glow of warmth at the thought. They were going to belong. She would make sure of it.

Patrick did up the buttons on his jacket, leaving the bottom one undone. He thanked God that he was a traditionalist and was wearing simple morning dress. His only nod to individuality was his grandfather's waistcoat, in blood-red silk embroidered with running foxes. He adjusted his tie, ran his hands through his dark hair so it was slightly dishevelled, and gave himself a curt nod of approval in the mirror. He looked at his watch. It was still well over an hour before he was due at the church.

He'd told Ned he would meet him there. Much as he loved his friend, Ned's sense of fun would have been too much to cope with. Patrick had visions of him turning up in his morning suit, wearing dark glasses like something out of the Blues Brothers, making tequila slammers and playing Huey Lewis and the News at full volume. Patrick wanted to prepare himself calmly. If a man ever deserved peace and quiet it was on the morning of his wedding.

But now he was ready, the house felt incredibly still. Too still. He couldn't sit here until it was time, doing nothing. He'd go mad. He picked up his car keys decisively. He'd slip into the Horse and Groom for one nerve-steadying Bloody Mary and get Mayday's seal of approval on his appearance. Patrick locked the door carefully behind him, realizing with a smile that the next time he walked over the threshold, he would be with his bride.

James stood in the kitchen in his morning suit, slicing up Marmite sandwiches into fingers and putting them into a Tupperware box. They needed a stash of food for the children, because it was anyone's guess what time they would actually get to the reception and be fed. Getting the children ready had been arduous beyond belief, but he had them all lined up in front of the television without a hair out of place while Caroline got herself ready.

He heard her clattering down the stairs. She burst into

the kitchen. She wore a Fifties-style floral dress, splashed with red tulips, with red peep-toe sandals.

'Wow,' he said. 'You look fantastic.'

'Thanks,' she replied. 'Are these the sandwiches? Well done. I'll stuff them in my bag.'

It was amazing, thought James, how much easier life was now they cooperated. It would never have occurred to him before to make the sandwiches, but just that one little task seemed to take the burden off Caroline, with the result that she was much happier.

He'd come clean to her, as Lucy had suggested. He'd fed the children and put them to bed early the evening after she'd come back, then sat her down with the horrible truth in black and white. And she had been amazing. Lucy was right. He had forgotten what a formidable business brain Caroline had, a brain that had become almost vestigial over the past few years. But she had gone through the figures with a keen eye.

'It's perfectly obvious,' she said. 'All we need to do is downsize. Get rid of this ridiculously huge house. We don't need a library and a garden room and an orchard and six bedrooms and an in-and-out drive.'

James opened his mouth to protest and she clamped her hand over it.

'We can keep it if you want to ruin us, and our marriage. But look – the house has gone up a hundred grand even since we bought it. If we sell this and buy a perfectly ordinary four-bedroom house with a nice big garden, we can shave two hundred thousand off our borrowings. That's a lot of tables and chairs you don't have to sell.'

James sighed. He couldn't argue with the maths. Caroline had opened the local paper and proceeded to put a red ring around half a dozen suitable properties. By the end of the week, Lyttleton House was on the market and they had been to view three smaller houses, none of which were as bad as James imagined.

Caroline, meanwhile, had never mentioned the diamond debacle. There was just no way of telling the story that didn't make her look guilty, and James wouldn't find it remotely funny. Least said, soonest mended, she had decided. But the episode had helped her regain her confidence. And now, as she lined the little ones up by the door ready to troop them out to the car, she looked over at James. He might be irritatingly anal and superior and sexist at times, but he was still a handsome bugger.

'Do you remember the day we got married?' she asked huskily.

James looked at her. 'Of course I do.'

'I've got my wedding knickers on.'

James gave a slow smile. He slid a hand up her thigh and underneath her dress. 'So you have.'

He put his arms round her waist. Instead of stiffening and trying to extricate herself from his grasp, she relaxed against him, nuzzling his neck.

'Do you think it would matter awfully if we were late?' asked James.

'Given that you're an usher and Connie's a bridesmaid, I think we would be toast,' Caroline replied, reluctantly peeling herself away.

Mayday was ushering the last of the drinkers through from the bar into the dining room for Saturday lunch when Patrick walked in.

He looked . . . perfect. Like the most dashing English

gentleman on his wedding day, his hair dark, the rose in his buttonhole just starting to open.

She couldn't face him. She went to run from the room, feeling like a foolish schoolgirl. But it was too late. He had seen her. He gave her a sheepish grin, as if to say what a prat he was to come in dressed as he was.

'I was early,' he said. 'So I thought I'd come in for a drink.'

'You've come to the right place, then.' Mayday managed a smile despite her heavy heart. 'Champagne?'

He shook his head. 'Just a Bloody Mary. I've got to drive to the church. And I don't want to slur my words.'

Mayday made him his drink, unable to think what to say. She'd never been tongue-tied.

'You are coming to the evening do?' he asked anxiously.

She nodded. She'd been invited, like all Honeycote Ales employees. There was no point in saying she wouldn't be there.

'It's . . . a lovely day for a wedding,' she finally managed to offer.

Patrick drank down his drink, then put it carefully down on the bar. 'Wish me luck,' he said, and held out his arms for her to hug him.

As they embraced, Mayday shut her eyes tight, almost unable to bear the sensation of Patrick's warmth on her body. She wanted to scream at him, 'Don't leave me!' She wanted to claim him as rightfully hers. But the miracle hadn't happened. He hadn't seen beyond the relationship they'd always had, even though she'd thrown him enough clues.

Suddenly, she pushed him away. 'You're going to be late.' Her voice was tight with tears.

'I guess you're right.' He let her go, reluctantly. She turned away so he couldn't see how hard she was trying not to cry. She went over to her handbag, rummaged in it for a moment while she gathered herself, then turned to him with a bright smile.

'Here's your wedding present.' She proffered a small package, wrapped in dark purple tissue paper tied with a violet ribbon. He went to open it, but she stopped him. 'Don't open it now. Open it later. When you're on your own. Just you.'

She was very insistent. Patrick looked at her warily. Knowing Mayday it was probably a couple of grams of coke. Best not opened in front of Mandy. He grinned and stuck it in his pocket.

'What is it? A gold-plated cock ring?'

Mayday pushed him gently. 'Go on. Bugger off and get married. See you around.'

She watched him go. So this was how it felt when your heart broke. It did hurt. A horrible, gnawing, grinding pain right at the very core of you. She wondered if it would ever heal, or if she would feel like that for ever.

The little church at Honeycote was bursting at the seams. Toned buttocks vied with broader beams for space on the slippery wood of the pews. Shafts of golden sunlight pierced the stained-glass windows, shining on the congregation. The organist, confident now she was in her stride, shifted her repertoire up a gear. Usually the service was over before she'd even had a chance to warm up, so she was taking advantage of the opportunity to demonstrate her musical prowess.

Every alternate Sunday, the stone walls were host to

nothing more exciting than dull tweeds and gabardine. Today, the church was crammed with a veritable rainbow of colours in every imaginable stuff – silk, chiffon, velvet, linen and lace. Hats, it seemed, were back with a vengeance, from straw cartwheels trimmed with fruit to ostrich-feather headdresses to dainty pillboxes. And the scent! Most of the seven deadly sins were represented, and several more weaknesses besides – Envy and Obsession and Passion mingled with the woodier base notes of the men's cologne.

In the front row, Lucy thought back to the day she had walked into this church, more than twenty years ago. She and Mickey had decided to get married at Honeycote rather than at her parents', because all their friends were nearby. Most of those friends were here again today, together with the next generation. And she thought she probably still loved Mickey as much as the day she married him. She had never regretted their marriage for a moment, despite the ups and downs. She'd seen Kay enter the church, together with Flora, and had given her a smile. Lucy could afford to be magnanimous. After all, she was sitting at the front with her husband while Kay slipped unobtrusively into a pew near the back.

Everyone was seated now. The initial cocktail party atmosphere had settled, the ritual two-cheek kisses and squeals of recognition over for the time being, although guests were still peering over their shoulders to see who had come in behind, wiggling their fingers surreptitiously in greeting. And raising eyebrows. Shrugging shoulders, as if to say, 'I don't know what's going on. Do you?'

Lucy nudged Mickey and frowned.

'Where is he?' she whispered.

Mickey shrugged. 'He'll be here in a minute. Don't worry.'

Lucy felt the tiniest flash of irritation. Everyone had been slaving away to make sure everything was perfect. She would have thought Patrick could have bothered to turn up on time.

Patrick couldn't resist pulling over to see what Mayday's present was. He had a feeling he would have to hide it, whatever it was. So he stopped at the top of Poacher's Hill, into the very lay-by where he had proposed to Mandy what seemed like a lifetime ago. He hastily undid the ribbon and unwrapped the tissue.

It was an iPod. Black, of course. Mayday wouldn't have chosen any other colour. There was a little silver plaque on the back, on which a single word was inscribed. 'Listen'.

Intrigued, Patrick put the headphones in his ears and pressed play. He expected something heavy and hard – some guitar-based thrash metal, some crazy anthem redolent of the mad times they had shared together over the years. But no. It was a tinkling piano and the minimal thrum of a double bass that he heard. The sweet notes of the intro to a song he thought he recognized. He frowned, listening, as a coffee-rich voice began to sing. It was Roberta Flack, singing 'The First Time Ever I Saw Your Face.'

Patrick was puzzled. This was so un-Mayday. He couldn't imagine her giving a sentimental ballad like this airplay. The melody, the lyrics and the production were all designed to tug at the heart-strings and bring tears to the eyes, as the singer poured out her feelings, declaring her love, her passion, the impact of the first time she met her lover.

Then, as he continued to listen, a slow realization dawned on him. This was a message. Mayday was telling him that she loved him. That she always had, from the first day they met. From the first time they had lain together, if he was to believe the song. From the first time she'd ever seen his face.

Bloody hell, thought Patrick. Mayday loved him.

In the front row, Sandra took a deep breath in, thanking God she had dropped two diazepam with her lunch. She'd chosen to wear a cream brocade coat dress, woven through with metallic threads, picking out the bronze for her accessories – St Laurent courts and a matching clutch. Which she was now clutching, knuckles white with anxiety. This eventuality hadn't been in her list of possible disasters. She had contingency plans for every technical hitch and natural disaster, but this hadn't occurred to her in her wildest nightmare.

Ned was bewildered. He'd called Patrick first thing that morning, just to check he was OK and see if he needed anything. His friend had seemed perfectly fine. Calm, but then Patrick always was calm. He exchanged worried glances with Bertie and James, who were also ushers, whilst trying not to cause alarm. The organist ploughed valiantly on, drowning out the rustle of hymn sheets and the occasional cough.

The vicar remained unruffled. It was par for the course, and he was in no hurry. Honeycote was a quiet parish; this was the first wedding he had presided over this year and he was determined to enjoy it. He was particularly looking forward to the reception – he'd been asked back to Honeycote House afterwards, and the Liddiard hospitality was famous. And he was partial to a pint or two of Honeycote Ale, which was bound to be on tap, even if there were rumours abounding that the Liddiards were as good as bankrupt – again! – and the brewery was about to be sold off. Patrick would tip up any minute, he was sure.

Ten minutes later, even the vicar was starting to have doubts. Twenty minutes was the longest he'd ever been kept waiting. The church clock struck the half hour solemnly. As if anyone needed reminding of the time – the invitation had stated two o'clock quite clearly.

Outside the church, Mandy's fingers tightened around her bouquet. Keith gave her arm a kindly pat, trying to reassure her. She wasn't the hysterical type, but it would be hard not to feel a little disconcerted. After all, it was the bride's prerogative to be late for the wedding, not the groom's.

Her bridesmaids clustered round her, concerned. Sophie got out her Rescue Remedy. Sasha produced a tiny bottle of vodka.

By the lychgate, Kitty was surreptitiously calling Patrick on her mobile phone. 'Where the fuck are you?' she hissed into his voicemail.

Georgina was about to stomp off to her Fiesta and go and find her brother. 'I'll kill him first,' she said. 'And then I'll bring him back.'

Even little Constance, who would normally by now be creating merry hell, sensed there was something very wrong and decided to keep quiet.

Patrick stared out over the landscape, tears pricking at his eyelids. Why the hell hadn't she told him before? For in that instant, her declaration made him acknowledge that he loved her too. They were soul mates, weren't they? He had always felt at home with Mayday. He never had to explain anything to her. She understood him, and he her, with a simplicity and a purity that was only shared by people who were meant to be together. There were never any expectations, and consequently no disappointments.

What was he supposed to do now? He could see the church at Honeycote down below. He could sense the anticipation of the congregation. And as the final chords of the song died away, the bells rang up through the valley, summoning him to his own wedding.

He sat at the wheel of his car. Should he turn round and drive back to Eldenbury? What would the future hold for him and Mayday? He'd have to leave the brewery. She'd have to leave the Horse and Groom. They would be cut off, excommunicated. What would they do? Where would they live? He could hardly take her back to Little Orwell Cottage – definitely not, if Kay was going to live there. They would struggle together, building a life. It wouldn't be fair, subjecting Mayday to the breadline.

Besides, he couldn't do it to Mandy. He wouldn't hurt her for the world. And leaving someone at the altar was the worst crime in the world. He had to go through with it. After all, he had never made Mayday any promises. He wasn't letting her down. If anything she wasn't playing fair.

Patrick brushed away his tears, thrust the iPod into his pocket and jumped into his car. Hopefully she would still be waiting for him. He turned the key in the ignition, slammed the car into first, and spun off down the road.

*

The vicar stepped out of the church into the crowded porch to confer with the bride. It was getting beyond a joke. This wasn't merely late; the wedding looked very much as if it wasn't going to go ahead. Not that he would voice his fear. It was up to the bride to decide when to stop waiting.

'What do you think we should do?' he asked politely, just as the Healey came screaming to a halt in the car-park and Patrick leapt out without even opening the door.

'I'm so sorry,' he said with an agonized expression. 'The car . . . it broke down.'

'You could have phoned!' Georgina was outraged by the lameness of his excuse.

'It's all right,' Keith placated them. 'He's here now.'

Sasha threw her arms round Mandy as Patrick disappeared into the church.

'You poor thing! Now come on – look gorgeous.'

'Out of the way,' said Kitty. 'You're squashing her.' And she started rearranging Mandy's outfit, to make sure she was absolutely perfect for the journey up the aisle.

Mandy's legs felt wobbly and her hands were still shaking slightly. It had been the longest half-hour of her life. She'd been able to sense the consternation of the congregation through the thick walls of the church, and her heart had fluttered with panic as any number of eventualities had flashed through her mind. Her father had been the one to keep it together. If it hadn't been for his solidity, his calmness, she felt sure she would have been tempted to run, unable to face the possibility of the ultimate humiliation.

'Don't you worry, love,' Keith had said, with such certainty in his voice. 'Patrick will be here.'

And he was right.

Inside the church, over a hundred heads snapped round to glare at Patrick accusingly. He put his hands up in mock surrender.

'Bloody vintage cars,' he said with a tentative grin. 'Always let you down when you least expect it. I'm terribly sorry to keep you all waiting.'

The congregation was placated by his charm, and he strode up the aisle to take his place next to Ned. The vicar joined them, hugely relieved. This was the closest he'd come to disaster in all his days.

Together, Mandy and Keith stepped into the cool of the church. Mandy suddenly felt overawed. The agonizing wait, the emotional rollercoaster, and now the attention were too much to bear. The aisle seemed a hundred miles long. Tears blurred her vision. She could just make out two tall figures at the altar. Ned and Patrick. This was it. This was really it. She was about to get married.

'Take your time,' Keith said gently.

'The Arrival of the Queen of Sheba' struck up. Mandy took in a deep breath to steady her nerves, threw back her shoulders and managed a trembling smile. The guests beamed back in approval, and some of them wiped their eyes, overwhelmed by her beauty.

She wore a fitted silk jacket with three-quarter-length sleeves and vintage diamanté buttons, tied at the waist with a wide blue satin ribbon. The skirt beneath was full and sheer, made of hundreds of squares of different lace that Kitty had painstakingly sewn into a cascading patchwork waterfall and then attached, at random, mother-of-pearl buttons, feathers, bows of silk ribbon, little silver charms and tiny bells. Peeping out from underneath the skirt were white kid boots laced up with the same blue satin ribbon that trimmed her jacket; and she held a simple bouquet of white tea roses and ranunculus. Her hair was loosely pinned up, and at her ears twinkled pearl and crystal droplets that caught the light. She looked the epitome of fairytale chic; elegant and enchanting.

Constance followed carefully behind Mandy, her breath sweet with the Refreshers that had been rationed out to her during the long wait, her fat little feet squashed into embroidered kid slippers, her fist clutching a wilting bunch of grape hyacinths. Then behind her, Kitty and Sasha, Sophie and Georgina, in white organza, still exchanging scandalized wide-eyed glances at the drama.

As Mandy joined Patrick at the altar, he saw her hands were shaking.

His heart melted. He cursed himself for putting her through what surely must be every girl's worst nightmare. How could he have doubted his love for her even for a moment? He supposed he was entitled to a last-minute panic, but even so he'd allowed himself to get rather carried away.

He picked up her hand and squeezed it tightly.

'I'm so sorry,' he whispered, and her smile of total forgiveness made his stomach lurch as he realized he had been tempted, just for a moment, to give it all up. He caught the vicar's eye, urging him to hurry, to make up for all the time that had been lost.

'Dearly beloved,' began the vicar, and Ned beamed round at the congregation giving them the thumbs-up, as if he had single-handedly resolved the situation himself. Then before he knew it, he was patting his pockets frantically for the ring and laughter rang around the church, followed by a smattering of amused applause as he produced it triumphantly.

Patrick slid the ring onto Mandy's slender finger. Her hands were no longer shaking. She looked down at it in wonder, the rich gold gleaming against her tan, then looked up at her husband as the vicar pronounced them man and wife.

This time the applause was thunderous. It was a full minute before the vicar could restore order. It was always hard to keep the congregation's attention from here on in, because they were champing at the bit to get on with the celebrations, but he was determined to keep them in their place while he delivered his mercifully short sermon.

Finally, it was all over. Patrick and Mandy walked back up the aisle to 'Ode to Joy' and went out of the church into the bright May sunshine, where they were pelted with rose petals. After endless hugs and kisses of congratulation, they leapt into Patrick's car for the short drive to the reception.

Patrick couldn't resist pulling in to the side of the road to look at his wife.

'Happy?' he asked.

'Ecstatic,' she replied. 'But don't you ever put me through that again.'

And she pulled him to her, smiling. As they kissed a cavalcade of guests drove past, tooting their horns in approval.

21

As each guest stepped into the garden at Honeycote House they gave a gasp of delight. It looked like a film set. Mismatched wrought-iron chairs were placed around mammoth stone tables; Lloyd Loom armchairs and velvet sofas were tucked under the shade of the trees. Silken maharajah parasols spattered with silver sequins that glittered in the sunshine were placed strategically around the garden. Cast iron urns that looked as if they had been plucked from the gardens of Versailles were filled with ice, on which rested chilled bottles of champagne for the guests to help themselves. Random pieces of sculpture and statuary peeped out from behind bushes, and in the very middle was an exquisite fountain with more bottles of champagne resting in its depths. A trio of maidens dressed in white played baroque music under a tree.

At the very bottom of the garden was a palatial white tent, open-fronted, its turrets held up by silver and white poles, the inside lined in white voile with hand-blocked silver butterflies. Dark wood sofas and chairs were scattered with embroidered cushions; white, silver and turquoise leather beanbags were conveniently positioned next to low tables smothered in ornate lanterns and etched tea glasses. Enormous palms were scattered around, and the entire interior was lit with pinpricks of light that flickered on and off. Here guests could relax out of the heat of the sun and shut their eyes for five minutes if they felt so inclined.

It was as pretty as a picture.

Lucy squeezed Bertie's hand. 'I can't believe how generous you've been.'

Most of the stuff had been brought over from his reclamation yard, or obtained from his contacts – the tent belonged to a friend of his, he'd got the parasols at a heavy discount from one of his suppliers and the fountain had been ordered by a customer who had done a runner.

'It's obvious I'm never going to have my own wedding,' he replied lugubriously. 'So I might as well get a vicarious thrill out of this one. After all, you lot are the closest to family I've got.'

Lucy rolled her eyes, not taken in by Bertie's self-pity, but gave him a hug nevertheless.

She looked around the garden with a smile. It was just as she had imagined. Everything was as it should be, even the weather – the sun was warm but not relentless, and there was the faintest breeze that carried the scent of blossom through the air.

Suzanna Blake had excelled herself. While the guests circulated and drank champagne, staff from the Honeycote Arms passed around sweet scallops with minted pea puree, white asparagus wrapped with palest pink Parma ham, rice balls filled with melting mozzarella and potato rosti topped with smoked trout. Later there would be poached chicken with a watercress sauce, followed by elderflower and champagne jellies that had been made in individual Victorian jelly moulds, and little pots of white tiramisu, tipsy with rum.

It was, thought Lucy, the perfect white wedding.

Kay was sitting in the shade of a willow tree, on a small wooden bench. The children were corralled into a small gazebo; a machine inside was pumping out bubbles that were causing much mirth.

'So – which side are you on?' A languid voice startled her. 'Bride or groom?'

She looked up at a tall man in an exquisite white suit, his features vulpine but undeniably attractive. He had a glass of champagne cupped in each hand, and as he passed her one his jacket fell open to reveal bright orange silk lining.

'Um . . .' She debated the query for a moment as she took the glass obediently.

'It's not a hard question,' he teased.

'No,' she countered gamely. 'But it's a long story. And it might shock you.'

He sat down next to her and stretched out his legs, showing deeply tanned feet in white suede loafers. On most men they would have looked atrocious, but he carried them off with panache. He smelt delicious. Kay took a gulp of her bubbles as he slung one arm along the bench behind her. He wasn't making a pass; his arms and legs were so long there was nowhere else to put them.

'I can assure you I am utterly unshockable,' he declared.

Kay didn't doubt it. His eyes glittered with mischief. Or perhaps cocaine. Or both. She took a deep breath.

'I'm . . . sort of related. To the groom's side. But I used to live in Honeycote. At Barton Court.'

'Oh.' He surveyed her quizzically. 'When it was a garden centre?'

'Yes.'

'Bit before my time. I only moved down here on a permanent basis a couple of years ago. But that means we're in the same line of business. I do garden reclamation.'

'Then you must be Bertie Meredith.' Kay was pleased she was able to identify him. She remembered his yard by the station in Eldenbury. And of course his reputation went before him, even though she'd never met him.

Bertie nodded. 'And you must be Kay Oakley.'

Kay tensed slightly. What had he heard? If anything.

'How do you know that?'

Bertie smiled enigmatically for a moment. 'Everyone thinks I haven't a clue who everyone is or what's going on. But actually I make it my business to know exactly what's what and who's who. And I never forget anything. I remember James telling me about you and Mickey.' He chuckled. 'I was ribbing him because I thought he was knocking off Lucy. He gave me a load of guff about comforting her because of you two.'

He smirked and turned sideways to look at Kay, to see what reaction he was getting. She was sitting bolt upright, taut as piano wire, jaw clenched.

'Shit,' said Bertie. 'I'm really sorry. You don't still . . . ? You don't look the type to fall for Mickey. He's a nice bloke, but . . .'

As a tear slid down Kay's face, he was even more horrified.

'Bugger. Have a hanky.' He burrowed in his pocket.

457

'I knew I shouldn't have come.' Kay was sobbing by now. 'They were so nice. They want us to be part of the family, but we're never going to be. You might as well know,' she gulped, dabbing at her eyes with Bertie's enormous handkerchief that smelt so divinely of him, 'because they've said it's up to me to tell people if I want to. That's my daughter, Flora.' She pointed in the direction of the children's tent, where Flora was leaping up and down with Constance, catching bubbles. 'And Mickey's her father.'

She waited for a reaction. Bertie gazed over at Flora for a few moments without commenting.

'Well,' he said. 'In my opinion there's plenty of room for more Liddiards in the world. They're a good bunch.'

'Actually, she's an Oakley,' said Kay stiffly, knowing she sounded rather prim. 'We're keeping my husband's name.'

'And he's . . . where?' asked Bertie, looking round as if expecting him to appear from behind a rose bush.

'Dead.'

There was a moment's silence, and Kay rather wished she hadn't been so blunt. But she felt weary of it all, especially when she realized that this was the first of many such conversations she was likely to have. She tensed herself for his reaction, wondering how long it would be before he made his escape. But he just put his head to one side and looked her up and down, rather as one might examine a racehorse.

'I'm rather glad I sat next to you,' he said companionably. 'I think you're the only person at this wedding with a past more lurid than mine.'

Kay went rigid with shock for a moment. Then she

burst out laughing, relieved by his total irreverence. He grinned as he drained his glass.

'You poor thing,' he went on. 'Widowed and made to play the poor relation. I expect you could do with a good night out.'

Kay looked at him. He oozed decadence. She wasn't going to go there.

'Mickey and Lucy will tell you, I'm an utter rogue. Totally incapable of remaining faithful. Utterly feckless. Completely unreliable. And congenitally late. So I imagine I'd suit you down to the ground. As no doubt you are remaining faithful to the memory of your dead husband. I'd be no threat to him. All I would be is the best fuck you've ever had in your life. Probably.'

Kay gasped. He was outrageous.

He grinned. 'Definitely better than Mickey, anyway.'

She should get up and walk away. She didn't need to be spoken to like this. But something was keeping her pinned to the seat.

Bertie was sitting on her dress.

He grabbed her wrist as she pulled the fabric out from under him.

'Hey. I'm sorry. Nerves always make me behave badly. Champagne makes me even worse. And weddings always remind me of what I'm missing.'

She looked into his eyes, about to retort that she wasn't surprised he'd never married, with manners like that. But she saw something in them that made her stop. It wasn't sympathy, because sympathy always made her want to puke. It was such an easy emotion to dispense when you had the upper hand. No, it was something more subtle. Compassion, perhaps? Or empathy?

She dropped back down onto the seat, unable to tear her gaze from his.

'Dinner would be nice,' she said faintly.

'Are you all right to get a babysitter?' he asked. 'If not, bring Flora as well, and I'll do you supper in the kitchen.'

Kay felt her heart flutter. What a sweetie. Most men wouldn't even register that babysitting might be a problem. There was definitely more to Bertie than first met the eye.

All too soon, it was dusk, and the evening guests were arriving. The wedding party was finally allowed down to the bottom paddock. Mandy and Patrick led them along the little path that went through the wood. Lanterns hung from the branches of the trees, lighting the way, until they turned a corner and found a huge archway woven through with ivy and roses. Tiny birds were perched amongst the foliage, and the sound of birdsong permeated the night air. It took a moment for everyone to realize that the birds weren't real, and their song was coming from cunningly secreted speakers. The effect was magical nevertheless, and everyone held their breath as they walked through the entrance.

There in front of them was a magnificent carousel. Two dozen white horses rode proudly up and down, the only hint of colour the gilt on their bridles and the red of their nostrils. Three thousand tiny bulbs lit up the inside and were reflected against a myriad squares of cut glass that reflected the ornate gilded carvings. The organ was playing 'The Arrival of the Queen of Sheba', the same music that had played Mandy up the aisle.

Around the perimeter of the paddock was a range of

tents and fairground attractions. Fat and thin mirrors and a glass maze; a stall cooking organic burgers and hot dogs; another dispensing candy floss, toffee apples and doughnuts. There was even a coconut shy.

'Mum,' breathed Mandy in amazement. 'It's fantastic.'

'I know it's all a bit over the top,' said Sandra happily, 'but I wanted something for you to remember. And once I'd started, I couldn't really stop.'

From the humblest Honeycote Ales employee to the upper echelons of the Eldenbury hunt, the guests swarmed enthusiastically over the fairground, whooping and shrieking with glee, letting their hair down. Soon every mount on the carousel had a rider, the air was thick with flying coconuts and howls of laughter greeted the reflections in the hall of mirrors.

Even Lucy, the arbiter of good taste and understatement, had to admit it was fantastic, as Mickey grabbed her hand and forced her onto the dodgems. James and Caroline were already in one car; Ned and Sophie were in another.

'I hate to admit it, but Sandra's got it absolutely right,' said Lucy to Mickey, taking the wheel. 'There's no way I'd have thought of this. But it's just what everyone wants. Everyone's equal in a fairground.' She put her foot down on the throttle and aimed straight for Eric, the brewery handyman, smashing him out of the way.

'Hey!' said Mickey. 'Steady on!'

The next moment they were bombarded by Ned. Their car spun round. Lucy was laughing helplessly, her elegant hairdo collapsing, her shoes long discarded. As they whirled off in another direction, Mickey caught sight of Bertie lifting Flora onto a white horse on the carousel, then leap onto the one next to her. Kay stood on the ground, her dress obviously unsuitable for a merry-go-round, but she was smiling. Everyone, noticed Mickey, was smiling. Even his po-faced, uptight brother.

It seemed that everyone loved a wedding.

Ginny collided with Sandra by the white chocolate fountain. She felt a rush of pity for her. She had pulled together such an amazing spectacle, yet here she was on her own, with no one to go home and swap notes with. No one to share the memories with.

'It's completely fabulous, Sandra. You've done a wonderful job.'

Sandra dipped a skewer of pineapple idly into the swirling sweetness. 'I wanted it to be special. I haven't been here for Mandy for the past few years, so I wanted to make it up to her.'

'Well, I'm sure you have. More than made it up. No one will ever forget this.'

Sandra gave a little nod and a smile. Ginny hoped she hadn't sounded too patronizing. She certainly hadn't meant to.

'By the way,' said Sandra. 'I'm impressed with your will power.'

She looked at Ginny with a sly smile. Ginny looked back, startled.

'What?'

Sandra drew a piece of pineapple off its skewer with her teeth.

'Alejandro was very put out. He said you were the first woman ever to resist his charms.'

Ginny felt her cheeks flush red. 'I couldn't imagine what he saw in me. I thought he was teasing.'

'Oh no,' replied Sandra. 'He adores older women. And I'll tell you something. You missed a treat.'

She tapped Ginny on the chest with her skewer, winked and waltzed off.

Ginny was left shell-shocked. Was Sandra winding her up? Was this her way of saying that she knew what Ginny had been up to? Or had Alejandro really made out Ginny had rejected him? Panic flooded through her. Was she going to spend the rest of her life worrying about the truth coming out? She couldn't bear it. The only way to stop the torture was to confess to Keith . . .

Then, as she stood there, she started to giggle. What would she say? 'By the way, I screwed the arse off Sandra's drop-dead-gorgeous twenty-three-year-old pool boy.'

No one would believe it in a million years. Her secret was safe. And best of all, it had taken years off her. She'd cancelled her appointment at the clinic in the end, but everyone kept telling her how amazing she looked, and asked what her secret was. If they only knew . . . Guests looked at her askance as she walked through the fair, her head thrown back, laughing.

Sandra knew she shouldn't have wound Ginny up, but she hadn't been able to resist it.

Amidst the wedding preparations, she had spent the week taking a long, hard look at herself. She couldn't maintain her smash and grab attitude to life any more. She had been so certain of getting Keith back, it had shocked her when he had rejected her outright. And of course he had been right, in retrospect. They couldn't go backwards. They could never recapture what it was that had brought them together in the first place. They were both totally different people. She had been foolish to imagine that it could ever have worked, that she could slip into the new life he had built for himself and become accepted.

If she wanted to share her life, if she wanted someone to enjoy the considerable fruits of her success with her, she had to do it for herself.

She had begun by placing an advert on an internet dating site.

'Successful mature businesswoman with a love of the finer things seeks a kind, generous and thoughtful gentleman to share . . .'

Share what? She didn't have any hobbies or interests. Her work had been her life. She hadn't even played golf for the past two years.

She rewrote it.

'. . . to rekindle a passion for golf and find out what else life has to offer.'

That would do. She didn't want to be too exacting. And if her mental image of her ideal man looked rather like Keith – with a hint of Julio Iglesias thrown in – then that wasn't so surprising.

Patrick stood still. For a moment, he was transported back more than ten years, to that night at Eldenbury fair. The smells and the sounds were almost the same: music, generators, candy floss, diesel. He shivered as he remembered the dark eyes, the full lips, and what she had done to him.

Mayday, as sweet and wild as the most out-of-reach

blackberry. He'd thrown her to one side like a piece of autumn fruit that hadn't quite made the grade. He felt sick with guilt. What was she doing, while the rest of the county celebrated his nuptials, gorging themselves sick and drinking themselves senseless?

He shivered, despite the warmth of the evening. Then he turned to find his bride beside him.

'Are you OK?' asked Mandy anxiously, and by way of a reply he took her in his arms.

'I've never been happier,' he told her, thinking that as lies went, it was the perfect colour. 'Shall we go?'

'Aren't we supposed to make an official departure?'

'Never mind that. No one will notice. They're all having too much fun.'

He took her by the hand, led her through the fairground, back up the path, over the lawns, and into the house. They stood in the middle of the kitchen, arms around each other.

'I remember the first time I came into this kitchen,' said Mandy dreamily. 'I fell in love with it, completely and utterly. It was so unlike our kitchen. It was mad, chaotic, full of people and laughter and music. And then you walked in . . .'

'I remember too,' said Patrick. 'I saw this girl sitting at the table. Next to Sophie. I couldn't keep my eyes off you.'

'And now here we are,' said Mandy. 'You're mine. And this kitchen's going to be ours.'

Patrick led her over to the kitchen table. It was a Liddiard ritual for guests to carve their initials into the wood. The entire top was smothered in letters.

'There's just one thing that needs to be done,' he said,

searching for Mandy's. He found them at the top left hand corner. M S for Mandy Sherwyn.

He handed her a Swiss army knife. She smiled and took out the blade, then scratched through the S and replaced it triumphantly with an L.

22

It was just over a week after the wedding. The fairground had been packed away, the plates and dishes and glasses washed and returned, false nails and fake tans had peeled off and faded, and the grass had grown over all the heel marks on the lawn.

Patrick was driving hell for leather through the little country lanes to Honeycote. His hair was still wet from his hasty shower. He'd only just had time to jump in and pull some half-decent clothes on. It was jolly hard work being a newly-wed, he thought with a grin. Lucky Mandy was having the week off. She had thank-you letters to write. And she was making a start on packing up Little Orwell Cottage so that Kay and Flora could move in. Lucy had been horrified when she'd seen the state of the flat at the Peacock, and had insisted that they shouldn't stay there longer than was necessary. After all, there was more than enough room for Patrick and Mandy at Honeycote House, even with Sophie and Ned there too. In the meantime, Lucy had found an architect and was drawing up plans for the stables to be converted. Rather elaborate plans, Patrick mused, involving floor-to-ceiling windows and mezzanine floors and spiral staircases. Whoever their potential investor was, he hoped they had their cheque book handy.

They were meeting the investor today. They all had bets on who it would be. Robert Gibson wouldn't be drawn on their identity. Patrick actually didn't care much, as long as it meant they could bloody move on. It wasn't as if they were going to be giving away a controlling interest any longer. Only James wanted to sell up completely. Mickey and Keith were both going to keep ten per cent, and stay on as consultants. Which left Patrick and the investor with forty per cent each. So whoever it was couldn't do anything they didn't agree with, or anything that wasn't in line with the Liddiard ethos. There was nothing wrong with a bit of fresh blood. And from what he had seen of the proposal, even if he didn't agree with every idea on it, it was certainly in keeping with what Honeycote Ales stood for.

He turned left and whizzed down the hill to the brewery. Robert Gibson's car was already there. Next to it was a gleaming Aston Martin. Bloody hell, thought Patrick. He couldn't think of anyone he knew with a car like that. James had an old one stuffed in his garage, but this was brand new, with a private plate he didn't recognize. MP. He ran through the few people he knew with initials that matched, but didn't think any of them were likely investors. Never mind, he thought. He'd find out soon enough. They must all be in the boardroom already. He was only five minutes late.

He jumped out of the car, ran his fingers through his hair, which was now nearly dry, and strode inside.

He smelt her perfume first. The scent of wild roses filled his head, propelling him to another time and another place, making his heart skip a beat. He would recognize it anywhere. It was the scent he had chosen.

And then he saw her. She was standing with her back to him, talking to the others. She was wearing a black dress that was severe and sexy at the same time. Extremely simple, extremely expensive – he knew that, because he remembered seeing the label when it was strewn on the bed at Claridges – and he was surprised it suited her. Her hair was straight and gleaming and her make-up subtle, though she still hadn't been able to resist her dark red lipstick. In her hand she held a leatherbound document wallet, and each place at the table had a similar wallet placed next to a glass of water and notepad and pen.

'Patrick!' Mickey moved towards him, his face wreathed in a smile. 'We thought you'd never get here. Come and see.' He put a hand on Patrick's back, ushering him across the room. 'I expect you'll be as surprised as I am. But it just goes to show, you shouldn't scoff at all those people who do the lottery. Mayday bought her ticket in the post office in Honeycote, apparently. Nearly six bloody million quid! All right for some. All right for us, actually, it would seem.'

Six million? Mayday? As the truth filtered in through his brain, Patrick took a guarded step towards her, trying to assimilate what this meant. To her, to him, to Honeycote Ales. She looked the epitome of a successful businesswoman. Polished, confident and focused. She peeled away from James and Keith as soon as she saw him.

'Patrick.'

They met in the centre of the room. Patrick felt all eyes were upon him as he put out his hand for her to shake and his cheek for her to kiss. A formal gesture with a hint of familiarity. It seemed the appropriate greeting. After all, everyone knew they were old friends and that they worked together. To keep too great a distance might seem odd.

'Mayday,' he managed. 'This is a . . .'

A total shock. A blow that had sent his senses reeling. Was it a stab in the back? Was this some sort of twisted revenge, because he had rejected her? Was she showing she could have him by the metaphorical balls? Was she going to taunt him, make him grovel, rub his nose in it?

He struggled to find a suitable response.

'A surprise,' he managed lamely, as Robert Gibson came across to shake his hand too.

'Sorry. I couldn't breathe a word before,' Robert said jovially. 'We wanted to keep the whole thing under wraps. It doesn't always do to advertise the fact that you've come into money – you get all sorts of strange people asking for handouts. And Mayday was particularly anxious not to overshadow the wedding.'

Patrick glanced at her sharply. And she smiled back. And in that moment, he knew that her intentions were not malicious. On the contrary, she had done it out of her love for him. So many times he had shared his fears and worries about the brewery with her, and expressed his desperate wish for a change in their fortunes. She was coming to the rescue.

She was doing it for him.

Keith came over to join the group. 'We better sit down and start thrashing things out,' he said, ever businesslike. 'There's a lot of small print to get through before we actually shake hands on a deal.'

Everyone moved to take their place at the table.

Patrick took the opportunity to move close to Mayday,

close enough to murmur in her ear. 'Why didn't you tell me?'

She looked at him. He couldn't quite describe the look in her eyes. Was it sorrow? Hurt? It certainly wasn't scorn or triumph.

'What difference would it have made, Patrick?' she asked softly. 'If you had known about the money? Would that have changed your mind?'

He felt as if he had been punched. He wanted to shout that it wasn't fair, that he hadn't chosen her because the sacrifices they would all have had to make would have been too great. Or so he'd thought.

He hadn't believed in their love enough.

Shaking, he took his place at the table. He had to say something. He couldn't endure the prospect of having her as a partner. It was no good pretending that he would be able to keep his distance. If he was going to be taking on more responsibility, he would have to liaise with her, consult her, have discussions with her. Probably every day. With that scent driving him demented, reminding him of their passion. He would go insane, trying to resist her.

But if he protested, they would be turning down a golden opportunity. Where the hell else were they going to get that kind of money melded with that kind of freedom? Because Mayday was perfect for Honeycote Ales. She understood exactly how it worked, and where it needed to go. He knew that because of what she had done at the Horse and Groom, because of all the conversations he'd had with her, because of the bloody document she had drawn up behind his back that gave him a glimpse of a future that was beyond rosy, and that he now didn't want to relinquish.

Besides, what he could say? What reason could he give the rest of the board for not wanting Mayday as a partner?

But if he said yes . . .

Could he trust himself?

Of course he could. He was a married man. He loved his wife. He'd made his decision over a week ago, on that hilltop overlooking Honeycote, made his pledge in the sight of God, and he was going to stick to it.

Patrick opened his document wallet as Keith called the meeting to attention. His head was swimming. He took a gulp from his glass of water as Mayday took the chair opposite him. He barely took in a word anyone was saying. Keith spoke first, welcoming Robert and Mayday. Then Mickey, who gave a heart-warming speech about what Honeycote Ales meant – to the family, to the board, to the workers, and to the community. Robert gave a brief official introduction to Mayday, explaining that he was in a difficult position with a foot in both camps, but how he hadn't wanted to miss out.

And then Mayday stood up. No one could keep their eyes off her as she spoke. Softly at first, but as she became more impassioned her voice gained in strength. She talked about growing up with Honeycote Ales, about waking up to the smell of malt in the air each morning, about the journey from Tizer to cider in the pub gardens through-out her childhood, her first underage drink, her first legal drink. How the pubs had provided her with a certain security throughout her troubled adolescence, about how when she had taken her first job at the Horse and Groom, she had suddenly become someone in her own right. She had felt she had an identity. Which was why she was still there now.

'When I won the money,' she said, 'the first thing I realized was I didn't need my job any more. There would almost be no point. I've got a bloody fortune. I don't need to get out of bed ever again if I don't want to. But I love the Horse and Groom. And the brewery. They are part of who I am. If you cut me, I'd probably have Honeycote Ale running through my veins.'

She laughed, and everyone laughed with her. They were, Patrick realized, completely absorbed in what she was saying.

'Buying into the brewery seemed to me to be the obvious thing to do. I don't want to blow my money on status symbols.' She gave an abashed smile. 'Well, I know you've all seen the car, but I've always been a bit of a girl racer. That's my one little indulgence. I want to do something constructive with the rest. Something I can be proud of. And I want something I'm interested in and I believe in. I don't want a knicker shop or a jeweller's. I want a challenge. And I want success. And I think Honeycote Ales can bring me all of that.'

She looked around the room. You could have heard a pin drop. Then Mickey started clapping. Then James. Then everyone else. By the time Patrick joined in, he realized that he had little choice.

As the applause faded away, he got to his feet. Mayday was still standing. The two of them locked eyes across the boardroom table. Memories of the past and visions of the future hung between them. Two young lovers who had shared their hopes and dreams. Friends locked together by a bond of steel they could never break. Was it folly, not to try and break that bond now, while he had the chance?

'Well,' said Patrick. 'I think there's only one thing we can say after that speech. And that is . . .'

He looked around the room. At his father and uncle. His father-in-law. Robert, who looked rather anxious. And Mayday, who gave him the sweetest smile, with those blackberry lips.

'. . . when do you start?'

As Mayday slipped into the front seat of her car, she shut her eyes for a moment, enjoying the comfort, the smell of the leather, the feel of the steering wheel at her fingertips and the prospect of the power she would shortly unleash when she started the ignition. It had been an incredibly long day. There had been so much to discuss. Poor Robert's pencil had flown over his legal notepad as point after point had been brought up. But it was over. The final vote had been cast. Hands had been shaken.

She owned forty per cent of Honeycote Ales.

She hadn't enjoyed the look of panic in Patrick's eyes when he had realized the truth. That hadn't been the point of the exercise. For over the past few days, she had come to her own painful conclusion about her relationship with him. She didn't want to be married to Patrick, and have the responsibility of a family, a heritage, and the Liddiard name. She would never be the most important thing in his life. And that wasn't good enough for Mayday. It was all or nothing.

This way, she was free. But she still had him. She always would.

She started up the car, and the purr of the engine sent a thrill through her that made her shiver. She drove up the hill out of the brewery drive, taking it carefully through the winding lanes. When she finally hit the main road that led to Eldenbury, she let her go. She knew the road only too well. Every bend. Every corner. The torque, the camber. Poacher's Hill reared up in front of her, nearly a mile of steep ascent. The Aston gobbled up the tarmac effortlessly. The needle nudged ninety. A hundred. It was like flying.

Shit! She could see the blue lights in the mirror, hear the warning siren. She supposed she'd asked for it. She'd shamelessly flouted the speed limit. With a sigh, Mayday pulled into the lay-by at the top of the hill, then sat and waited demurely with her hands in her lap, looking down on the village of Honeycote below.

'I'm sorry, officer,' she said, as the door opened, and looked up into Rob's astonished face.

'Mayday!' he stammered. 'What the hell . . . ? What are you doing in this?'

'Speeding?' She grinned at him impudently.

'Tell me you haven't nicked it.'

'Of course not. I won the lottery, didn't I? What do you think?'

Rob towered over her, at a loss for words. She ran her eyes up and down him. She wondered exactly what was underneath that uniform. He might fool the public with those sleepy brown eyes and those curls, that slow way of talking, but underneath he was a powerhouse. She had seen the bulge of his muscles under his clothes, imagined his rock-hard thighs, the strength in his arms. Once or twice she'd seen him in action, pushing a drunk and disorderly up against the wall, sorting out a fight that had gone wrong. And she'd been impressed with what she saw.

'Come on,' she urged. 'Get in.'

'I'm on duty,' he protested.

Mayday said nothing, just held his gaze and pressed her foot down on the throttle. The engine purred as softly as a newborn kitten.

Rob only hesitated for a moment. It was a no-brainer, really. The chance to ride with Mayday? In a brand new Aston Martin? It was two of his dreams come true. He would never as long as he lived get an opportunity like this again. And so what if he did get sacked? It would be worth it. Anyway, there were plenty of security firms around at the moment looking for ex-coppers.

He jumped into the passenger seat. Mayday gave a whoop of glee and barely waited for him to shut the door before accelerating off at a speed that nearly took his breath away. Rob shut his eyes. Even on his police driving courses he hadn't done nought to sixty in such a short space of time. He knew he should be telling her to slow down, but the adrenalin rush was irresistible. Mayday's perfume filled the air. Roses, he thought weakly, but not the sort of roses he was used to, cellophane-wrapped in a black bucket. These were intoxicatingly wicked roses, opium-drenched blooms that made you do things you'd never dreamt of when you inhaled their narcotic scent.

'Where to, Rob?' she asked, looking deep into his eyes, which he had now managed to open.

'Um . . .' He didn't have a clue what he was supposed to say. 'I ought to get back to the station.'

She just laughed. A deep, throaty, wicked laugh, then pressed down on the accelerator. Rob wondered where was she taking him, panicking slightly, then decided he didn't care.

The music system kicked in. The familiar riff pounded through their bodies. Steppenwolf. It could have been written for her.

She had everything. Beauty. Money. Power. Freedom.

But she was still born to be wild.

The Honeycote Wedding Guide

For most people, weddings are torture. There's the agony of deciding what to wear, what to buy as a present and where to stay, only to be rewarded by an excruciating afternoon standing around while the wedding photographs are taken, a nondescript three-course meal sitting next to someone you have never met before and never want to see again, followed by interminable speeches, all the while wondering whether it would be rude to leave before the bride and groom.

And weddings have become more and more competitive. With the average cost nearly topping £20,000, one has to query the point of a 50-foot Swarovski-studded train, horse-drawn carriages and rivers of vintage champagne. It is largely a façade, and not a true reflection of what the bride and groom represent at all. A momentary madness seems to take over when planning a wedding, turning the most unassuming of couples into profligate show-offs, ably egged on by the in-laws-to-be, more often than not.

The perfect wedding is not about spending money. What matters is getting the people who are important to you together, for them to enjoy your union, and then buggering off before drunken oblivion or total boredom set in. What doesn't matter is a phalanx of overdressed bridesmaids, wedding favours for the

guests and an official master of ceremonies in full regalia. Fine if that's what you've set your heart on, but there is no need to feel pressurised into all the bells and whistles.

So with the help of the Liddiards I have put together a guide to a short but sweet and stylish wedding. And never be afraid to enlist the help of friends – amongst them will be keen cooks, photographers, florists, all eager to help. Their contribution would be a much more welcome present than a set of matching saucepans.

I recommend a two o'clock ceremony followed by tea and cocktails. All done and dusted by five so the bride and groom can escape and be alone together . . .

Mickey Liddiard's Wedding Cocktails

No one knows better than Mickey the importance of alcohol at a social function. Two or three of any of these concoctions will make sure your reception goes with a swing. But remember – have plenty of water and non-alcoholic alternatives available so the aged aunts don't start a handbag war after one too many.

BLUSHING BRIDE

70ml champagne
30ml lychee juice
A few drops of grenadine

Combine the champagne and lychee juice. Add the grenadine gradually so the colour spreads through like a blush.

MAID OF HONOUR

40ml gin
20ml rhubarb puree
15ml elderflower cordial
10ml syrup from a jar of stem ginger
25ml cranberry juice
50ml soda

Whizz it all up in a shaker with crushed ice and pour into a glass.

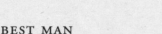

BEST MAN

40ml vodka
1 freshly squeezed lime
4 basil leaves
2 teaspoons sugar
Soda

Muddle the basil leaves and sugar as if making a mojito. Fill the glass with crushed ice, then add the vodka and lime juice. Top up with soda and garnish with a basil leaf.

WEDDING VEIL

25ml gin
20ml fresh lemon juice
10ml sugar syrup
Blackberry liqueur

Mix the gin, lemon juice and sugar syrup together in a glass with crushed ice, then slowly drizzle liqueur into the mix until it sinks to the bottom. Garnish with fresh blackberries.

TILL DEATH US DO PART

50ml Grand Marnier
Prosecco
Cranberry juice

Mix all the ingredients and chill well.

The standard pub measure for spirits is 25ml.
Please drink responsibly.

Lucy Liddiard's English Country Garden Tea

The most important thing is to keep the food plentiful and keep it coming so no one is necking back the cocktails on an empty stomach. Most people will have access to obliging teenagers eager to earn twenty quid – get a small team together and give them instructions to keep the food circulating so no one goes hungry.

Kick off with the traditional sandwiches – smoked salmon, cucumber and egg are popular – together with some savoury bites. Use a variety of white, wholemeal and granary bread. Follow with some substantial buttered tea bread, then finish with scones with cream and jam, biscuits and cakes. Here are a few of Lucy's favourite recipes to inspire you.

CHICKEN AND ALMOND SANDWICHES

Mix finely chopped chicken fillets with thinly sliced celery and flaked almonds. Bind together with mayonnaise. Make sandwich fingers with best thin white bread, cutting off the crusts of course!

PESTO PASTRY HEARTS

2 sheets puff pastry
2 tablespoons pesto – one red, one green
30g butter
40g grated parmesan

Divide the butter between two bowls then mash one with green and one with red pesto. Spread on to the pastry sheets and cut out hearts with a shaped pastry cutter. Place on lightly oiled baking trays and bake in a medium oven for 10 minutes until puffy and golden.

ROAST BEEF CROSTINI
1 thin French stick
Mayonnaise
Wafer thin slices of rare roast beef
Horseradish

Slice loaf into thin slices and place on an oven tray. Bake in a medium hot oven for 15 minutes, turning once – be careful not to burn, you want them gold not black! When cool, spread with mayonnaise, top with a slice of beef, and garnish with horseradish.

You can also do these with smoked salmon topped with a little horseradish mixed with crème fraîche, Parma ham garnished with a slice of fresh fig, or pesto and a slice of goat's cheese finished off with a basil leaf.

CARAMELISED ONION AND FETA TARTLETS

2 large sliced onions
Butter
1 tablespoon brown sugar
2 teaspoons balsamic vinegar
30g feta cheese
Jar of sun-blush tomatoes
2 packets ready prepared croustades – available from good
*   supermarkets or delis*

Cook the onion gently in the butter until soft and golden – at least 30 minutes. Add the sugar and vinegar and a tablespoon of water, stirring carefully so the onions caramelise but don't burn. When cool, fill the croustades with a teaspoon of onion mixture, then top with crumbled feta and a snip of sun-blush tomato.

TEA BREAD

1 1/2 cups best mixed dried fruit
1 tablespoon glace cherries
1/2 tablespoon brown sugar
1/2 pint cold tea –nothing fancy, just builders' tea
1 egg
2 tablespoons of thick-cut marmalade
2 cups self-raising flour
A pinch of mixed spice

Soak the fruit and sugar in the tea in a large mixing bowl overnight until plump and juicy. Add the flour, beaten egg, marmalade, salt and spices and mix together thoroughly. Pour into a greased loaf tin and bake in a medium hot oven for 1½ hours. When cool, serve thickly sliced and spread with cold best butter.

PERFECT SCONES

350g self-raising flour
100g caster sugar
85g butter
175ml plain yoghurt

Rub the butter in with the flour and sugar until it resembles breadcrumbs (as if making pastry). Tip in the yoghurt, mixing with a knife until you have a smooth dough. Knead the dough lightly on a floured surface, then roll out to about an inch thick. Stamp out tiny rounds with your smallest cutter, then repeat until all the dough is used. Place the scones on a baking tray and bake for 10–12 minutes in a medium oven until they are golden.

Split and serve filled with cream and jam – strawberry is traditional, but ring the changes with damson, boysenberry, raspberry or apricot. Lucy gets her jams from the WI in the farmers' market.

PANSY CAKES

These pretty cakes are bedecked with sugar-frosted pansies from Lucy's garden. You can use any edible flowers – just brush them with egg white and sprinkle with caster sugar – or buy sugar flowers if this all seems too time-consuming!

100g butter
175g self-raising flour
175g caster sugar
1 teaspoon baking powder
2 eggs
1/2 cup of milk
Zest of one lemon
Juice of one lemon
100g caster sugar

Put the butter, flour, baking powder, sugar, eggs, milk and lemon zest in a food processor and whizz until glossy and smooth (you could do this with a wooden spoon but it will be an arduous task!). Pour into a greased and lined square cake tin. Bake for 35 minutes in a low oven until golden and firm.

Mix together the extra sugar and the lemon juice, then drizzle this over the cake while it is still warm so it soaks in. When cool, cut into bite-sized squares and top with the frosted flowers.

CROQUEMBOUCHE

A towering cone of profiteroles, a croquembouche makes a spectacular centre piece for a wedding, and is stunning when studded with silver almond dragées and miniature sparklers. Lucy makes hers with a lemon cream filling and dips them in white chocolate. Both Delia and Nigella have reliable profiterole recipes.

LEMON CREAM
4 egg yolks
3oz caster sugar
2 lemons – zested and juiced
2oz butter
$^1/_2$ pint double cream

Cook the egg, sugar and lemons gently in a pan for five minutes until thick. Remove from heat and beat in the butter. Chill in the fridge. When ready to fill the profiteroles, whip the cream and then fold into the lemon mixture.

Fill an icing bag with the lemon cream and use to fill the profiteroles, then dip them in best white chocolate.

Lucy makes baby meringues with the remaining egg whites.

Mandy Sherwyn's Alternative Wedding Presents

When most people get married these days, they have usually lived together and built up a home, so they already have most of the things necessary for starting married life. And there is nothing duller and more prosaic than a department store wedding list, especially when you get to it late and there is only a gravy boat left. So with Mandy's help here are a few suggestions for a more imaginative present list.

BUILD A LIBRARY

Look up a list of the nation's top one hundred books on the internet, replacing any you already have or don't fancy with choices of your own. Guests can buy a single book, or the complete Dickens/Harry Potter/Jane Austen. Also add to the list bookshelves, reading lamps and a set of library steps. You will have years of pleasure curled up on a sofa or lolling in a hammock and working your way through your list.

BUILD A MUSIC LIBRARY

This is great if you have a lot of young guests who don't necessarily have a lot to spend on a present. Build up a list of every album, every track you have ever loved and all the ones you think you should listen to, which your guests can then purchase online for you. Every time you play one of these songs you will remember your friends and family. Add to this his and hers iPods, a docking station and top quality speakers for the wealthier guests!

PLANT A GARDEN

Employ the services of a landscape gardener and get them to help you draw up a planting plan. Guests can then purchase plants or bulbs either through a website or a local garden centre. Add outdoor seating, pots and lighting to the list and enjoy the months after your wedding watching your garden come to life.

START A WINE CELLAR

A local wine merchant will be only too delighted to create a list for you – from light fresh wines for summer drinking to heavy, robust winter reds. Throw in some sparkling fizz and a couple of bottles of serious port and you will have the perfect drink for every social occasion in your cellar. Guests could also purchase crystal glasses, decanters, corkscrews or even a wine fridge!

BUY A WORK OF ART

Choose a stunning painting together that can be your future legacy. Divide the picture into square inches (not literally!) – guests can purchase as many as they like. Hang the painting over your fireplace and enjoy for the rest of your life – choose well and it will be a wise investment.

Patrick's Wedding Night Suggestions

Not everyone has the time or the money for a romantic honeymoon in the Maldives or Tahiti. But a special first night with your bride is a must – every couple needs some time out together after all the frenetic planning, preferably in unashamed luxury. Here is a selection of hotels to suit all tastes.

SOHO HOTEL

Understated townhouse chic in the heart of London. Enjoy a trip to the theatre or some serious shopping, then hang out for cocktails before slipping into the Egyptian cotton sheets.

LYGON ARMS

Quintessential Cotswold charm. Slip in some antiques shopping or peruse the estate agents for your own chocolate-box cottage before tucking into champagne and amuse-bouches in front of a roaring log fire.

WATERGATE BAY

For the outdoor type – try an afternoon's kiteboarding or surfing or just a walk on the stunning beach, then book a table at Jamie Oliver's Fifteen restaurant and enjoy local fish.

ROYAL CRESCENT, BATH

Roam historic Bath and while away the afternoon in the amazing Thermae Bath Spa, Britain's only natural thermal spa, before enjoying dinner at this classically elegant hotel.

LE MANOIR AUX QUAT' SAISONS

A must for gourmands, this beautiful house set in a walled 17th-century garden is the perfect foil for Raymond Blanc's magnificent cooking, largely supplied by the hotel's own herb and vegetable gardens.

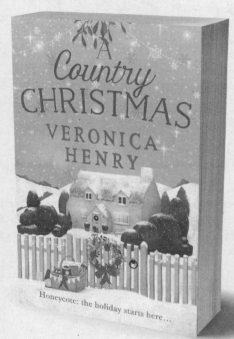

**Don't miss bestseller Veronica Henry's
next delightful novel**

*A Family
Recipe*

Laura Griffin is preparing for an empty nest.
The thought of Number 11 Lark Hill falling silent –
a home usually bustling with noise, people and the fragrant
smells of something cooking on the Aga – seems impossible.
Laura hopes it will mean more time for herself, and more
time with her husband, Dom.

But when an exposed secret shakes their marriage,
Laura suddenly feels as though her family is shrinking
around her. Feeling lost, she turns to her greatest comfort:
her grandmother's recipe box, a treasured collection dating
back to the Second World War. Everyone has always adored
Laura's jams and chutneys, piled their sandwiches high with
her pickles . . . Inspired by a bit of the old Blitz spirit, Laura
has an idea that gives her a fresh sense of purpose.

Full of fierce determination, Laura starts carving her own
path. But even the bravest woman needs the people who
love her. And now, they need her in return . . .

**A deliciously feel-good story from bestseller
Veronica Henry about the heart of the house:
the kitchen. Pure food for the soul!**

Coming May 2018

Discover Your Next Read from
VERONICA HENRY

Home isn't always where the heart is . . .

Jamie Wilding's return home is not quite going
to plan. A lot has changed in the picturesque
Shropshire village of Upper Faviell since she
left after the death of her mother. Her father
is broke and behaving like a teenager. Her best
friend's marriage is slowly falling apart. And the
man she lost her heart to years ago is trying to
buy her beloved family home.

As Jamie attempts to fix the mess, she is forced
to confront a long-standing family feud and the
truth about her father, before she can finally
listen to her own heart.

**Upstairs, downstairs . . . it's all going
on at the manor**

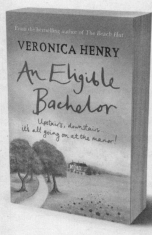

When Guy wakes up with a terrible hang-over
and a new fiancée, he tries not to panic. After
all, Richenda is beautiful, famous, successful . .
. what reason could he have for doubts?

As news of the engagement between the
heir of Eversleigh Manor and the darling of
prime-time television spreads through the
village, Guy wonders if he's made a rash
decision. Especially when he meets Honor, a
new employee of the Manor who has a habit
of getting under his skin. But Honor has her
own troubles – a son who's missing, and an
ex-boyfriend who has made an unexpected
reappearance . . .

It was the opportunity of a lifetime – a rundown hotel in Cornwall, just waiting to be brought back to life

When the rundown Rocks Hotel comes up for auction in Mariscombe, Lisa and her boyfriend George make a successful bid to escape and live the dream. But their dream quickly becomes a nightmare. Their arch-rival, Bruno Thorne, owner of Mariscombe Hotel, seems intent on sabotage.

Meanwhile, local chambermaid Molly is harbouring a secret that will blow the whole village apart. Then an unexpected visitor turns up on the doorstep. It seems everyone in Mariscombe is sailing a little too close to the rocks . . .

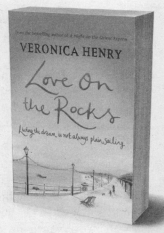

How far would you go for love: a white lie, a small deceit, full-scale fraud . . . ?

When Charlotte Briggs' husband Ed is sent down for fraud, she cannot find it in her heart to forgive him for what he has done. Ostracised from their social circle, she flees to the wilds of Exmoor to nurse her broken heart. But despite the slower pace of life, she soon finds that she is not the only person whose life is in turmoil.

On Everdene Sands, a row of beach huts holds the secrets of the families who own them

'FOR SALE: a rare opportunity to purchase a beach hut on the spectacular Everdene Sands. "The Shack" has been in the family for fifty years, and was the first to be built on this renowned stretch of golden sand.'

Jane Milton doesn't want to sell her beloved beach hut, which has been the heart of so many family holidays and holds so many happy memories. But when her husband dies, leaving her with an overwhelming string of debts, she has no choice but to sell.

Secrets, rivalry, glamour – it's time for the party of the year . . .

Delilah has lived out her tempestuous marriage to hell-raiser Raf in the glare of the media spotlight. Now planning a milestone birthday, she has more on her mind than invitations.

Raf has been offered a part in a movie he can't refuse. But will he succumb to the temptations he's struggled to resist for the last ten years?

Delilah's three daughters are building careers of their own, only too aware that the press are waiting for them to slip up. For the Rafferty girls might look like angels, but they are only human.

It's the perfect recipe for a party like no other . . .

A short break can become the holiday of a lifetime

In a gorgeous quay-side hotel in Cornwall, the long weekend is just beginning . . .

Claire Marlowe owns 'The Townhouse by the Sea' with Luca, the hotel's charismatic chef. She ensures everything runs smoothly – until an unexpected arrival checks in and turns her whole world upside down.

And the rest of the guests arrive with their own baggage…

Here are affairs of the heart, secrets, lies and scandal– all wrapped up in one long, hot weekend.

A new life is just a ticket away

The Orient Express. Luxury. Mystery. Romance.

For one group of passengers settling in to their seats and taking their first sips of champagne, the journey from London to Venice is more than the trip of a lifetime.

A mysterious errand; a promise made to a dying friend; an unexpected proposal; a secret reaching back a lifetime. As the train sweeps on, revelations, confessions and assignations unfold against the most romantic and infamous setting in the world.

Return to Everdene Sands, setting for the _The Beach Hut_, and discover secrets, love, tragedy and dreams. It's going to be a summer to remember . . .

Summer appeared from nowhere that year in Everdene and for those lucky enough to own one of the beach huts, this was the summer of their dreams.

For Elodie, returning to Everdene means reawakening the memories of one summer fifty years ago. A summer when everything changed. But this summer is not all sunshine and surf – as secrets unfold, and some lives are changed for ever . . .

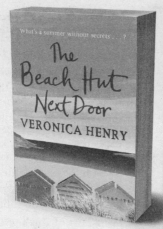

Pennfleet might be a small town, but there's never a dull moment in its narrow winding streets . . .

Kate has only planned a flying visit to clear out the family home after the death of her mother. When she finds an anonymous letter, she is drawn back into her own past.

Single dad Sam is juggling his deli and two lively teenagers, so romance is the last thing on his mind. Then Cupid fires an unexpected arrow – but what will his children think?

Nathan Fisher is happy with his lot, running picnic cruises up and down the river, but kissing the widow of the richest man in Pennfleet has disastrous consequences.

Vanessa knows what she has done is unseemly for a widow, but it's the most fun she's had for years. Must she always be on her best behaviour?

Everyone has a story . . . but will they get the happy ending they deserve?

Emilia has just returned to her idyllic Cotswold hometown to rescue the family business. Nightingale Books is a dream come true for book-lovers, but the best stories aren't just within the pages of the books she sells – Emilia's customers have their own tales to tell.

There's the lady of the manor who is hiding a secret close to her heart; the single dad looking for books to share with his son but who isn't quite what he seems; and the desperately shy chef trying to find the courage to talk to her crush . . .

And as for Emilia's story, can she keep the promise she made to her father and save Nightingale Books?

A gorgeous escapist read for anyone needing a hug in a book.

Hunter's Moon is the ultimate 'forever' house. Nestled by a river in the Peasebrook valley, it has been the Willoughbys' home for over fifty years, and now estate agent Belinda Baxter is determined to find the perfect family to live there. But the sale of the house unlocks decades of family secrets – and brings Belinda face to face with her own troubled past . . .

'A delight from start to finish' Jill Mansell

Pick up the next charming story by Veronica Henry today!